WAR OF THE ASHERS

THE PETROS CHRONICLES

DIANA TYLER

To my husband this book is affectionately dedicated.
Thank you for loving me and encouraging my writing
every single day.

CONTENTS

HERMES	1
ATTACK	9
TRUTH	17
TRAITOR	25
PORTAL	33
ESCAPE	42
ALLIES	50
PUNISHMENT	58
KINSHIP	65
ORPHANS	75
WARNING	83
LETO	92
HESPERIDES	101
PREMONITIONS	111
MEDUSA	120
ENEMIES	130

PROPHECY 138

CAVE ONE 150

AISON 158

DISCORD 166

MERCENARY 175

BLOOD 183

ULTIMATUM 191

CURSED 200

HERMOGENES 208

ANSWERS 218

LYCAEA 226

PRODIGY 239

PARADOX 246

POISON 255

PAWNS 265

MNEMOSYNE 275

CHIONE 286

REFLECTION 296

IMMORTAL 307

FREEDOM 314

ORPHEUS 323

AMBROSIA 334

ADMISSION 344

KRATÍRAS 353

MISSION 362

CORINNA 373

PRISONERS   384
MEMORIES   393
DÝNAMI   404

THE PETROS CHRONICLES BOOK 3   411
AFTERWORD   420
ACKNOWLEDGEMENTS   421
ABOUT THE AUTHOR   423

CHAPTER ONE
HERMES

For the first time in thousands of years, Hermes felt tired. He'd been tracking the mortals' scent all night, his winged sandals fluttering through the trees, his golden wand lighting the way. He knew it was only a matter of time until the Asher's invisibility wore off, and then they'd all be as good as dead.

The Moonbow had been waning for the last half hour as warm streaks of sunrise sprayed its arches with the rosy foam of dawn. It had been watching him since he emerged from Lake Thyra with his treacherous heart set against his brothers, the hell-bound lords of the Underworld, who would doubtless condemn him to a century of torture once they learned of his present errand.

But the Moonbow had bewitched the wandering messenger. Hermes could feel no fear nor contemplate remorse as long as its peaceful bands hovered over him. What he was doing was undeniably out of spite for his brothers, yet for some reason he couldn't help but feel that the Moonbow was smiling on him, nudging him onward even as his immortal limbs grew weak and heavy in the air.

Hermes' mind drifted as he stared through a net of leaves into the fading Moonbow that filled it. His thoughts traveled back to the last time he could recall ever feeling so weary. It had been immediately after the War against the All-Powerful, the night he and his brothers, the bold triumvirate, were expelled from heaven along with countless other rebels, all of whom had been hypnotized by Apollo's promise of unending power and a paradise of their own to rule as they pleased.

Hermes had been in on the lie from the start. Together with Poseidon, Apollo, Zeus, Hades, and the Titans, he had been plotting the coup for what seemed like eons within the timeless stretch of eternity. It was called "the War," but no swords were wielded nor chariots mounted until the dreaded end, which each black-hearted devil knew full well was coming.

Before word of their treason reached the All-Powerful, the weapons had been innocuous words, whispers of rumors that infected heaven's streets like an insidious plague. The symptoms were mild at first, hardly noticeable. A few complaints, a few disputes, a furious brawl here and there when the devout grew defensive and could stand the heresies no longer.

In the beginning, the revolt comprised only a few small circles of murmuring adherents. But, little by little, even the most pious ears were tickled and the strongest minds corrupted. To Hermes' surprise, there were soon enough of them to form an entire army that could rise up, dethrone the All-Powerful, and make greedy gods of themselves. It was then that the faithful took up arms against the rebel forces and drove them outside the city walls, as ruthlessly and swift as when a ferocious squall besets a sailboat.

Spirits, every one of them, the rebels awoke in one piece, their wishes granted. Around them now was a kingdom all their own, far from the stifling sovereignty under which they'd served and worshiped for untold ages.

The world was a newly created planet called Petros, meaning *stone*, named for the rocky terrain and jagged mountains that defined it. The atmosphere was so dense that many rebels swore that the fingers of death, which did not yet exist, were wrapping around their throats. For millennia, they'd been accustomed to the pure, rarefied air of heaven; now their lungs labored and burned with every breath.

The anemic color of the clouds hanging low over the sickly green hills was a sore to the rebels' eyes. They kicked the weeds and cursed the thorns as they hiked to the highest peak on which the three would erect their thrones and rest their flimsy shelters, all pigsties compared to their former abodes.

Hermes, one of the few with the gift of flight, had fallen from the sky halfway to the top of the summit and awoken half a day later, hoping it had all been a terrible dream, a hallucinatory warning from his subconscious. His conniving mind stopped scheming, slowing to assess the bruises and aches racking his body, this frightening pain he had never before experienced. His ichor blood felt frozen as regret gripped his muscles and sorrow seeped into his bones.

He wanted to cry out to Duna, to confess that he'd made a grave mistake and that he'd do anything to escape this loathsome world and reenter heaven's gates. But the darkness within him would tolerate no remorse, nor would his brothers let him lie idle for long, pitying his wounds and rethinking his choice. Give it some time, they'd said, for we have it here. And in time we shall all be kings.

They had been right. In time, the fatigue had worn off, the bruises had healed, and repentance had become as vulgar a notion as revolution had once been. Petros had become home, and Hermes had made himself one of its sovereigns.

For thousands of years, he had been an indispensable part of the oligarchy, and then of the counterfeit trinity after Apollo had imprisoned the Titans and his siblings within the bowels of Tartarus, and adopted Hermes and Hades as brothers. It was then that Hermes, true son of Zeus, began to prove himself more clever and cunning than his two "brothers" combined. It had been his duty, his greatest pleasure, to bend mortals to his will, to convince even himself that his gods-breathed, grandiose lies were true.

And then the Vessel had risen; just as the oracles had prophesied two thousand years before their birth. The whole Underworld knew the Vessel would be an Asher, one of the gifted mortals who received supernatural abilities when they reached eighteen. And because the All-Powerful had ordained long ago that there could only be one Asher per family, Hermes was sure the girl called Chloe was the one. He didn't consider that her twin brother could be a threat as well.

That oversight was Hermes' undoing.

Apollo and Hades blamed him for the Ashers' escape. He was their eyes and ears, they'd said, but he might as well have been blind and deaf, and unforgivably brainless. He wasn't needed anymore. They had their blessed Fantásmata, their brainwashed, power-crazed disciples with whom they communicated through drug-induced channeling and cataleptic trances.

Hermes was nothing but an underling now, an impotent peon like the other rebels who stood guard around Hades' gates, as if they could ever fend off the All-Powerful for even a second were he to descend to their sulfuric depths. If he chose to, he could thresh them like wheat and grind them to grain with a single breath. The question of why he didn't had settled over Hermes' mind like a fog, filling the void where his ruses and plans once dominated. He would rather be annihilated than continue living with countless gallons of mortal blood staining his conscience.

Perhaps this was his punishment, one much worse than being bound in Tartarus or cast into the Vale of Mourning.

Just hours ago, he'd been certain that the greatest torture was to possess a hubris matched only by two other spirits in the universe, and have no purpose or outlet with which to gratify it. But something in the air this night, perhaps the Moonbow itself, had convinced him otherwise. The greatest torture was not to be deprived of satisfying his pride, but to recognize its repulsiveness, to feel the unbearable weight of blood caked on his hands, to carry guilt like a yoke upon his shoulders, and to remember a peaceful existence before any of it.

Hermes' heart quivered, one side fighting to beat fast with swelling offense and anger, the other side resisting, for it knew that blaming his brothers for his dismal fate was futile. Evil had been stagnant within him all along, and they'd known how to draw it out, capturing it like sap from a tree. But he wasn't dumb; the All-Powerful had created him to be one of the shrewdest of all. While others might have been manipulated and deceived, Hermes was fully aware of the choice he was making. There was no one to blame but himself.

Unable to fly any longer, Hermes grabbed onto the nearest tree branch and sat down. He leaned his head against the trunk and breathed in the Petrodian air. It had once tasted so vile, but it was now nectar compared to the choking swelter of hell.

The amber glow surrounding the Moonbow dissolved into the clear blue canvas of sky. He pointed his wand at it, commanding it to stay, but of course it was impervious to his magic. It came and went as it wished, offering solace, delivering warnings, chasing down destinies, answering only to the All-Powerful.

Who would Hermes answer to now? He'd betrayed the All-Powerful. He'd been ostracized by his brothers. But he had not antagonized the Moonbow, the silent messenger that overlooked the deeds of mortals and spirits both. Perhaps by helping the Ashers it loved, he could win its favor. He could do something noble, that might reach the All-Powerful's ear and lighten the load of guilt bearing down on him.

Hermes jumped as his reverie was shattered like glass by the sound of a man's voice a stone's throw away.

"Damian, look," the man shouted.

Hermes looked down through the density of looming Folóï oaks, but saw nothing but a red fox scampering past. And then he saw it, a faint glimmer spanning four feet of air on which transparent waves rippled and shook as if pebbles were skipping across it.

"It's fading again," came the same disembodied voice, much quieter this time.

Slowly, the see-through apparition became obscured as flesh tones and flashes of clothing suffused it. Hermes could make out four human forms, all still hazy as they regained their corporeality. Only one was familiar to him, the one named Ethan, whose voice he had heard.

Ethan and an older man and woman had their hands planted firmly on the fourth person's shoulders and wrists, clinging to him like children to their mother. Reluctantly, as they regarded the sunshine and shadows on their skin, and crunched the leaves beneath their feet, they removed their hands and stepped away.

So this was Damian, the Asher who had escaped Hermes' notice. The one responsible for his demise.

"No one to blame but yourself, old man," Hermes muttered to himself. Then he rose from the branch and flew down to the ground, smiling softly at the thought of both vengeance and redemption being irresistibly within reach.

CHAPTER TWO
ATTACK

"I see them! Up there!"

Hermes' keen ears rang as his head whipped around. The guards were closer than he'd anticipated; clearly they too had simply been biding their time until the Asher's doma ran dry.

Hermes floated toward the four fugitives and held out his palms to show them he meant no harm. Then he opened the satchel on his hip and plucked from it four tiny pomegranate seeds, souvenirs from Circe's isle that he'd been saving for a special sort of mischief. He couldn't help but grin as he cupped them in his hand.

"You'll have to trust me," Hermes said.

"Who are you?" The woman's hands trembled as they clutched the man beside her. Her husband, Hermes assumed.

"It's Hermes," said Ethan, smirking at Hermes' dog-skin cap and winged sandals. Hermes' cheeks flushed with pride, and he gave a modest bow. "You're the most notorious con artist in history. Why should we trust you?"

Hermes didn't have time to retort. He could hear the guards' footsteps growing louder. The guards would see them at any moment, and Hermes couldn't make anyone but himself invisible. But the seeds...

"The councilman's guards are closing in on you." Hermes tapped the top of his ear. "I can hear far better than the bloodhounds they have with them."

"You haven't answered Ethan's question." Damian threw back his shoulders and stepped forward. "Why should we trust you?" He cracked his knuckles and set his jaw.

Hermes smiled. The Asher had no idea whom he was dealing with. "It's because of you that I'm here, Damian. Why I'm as wanted a man as you are."

"What are you talking about?" Damian asked. "Wanted by who?"

"I'll explain later," Hermes said. "That is, if you're not all executed first."

"What's that in your hand?" Moris asked as he peered through his smudged glasses.

Hermes took a seed and gave it to the older man. "It's your salvation. Eat and see."

Ethan dropped his black carbon helmet and reached out to grip his father's arm. "Don't do it, Dad."

"I swear to you the effects will be temporary," Hermes said. "On Petros, this magic is forbidden to last longer than a few hours. Like your doma"—he inclined his head toward Damian—"everything has its limits."

Ethan's father pulled away from his son and brought the seed to his lips. "There's only one way to find out if he's telling the truth."

"Moris..." Lydia whispered, her face awash with terror as she watched her husband swallow the seed and begin to shake. "Moris!"

"Just be patient," Hermes cooed. His eyes widened with glee as he watched the metamorphosis commence. It always started with this kind of unbecoming spasm: the limbs twitching, the head jerking, the eyes rolling. And then...

"My gods, what's happening?" The woman covered her mouth and dropped to her knees.

Moris was shrinking, and tawny hair was sprouting from head to toe as his clothing disappeared.

Ethan lunged forward and seized Hermes by the throat. "You picked the wrong day to mess with my family."

"Ethan, look," said Damian.

Ethan tightened his grip as he turned his head. Behind him stood a tan, sturdy-looking ibex staring at them with large yellow eyes.

"Disguise," said Hermes, as he broke free with ease from Ethan's grasp. It took every ounce of self-control to keep him from breaking the boy's knees with a single blow of his wand. "It's the only option you have as long as his doma isn't working." He clenched his jaw as the guards' footsteps pounded like a drumbeat in his ears. "Choose quickly."

Lydia rushed forward and stole a seed from Hermes' hand. Ethan started to object, but she hushed him and gulped it down. A few seconds later, she was a plump, perfect little squirrel.

Ethan raked a hand through his hair as he yelled, then sighed, at the plight of his parents.

Hermes suppressed a laugh. If this mortal were so overwhelmed by the child's play of Circe's enchantment, how would he react if he ever glimpsed the horrors of hell itself? It would likely be too much for his delicate heart to take.

"Come on, Ethan," Damian said, as he paced between the two creatures. Both were sitting still as statues, their pricked ears attuned to the enclosing enemy. "What do we have to lose?"

"What if he's wrong?" Ethan's voice cracked with fear. "I'd rather be dead than live as an animal." He glanced at his parents and blinked back the tears welling in his eyes.

A foreign feeling tugged at Hermes' heart; he knew it vaguely as empathy. He locked eyes with Ethan and spoke with more earnestness than he ever had before. "You have no reason to believe that I'm telling the truth. But I assure you, I am."

Ethan gave a curt nod and held out his palm. Hermes dropped the two remaining seeds into it and then floated up into the autumn-colored canopy of trees; rather than the feeling of power propelling him, he felt the weight of guilt falling off his soul like shackles.

"On three?" Damian took a seed from Ethan.

"If we're stuck like rodents or goats or whatever else for more than a day," Ethan said, "I'm going to hunt you down and kill you for talking me into this." He patted Damian's shoulder and held the seed over his tongue. "On three."

"One," began Damian, "two, three..." And down went the mystical seed from an infamous imp he'd grown up believing was nothing more than a fairytale character. This was insanity.

Damian's heart pounded as his knees buckled and every muscle in his body went rigid. He trembled uncontrollably as what felt like hot electricity surged through his veins, shocking every inch of him from the inside out. His stomach twisted with nausea as the world around him spun in circles. Struggling to focus his vision, he saw Ethan watching him, the seed still in Ethan's hand, his face painted white with fear. So much for "on three."

Unlike Moris and Lydia, Damian wasn't shrinking; instead, he was growing taller, wider and heavier, from head to toe. He closed his eyes; he didn't want to see what he was becoming.

"What in the..." he heard Ethan say. "You're a *bear*?" He sounded incredulous, and not a little peeved.

Have fun hunting me down. Damian laughed silently. At least his mind was still his own. He opened his eyes to see six armed guards rushing toward Ethan. Damian pitched his weight forward and fell onto all fours.

"There!" one of the guards yelled and pointed at Ethan. "Freeze, Mr. Ross. Put your hands behind your head."

Damian didn't have time to weigh his options. He opened his jaws as wide as he could and let out a deafening roar. The forest went quiet. The guards stopped dead in their tracks. All eyes were on him, waiting for his next move.

Unsure what signs of aggression were normal for bears, Damian did what came naturally. He dug his claws into the earth and pawed at it, then flattened his ears as another roar bellowed from his belly. He shot a glance at the guards, whose guns were trained on him. With a snort, he pivoted on his back feet, swinging his body around toward Ethan.

"Looks like the bear will take care of him for us," one of the guards said.

This might actually work, Damian thought. He lowered his head, nose to the ground, and charged Ethan, knocking him down with his powerful paws before Ethan knew what had hit him. Careful to use his gums instead of his teeth, Damian clamped his mouth around Ethan's shoulder and shook him violently until he fell limp. He'd gotten the message.

Damian lifted his head toward the guards and roared until his lungs felt ready to explode.

"Let's get out of here," the guard whispered. "Let it enjoy its dinner. We'll come back at nightfall."

The guards holstered their weapons and slowly backed away. Damian could hear their breaths released like air from a burst balloon.

He buried his nose into Ethan's torso, nudging and jabbing as he feigned ravenous grunting sounds. A few seconds later, Lydia jumped into view and perched on a tree root above Ethan's head, her bushy tail wrapped around her, tiny paws joined at her heart as she looked down on him. Moris followed, making a shrill bleating noise as he pointed his hoof in the direction of the guards.

"They're gone," Ethan said, as he squeezed his eyes shut and hissed in pain.

Damian had been rougher than he'd intended, but at least Ethan was alive. By some miracle, they all were. He sat back on his haunches and did his best to apologize to Ethan with a shrug of his shoulders.

"Yeah, I know," said Ethan. "You did what you had to do." He lifted himself to a sitting position and rubbed his chest. "I'll survive." He patted Damian on the elbow and laughed. "And we thought you were a good wrestler before."

Damian snorted and shook his head, then searched the sky for Hermes. He could use some assurance that he wouldn't be this way forever.

"It'll be okay, Damian."

Damian stared blankly at Ethan. He knew Ethan didn't really believe that. If he did, he would've eaten the seed, too, instead of backing out at the last moment, leaving the three of them to be the guinea pigs, almost literally.

"Ethan?" a woman's voice called quietly.

Ethan's eyes widened and a stunned smile spread across his face. "Chloe!" he shouted at the sight of Damian's sister. Apparently forgetting all about his pain, he leapt to his feet took off running.

His outsized bear's heart still pounding, Damian watched as Ethan jogged into a soft shaft of sunlight and embraced Damian's sister; his sister, whom he had forsaken and written off as a rebel who'd stuck her nose where it didn't belong; his sister, whom he had watched walk unwittingly through a portal to hell and refused to go after; his sister, who he finally realized was stronger and braver than anyone he'd ever known.

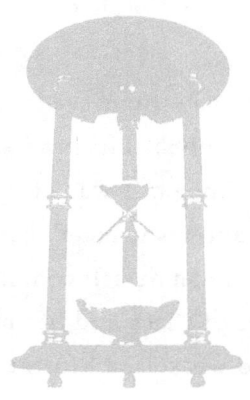

CHAPTER THREE
TRUTH

I thought that bear killed you," Chloe said, her eyes darting back to the animal sitting strangely still, watching them closely. *What in the world is it doing*, she thought. *And what kind of bear attacks without drawing blood?*

"It's not a bear." Ethan pulled back just enough to look into her eyes. "It's your brother."

"What?" Chloe watched as the bear leaned back against the tree and smiled at her like an oversized stuffed animal. "That's *Damian?*"

The bear raised a paw and waved at her.

The ibex beside it bobbed its head and *baahed*.

If Chloe hadn't known it was possible for men to be turned into beasts, and if she hadn't been an enemy of the state, she would have had herself committed.

"How..." Images of Circe and her menagerie of birds, foxes, polecats, and weasels, all former warriors, flashed through her mind's eye.

Before Chloe could finish her question, Ethan pulled her close again, and she rested her head on his chest, listening as his rapid heartbeat gradually slowed. They could discuss everything later. Right now, they just needed to breathe.

After several long, still moments, Ethan let go of Chloe and she wiped the tears from her cheeks. She slipped off her shoes and sank her toes into a mound of crisp, cool, multicolored leaves, then closed her eyes as she lifted her chin to the sky, letting the light breeze caress her skin.

It was good to feel things, even things as simple as fallen leaves and air in motion. Neither existed where she had come from, up there, millions of miles away from Petros in that indescribable in-between realm perhaps no one else had ever seen—no one living, anyway.

She'd felt like an alien as she had stood there, face to face with Orpheus, a man who had tasted death twice ,and finally, after thousands of years of suffering, found happiness. He'd been sent to ask her forgiveness, and to encourage her not to lose faith. It was as if he had known her troubles were only just beginning.

"Where were you?" Ethan asked.

Chloe grabbed her shoes and they walked toward the tree. She stopped in front of Damian and tried to force a smile, but her muscles refused to move. "I was in hell," she said finally. Rather than answering Ethan's question, she had made an unsolicited statement to her brother. She needed to see his face when she said it.

Damian held her gaze. She knew that if he could speak he'd defend himself until he was blue in the face. He'd scold her for having followed the woman into the mist in the first place. He'd tell her it was her fault that he and the Rosses had been turned into woodland creatures. And when he was done, Chloe would be so wracked with guilt she'd probably turn herself into the councilman.

But Damian couldn't speak, and she was free to explain to him, without interruption, precisely what she'd endured, how she'd been tortured, all because he'd been too much of a coward to try and save her.

"Do you have any idea what I've been through, Damian?" Her voice quavered, not with anger, she realized, but sadness. She'd been betrayed, and despite her father's words admonishing her not to dwell on the past, she couldn't rid the betrayal from her mind. She'd been too distracted before to pay the pain any attention, but now, in this long-awaited moment of reprieve, she felt the sharp stab of abandonment all over again.

"I was in prison down there," she continued, tears burning as they appeared in her eyes. "All alone except for two tormentors who were all too happy to keep me company. It was Phobos who told me you'd betrayed me. I wish it had been harder to believe."

Her breath caught in her throat as Phobos's wicked voice echoed in her ears: *She's neither loved nor lucky.* And she'd believed it, so much so that she'd wanted nothing more than to drink from the River Lethe and have all her memories erased, not least those of her parents dying and her brother leaving her to rot.

Damian dropped his head and rocked off the tree onto all four of his humongous legs. Then he started walking.

"Go ahead, Damian," Chloe called after him. "Walk away. Turn your back like you always do."

"Chloe," Ethan said, placing a gentle hand on her shoulder, "your brother is the reason my family and I are alive."

A lump the size of her fist sank into Chloe's stomach. "What are you talking about?"

"The councilman was going to kill my mom and me," said Ethan. "And he was forcing my dad to be the executioner. Your brother risked his life to save ours."

Chloe shook her head. "That's impossible. There's no way a person could have—"

"He's like you, Chloe," he said sternly.

Chloe's mouth fell open as the lump in her abdomen expanded and pressed into her ribs, causing every breath to ache. Surely Carya would've told her if Damian had a doma, too. "What..." she rasped. "What do you mean like me?"

"Damian has a power. He can make himself and anyone he touches invisible."

"I didn't know." Chloe placed her hand on the tree and tugged on a piece of peeling bark. "I'm sorry."

"He's more like you than you thought, huh?" Ethan said with a smile. "He's brave."

Chloe pushed away from the tree and gave a sigh. "I guess I owe him an apology," she said, resisting the temptation to demand why Damian hadn't been brave for *her*. What mattered now was that they were safe, at least for a little while.

The ibex bleated and stomped his hoof.

"I think Dad's saying we need to go," said Ethan.

The ibex nodded and turned to follow in the direction Damian had gone.

"Wait," said Chloe. She stared at the peculiar ibex, then up at the squirrel above their heads, whom she would swear was eavesdropping on their conversation. "Don't tell me those are your parents."

"So you can believe that your twin brother is walking around the Eirenian woods as a brown bear, but it's too far-fetched to believe that my mom's a squirrel and my dad's a goat?"

Chloe laughed and started walking. "Well, if you put it that way. I guess...for some reason I thought it was just my family that got caught up in this stuff."

Ethan shook his head. "No, ma'am." He reached into his pocket and opened his palm, revealing a bright red pomegranate seed. "The guards found us before I could eat mine. You could've been talking to a hedgehog right now."

Chloe pressed a hand to her chest and stumbled. "Where did you get that? Did Circe give it to you?" She lowered her voice so his parents wouldn't hear. "That's *permanent*, Ethan. I've been to Circe's island. I was supposed to eat one so I wouldn't be a problem to the Fantásmata."

Her blood warmed as she thought of Orpheus. If it hadn't have been for Orpheus, the witch would have forced the seeds down her throat and right now she'd be on that island living an immortal existence in Circe's accursed zoo. Orpheus had carried goodness in him all along.

"He said the magic only lasts a few hours in Petros." Ethan slipped the seed back into his pocket.

"Who said?"

The squirrel scurried past them and stopped in front of Ethan.

"Are you hitchhiking?" he asked.

Lydia nodded, then leapt into his arms.

Now Ethan's mom could definitely hear everything they said, but Chloe wasn't upset about it. They were all in this together now. What good would it do to keep secrets?

"Hermes said," Ethan said, answering Chloe's question.

"Oh no," Chloe groaned.

"You know him?"

"I've been duped by him, if that's what you mean. You can't believe anything he says." She looked down at Lydia sympathetically. She wished she had something more comforting to say. "When I stepped through the portal, he welcomed me on the other side of the River Styx."

"No way. That really exists?"

Chloe rolled her eyes. "I'm not the only one picking and choosing what's believable and what's not."

"Okay, okay, so you crossed the Styx, and then what did Hermes do?"

"Long story short, he promised he'd shed some light on my...situation. But instead he deposited me at the Fields of Asphodel, which is absolutely the most depressing place you can imagine."

Ethan drew a deep breath. "I'm so sorry, Chloe," he said.

He was looking at her with the greatest measure of pity she'd ever seen on a person's face. She hadn't been looking for his pity, but it felt good nevertheless.

"Thank you." She looked down at the shoes in her hand. "I guess I should put these on." She did so, but when she straightened, the expression of pity on Ethan's face had only deepened.

"It isn't your fault, Ethan."

She looked down at Lydia, who was looking off wistfully into the distance. "Mrs. Ross, I could be wrong. Maybe Hermes was telling the truth."

"Time will tell," said Ethan.

Chloe nodded slowly as his words flicked on a light switch in her brain. "Maybe time won't have to."

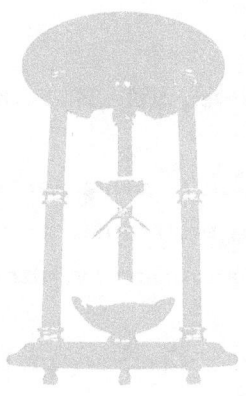

CHAPTER FOUR
TRAITOR

Ethan stopped walking, waiting for Chloe to expound the idea still percolating in her mind.

"If I can take us out of here," she said, "out of this time, we can find out right now if what Hermes said was true."

"So you can time travel?" He looked at her as if she'd just admitted to being able to fly to the moon and back. And that was almost true.

"It seems that way, yes." She paused. "Is that cooler than Damian's invisibility?"

"In my opinion? Definitely. That's the coolest thing I've ever heard."

Chloe smiled softly, trying not to think about the implications inextricably linked to possessing domas, namely the damage and death they attracted to herself and her family.

"What if Hermes wasn't telling the truth?" Ethan asked.

"My plan doesn't go that far yet."

"Fair enough. We'd better catch up to your brother before he loses us." Ethan looked down at his mom. "Hold on tight, Mom." Then he whispered over his shoulder to Chloe, "I really hope it works."

They took off jogging, slowing after half a minute when Chloe got a stitch in her side. "I've really gotta work on my endurance if running's going to be a regular part of my life," she said, as she bent over and grasped her knees.

"Chloe, look." Ethan pointed to his right, at a narrow path filled with footprints of various shapes and sizes, the biggest and most distinct of which belonged to a bear.

Chloe followed behind Ethan through the meandering pathway and shivered at the tall, white asphodels filling the spaces between the trees. In the Underworld, the spirits of the dead were obsessed with them. With their memories washed away and their identities forgotten, the flowers that grew in the meadows were their only possession, and, as if compelled by an unseen taskmaster, they spent every waking hour hoarding them. Thank Duna Orpheus had freed them from that hell.

"He found water," Ethan said.

Chloe looked past Ethan at the sea-green river winding through the saddle of low hills below them, its surface sparkling like diamonds in the morning light. Damian was sitting on the bank with his back to them.

Chloe placed her pinkies in her mouth and whistled. "Damian, it's us," she called. She caught Moris stumbling past in her periphery, his huge, backward-curling horns seeming to drag him down the slope.

"We're sure that's Damian, right?" Ethan whispered.

"It would be like me to let a man-eating predator know where we are."

Moris joined the bear and took a voracious drink from the river. Damian lowered himself back down and began eating from the neat pile of berries stacked next to him.

"Guess that answers your question," said Chloe, then she cupped her hands around her mouth and called out, "You shouldn't be out in the open like that!"

Damian turned his head to the side, just enough to acknowledge that he'd heard her, then turned away and continued to snack.

"Chloe, the councilman is looking for four humans. I think Damian and my parents are just fine." He gave her his pity look again, only this time it was mixed with unsettling concern.

"Why are you looking at me like that?"

"When's the last time you slept?"

"Does getting knocked unconscious in Hades count?"

Ethan looked away and rubbed the back of his neck. How did she expect him to respond? "No, no, it definitely does not count, Chloe."

His mother chirped in agreement. "You need to sleep."

Just hearing the word "sleep" made Chloe's eyelids droop. "Sleep is a luxury we don't have right now." She was on the verge of slurring her words.

"May I see your jacket?" Ethan said.

"Ohhhkaaay..." Chloe took it off. "I apologize for the smell. I think I need a bath worse than I need sleep."

Ethan laughed as he took the jacket. "I'll hold my breath," he joked. He set Lydia on a nearby branch, spread the jacket on the ground, then pulled the sleeves inside out, folded it lengthwise, and rolled it up. "Your pillow," he said, handing the bundle to Chloe. "I would've given you my vest to sleep on, but it's bulletproof." He gave a wry smile as he drummed his fingers across his chest.

"Well, I guess I know my place in the hierarchy here, but I told you, I'm not sleeping. We have to get out of here."

Ethan crouched down and set the black helmet he'd been carrying by his side. "Hermes said they'd be human again in a few hours." Chloe opened her mouth to interject, but Ethan was too quick. "Even if he lied," he said slowly, punching every syllable, "we can use your power to go back, right? We can go back in time to when Hermes showed up and tell him to go back to where he came from."

Chloe pursed her lips and tilted her head side to side as she pondered. "Yeah...I guess logically that works." She could almost feel her brain throbbing as she tried thinking it through. There was no denying she needed sleep. She doubted her doma would even operate if she let herself get too exhausted.

"Perfect. So you take a little nap, and I'll wake you up in a couple hours. Then we'll go from there." Ethan held out his hand. "Deal?"

Chloe took his hand and shook it. "Deal."

She stuffed the makeshift pillow under her head and closed her eyes. Immediately, her father's face materialized in her mind, his warm green eyes, lined with faint wrinkles and moist with happy tears, smiling at her. Even though she'd reunited with him in the Fields of Asphodel, where he was a spirit and she a prisoner, she'd wished with all her heart she could stay there forever. But she'd been told to be brave; the fate of every listless soul in Hades was depending on her to liberate them. And according to Orpheus, she had succeeded.

Now it was her own world that needed liberating, and she hadn't the foggiest clue where to start.

"Ethan, I'm turning back."

Chloe opened her eyes to see the squirrel's undersized head swelling by the second atop its shaking body.

"I'm turning back!" Lydia repeated, her voice like a chipmunk's.

Next, her hands replaced her paws and her tail disappeared as the olive green of her hospital gown covered her up completely like a billowing tent. A few moments later, her legs and arms shot out of the gown and she rolled onto her back with a groan, a woman once more, albeit a frazzled one.

Chloe jumped up and ran to her. "Mrs. Ross! Are you okay?"

"Fantastic. Just a bit of a headache," she said, rubbing her forehead as she turned onto her side and pushed herself up.

Ethan knelt beside his mom and hugged her until she winced and pulled away.

"Sorry, son, but I'm a little tender. I'm not sure what that process entails physiologically, but it leaves one feeling like they just got mauled by a bear." She smiled and squeezed her son's hand. Then she looked toward the river and brought a hand to her mouth as she spotted her husband walking in circles, scratching the places where the horns had been. "Moris..."

Moris stopped abruptly and pushed a finger to his ear.

"Moris?" Lydia called. "Moris, what is it?"

Moris's eyes skimmed the ground. He was listening intently...to what?

Chloe looked past Moris to Damian. He was lying on his back, still and stiff as a board, but he was human again.

After a few spasmodic twitches, he rotated his wrists and ankles, and nodded his head up and down as if to make sure he'd been properly put back together. Carefully, he rolled up, threw his hood over his head, and gazed off into the foliage beyond. Then he resumed eating berries as if nothing had happened.

Chloe put on her jacket and stepped out of the trees. "I'll be right back."

"Don't be long," Ethan said. "We shouldn't be out in the open."

"I won't be."

When she was halfway to her brother, Moris cleared his throat and lowered his finger from his ear. His face was flushed and glistening with sweat.

"Hi, Mr. Ross." Chloe held out her hand. "I don't think we've ever officially met."

He took her hand reluctantly and held it as he spoke. "Yes, sir. Thank you, sir," he said, the color draining from his face.

"Are you okay?" Had the ibex debacle driven him nuts?

Moris gave a curt nod as he let go of her hand. "It was the councilman." He twisted his thumb and forefinger into his ear canal and produced a gray earpiece. It reminded Chloe of a bloated tick.

A rush of heat surged through her body. "He's been listening to you the entire time? Since the escape?"

Moris shook his head and found an iridescent beetle crawling across a rock to stare at through his bifocals.

Chloe stepped between him and the beetle and raised her voice. "Mr. Ross, please answer me. How long has he been listening?" On her periphery, she saw Damian jump to his feet. She cast a look back at Ethan. He jogged over, Lydia trailing behind him.

Moris reached into his pocket and pulled out a square device on which a neon light blinked green. He pushed a switch on its side, and the light went dark. "I had it off the entire time. Until just a few moments ago, when I turned human again."

Ethan parted his lips, but he was too dumbfounded to speak.

His mother spoke for him. "Morris, why? After everything—"

"He says he'll grant amnesty for us, Lydia," said Moris, as he took his wife's hand and kissed her temple. "For you, me and Ethan, if we go back now and tell them what we know about Chloe and Damian." He adjusted his glasses and pushed the earpiece back into his ear.

Chloe could see that any shame Moris had felt was giving in to his primal sense of self-preservation. Humans were more animalistic than they cared to admit.

CHAPTER FIVE

PORTAL

He's lying!" Ethan exclaimed. "He told me he was planning to kill you both as slowly as possible. What makes you think he's changed his mind?" When his father didn't answer, he kicked the dirt and held the crown of his head with both hands. "I can't believe this," he mumbled.

"Because I've helped him," Moris finally replied as he fiddled with the end of his sleeve.

Ethan grabbed the sleeve and yanked it hard, revealing a black pea-sized microphone. "How *could* you, Dad?"

"They'll be fine, son," said Moris in a calm, parental tone. "The GPS has given them our location. We can get out of here, and so can Chloe and Damian." He turned to Chloe. "What's your...talent?"

"Time travel."

"I rest my case," said Moris.

Lydia tucked her hair behind her ears and drew her husband's arm around her waist. "Moris is right. By law, the Fantásmata must show clemency toward convicted individuals who have cooperated with them. And, given that we haven't even been tried, let alone convicted, we're guaranteed that at least."

"Did you not hear what I just said?" Ethan said. "The councilman said he was going to kill you when he tracked you down." He nudged Chloe's elbow. "Chloe, please back me up on this."

"We're turning ourselves in," said Moris. "We're not fugitives. By law, he's prohibited from laying a hand on us, and, worst-case scenario, we'll serve some time for aiding and abetting."

Ethan's arms collapsed to his sides. "I can't believe this," he said again. He shook his head and looked at Chloe, his face a giant question mark.

"I don't think the councilman abides by the laws," said Chloe.

"That's the understatement of the century," Damian piped up as he stormed toward them. He stood in Moris's face.

"Have you lost your mind?" The vein in Damian's forehead bulged as he fought to keep his temper in check. "You're dealing with a *maniac*. You're no use to the councilman now; you're a threat. He'll kill you both just to keep this whole thing a secret."

Chloe's spine turned to ice. She didn't want to tell Damian like this, but it might be the only thing that could convince the Rosses to stay...

"That's why he killed our parents," she said, her voice barely above a whisper.

Damian stepped back as his fury was transformed into grief.

Chloe went to him and hugged him hard, as if to absorb his pain. "I'm so sorry. The councilman told me—"

"I knew," he whispered. "I knew." And then he crumbled to the ground, buried his head in his hands and wept.

"Chloe, you both need to get out of here," said Ethan.

I know, she mouthed to him. Then she knelt beside Damian and scratched his back, just as their mother used to. "Being in hell wasn't completely terrible."

Damian's shoulder blades twitched. "Just leave me alone for a second, Chloe." He pulled his knees to his chest and hid his face between them.

"I saw Dad." Chloe took her hand off his back as she sat down. "In Hades."

For a few seconds it appeared that Damian had stopped breathing. Chloe looked at him. Sitting there, arms wrapped firmly around his knees, forehead pressed atop them, he resembled his five-year-old-self pouting in time-out.

After a long while, he lifted his head and squinted into the still-rising sun. A lone tear slid into the corner of his mouth. "Mom and Dad are in hell?" His mouth fell open as if he'd just been punched in the gut.

"Yes. No. I mean they *were*," Chloe stammered. "It's a long story, but what's important is that heaven isn't a myth." She placed a hand on Damian's. "Death isn't the end."

Damian took a deep breath and laid his other hand on top of hers. His frown turned upwards into a hopeful, albeit weak, smile, the first he had directed at her in years. Then the smile evaporated. "I guess we'll be reunited soon, then."

"Not yet. I have a doma, too, and it might just save our lives."

Chloe's eyes met Ethan's as she stood. His parents were nowhere in sight. "Where they'd go?" she asked, as her eyes frantically scanned the trees.

Ethan's silence answered for him.

Damian got to his feet and stuffed the remaining berries into his hoodie pocket. "You're staying, Ethan?"

Ethan didn't answer. It seemed plain to Chloe that Ethan didn't know what he was doing.

"You know your parents are about to commit suicide, right?" Damian pressed.

"I know." Ethan cracked his knuckles as he knelt beside the river. "It's like my dad's been brainwashed." He cupped a handful of water and took a drink. "And my mom's too scared to leave him."

"And you're not too scared to leave *them*?" Chloe asked.

Ethan rose and stared blankly into the river, a pure, untouched oasis in a world teeming with corruption the vast majority of Petrodians knew nothing about. "My mom told me to stay behind. In case they're wrong." He turned away as he brought a fingertip to his eye.

"Ethan, no," said Chloe, determination hardening her voice. "I'm not going to let this happen. I'm not going to stand idly by and watch your parents just waltz right into his trap." She went to the river and quickly splashed her face.

"And how do you intend to stop them?" Damian said flatly. "My power isn't working right now. I've been trying for half an hour." He kicked the ground and sent pebbles skidding into the water. "And even if it was, I think I'd have a hard time rescuing a traitor."

"We won't need your doma," said Chloe. "I'll use mine. I'll go back in time, back to a few minutes ago when you all were animals. I'll take away all his fancy spy gear and throw it in the river. Then I'll whisk us away before they can go back to the council." She took a breath. "Easy."

Ethan raised an optimistic eyebrow.

Damian sighed and shook his head, but not even he could find a hole in her plan, nor a legitimate reason to protest. It was their best shot.

"Okay, if there are no objections, I'll be going now," said Chloe.

She closed her eyes and visualized the moment when Ethan had taken her jacket and made it into a pillow. She waited for the feeling of weightlessness to follow, for every sound and sensation but that one to be blocked from her awareness. But it didn't come. She could still hear the birds, feel the breeze, and smell the sweetness of the junipers. Why wasn't it working?

She heard Damian walking toward her.

He put his hand on her shoulder and shook her gently. "Chloe, tell me you can see her, too."

Chloe opened her eyes and saw Carya standing within arm's reach, encased inside a thick, winter-white haze. The messenger lifted her arms and punched her white fists through the canopy around her, producing a loud whooshing sound as the radiant wisps drifted and fell to the ground, covering it with ethereal frost.

A familiar chiming noise tinged in Chloe's ear. She'd seen Carya perform this exact ritual before. She was making it possible for Chloe to communicate with the ancient Petrodians. Had she come to call Chloe back there, back to Iris?

"Ow!" Damian pressed his hands to his ears. "What was that for?"

"Carya just made you bilingual," Chloe answered. "You understand Próta now."

Damian rubbed his ear with his finger. "A few days ago I would've called you crazy if you'd said something like that."

Ethan stepped closer to the strange girl and circled her, his mouth agape. His face blanched as if he were seeing a ghost. And, Chloe supposed, effectively he was. "Is that... are you..."

"It's Carya," said Chloe. "Don't ask her any questions. She won't answer you."

Carya giggled, and as she did, shimmering specks of snow-white dust were ejected from the haze and danced around Chloe's face.

"The domas which you seek to use
*   are bound by timeless laws,*
Ordained to prevent exploits of power
*   and quests of unjust cause.*
Every limit is different, each
*   encoded by Duna's hand,*
For he knows well each Asher's heart, how
*   they quake and shift like sand.*
Damian, lest you hide forever, your
*   doma is not without end,*
It is yours to control three hours each day,
*   then shall blow away like the wind.*
Chloe, lest compassion lead you to
*   try and erase every tear,*

You may use your gift twice in twenty-four
    hours, and then it will disappear.
To the past you may travel freely and
    to your former time return,
But the future lies only with Duna,
    for it is only his concern.
For this world is not perfect, and never
    shall be; you cannot make it so,
But there is a battle you are all meant to
    fight, a far-off place you must go.
An ephemeral portal is the river now;
    it waits for you to dive in,
In a tunnel of fire you will emerge,
    then your journey will begin."

"This is the part where she leaves," Chloe said out of the corner of her mouth.

"I know," said Damian. "She appeared in my room once, the day I got my power. She isn't the most accessible person ever."

With an elegant wave of her hand, Carya beckoned them to follow her. Her long white robes trailed behind her as she floated soundlessly to the river's edge, then stood completely still, the breathtaking picture of a patron goddess keeping watch over some hallowed glen.

"Does she want us to follow her into the river?" Ethan asked. "And then pop out the other side in a fiery tunnel?"

"That was my interpretation," said Damian, cramming his fists into his hoodie pocket.

Ethan flicked his helmet and then spun it backwards in his hands. "I think I'd rather take my chances with the councilman."

"Duna wouldn't lead us somewhere if he didn't have a plan for us," said Chloe.

Carya smiled at this and gestured at the river. Tiny crystals fell like water droplets from her fingers and infused the waves with an otherworldly shade of turquoise.

"We don't have to be scared," Chloe said.

Damian folded his arms. "And what if his plan involves us being asphyxiated?" he asked.

Ethan laughed.

At least they still had a sense of humor. Chloe had a hunch they'd need it.

"Carya has done nothing except help us, or try to warn us," said Chloe. "The last thing Orpheus told me was that I couldn't lose faith. I promised him I wouldn't." She walked to Carya's side and inhaled the sweet aroma of lavender, lemon, and the hint of thyme emanating from the translucent cloud around her. "Stay here if you want. But I'm going."

And with that, Chloe dove headfirst into the river.

CHAPTER SIX
ESCAPE

E than's heartbeat accelerated as he scanned the river in disbelief. Chloe had just returned from hell. How could she so readily dive into some mysterious portal she knew nothing about except that it led to a "tunnel of fire"? She was either an adrenaline junkie who'd lost her mind, or she really did have faith in this new god called Duna. He knew which it was, and only wished he could be so confident.

The glowing girl named Carya bowed her head, then vanished with a brilliant flash of light, leaving Ethan and

Damian alone with only two options before them: take their chances in the river, or be captured at any moment by the councilman's guards and hope that by some miracle they would be pardoned.

It wasn't a difficult choice to make, yet one thing held Ethan back. "What about my parents?" he asked softly, half hoping Carya would return and tell him they'd be all right, or explain how he might save them.

At least we could have waited one day for Chloe's doma to come back. As he thought the words, he knew they were nonsense. In twenty-four hours, they'd all be locked away in a cell, waiting to hear by which sadistic method of execution they'd die, if they weren't dead already. They didn't *have* one day. His parents had made their decision, and there was nothing anyone could do about it.

"I'm really sorry, Ethan," said Damian. He sounded sincere.

Ethan gave him a nod. "Thanks. I know you know how it feels to have your parents taken from you."

The words felt odd as soon as he said them. Damian's parents had been murdered, whereas his own parents had left him of their own accord. But deep down he knew they were all still victims, innocent prey being lured into a snare. Even after all that his father had witnessed, the councilman's influence through the years had been so powerful, so all-consuming, that it had warped Moris's judgment. It was manipulating him still, forcing him to do his bidding, even when that bidding meant delivering himself, and his wife, up for death.

"It's the worst feeling in the world," Damian said.

Ethan watched a gray heron circle above the river and land on the opposite side. He remembered that in the ancient myths, the heron symbolized the eternal struggle between good and evil, a struggle that, they were taught in school, had been won long ago. And now Ethan knew which side had been the victor.

"And I'm sorry for what I said about your dad," Damian continued. "I shouldn't have called him a traitor."

"It's okay. I'd probably do the same if the tables were turned."

Damian zipped up his hoodie to his chin and watched the heron wade into the turquoise water. He sighed. "I left my sister at the Lake Thyra portal. I don't intend to abandon her again." He clapped a hand on Ethan's shoulder. "You've been a better brother to her than I have."

Ethan jumped as a dart pierced the side of Damian's neck, knocking him out instantly. Ethan turned to see no fewer than thirty guards, all in tactical gear like his, form a perimeter at the edge of the trees. They raised their weapons and aimed at Ethan; another dart struck him in the chest, penetrating only his aluminum chest plate.

Before they could fire another, he dropped his helmet, bent down and yanked the dart from Damian's neck, then pushed him into the river as bullets started to fly. Ethan dove in and dragged Damian under. He heard yelling, splashing, and a barrage of gunfire. The water churned with the desperate strokes and kicks of Ethan's limbs.

And then the cacophony was replaced by perfect silence as a flicker of orange, no larger than his hand, appeared in the murky depths below.

☾

"Ethan!"

It was Chloe's voice, but Ethan's eyes were too busy adjusting to the light to see her. How long had he been swimming? It felt like hours. He tilted his head to either side, letting the river water stream out of his ears.

"Did Damian make it?" he asked.

"He's right here beside you," said Chloe. She was breathless, panicky. She placed her hand on Ethan's arm. "What's wrong with him?"

Ethan's vision slowly returned. The first thing he saw was a blazing wall of fire not ten yards away, the heat of which quickly replaced his shivers with beads of sweat.

"He got shot with a tranq. It'll wear off, but we've got to get him out of here."

Ethan looked around. All he could see was black, billowing smoke overhead and a narrow pathway bisecting the fiery walls. It seemed impossible that the flames weren't devouring the path and everything in it.

Chloe helped Ethan to his feet. He started to pant as sweat trickled down his back beneath the thick foam padding of his suit. He had no doubt he'd self-combust if he stayed inside it much longer.

"Can you help me get all this off?" he asked, tugging on his elbow pads.

Chloe began removing his gear, piece by piece, until all that remained were his black, polycotton pants. He caught Chloe glancing at his naked chest and arms, and a burst of heat, not from the fire, filled his face. He bent down, lifted Damian up and threw him over his shoulder, his body a dead weight.

He hadn't had time to check Damian's vitals. He could be dead for all Ethan knew.

"Come on," said Chloe. "They're up there." She covered her face with her jacket and took off running.

Ethan coughed. "Who's up there?"

"You'll see."

With his legs leaden and lungs burning, he ran with Chloe for half a mile. They were so hopped up on adrenaline, neither one of them needed a break. Their survival instincts drove them on. They wouldn't stop until they had found a way out—or dropped dead trying.

Up ahead, four shadowy figures came into view.

Chloe smiled and slowed her pace. "They're the good guys," she said.

"We could use some good guys," Ethan grunted. He was suddenly aware of a massive cramp in his left trapezius and a dull ache in his lower back. Hunger, thirst, pain and exhaustion were also making their presence known. He couldn't carry Damian much longer. "Any chance one of them is a dude?"

"Yes, two of them, actually, if you count the Centaur." Chloe gave him a playful sideways glance, this time looking only at his eyes.

"Even better." He adjusted his grip on Damian's wrist and resumed his weary jog.

"Iris! Tycho!" Chloe shouted, but the roar of the flames swallowed her voice.

They pushed onward, using every bit of strength to close the gap that separated them from the others. Ethan could only hope they had domas or some other life-saving trick up their sleeves.

Just before the world started to dim and his feet refused to continue, the half-horse, half-human creature stopped and turned to face them. He gave a high-pitched whinny, alerting the other three to the sudden company, and then galloped toward them, scowling. A scabbard bound to the Centaur's waist revealed the bronze hilt of a sword.

He definitely didn't look like a good guy to Ethan.

"What are you doing here?" the Centaur barked. Then he looked them up and down as though he was trying to make sense of their strange attire. "Who are you?"

"I'm an Asher," said Chloe. "Like Iris. And so is my brother." She touched the side of Damian's leg, hanging limply from Ethan's torso. "He's sick. Please...can you carry him for us?"

The Centaur gave a coarse laugh. "You've caught me in a merciful mood. I'm afraid there isn't time for me to be ornery." He turned sideways and jerked his thumb toward his back. "Throw him aboard."

Ethan positioned Damian across the Centaur's body as carefully as he could, trying simultaneously to keep Damian's body stable and his own stressed knees from buckling. Insisting that Chloe ride too, he helped her up, and then sighed with relief as his muscles and joints relaxed. He smiled his thanks to the Centaur and closed his eyes, craving just a split second of rest.

The Centaur laid a heavy hand on Ethan's shoulder. "Don't fade out now, kid. The fire's almost over."

Ethan opened his eyes and shook his head, willing his body to forget its appetite, discomfort and fatigue. "I won't."

He tried his best to appear undaunted as he looked up at the Centaur towering a good two feet above him. There was something familiar about him, something in his narrow, deep-set eyes that gave Ethan the eeriest sense of déjà vu. "I've seen you before."

"Come on!" one of the women up ahead called to the Centaur. Her arms were outstretched to either side, palms erect as fire flowed out of them like gushing rapids.

Chloe stared. Was *she* the one creating the fire?

"Ethan, you're worrying me," said Chloe. "That's impossible. There's no way you've seen him before. Not unless you can time travel, too." Then she kicked the Centaur's flanks lightly and clicked her tongue.

The Centaur snorted and threw back his bald head. "I'm not a donkey to be spurred and goaded on!" he yelled.

"I'm sorry," said Chloe, patting his withers. "I wasn't thinking."

Even in the flame-cast shadows, Ethan could see her blushing.

The Centaur hacked and spat on the ground, reared up—just enough to teach Chloe a lesson—and trotted off toward a faint circle of sunlight...the way out.

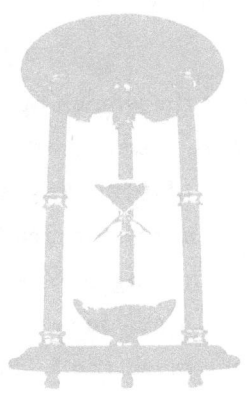

CHAPTER SEVEN
ALLIES

Chloe wished there was time to assure Ethan that everything would be okay. She remembered her first experience in the tunnel and how terrified she'd been. She had been certain that she would die there, and she'd have nothing to blame but her own stupidity for eating a walnut given to her by some innocent-looking urchin in the backseat of her car.

She hadn't known that the urchin was a messenger from Duna, or that the walnut was providing a foretaste of her doma. She'd only known that she wanted answers, and she was willing to take any risk to find them.

At this moment, all Ethan knew was that if they were lucky, his parents would soon be tried for treason, and that his own demise wasn't far behind.

"Come on, Charis," Chloe whispered. "Any minute now..."

As if reading her thoughts, the redheaded woman disappeared for a few short seconds. When she returned, she lifted her arms, signaling to her mother that it was safe to stop the fire.

Iris closed her hands and doubled over, her back heaving and arms shaking at her sides. Tycho ran to her and drew her into his arms. Her charred palms leaked tendrils of smoke like blood.

Gradually, the walls of fire weakened until only dark gray whorls of smoke were left. The air was humid and thick with the smell of dry dirt and burning grass.

Chloe looked back at Ethan, who was a good ways behind, moving at a snail's pace, his eyes barely open. "Ethan, look!" she called to him.

She smiled as rain splashed onto his nose and forehead. He tilted his chin to the sky, opened his mouth, and welcomed the downpour.

The Centaur stopped abruptly. "Girlie, your ferry ride has ended."

"Thank you, Mr. Centaur," Chloe said, sliding off his back.

Damian's elbow jerked. "Chloe?"

His voice was so hoarse Chloe could hardly hear him. "Are you okay, Damian?" she asked, brushing his hair off his sweaty brow. "How do you feel?"

"What's going on?" Damian sniffed the air and grimaced. "What's that smell?"

Chloe wondered if the sour scent of the Centaur had woken him.

The Centaur turned his head toward them and ground his teeth. "I save your atrociously adorned skins and this is the thanks I get? Childish insults?"

"Take it easy, Mr. Centaur," said Chloe. "No need to be so sensitive about your body odor. We've all got it."

The Centaur muttered under his breath and started walking again.

Damian's eyes widened as he lurched forward, finding his balance on the Centaur's back. "The horse is talking?"

"Shhh!" Chloe snapped, trotting alongside them. "He's a Centaur."

Damian's features froze as all the color drained from his face. He braced himself on the Centaur's withers and slowly pressed himself up. "Oh my gods..."

"What?"

Damian leaned forward, straining to get a better look at the Centaur's face. "Katsaros?"

The Centaur ran a hand over his bald head, on which a black serpent was tattooed. "Is that some sort of joke?"

He halted again. "Get off me, kid. If you're well enough for insults and jokes, you're well enough to walk."

Ethan caught up with them and eased Damian off the Centaur's back. "How are you feeling?"

"He's about to be feeling a hoof in his spleen if he doesn't shut his trap," said the Centaur.

"Your name is Katsaros," Damian said. "I met you. Ethan and I both did." His eyes darted back and forth between Ethan and the Centaur, waiting for one of them to confirm this, but neither did.

"I'm afraid that whatever sickness the girl says you've got has turned your brain to mush." The Centaur laughed. "Do you have any idea what 'katsaros' means in our language?" Damian shook his head. "Curly-haired." The Centaur pointed to his shaven scalp. "Does it look like that description belongs to me?"

Chloe looked the Centaur up and down. His bare chest and bulging arms, though undoubtedly strong, were covered in curly chestnut hair. "It does, actually," she said. She reached out to touch his arm, but he sidestepped away with an aggravated neighing sound. "And guess why we're even able to understand your language."

The Centaur made a mocking face. "You've stumped the odiferous Centaur. Tell me."

"Because of Carya," said Chloe. "She did something to our ears."

The Centaur scratched his head, stupefied. "So that's what that was. The little sprite paid a visit just this morning." He tugged on his earlobe. "They're still ringing a bit."

"What's going on?" came Iris's voice.

Chloe spun around to see Tycho, Iris, and their teenage daughter Charis standing before them. Unlike the last time she had met all three of them, they didn't look particularly pleased to see her.

"Who are you?" Tycho asked Chloe, his voice stern but not angry.

"Tycho," said Iris softly. "Don't you remember her? She's from the ship that day."

Tycho's jaw fell as his mind registered her face. "Our friend Chloe!" He leaned forward and kissed her on both cheeks. Iris and Charis did the same.

"Yes, but I'm not alone this time." Chloe looked around. The smoke had finally cleared enough for her to see the barren plain around them and the jagged mountains in the distance, their snowy peaks piercing the clouds.

Without the faintest warning, the earth beneath their feet began to quake. A strong gust of wind whistled through the grass and kicked gritty dust into their eyes.

"Mania…" said Iris. "We've got to get off this plain. We're open targets here."

Fear fell like a shadow across Charis's face. "There are outlaws in these mountains, Mama."

"There's no need to worry," Charis's father said. "They're mostly refugees, as well as a few centaurs. And we know their hearts are softer than they let on." Tycho grinned at the Centaur.

The Centaur threw back his head with a laugh. "Lightning doesn't strike the same race twice, I'm afraid." He glared at Chloe and Damian. "But our kind doesn't make trouble...till trouble comes knocking at our door."

The ground shook again, this time nearly sending Chloe backward into the dirt. Ethan grabbed her arm and held her steady until the tremors passed.

"Your threats will have to wait until we reach shelter," Iris said in a firm, maternal tone, defying anyone to ignore her.

The Centaur piped up again after a few moments' pause. "Are we really going to trust these three ragamuffins so easily?"

Iris's posture straightened at this.

"Call me paranoid," the Centaur said, "but what if they've been sent by Mania to do a reconnaissance of our position, or worse? Perhaps the lass was a friend once, but who's to say she hasn't been corrupted?"

Chloe looked helplessly at Ethan, who stood close, ready to catch her should the shaking start again. She could neither prove they weren't on Mania's side, nor that she and Damian were Ashers. But by the way everyone was staring at her, they obviously expected answers before they took another step.

"The stone on your necklace," said Damian. He was looking at Iris. "It's jasper, isn't it?"

The warm wind blew across Iris's auburn hair as she nodded.

"It was handed down through generations, starting with you, I assume." Damian's glance swung to the Centaur. "You—well, you in the form of a middle-aged man named Katsaros—recited a poem that went along with it." He looked down and frowned at the sun-scorched grass. "I can't remember the words."

"You're from the future?" Charis asked.

"At least two thousand years from now," Damian answered.

Chloe whipped her head toward the Centaur. "That would be why we're so atrociously adorned."

"I would show you my powers if I could," Damian said, before the Centaur had a chance to retort. "But Carya recently informed us that domas have limits." He lightly elbowed Chloe's arm. "We both reached ours earlier today."

"Today..." Charis began.

"You mean two thousand years from now," Tycho said, finishing his daughter's thought.

"Duna dwells outside of time," said Iris, with the sage wisdom of a goddess. "And so do his laws." She pointed to the western sky. A black thunderhead sailed past the sun, covering the plain in darkness. Like waves in a squall, it churned with fury, swallowing the horizon in a matter of seconds.

"I am honored to meet you." Iris gave Damian a slight bow, and Charis and Tycho followed suit. "The three of you must be strong indeed if Duna saw fit to send you here."

Already Chloe felt fear—the same fear she'd felt in Hades—gripping her heart and shortening her breath, but she made herself speak anyway. "We're here to help you, Iris," she said. "Whatever it takes."

It was too late to turn back now.

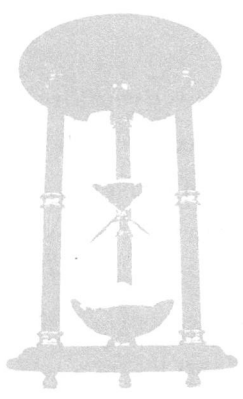

CHAPTER EIGHT

PUNISHMENT

Hermes sat on the palace parapet between the towers overlooking the miry gorges and the smog-filled valleys of Hades. The chimera stood watch beside him, its leonine head scanning the horizon for brazen souls trying to flee for the Styx or get their hands on Hermes' brothers. It was funny, Hermes mused, that this horrific, fire-breathing creature, the stuff of children's nightmares and the most monstrous of myths, was his only companion in the world.

When Hermes wasn't busy doing Apollo's bidding and creating chaos for the mortals, he would alight upon this lofty corner of hell and let his mind daydream about heaven and what was happening there. What dark outer reaches of the cosmos were being stirred into life with a touch of Duna's finger? What unmapped galaxies were his former countrymen exploring, with their blinding wings of gold and lightning-fast chariots? What glorious music, the kind that emblazons upon one's heart epic tales of love and valor and sacrifice without a word being sung, was emanating from Duna's throne room?

Had anyone there seen or heard what he had done for the Vessel and her brother? Did Duna know that Hermes, dastardly rogue and sworn enemy of humankind, had divorced himself from the blasphemous trinity that had corrupted thousands of faithful *ágioi*—the holy ones—and bred vile monsters such as the one standing guard beside him? If he did know, was there even a hairsbreadth of a chance that he might call him up to heaven's gates and bestow mercy?

"There you are."

The chimera's snake tail hissed at the sound of approaching footsteps. Hermes didn't need to turn around. Only one voice in the world chilled his bones as Apollo's did.

"Where else would I be?" he said.

Arrayed in a gossamer nimbus of light, Apollo stilled the chimera's tail. On his periphery, Hermes watched his brother pull from the scabbard opposite his sword a pair of ivory pipes and begin to play the ghostly lullaby reserved for all the hybrid beasts, from the gorgons and harpies to Cerberus at the Styx.

After a few seconds, the chimera's mammoth-sized body fell to the ground with a thud that vibrated in Hermes' ribs.

"You're not one for idling away the hours like some starry-eyed philosopher," said Apollo, taking his seat beside Hermes.

"Unlike you, brother," Hermes began, although he knew better, "the All-Powerful has granted me the privilege of beholding the stars on the rare occasion that my pride doesn't hinder me from looking heavenward. That they sometimes fill my eyes is perhaps the only beauty still afforded me."

A guttural growl rumbled in Apollo's throat. The light around his body dimmed as a furious heat pulsed through it, burning Hermes' skin. The dark lord balled his hands into fists, arms shaking as he fought to restrain his temper. "Why this sudden hatred of me, Hermes?" Apollo asked between clenched teeth.

"You cast me away like some leprous beggar," answered Hermes. He had nothing to lose by speaking his mind. Their chance to make amends had been dashed the second he had given the boy and his friends those seeds.

"You failed your mission," Apollo said, his voice rising. His cerulean eyes flashed black like onyx pearls. "It was because of you that the Ashers slipped through our grasp. Your negligence is the reason the fugitives escaped their execution."

The luminescent web around Apollo faded with a sharp fizzing sound. Vines of anemic light slid from the crown of his head and reached the granite wall, dripping to the ground a hundred feet below. His gilded armor gleamed red, glowing with the ire boiling deep in his bloodless veins.

"And what of the girl?" Hermes asked. "Am I to take the blame for her disappearance from the Vale? Was she not entrusted to the watchful care of Deimos and Phobos?" He watched Apollo's hand jump to the hilt of his sword, gripping it so tightly that Hermes expected his brother's white knuckles to pop through the flesh.

"The girl didn't escape!" Apollo barked, then got to his feet and drew his sword. "She vanished, or so the witnesses say. Deimos and Phobos were helpless to prevent it." He pressed the sword's tip to Hermes' chin and lifted up his brother's face. "But you..." he seethed. "Aren't you the gifted one among us three? The one with the power to fly, to shapeshift, to charm, to traipse around all Petros, unseen if you choose?"

Apollo paused to give Hermes time to refute these charges, but no denial could be made. "And still two mortals eluded you. Two children whose powers only recently manifested."

"Let's not beat around the bush, brother," said Hermes. "I'd wager you've had more eyes than Argus watching me of late. No doubt one of your devils has informed you of my perfidy." He pulled his head back and placed his neck against the side of Apollo's blade. "Take my head and throw it to the furies. And when it grows back, chain me beside my father below and let his bolt be my bane for eternity." He stared down at the blade, daring Apollo to deal the deathblow. "I care not what you do to me."

Apollo sneered down at the silver blade, contempt curling his lips into a bloodthirsty snarl. "Do you have any idea what you've done?"

"Of course," said Hermes, unfazed by the pressure of the sword pushing harder against his jugular. "We've committed high treason against the All-Powerful." He couldn't help but chuckle. "We ascended the heights of hubris and staked our claim as the most imbecilic numbskulls in the history of all creation."

With one swift motion, Apollo flipped his sword in the air and thrust its pommel hard into Hermes' chest, knocking the wind out of him. "If you weren't immune to every poison and potion of our realm, I'd suspect someone played a trick on the chief of tricksters."

"It's no trick," Hermes wheezed, as he fell onto his hands and knees. "What's done is done. I'm ready to face my punishment, from you and the All-Powerful both."

Apollo spun the sword on its tip and let it clatter onto the ground. He crouched before Hermes and pulled him up by the cowl of his cloak. "You think the All-Powerful cares about a sniveling worm like you?"

He pushed Hermes against the sleeping chimera's belly. The monster stirred as the snake tail impulsively whipped against Hermes' shin.

"You think he cares about a spineless, two-faced fox who acts without creed or convention? He sees straight through you, as I do." Apollo spat in Hermes' face, then again when Hermes wiped away the spittle. "You disgust me."

Hermes felt as if scales, which had hitherto blinded him from the truth, had been peeled from his eyes. He was beginning to think and see clearly for the first time since before the War, before the rebellion that had cleaved heaven in two. He lifted himself from the ground and drew his wand from the small leather sheath on his belt.

"You will lose, brother."

Hermes reared back and heaved the wand over the wall. Next to go were his winged sandals, which he offered to the goat head bleating greedily from the chimera's back. It gobbled down the snack then promptly belched with satisfaction.

"Your success in blotting out Duna from the pages of history has been nothing more than an illusion." Hermes dunked his fingers into his satchel and brought out gold grains of sand from Circe's bewitched island of Aeaea. He threw them into the air and then, using his fingers, directed them to collect before Apollo's face in the form of a diadem.

Unable to resist its beauty, Apollo reached for it, but the crown broke apart and the sand gathered again into seven separate arches.

The Moonbow.

Apollo roared at the top of his lungs. Even the lion head of the chimera ducked its head in fear.

But Hermes had never stood stronger. He waved the Moonbow toward him, and then sent it up into the false dome of sky pushing against Petros's crust. "The Moonbow and all it stands for—sacrifice, salvation, freedom, triumph—will prevail."

"You know *nothing*," Apollo roared. "I've been silencing and destroying Ashers for generations. I silenced our father, Zeus, and that sea monster, Poseidon. Do you think I'm afraid of these children just because there are two of them?"

Hermes walked forward, stood within inches of Apollo's face and gave his answer clearly, drawing it out with an orator's flourish. "Yes."

Apollo stepped on the hilt of his sword and it sprang with eagerness into his hand. A second later, Hermes felt the cold steel pierce his abdomen. Apollo leaned into him, driving the blade deeper and deeper until not an inch of it was visible.

"Get used to this," Apollo whispered and then kissed Hermes on the cheek.

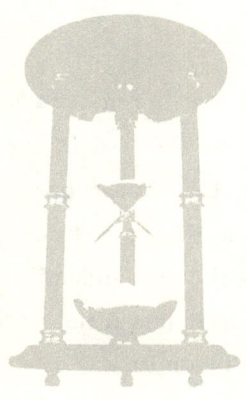

CHAPTER NINE
KINSHIP

Damian jolted awake at the sound of metal clashing against metal. His eyes flashed to Chloe, who was sitting cross-legged on a straw mat, stuffing her mouth with bread.

"Sorry," she said, breadcrumbs spilling from her lips. "Did I wake you up?"

Damian shook his head, then winced at a crick in his neck and frowned at the lumpy makeshift pillow he'd made of his hoodie. "No," he said, pointing outside, "that did."

The door of the tent they'd been assigned to fluttered open long enough for Damian to see Ethan and Tycho sparring with swords, their bodies backlit by a peach sunrise peeking over the mountains. A huge, gray wolf-like dog stuck its nose inside the tent and sniffed the air. It seemed to be deciding whether it wanted to further investigate these new people or be on its way.

Chloe held out her bread, and the canine bounded toward her and poked at her hand with its snout. "You hungry?" Chloe scratched its back then patted its belly. "You sure don't feel like you're underfed."

"It's a dog, Chloe. They're always hungry." Damian rolled his eyes as his sister gave the dog her bread. It scarfed it down without chewing. "You know animals aren't supposed to have people food, right?"

"Not everyone reads the signs at the zoo."

The dog neared Chloe's face and smelled her hair and ears. "That tickles!" she squealed.

The dog's wide jaws smiled at her excitement, and its tail wagged back and forth in a frenetic blur. It crouched down in a playful pose, floppy ears alert, tail fanning the ground.

"What does it want?" Chloe asked.

"For you to play with it," Damian answered.

Without hesitating, Chloe got on all fours and emitted a pathetic series of barks. The dog tilted its head to the side, then, as if it could think of nothing better to do, trotted forward and graced her cheek with a slobbery lick.

"Ewwww!" She wiped the drool from her face and rubbed her hand on the hard dirt floor.

"I see you've met Artemis."

Damian glanced up to see an old man in white robes standing in the opening of the tent. He stooped and stepped inside, then pointed an authoritative finger at the dog. "Artemis, out!"

The dog spun around and sat on its haunches, like a soldier at attention.

"Haven't you got a corncrake to catch?" the man said.

"Clever name," said Chloe. "Artemis was my favorite goddess." Hearing her name called, Artemis's taut body relaxed and she cuddled close to Chloe's side. "So you're a girl." Chloe grinned and stroked the dog's head. Artemis panted happily as her tail made a swishing noise on the floor.

The old man furrowed his brow as he squinted at Chloe from beneath his bushy salt-and-pepper unibrow. "A pagan goddess. If the hound were mine, I'd change her name and sprinkle holy water on her."

Damian stood and wiped the dust from his jeans. "I'm Damian. This is my sister, Chloe."

"I've been informed," the man said as he lifted his chin and squared his shoulders, then placed a hand over his ear lightly. "I was informed by the messenger. She gave me quite a fright when she invaded my quarters like a ransacking thief."

Chloe laughed, but stopped when she saw the man was not the slightest bit amused.

"You are Ashers, is that right?" He looked Damian up and down, suspicion deepening every wrinkle of his face as he studied him.

"We are," said Chloe. Maintaining a hand on Artemis's neck, she stood up. "I hope that's okay with you."

Artemis stopped panting. Her tail stopped wagging. She could sense the tension in the cramped space.

"Of course." The man combed his long hoary beard with his fingers. He turned to Damian. "After what Iris has done for our world, any Asher is a friend of the temple." The man's mouth smiled, although his lusterless eyes remained cold. He extended his hand to Chloe. "My name is Archelaos. I became high priest after Anatolius was assassinated."

"High priest at the temple," said Chloe. "I don't know if Carya told you, but my doma allows me to travel through time. During one of my trips, I saw the temple destroyed. There was nothing left except ruins."

The man's hand lowered shakily to his heart. Sensing his distress, Artemis went to him and brushed up against his legs, then licked his fingers.

"I take it that's in the future," Damian said to Chloe. She shrugged as the old man staggered back. "Way to go, Chloe. You're gonna give him a heart attack."

The man quickly righted himself as if he were ashamed of his startled reaction. The hand on his heart returned gracefully to his side as he closed his eyes and inhaled deeply through his nose. "How susceptible the flesh is to fear." He opened his eyes. "How quickly it forgets that it does no good to fret about the future."

"Maybe that's why we're here," Chloe said. "To change the future."

Carefully, the old man knelt beside a terracotta jar. He picked it up by its vertical handles and poured water into a shallow bowl. Artemis neared it, her pink tongue reaching for a drink, but the man shooed her away.

"Worthless mutt," he rasped.

He washed his hands in the water and reached for a folded towel that had been placed on the tent's solitary bench. "They say the Ashers are sent by Duna, that their powers flow from him and operate for our good. But I'm not convinced." He dried his hands and then eased himself up from the floor. "Whatever becomes of you and your friends out there, my hands, and my conscience, are clean."

(

A chill hung in the air, even though, from the sight of the red and yellow wildflowers dappling the foothills, Damian knew it was spring or early summer. He was surrounded by

tents, and scores of people—men, women and children—
milled about as if this rocky countryside were a proper city.

One-wheeled carts filled with timber creaked along
the uneven earth toward what appeared to be small houses
under construction. There was only one finished building,
which, from the puffs of smoke rising from its chimney and
the repetitive banging of hammers, Damian assumed was
a forge.

Going the opposite way, toward the mountain, were
young, suntanned women with wicker baskets on their
arms. In the plain below, spans of oxen pulled their plows
while unchaperoned children zigzagged between the rows
in high-spirited games of chase.

Damian and Chloe asked around for Ethan and the
others, but they soon learned that the communication
barrier between themselves and the general public hadn't
been broken by Carya's magic. It was probably for the
best, they decided; no information was better than a little
information that could easily morph into gossip and rumor.
As far as Damian was concerned, having Archelaos's distrust
was already a problem.

They found a boulder to sit on and watched as the old
man darted and weaved through the hubbub. When an
attendant approached holding the reins of a sorrel steed, the
old man mounted and cantered down the hill, out of sight.

"No heart attack," said Chloe.

Damian blew air out his nostrils, his version of a laugh at one of Chloe's quips. "Not yet."

He turned to Chloe and, for the first time since they'd reunited, realized how desperately she needed a bath. Her dirty-blond hair was darkened by the buildup of oil and dirt, and ash covered her pale skin. Her eyes, framed by puffy blue circles, were glassy, and every inch of her clothing was begrimed. But she didn't seem to care. He knew she had never cared about anyone's opinion of her, least of all his.

"So tell me about this Mania person," said Damian.

"I'm only assuming she's a person," said Chloe, smiling at Artemis as the dog walked by, heeling at the side of a young man carrying a bow, a quiver of arrows strapped across his chest. "From what I saw, and what you saw last night..." Chloe paused and stared vacantly into the distance. "She's more like a storm."

"Why did you go back to see the temple destroyed?"

"I didn't mean to, really," Chloe said, pulling her hair back into a ponytail. "I've only used the doma a few times, but it seems to respond to prayer. When I used it to go to the temple, I just prayed for Ethan to survive."

"Survive what?"

"Apparently the councilman rigs all the guards' suits with bombs. Crazy, right?"

Damian's stomach balled into a knot as his mind flashed back to his own brush with death, when he'd helped Ethan and his parents escape the council building. "He's a maniac."

"You can imagine how nuts Mania is if there's a word named after her."

"So why do you think the prayer led you to the temple? Why not to the councilman's so-called coronation?" Damian felt his neck grow hot. There was nothing he'd like more than to stick that needle into the councilman's puny little arm and watch his life ebb away.

Chloe picked at the dirt beneath her fingernails. "I thought it was because Duna wanted the councilman to see the world like it was before. When people were free and there weren't any secrets."

She lifted her gaze to a group of little girls braiding each other's hair beneath a shady plane tree down the slope. Not far from them, a half dozen boys kicked a ball back and forth.

"There was a celebration going on before Mania got there," she continued. "And it was so much better than the Lycaea Festival." She looked at Damian as if she might elaborate, but instead pressed her lips together and reached for the cup of water on the grass beside her.

"But the councilman's perspective wasn't changed, obviously," said Damian.

He saw Ethan and Tycho trudging up the hill, their faces glistening with sweat, their bare shoulders pink with the start of sunburn. Charis, holding Iris's hand, appeared at their side and smiled shyly when her eyes met his. Iris's jasper stone glinted in the sunlight as she waved at them.

"No," answered Chloe. "That's why I don't think that was the reason Duna led me there."

"Then why?"

"I think he wanted to show me what I'm supposed to stop."

Whether she'd intended it or not, Damian felt the sting in her words; she was expecting to go after Mania alone, to change the course of history on her own. And why would she think any differently? Why would she think that he, her own flesh and blood, who'd left her to rot in Hades, would help her now? Even if he had helped the Rosses, he hadn't lifted a finger when Chloe had needed him most. She had no reason to trust him.

"I know I haven't always been there for you—" Damian stopped himself. He couldn't sugarcoat this. "I know I deserted you, is what I meant to say."

Chloe lowered her head, her long bangs hiding the side of her face.

"What you said, back in the woods... It was all true, I was a coward. I had the power to save you, and I just walked away."

Chloe took a deep breath and sat up straight. She cleared her throat to speak. "You know what Dad told me when I saw him down there?" Damian shook his head, puckering his lips to keep from crying. "He said the Fantásmata haven't made it easy to act brave or take chances. He said he should

73

have told us about his doma, but he was too afraid, just like all the Ashers in our family before him."

Damian sighed. "You aren't afraid."

Chloe turned to him. "I'm terrified. But we can't let that stop us." She scooted closer and wrapped an arm around his waist, resting her head on his shoulder. "The past is in the past."

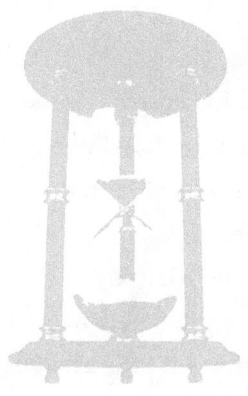

CHAPTER TEN

ORPHANS

It appeared to Ethan that Chloe and Damian had made amends. Chloe's head was resting on Damian's shoulder and he didn't seem to mind.

"Sleep well?" Ethan asked as he removed a damp rag from his neck and wiped his brow. "We tried waking you up this morning so you could come with us. I swear, you two could probably sleep through an earthquake."

"We may very well find out soon," Damian joked.

Chloe raised her head. "Where'd you go?" she asked Ethan.

Damian pinched his nostrils closed. "Did you find a lake or waterfall or something for Chloe to shower in?"

Chloe elbowed his ribs. "You don't exactly smell like a spring bouquet yourself, Damian."

Ethan laughed. "Be nice, kids."

It was nice to see them getting along. Even before this whole Asher thing started, Ethan had never known them to be particularly close. The majority of their classmates didn't even know they were siblings, let alone twins.

He turned at the sound of clip-clopping hooves sauntering up the rocky path. The Centaur was munching on an orange and wore a wide-brimmed hat on his head. If only Ethan's friends at school could see this.

"What are you gawking at?" the Centaur said, his mouth full of the orange flesh of the fruit.

Ethan blinked and turned away. He hadn't meant to stare. "Nothing. You're just..."

The Centaur spit out a seed. "Just what, man? Spit it out."

"You're different," Damian answered for Ethan.

The Centaur leaned sideways so he could look past Ethan into Damian's eyes. He jabbed a finger at him. "Don't even start with me, kid."

"You'll believe me one day," said Damian. "One day when you're dead."

The Centaur threw the orange skin into the dirt and stormed forward, nearly knocking Ethan off his feet. "Are you threatening me now?" He grabbed Damian's arm and yanked him off the boulder.

Damian wiggled his fingers tauntingly and shifted his weight from one foot to the other.

"Hey!" yelled Chloe. Was Damian really going to try and wrestle an eight-foot Centaur? She jumped up and stood between them, holding her brother back with her hand.

"I'm not threatening you," said Damian, in the most threatening tone he could use. He spun away from Chloe's hand and stood in front of the Centaur.

Ethan scanned the area for a stick, a rock, a bucket, anything he could use to intervene should things get ugly. He wanted to tell Damian to see if his doma worked so he could become invisible, but that would just put Ethan on the Centaur's blacklist, and he didn't have a power with which to defend himself.

"All I'm doing," Damian said, sounding only a smidgen calmer, "is telling you that I met you in the future. And you were different." He took a step back, giving the Centaur some breathing room. "Way different."

The Centaur scratched his chin where the hat's strap ran across it. "And why, pray tell, did I come back from the grave to visit the likes of you?"

"Because Duna sent you to teach me." Damian looked away, and Ethan could almost see the weight of remorse bearing down on his friend's shoulders. "You said you were living proof that faith can save the soul of any wretch, even a murdering, thieving, lying, cheating Centaur like you." Damian threw up his hands before the Centaur could retaliate. "Those were *your* words, not mine."

Ethan looked at the Centaur, but he didn't appear angry. Quite the opposite: he'd pulled the hat over his face, trying in vain to hide the fact that he was crying like a child.

Chloe looked at Ethan and shrugged.

He shrugged back and waved her over to him. "Maybe we should give them some bonding time," he whispered.

Chloe smiled and shook her head. "Life just keeps getting weirder and weirder, huh?"

"We've come a long way from the gryphon fossils back at the museum."

They walked down the road toward their tents. Ethan folded his arms across his chest, suddenly self-conscious about being half naked in front of a girl. If they'd been back in their time, he would have been suspended from school and probably jailed for *aprépeia*, indecency. It had never made sense to him that sexual intercourse was permitted at fourteen, yet being shirtless was a crime. Just more rules with which the Fantásmata reinforced their control and kept people more preoccupied with staying in line than seeking the truth.

"Did you really meet the Centaur like Damian said you did?" Chloe asked him.

"I met Katsaros. Remember the overweight PE instructor we had in grade four?"

"That was the Centaur?" Chloe said, incredulous.

Ethan laughed. "No, but he looked a lot like him, except Katsaros wore corduroy pants and suspenders instead of a sweatsuit."

"You're kidding."

"Afraid not."

Chloe looked over her shoulder. "Sounds like it was an effective disguise."

"I guess when things got desperate enough, he showed Damian who he really was."

Chloe became quiet as she slowed her pace.

Ethan could see that he'd touched a sore spot. "So it seems like you and Damian have patched things up," he said, hoping he'd been correct in his earlier assessment.

"We're in this together now," she said. "Whatever he did or didn't do, it doesn't matter now."

Ethan smiled his agreement as two children sprinted past, the older chasing the younger and yelling angrily in Próta.

"And if it's true what Damian said about the Centaur changing from a murderer to a man of faith," Chloe said, "then who am I to think Damian can't change, too?"

"That's a good point. You may not have had your parents for long, but I think they taught you a lot in the short time you did have. They'd be proud of you."

"I hope so." Chloe looked up to the sky and smiled softly. Then, as if just remembering something, she dropped her gaze and turned to him. "Where did you go this morning, with Iris and Tycho?"

Ethan walked toward a copse of olive trees and stood under the shade. "How about I show you?"

Chloe smiled and put a hand on her hip. "I don't need a chaperone."

Ethan tried not to stare at her; at how pretty she looked, even covered in mud and grime and whatever other hell-borrowed substances were stuck to her clothes and skin. He couldn't put words to what made her so attractive to him. It wasn't so much what she looked like but what she did that drew him. The way she laughed and talked and asked questions, always hungry to learn. The way she didn't care what anyone thought or said about her. The way she wasn't afraid to express her emotions, to stand up for herself when necessary. And the way she let go of bitterness and extended forgiveness so readily.

Even without the doma, Chloe was the most unusual girl he knew, in the best of ways.

"I think I'd like to find a river or something first," said Chloe, yanking a short twig out of her hair. She tossed it at him and smiled when he caught it. "I'm starting to smell myself, not a good sign."

"I don't know. Bad things seem to happen whenever you get too close to a body of water." Ethan twirled the twig in his fingers. "First Lake Thyra, which took you to Hades, then the river back home..."

Chloe leaned against the gnarled trunk of the nearest tree. "Hey, neither of those examples ended poorly. I got out of hell, didn't I? And this place isn't all that bad. There's just a storm-generating, humanity-hating, maniacal Asher to contend with. No big deal."

Ethan let the twig fall to the ground as his thoughts traveled back to the river. "I wish it could've ended well for my parents." He hadn't said it to make Chloe feel guilty, but looking at her now, he could see that was exactly how she felt.

She pushed off the tree and went to him. "Ethan, I'm so sorry." She reached out as if to touch his hand, but stopped herself. "That was a really dumb and heartless thing for me to say."

Ethan shook his head. "No. Don't apologize." He looked at her and forced his cheeks into a smile. "It's been on my mind all day."

"You'd think that I, of all people, would be more sympathetic."

"I just want to know what happened to them." Ethan wanted to cry, to feel some sort of release, but he couldn't. He was utterly numb, as if his body and mind were in a state of shock. "I want to know where they are, if they're even still alive."

"I know."

Ethan knew that Chloe understood. She and Damian were the only orphans in modern history. Everyone else lived until age seventy-five, at which time they were murdered in the Fantásmata's twisted coronation ceremony. One day, Ethan hoped, everyone would know the truth, that the eagerly anticipated graduation from elderhood to sovereignty was nothing more than a ritual execution.

Chloe stilled and closed her eyes, just as Ethan had seen her do by the river before Carya had shown up.

"Chloe, what are you doing?"

"Shhh! I have to focus."

Before Ethan could try to stop her, she was gone.

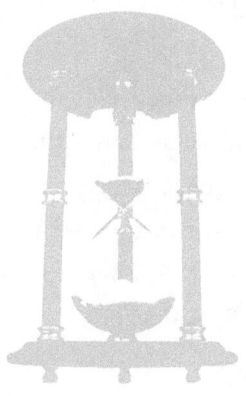

CHAPTER ELEVEN
WARNING

E ver since the night she'd eaten the walnut Carya had given her, Chloe had grown accustomed to darkness. From her time in Hades' prison to the handful of occasions she'd used her doma, darkness seemed to accompany her everywhere she went. It had frightened her at first, but now it was almost a comfort, like the threadbare blanket she'd clung to as a child because it ensured she was never alone.

Chloe was suspended in darkness now. She couldn't even see her hand before her face, nor could she feel any sort of floor beneath her feet. Was she in space again, a part of space without stars or suns to illuminate it?

And then a soft breeze, accompanied by the enlivening scent of lavender, blew through her hair.

"Carya? Is that you?" She felt a small, warm hand take her fingers and gently squeeze.

> *"Do not be alarmed by what you shall see,*
> *This is but a vision of a future that could be.*
> *Death will come for them again, and*
> *   again will Ethan grieve,*
> *It is best to let them rest, and*
> *   in your heart believe*
> *That they received the truth, which*
> *   those in hell now know;*
> *Their spirits flew to heaven, free*
> *   from suffering here below."*

The lavender smell disappeared and was replaced by the nauseating odor of rotten eggs and acrid smoke blended together.

"Carya!" Chloe yelled. She covered her nose as rocky ground rose under her feet and dim light pierced the center of the blackness, expanding like ripples on water. "It's rude to just leave people, you know. Especially after giving them creepy messages."

"Mom! Dad!"

Chloe jumped and turned as she heard Ethan shouting behind her. He was in a small wooden boat, rowing frantically toward the shore. Only a thin sliver of orange sunlight was left hanging on the horizon. As far as the eye could see, the waves were like a battleground covered with flotsam: dead fish, and fragments of shivered oars. What had happened here?

Chloe looked over her shoulder at Ethan's parents running toward her, sheer panic clinging to their faces like plaster masks. The sleeveless robes they wore were ragged and unraveling at the edges.

Behind them charged two unnaturally large bulls whose pounding hooves made the pebbles jump as the earth shook beneath them. From their mouths and nostrils issued a ceaseless spray of fire, the smoke polluting the air with the choking stench of rot. Their entire bodies, from the tips of their horns to the twitch of their swishing tails, were made of solid bronze.

"Automatons..." Chloe said, her heart skipping a beat. Her mind flashed through snippets of stories about these creatures, twin bulls forged by the god Hephaestus as gifts to an ancient king. A hero called Jason had once subdued them, but for whatever reason—a reason she thought was probably linked to Mania—they'd been unleashed to terrorize once again.

Chloe snapped back to reality and commanded her legs to move. She dashed toward Moris and Lydia, hoping she'd be able to make contact and focus long enough to get them out of there. She stopped and held out her arms, yelling for them to take hold of her, but they didn't seem to see her.

She stepped into Moris's path and he ran right through her, as did one of the bulls five seconds later.

"It's just a vision... It's just a vision..."

And then silence, followed by a helpless cry from Ethan and the sound of his body splashing into the water.

"No!" he screamed.

Chloe couldn't bring herself to turn around. She knew exactly what she would see: Moris and Lydia mangled and bleeding on the ground, and Ethan standing on the beach, powerless to save them—if they weren't already dead.

"But *I* can save them," she whispered, hoping Carya could hear.

She didn't have to close her eyes for darkness to return. It fell over her like a cloak and drew her back to the black in-between space where the messenger was waiting.

"Your heart is good and so you wish to
    spare your friend from pain,

But one way or another, they will
meet their death again.
Do not overwhelm yourself with
choices not yours to make,
Stay focused on the quest at hand,
for all of Petros's sake."

A deluge of warm liquid crashed down on Chloe's head, drenching her from head to toe. It wasn't water; it was thicker, like olive oil and shea butter mixed together, and smelled of pine and juniper.

Over the next few minutes, something that felt like a giant loofah went to work scrubbing her face, hands, head and neck. She could taste the grit and bitterness of mud as it dripped and slid between her lips. After the loofah was set aside, a blunt metal tool scraped away the excess soap as a hot mist lightly sprayed her skin. It was only then that she realized she was naked.

"Should I add 'personal hygienist' to your résumé, Carya?"

"There is much more to a leader
than appearances and smell,
But it will not serve you to resemble
a homely imp from hell."

Carya giggled softly as Chloe's jaw fell in astonishment. "Well, that's a little harsh," Chloe said.

But despite the levity of the moment, Chloe couldn't help thinking of Ethan, of the grief she'd seen taking hold of him as shock began to wear off and all the distractions subsided. They'd been too busy escaping from the guards, running through the fire tunnel, and fleeing to the mountains to think about anything other than survival.

Now Ethan was in the same place she'd been in eight years ago. His parents were dead, the latest victims of the Fantásmata. The only difference between them was that it could all be undone. Perhaps even her own parents' death could be undone.

Chloe shivered as the what-if scenarios escalated in her brain. What if she went back eight years and slit the tires of her parents' car, preventing the car accident that had presumably killed them? What if she traveled farther than that and removed every shred of evidence that revealed her father's identity as an Asher? Their family would be free, wiped off the Fantásmata's radar, therefore protecting the Rosses by blocking their involvement in the first place.

Carya was right. Chloe had wanted to spare Ethan from that pain, but she also wanted to spare herself. Even though she knew her parents were in heaven, she still longed to be with them in *this* world, in *this* time. She remembered thinking to herself in the Vale of Mourning that she would be more than happy to remain in hell as long as it meant being reunited with her parents. Now she was infinitely more willing to live in a fallen world run by tyrants, as long as her family was together again.

And as quickly as the what-ifs came, they swiftly dissolved as two wrinkled faces materialized before her mind's eye: Calix and Anastasia, the old couple from the Vale that Carya had entrusted with a message for Chloe. She envisioned how they'd danced together, overcome with rapturous bliss for the first time in centuries. In fact, with their memories erased from the River Lethe, they had no remembrance of happiness. In that moment they'd felt it in its purest form, all because hope had been returned to them.

She remembered Anastasia's last words to her: "Child, you must be brave. All of us can be restored if you'll trust Duna, the god who answered us when we didn't even know his name."

If Chloe returned to the past and undid her parents' deaths, Calix and Anastasia and all the other souls who'd been freed from hell would still be there, and she would be destined for it, too. There, in that dusky dungeon of a valley, where listless spirits trudged through death without remembering a single fact about their lives or the people they'd loved.

Chloe didn't know she'd been crying until a salty tear trickled into the corner of her mouth. She wiped it away as waves of heat, like a summer breeze, fanned across her body. Her scalp tingled as she felt Carya's hands braiding her hair. Seconds later, a woolen robe was draped over her shoulders and Chloe pulled it around her, adjusting it as best she could in the dark.

"Thank you," she said. "Any more warnings or sage advice you want to give me? I can use all the help I can get."

Carya kissed her on the temple as light, fainter than daybreak's first breath, permeated the mysterious ether in which they hovered. Chloe smiled when she saw the deep blue of Carya's robes and the lovely auburn of her waist-long hair. How frightened Chloe had been the first time she'd seen Carya sitting in the backseat of her brother's car with two walnuts in her hand. She'd thought she was hallucinating, on the verge of a mental breakdown.

"I meant to thank you," said Chloe.

The messenger dropped her head coyly, the coronet of pearls atop it glowing like midnight stars.

"For saving my life on Circe's island, and"—Chloe hesitated, reluctant to say the words—"for stopping me from going back to the river. I just..."

Her throat burned as she fought to stay her tears. She smiled and gazed about the hazy sphere encompassing them; it twinkled with opalescent shades of amber, gold, and yellow sapphire, all alternately intensifying and fading as if to a rhythm reserved only for heaven and its denizens to hear.

"I will tell him what you said, though," Chloe continued. "They're in heaven now. With mine."

"You asked for wisdom and a warning
*   to light your path ahead,*
And both did you receive within
*   your vision of the dead.*
A great power has been given you, a gift
*   to change the times and seasons,*
And some may have you do so for
*   their own self-serving reasons.*
You must not be swayed by
*   compassion, fear, or pity,*
This your mission, this alone: preserve
*   the truth of the holy city."*

CHAPTER TWELVE
LETO

The cool evening air drew Leto out of her house and into the moonlit tranquility of the courtyard. Jasmine blooms cast their fragrance along the unvarnished beams of the pergola while violet vines of wisteria spilled sleepily over its face. Firelight from the hearth inside shone just enough to shed an intimate glow upon the haven.

Leto smiled up at the seven Hesperides glittering like gems along the wing of the dragon constellation. Whenever she saw these stars she knew her lover was near, for they always heralded his arrival. It had been weeks since Hermes had come to her, and now, in light of her most recent conquests, she couldn't wait to see him as she guessed at the praises he might give her.

By her hands, the port city of Ourania lay in ashes. With every trireme, punt, and scow destroyed, the survivors had fled on foot into the mountains. They would have found no river on which to journey elsewhere, for in a calculated act of preemption Leto had ravaged them all, one by one, with a relentless assault of whirlpools and winds. Rallying every ounce of stamina and strength she could muster, Leto had stoppered every spring and sucked up every last drop of water before sweeping them into the sea.

Now, with the rivers rendered useless and every port either burning or blockaded, Iris and her cohorts were isolated and well within reach. Leto would have killed them already if not for the resilience of Iris's doma.

The fire had held out longer and burned hotter than Leto could have predicted. But she would be prepared next time. As soon as the Ashers were eradicated and every relic razed, all of Petros would be hers to rule forever, with her prince of Hades at her side.

Leto's heart began to flutter as the prospect of queenship swirled in her imagination like sparkling wine. She sat on the bench beside her favorite fountain: a marble statue comprised of half a dozen bottlenose dolphins, each with fresh spring water spouting from their buoyant bronze mouths.

The fount had been given her by the gorgon, Medusa, back when Leto was still a beautiful maiden and could not make statues of flesh-and-blood beings. She and Medusa had grown up together at the desert fortress known as Ēlektōr, along with hundreds of other children raised to be warriors from the time they could hold a stick. But after Leto's father, Diokles, had been slain, the seditious armies of Ēlektōr disbanded and dispersed before any arrests could be made.

Only Leto had remained there, an orphan with nothing and no one, and nowhere to go. She had spent ten years alone in the abandoned desert, subsisting on lizards, beetles, and the occasional mouse when she could catch one.

At night, she had slept on the hard cella floor inside the temple, two-thirds of her body wedged inside the niche that had once housed the sacred amber tablets. The light emitted from the terracotta lamps around the chamber had done little to comfort her. The only solace she found was in remembering her father's promise to her: "All will be better when you become a woman."

And so, despite the increasing temptation to end it, Leto had clung to her life. She had made up her mind that if she was still alone in her forgotten circle of the Underworld on the final day of her eighteenth year, she would hike up to the fortress summit and cast herself into the dry gully below.

But in the seventh day of her eighteenth year, on the coldest day yet in the month of Gamelion, something extraordinary had happened. In an instant she had known that her father's words were true.

It had all been ignited by a common spark of anger. Leto had just left the old mess kitchen after rummaging through the victuals for wine to keep her warm. The wintry desert air felt like icy fangs biting into her skin, and her bare toes were red and waxy with frostbite. The woolen cowl pulled over her head was so full of holes she thought it would make a better fishing net than a shield from the wind.

"Lord Hades of the dead, if there is a portal beneath my feet through which the shades can see, let my father behold me now!" Leto had cried out with contempt so strong it briefly tamed the pitiless chill. "Let him see what has become of his beloved Leto, a name that means 'hidden,' 'forgotten.' Well, how very prophetic."

She stretched out her arms and looked up into the white waning moon, her ravishing pale face its only equal. "It's a shame that his final oracle, that womanhood would bring me honor, has not proved so precise."

It was then that the sands had begun to swarm. Each "grain" was a tiny ant, and the insects coalesced and marched toward her in organized, fleet-footed ranks.

The ground became warm beneath her as a savage wind erupted from a fresh-carved fissure in the earth between her feet. This unworldly gust gathered the army of ants and flung it against the unfeeling air, where it hung in silence like a crude mosaic.

The wind died down as the moon hid its face behind a cloud. Leto jumped to one side of the crevice and studied the shapeless sand from afar. If Hades were to kidnap her, as he had the maiden Persephone, she would not run; instead, she would welcome him. Anywhere, even the throne room of hell, would be a brighter place to spend her days than here, alone in the ruins of her father's failed regime.

"Perhaps this is what he meant," Leto whispered to herself as she crouched down and drew carelessly, defiantly, in the sand that remained. Perhaps he had meant that after her suffering had run its course, she would be deemed worthy of becoming a hapless mistress of Hades.

She laughed and removed her cloak, but as she let it fall, it wrapped itself tightly around her waist and dragged her toward the frame that was still floating in the air. She dug her nails into the wool, tearing at it like a vulture claws at a carcass until it released her and dropped limply at her feet.

"Show your face, you gutless coward!" Leto shouted. "I am afraid of no man, no matter what side of this cleft he hails from." She gestured to the fissure and spat into it, rousing the wind from its slumber.

The breeze, far gentler than before, moved slowly into the sand portrait and caressed its surface, mixing the grains together like paint on an artist's palette. Soon, Leto saw a face taking shape as great swaths were cut away, as if struck by a sculptor's chisel.

"Leto..." the grains moaned softly. "The time has come for your impartation."

Dumbstruck, Leto stared at the specter spinning in the air, its edges tapering, the amorphous mass elongating as the form of a man appeared. He held a short golden staff at his side and wore a furry hat on his head.

"You felt it moments ago, did you not?" the man said.

Leto drew her dagger from her belt and thrust it toward the ghost. "Who are you? Are you one of the ghosts of my father's men come to take his revenge?"

The ghost raised his staff and twirled it in the air, guiding the grains in elegant spirals back to the earth. "I am no ghost, and nor am I an enemy. I am a friend." He slipped the staff into its sheath and bowed before her, kissing her hand with ice-cold lips. "My name is Hermes, messenger of the Lord of Death and tutor of despondent desert orphans."

He stood and grinned at her, then looked down at the dagger still held firmly in the hand he'd kissed. "Put it away, child. You have far more powerful weapons within that hand than without it."

"You're mad. I felt nothing moments ago." Leto stepped back and bent down to fetch her cloak.

"Are you cold?" Hermes asked. "No need for a cloak. Simply put heat in the sand as you did before."

"That wasn't me," she protested, "but the earthquake from which you emerged."

"Nay, I only emerged when the signal had been sent that you, my dear, had received your power."

Leto frowned at him as she put away the knife. Kicking the cloak, she knelt down and dipped her fingers into the sand.

"That's it," said Hermes. "Tell the earth what you want it to do. Command the elements with your thoughts."

"Elements..." Intrigued by the word, Leto stood and waited.

Hermes' eyebrows narrowed as he scratched his ear. "Don't stand there like a post. You must do something for the doma to be activated."

And then she felt it, the breeze she'd been waiting for. *Push him!* No sooner had she thought the words than Hermes fell back onto his rear end and half groaned, half growled with displeasure.

"I was going to teach you about the wind after your lesson with sand," he said, getting to his feet. He brushed the sand from his indigo tunic and faced Leto, a smug expression on his features. "You will not make sport of me, my desert flower."

He was whispering, as if the satyrs and nymphs were listening—and perhaps they were, Leto thought.

"I may be a humble messenger," he continued, "but I'm still more powerful than you can ever hope to be."

Leto smiled as the wind collected around her, warming as it blew against her face and through her white-blond hair. She told the sand to twirl like a tornado, and it gathered itself to the size of a cypress and spun fiercely into the distance. She told the cloud that hid the moon to split apart into pieces, and it obeyed.

She could almost see the moon shuddering as it sat exposed within its starry cradle. Maybe one day she could tell even the sun and moon when to rise and set.

"You called yourself a tutor," said Leto, as another cloud sailed toward the milky moon. She wrote her name upon it with her forefinger as easily as if her finger were reed on parchment. "I seem to be teaching myself just fine."

Hermes unsheathed his staff and raised it behind his head as though it were a javelin. He ran a few steps and, with an agile lunge, threw the wand toward the cloud. Up, up, up it flew, flying like a wingless bird until it landed in the middle of Leto's name and set the cloud ablaze. The smoke was so dense that it blotted out the moon and stars, shrouding the desert in darkness.

Leto felt her heartbeat quicken as she contemplated her next move. Her father had always admired her stubbornness, even encouraged it, but had she gone too far by defying an immortal? From all she knew of the so-called gods, they didn't tolerate human hubris for long.

"You are powerful, yes. And brave."

Leto jumped at the feel of Hermes' whisper on her neck.

He wrapped her cloak around her shoulders and chuckled darkly. "But courage must be tempered with wisdom, and power honed with discipline." He touched her shoulders and turned her toward him.

Leto watched his staff float back into his hand as the smoldering cloud fell from the sky in a heap of ashes, giving the stars room to shine again.

"To what end?" she asked, her pulse slowly settling.

"Ah, that is the beauty of it." Hermes' cold hand took hers, sending an electrifying chill down her spine. "To your power and reign there shall be no end. All that is required of you, my fair flower, is to be an amenable pupil."

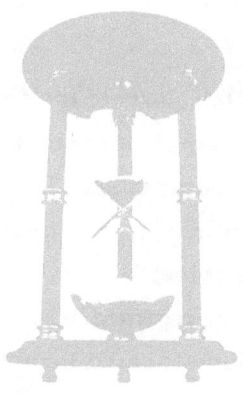

CHAPTER THIRTEEN
HESPERIDES

I wondered when you'd come," said Leto, as she held a pail to one of the stone dolphin's mouths and collected water. "I was beginning to think you'd found another desert bloom to coddle and charm." She watched from the corner of her eye as the golden wings of Hermes' sandals fluttered into focus, flapping as fast as hummingbird wings above her head.

"Desert blooms are beautiful, but their allure stops there." Hermes slowly lowered himself onto the fountain's pillar, which connected all six of the dolphin spouts. "You, my darling, have far surpassed the ranks of ordinary fauna, whose beauty reaches only eyes and nose."

"And what creature do you compare me to now? A scorpion, or a horned viper?"

Leto laughed as she regarded her reflection in the water. Judging by looks alone it could be assumed she was one of the most beneficent of goddesses, Hestia perhaps. As a young girl she'd been nicknamed Kallisto for her silky white hair, ivory skin, and eyes as gray as a turtle dove. Her beauty, Hermes said, was her greatest ally. Who could help but trust her? Anyone who looked upon her would expect nothing but divine secrets and primordial blessings to trickle from her cherry-colored lips.

"Your name is Mania," said Hermes, and he kissed her, his cold lips like melting snow against her own, "for you are Fury."

"So you are pleased with me, then?" she purred, as he nibbled playfully on her ear.

Hermes smiled and traced the length of her smooth, statuesque neck, then doffed his cap and set it on her head.

"What are you doing?" Leto asked, looking down at her reflection. "It looks sillier on me than it does on you."

"Soon, very soon, it will be replaced by a royal diadem."

Hermes drew his wand and waved it before the cap, sending faint sparks of light through the midnight air. He bent over the pail, and with one pass of the wand the water became a sheet of perfect glass.

"How splendid you look." He picked up the pail and flipped it sideways so she could see.

Leto's cheeks flushed as red as roses, and for a moment she was breathless. Upon her head sat the most beautiful golden crown she'd ever seen. Around it were impressed intricate palmettes in low relief, and from the top sprouted foliage and rosettes, all intertwined like fine lace and highlighted by blue enamel and green berries made of glass. An intricate Hercules knot, from which two tassels hung, lay at the center, serving as a protective amulet as well as a symbol of marriage.

"Hephaestus could not have crafted a finer one," she whispered, her eyes locked, trance-like, on the diadem.

"And Aphrodite could not have looked more stunning beneath it."

Hermes set down the pail and reached for the crown, but Leto shuffled back, clutching it tightly with both hands.

"Why must you tease me, my love?" she whined. "I have done all Apollo asks." She removed the crown and held it at her breast to admire it more closely. "What will it hurt to give me just this one piece of my reward? Iris is as good as dead."

"Patience, my furious flower." Hermes almost sang the words as he floated toward her.

Leto giggled when she saw the tuft of red hair sticking up where his cap had been. He made it so difficult for her to be upset with him for long.

"We have more than Iris to worry about now," he said.

Frustration seethed within Leto as she squeezed the crown, her hands stinging as her palms pressed hard against the pointed leaves.

"Iris and her companions were routed from Ourania last night," she said. "They're hiding like shrews in the hills. What other threat is there to trouble us?"

"Iris and her daughter are not the only Ashers left." Hermes came closer and touched her cheek. The coolness of his blood combined with the gravity in his voice made Leto shiver. "There is at least one other, and perhaps as many as three."

He pulled his hand away and unsheathed his wand once more, then pointed it toward a lifeless row of cressets, their metal baskets silvery blue in the starlight. With a swift series of jabs, he set them all ablaze. By their fire, Leto could clearly see the disappointment flaring in his eyes.

"That's impossible!" she shouted, flinging the crown like a discus across the courtyard. "I saw but four when Iris created the pathway: herself, her family, and that godsforsaken Centaur that tromps around with them."

"Yes, but from your vantage point you could not perceive the accompanying travelers. The Ashers."

Leto flexed her fingers at her sides, causing the earth to shake and the sturdy fountain to totter. She'd never learned how to master her temper.

"They passed into the tunnel and accompanied the others to their current refuge," he added.

Leto rolled the pail toward her with her heel, and then with a rabid yell kicked the mirror Hermes had made, transforming the glass back to water, which shattered and spilled at his feet.

"If this element would obey me," she said, indicating the puddle, "if the storm clouds I conjure would produce rain, Iris's precious fire would be extinguished with a snap of my fingers."

Hermes laughed as he always did at Leto's tantrums.

Fuming, she sat on the bench as a bright bolt of lightning struck a nearby poplar tree, splintering the trunk before the top half crashed to the ground. She gave a mild sigh of satisfaction.

"Control yourself, Leto." Hermes snapped his own fingers, calling back the crown from the shadows. He dusted it off and tapped it twice with his wand, returning it to the form of his unremarkable fur cap. "Your behavior suggests that you think I or my brothers are to blame for your doma's shortcomings. I hate to inform you that the rightful recipient of your rage is the All-Powerful, and he cares little for your juvenile murmurings and complaints."

Leto sprang up from her seat once more. "The All-Powerful is cruel and unfair!"

"You won't find me claiming the contrary."

"Then what *are* you claiming, my love?" she asked, sardonic disdain dripping from her lips.

"Humility was never your strongest aptitude." Hermes flipped his wand in the air and caught it behind his back. Pointing it up at the sky, he hooked the full moon like a fish and reeled it in until it hovered above their heads, no larger than a cantaloupe. "I've made my peace with how far my powers reach."

Leto looked up in awe at the beaming orb, then went up on tiptoes and brushed it lightly with her fingers. The hair on her arms stood on end as she felt the powdery dirt of a foreign world. She jumped up, straining to pull the moon down, but it drifted higher, not stopping until it was once more nestled among the stars.

"You see," said Hermes, "the ultimate authority belongs to the All-Powerful. And there's nothing anyone can do to change that."

Leto gave a heavy huff as she crossed her arms. "Your pessimism turns my stomach. Just because neither you nor your brothers have been able to undermine him doesn't mean it's impossible to do so."

A wry smile played on Hermes' lips. "Your conviction is admirable, albeit sorely delusional."

Impelled by another torrent of anger, Leto stirred a breeze with her right hand and sent it rushing into Hermes' chest. The force of its impact thrust the messenger into one of the pergola's beams, shaking the structure from base to roof.

"The only time I've ever entertained delusions," she said, "was the day I thought that you, a pathetic sycophant masquerading as hell's most revered polemarch, would have the courage to help me in my mission."

She strode toward Hermes slowly, eyes focused and hands rigid as she waited for him to retaliate. But he remained seated, slouched against the beam, his ankles crossed casually as he combed his fingers through his cinnamon hair. His cap had been displaced once again and now perched on the pergola's roof, wedged between sprigs of wisteria.

"Has the question of why you were unable to pursue Iris into the mountains even crossed your mind?" Hermes pointed at the cap with his wand and lured it back onto his head.

Leto's eyes darted to the stone pathway where the stray cat was sleeping. She tried to devise a response, but her mind was frozen, halted by infuriating images of the tunnel and the invisible barricade that had sabotaged her chase. She'd been aloft in the clouds, suspended by winds of her own making, every muscle and tendon taut as she held out her hands and amassed phalanxes of thunderclouds around her. All it would have taken was a single bolt stabbing through a chink in Iris's fiery armor to end her life and begin Leto's reign.

"The All-Powerful thwarted me," Leto said.

That had to be the answer. Who else could have been responsible for constructing an impenetrable wall invisible to the naked eye? She had felt it, a wall as solid as marble, running the width of the valley and reaching to the thinnest layer of the atmosphere, where Leto's breathing waned. It was from behind that bulwark that she'd watched them escape into the forsaken hills of the refugees and bandits. She had half a mind to think their luck would be no better there than in her midst.

Hermes stood, and with his wand traced a triangle shape in the air. He rapped lightly against it with his knuckles; it sounded as though he were striking stone. Leto mirrored him as he raised his palm to it, but their touch was impeded by the invisible wall he'd erected between them.

"The All-Powerful seldom works so spectacularly," said Hermes. "It wasn't his hands that constructed the wall but the desperate prayers of his disciples pleading for protection." He stepped around the unseen shape and tenderly cupped Leto's cheek. "You inspire fear in all but me." Then he beckoned Leto to follow him toward the courtyard wall.

He pointed up at the Hesperides, and with his wand, connected the stars with an amber streak, as brilliant as a meteor's tail. "You're familiar with the tale of the seven sisters?"

"I know they guarded the golden apples of Zeus, along with Ladon the dragon," she said. "What does that have to do with anything?"

"Did you know the apples were once stolen?"

Leto shook her head as she sighed. "No, schoolmaster. Do enlighten me."

"Hercules, greatest of the demigods, was sent by King Eurystheus to steal them, just one of the many feats the hero performed." Hermes' eyes jumped wistfully from star to star as he spoke. "Hercules' quest to obtain the apples was not without peril. He did battle with Ares, wrestled two of Poseidon's sons, slew the eagle that afflicted Prometheus, and, finally, dined with the Hesperides, who then gave him the apples freely, without a fight."

"Oh, Hermes, I do hope this prattling is headed for a conclusion of reasonable interest to me." Leto feigned a yawn. "I was hoping our meeting tonight would end in something slightly more exciting than tedious woolgathering."

The Hesperides dimmed as Hermes dragged his wand away from the constellation and set it on the wall. His temple protruded as he clenched his jaw. His patience with Leto was wearing thin.

"The lesson is this." He turned and stared at her sternly until he knew he had her attention. "The Hesperides were won over not with force, but friendliness."

"And so," said Leto, turning with a smile toward the stars, "I will befriend the Ashers."

Hermes nodded.

"And what of the wall that separates them from me?"

Mischief glinted in Hermes eyes. "If I know anything about mortals, it's that they're hopelessly proud and invariably reckless. And Ashers, as you well know, my queen, are known for their proclivity to seeking out adventure; they think themselves invincible." He laughed. "These three won't remain hidden for long."

"And you think they're stupid enough to pass into my territory."

"I think they're young people in a new world with heads full of questions, and domas they don't yet understand. Why would they stay behind bars?"

Leto smiled. "So I will let them come to me."

CHAPTER FOURTEEN
PREMONITIONS

Damian sat on a settle by himself in the tent eating a bowl of cold lentils, finally relaxing after the premonitions had passed. Artemis lay sleeping at his feet as the bush crickets began their nightly noise outside.

Chloe walked in quietly, holding a candle and wearing a lilac robe. Her hair was damp and her face free of dirt. Evidently, she'd had a bath.

"Where were you?" Damian asked.

Chloe shrugged. "I honestly don't know. I was with Carya somewhere." She yawned and reached for a ewer resting on a small wooden table. She took a sip straight from the wide ceramic mouth.

"That's wine," said Damian. He'd accidentally drunk from it earlier and spewed the stuff onto the ground.

Chloe didn't seem to mind, however, and smacked her lips. "I know. Circe's was better."

Damian swallowed the last bite of his supper. "What are you talking about?"

"When we have a good hour or so, I'll tell you." She knelt beside Artemis and scratched behind the dog's ears. "Where is everyone?"

Damian pointed outside. "Around a fire somewhere, eating the rabbits Artemis killed." His face twisted with disgust. "I watched Tycho and Ethan skin them. It was the nastiest thing I'd ever seen."

"Ethan skinned a rabbit?" Chloe laughed.

"Yep." Damian reached down for his cup of water and took a drink. "It seems everyone's adjusting to this nightmare rather well."

"Nasty-tasting beverages. Bloody animals. Smelly dogs. What's not to like?" Chloe said as she sat beside him.

"You forgot to add 'a sister that still doesn't trust you.'" Damian leaned onto the arm of the settle and propped his head in his hand. "I wish you'd be honest with me and tell me where you went."

"I *was* being honest." Artemis lifted her head and wagged her tail at Chloe. "I told you, I was with Carya. We were in some black void. If I had the latitude and longitude coordinates, I'd give them to you."

Damian sat up again and turned toward her. "Do you remember, when we were kids, any of the times I came into your room and found you holding that stuffed lion, crying?"

"Leo," Chloe whispered. "You ripped his nose off when we were four." She furrowed her brow, angry at the incident all over again.

"Chloe, focus. You remember those times, then."

She nodded. "Not as clearly as I remember you defacing Leo, but I remember."

"I'm sorry about Leo, okay? If we stumble across a toy store here in the boondocks, I'll be sure to buy you a new lion."

"Thanks." Chloe smiled. "So, back to your story."

"I would get these feelings, kind of like hunger pangs." Damian pressed his fingers to his abdomen. "They almost made me sick sometimes. Then I'd see you crying, in my mind, and I'd get sad, too." He looked up to see Chloe's eyes moist with tears.

"I always felt better when you hugged me," she said. "I didn't feel so alone anymore."

Damian pressed his lips together to keep from tearing up himself. He'd been so proud the day he finally ignored those psychic feelings, when he walked past his sister in the playground at school. Or when he passed her in the halls at home and pretended he didn't know she was struggling. Over time, the telepathic bond he had with Chloe had been so suppressed that it disappeared completely—until the day she stepped into the portal to Hades. The day he'd been too selfish and afraid to save her.

"I, uh..." Damian began as he nervously scratched his neck. "I'm sorry I stopped." Artemis stood and rested her chin on his knee as if to comfort him. "I'm sorry for a lot of things."

"I told you, I'm leaving the past in the past," said Chloe. "I meant it."

"I guess I'm having a harder time doing that than you are."

"Not entirely." Chloe brought her hair to one side and fiddled with the silver brooch that secured the larger panel of her robe to her shoulder. "I wasn't completely honest with you about where I went."

"I know," said Damian. "I saw it."

He drew a deep breath through his nose as the images flickered past once more: Ethan's parents running; eight giant hooves pounding; flames gushing from the bulls' bronze mouths; debris floating on the sea; bone-chilling terror on Chloe's face as her heart beat like a drum; the bloody tangle of limbs where Ethan's parents lay fallen.

"You saw them die?" Chloe asked.

Damian rubbed his forehead as if the movement might erase the memories—memories of something that hadn't even happened.

"I'm so sorry you saw that," said Chloe.

"Why did *you* have to see it?" Damian looked at her intently once again, anxious to see whether she'd hold back the truth or reveal it.

Chloe sighed and smiled softly. Artemis curled herself into a ball and laid her head on Chloe's foot. A few moments passed in silence, but just when Damian felt convinced the conversation was over, Chloe opened her mouth again.

"I can't put out every fire," she said. "It isn't my job to save Ethan's parents." She sounded robotic, as if she believed what she was saying but didn't yet accept it.

"Carya showed you one version of the future if, hypothetically, you went back and saved the Rosses. It's not written in stone, is it?"

Chloe shrugged. "I guess not." She sat up straight. He could see she already knew where his thoughts were taking him. "Damian, her point was that death isn't something to be manipulated. People make their choices, and the family they leave behind has to move on."

"Like our parents made their choices?" Damian said, indignation burning behind his eyes. "Our parents were *innocent*, Chloe." He rocked himself out of the settle, causing Artemis to yelp as he accidentally stepped on her tail. "They didn't choose to die the way they did."

"I can't save them, Damian." Chloe's voice was so low, so broken, that he could hardly hear her. "Please try to understand..."

Damian shook his head, giving himself a few seconds to try and see things a different way. But it was useless.

"How can I?" Chloe said.

He paced around the tent, and then stopped abruptly by the opposite wall. He knew that what he wanted to say would hurt her, but she had to hear it. It was the truth.

"If I had your doma, Chloe, there's not a god in hell that could stop me from saving Mom and Dad."

He felt the sting of his own words boomerang back to him as Chloe stared at the ground, speechless and stunned. Then she got up, swept the edge of the robe over her shoulder, and walked out of the tent with Artemis panting at her heels.

(

Damian tried falling asleep for over an hour, but he was kept awake by the cacophony of crickets, barn owls, and musical instruments playing outside.

Chloe hadn't come back in again. Artemis had checked on him once without so much as a tail wag, and then left him alone after licking the empty bowl that had held his lentils. He couldn't blame Artemis for her sudden indifference toward him; he'd been harsh with his sister, but he wasn't sorry. The truth hurt sometimes.

After he'd had enough tossing and turning on his sorry excuse for a bed, Damian got up. Surely enough time had passed for him to use his doma again.

Each of the previous times he'd become invisible, it had happened quickly, involuntarily, activated not by will but emotion.

The first time, he'd had no say in the matter whatsoever. The walnut from Carya had contained some sort of magic. After that, it had been a strong desire to save his sister that made his physicality disappear. Likewise, it had been his eventual cowardice that had brought it back. And later, when he helped Ethan and his parents escape, his doma had been precipitated by an overwhelming sense of duty, as if saving them could simultaneously redeem him and stop the Fantásmata.

Channeling that same sense of purpose, of ineluctable responsibility, Damian felt the electrifying tingle pulse in his hands and feet, then race up and down his body. Within a matter of seconds, he was completely invisible.

The air outside the tent was unseasonably thick and muggy, and carried the smells of dying campfires and imminent rain. The hills were dark and quiet, and everyone was asleep inside their tents under a full moon that kept watch overhead.

He'd never seen so many stars. There was no smog here and so no discernible barrier between Petros and space, no distinction between order and chaos. Everything seemed so pure, untainted by pollution, not cluttered with industry. It was as though Petros was an infant kept safe in the arms of the cosmos.

Damian's thoughts were interrupted when he heard the pattering of paws on the rocky soil. He glanced back to see Artemis trotting toward him, her hackles raised in suspicion.

"How can you see me?" Damian said.

Then he remembered the fat dachshund he'd run into at the Rosses' house just after he learned they'd been evicted. He'd been invisible then, too, and still the dog had seen him—and bitten two of his fingers. He realized that animals must have powers, too; they could see him despite his doma.

Artemis wagged her tail and ran to him, her blubbery dewlap flapping as she panted.

"I guess you've forgiven me, then."

The dog sat down and canted her head to one side, as if asking him to say it again.

"Wanna do a little exploring?" Artemis' ears pricked forward. "You can be my tour guide."

Damian scratched the top of her head and walked toward the path leading into the valley. When he didn't hear her following, he turned back and watched her go to the door of a tent and lie down.

Maybe the dog had been trained not to venture off, but Damian hadn't. He was done waiting around to receive snippets of information and disturbing premonitions based on what Chloe was learning and seeing. He wanted to see for himself.

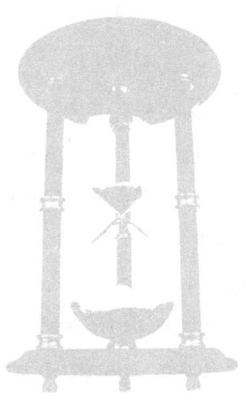

CHAPTER FIFTEEN
MEDUSA

It was nearly sunup and Damian was still walking through endless fields, waiting to find civilization. He wondered if it even existed, or if the people here were all nomads living in clans and tribes.

Every few minutes, his eyes scanned the horizon for signs of Mania. It was not that he was afraid of her; in his invisible state he was impervious to the weather. He just hoped she hadn't released any Asher-hunting canines to track him down. *I should've taken one of Tycho's swords*, he thought.

"Have you lost your way? Or perhaps your sanity?"

Damian jumped at the sound of a woman's voice coming from a rocky outcrop.

"Do not come this way," said the woman, "unless you want to become part of this rock."

"Who are you?" Damian stepped closer as he skimmed the ground for a stick to fight with or a stone to throw. "Are you a centaur? How can you see me?"

The woman laughed, then hissed, and then did both together, the sounds blending into a haunting harmony.

"You really *are* mad, aren't you?" she said. "Do you think yourself a dandelion seed floating in the breeze?"

"*I'm* mad? You're the one making snake noises." And then it hit him. He remembered a lesson from his ontology and mythology class that mentioned a hideous woman with wings and claws and venomous snakes for hair. "You're Medusa."

The hissing stopped. "See for yourself, if you're brave enough. I promise I won't turn my face to you."

"I am brave, but I'm not an idiot. You can stay right where you are. I'm leaving."

Damian picked up his pace, jogging around the outcrop toward a hilltop he'd been eyeing. Maybe he could see the coast from there, or some evidence of a culture. He didn't even know what year he was in.

"Are you trying to find Mania, little dandelion?" Medusa called after him. "If so, I'm afraid you're headed in the wrong direction."

"My name is Damian," he said, still refusing to turn around. He heard the snakes start hissing again. "What do you know about Mania?" He heard something plop onto the grass near his foot. He looked down and saw an ivory-handled mirror, as polished and clear as any modern one back home.

"It's obvious you've heard of me." Her voice seemed incongruous in light of the unflattering descriptions of Medusa in the myth books. It was sweet, soothing, with a smoothness that was almost hypnotic. "Don't you wish to see if the rumors are true?"

Damian couldn't deny that his curiosity was piqued.

"Use the mirror. Hephaestus made it for me. That's the only way he could look upon me without turning to stone. He was my lover, you know. His heart was so riven with pity for me that he escaped Tartarus to find me. We were happy, for a time."

"No, actually I didn't know." Damian knew a little about the crippled god of metalworking and fire who had been expelled from Olympus by his own mother because she considered him too ugly to be her child. But those were all children's stories. Like Medusa, like the Centaur... Why had it all been painted as fiction?

Damian could hear her walking toward him.

"I suppose it's a bit of a secret. But I feel I can trust my secrets with mad country wanderers."

Damian picked up the mirror and spun it in his hand. "I'm not mad. And I'm from Eirene. But you're right," he conceded, "I am lost."

"And looking for Mania?"

Damian nodded and held the mirror so it reflected the morning sky. "What would stop your reflection from killing me?"

"You don't know Hephaestus well at all. The materials of his forge are resistant to even Athena's curses."

"Athena turned you into a..." What should he call a winged woman with snakes coming out of her head?

"A gorgon. Yes. Jealousy will drive women to do unspeakably cruel things to others of their own sex." The snakes fell silent as sadness quivered in her voice. "It's a cancer that's eating away at Leto even as we speak."

"Who's Leto?"

"Everyone else in Petros knows her as Mania."

She was standing a few inches behind him now. He almost felt her loneliness as a magnetic force, drawing her to him. Despite himself, Damian raised the mirror. He tried not to gasp but failed. The myths didn't do justice to just how grotesque she really was.

"No need to pretend my looks don't alarm you," she said. Her gaze, and the gaze of all the serpents' eyes, fell to the ground. "I'm under no illusion that I'm anything but hellish."

Damian waited for her eyes to meet his before he replied. His mother had once told him that eyes reveal more about a person than anything else, and from the quick glance he'd had of Medusa's, she wasn't the man-killing monster of lore.

"I'm sorry people have treated you unfairly because of how you look," he said, hoping she wouldn't be insulted. But she had told him to be honest.

"Unfairly?" She laughed. "Unfairness is when two children perform their chores with equal excellence and only one receives a sweetcake for their labor. Unfairness is a virtue compared to what my fellow man has done to me."

"So what you did to them was in self-defense?" Damian recalled the drawings of men's stone faces contorted in eternal expressions of horror.

Medusa's yellow eyes darkened to a softer, more human caramel. With a bony, sunspot-covered hand, she stroked the side of a snake as if it were a tendril of hair. "Most of the time, yes. Other times..." Her wings relaxed along her back, their charcoal tips nearly touching the earth. "Other times my temper got the better of me."

She folded her arms across her chest; two ribs protruded from her sunburned sternum. The ochre robe she wore appeared to Damian to be many sizes too big—if ancient robes came in sizes.

She sauntered back to the outcrop and slid down its black side, snakes standing erect to keep from being squished against it. "I was never proud of what I did," she said. "I never wanted to become the monster Athena made me out to be." She drew her knees to her chest and rested her chin upon them, her wings wrapping around her like twin shields.

Walking backward, Damian approached her and sat a few feet away. He couldn't let himself become too trusting, no matter how much of a victim she portrayed herself to be.

Sensing his nearness, Medusa lowered the wing closest to him and wiped rheumy tears from her face. "It's why I'm here now. I swore I would never frighten another child, nor kill another man." She looked east toward the halo of sunlight crowning the hills. "My days of terrorizing are over. It's Leto's turn now."

"How do you know her?" Damian lowered the mirror so he couldn't see the brood of snakes as they writhed like worms dug from the soil.

Medusa straightened one leg as she pulled a pear from a fold in her robe and bit into it with her yellow, horse-shaped teeth. "Where are my manners?" she said, her mouth full of half-chewed chunks of fruit. She held the pear out for him to take. "Care for a bite? I promise it's fresh. Hephaestus brought me bushels of fruit from Hera's garden years ago. They never go bad."

Any appetite Damian might have had was long gone now. Even so, he forced his head to nod. "Thank you," he said, and reached over his shoulder.

He watched through the mirror as Medusa handed him the pear, nearly a third of it already gone. Her long fingernails lingered for a moment, hovering over his neck as if she were tempted to touch him. Then she pulled away quickly and crawled behind the rock. She returned seconds later holding a wineskin.

"Her name alone compels me to take a swig of wine." Medusa raised the wineskin to her lips. "Let me ask you something before I tell you anything more about Mania." She intoned the name, drawing out each syllable with unambiguous loathing.

Damian took a nibble of the pear and swallowed it down fast. "Do you care to know why I want to see her?"

"No," said Medusa as she passed him the wine. "I want to know why you have a death wish."

Damian took a drink, trying not to wince at the medicinal taste. "I don't have a death wish."

The wing closest to him twitched and Medusa stared at him blankly. He lowered the mirror and turned his profile to her.

"What?"

"Oh, nothing. It's just that I was beginning to believe you weren't mad after all."

Damian took a deep breath to quell his nerves. Medusa wasn't the only one with a temper. "Would you believe me if I told you I'm from the future?"

Medusa, and all the snakes, looked him up and down. He was still wearing his jeans, sneakers, and navy-blue hoodie. "It would explain a lot if you were." She gave a wide grin and took another swig of wine. "That makes you either a god"—she drained the wineskin and tossed it aside as she wiped her mouth—"or an Asher."

Her pupils dilated as skittish sunlight touched her skin. "You want to join her?" She almost whimpered the words, as if he'd just transformed into another of her enemies.

Damian shook his head. "No. I just want to see what she's doing. I want to know how one Asher was able to completely corrupt the world I come from."

Medusa's countenance brightened. Even the knot of snakes relaxed until their heads drooped to her shoulders. "The oracle!" She pushed herself off the wall as her wings, weary and worn, clapped open to their full span. Dead, gray feathers fell to the ground, but she didn't seem to notice. She closed her eyes and lifted her arms to the sky, muttering inaudibly.

Damian lowered the mirror; he was curious to look at her without it while her lethal eyes were shut. Turning around, he saw not a fearsome monster but a beautiful woman with golden hair and glowing, sun-kissed skin. Her wings were as white as Olympus's peaks.

"You're beautiful," he whispered.

He couldn't stop himself. He went to her, overcome with unprecedented lust. He knew a spell was compelling him, but he was helpless against it. He yearned to get closer, to smell her hair, to kiss her lips, to see what breathtaking shade her eyes were. But as he reached out to caress her cheek, she grabbed him by the wrist and jerked her face away.

"Turn away, Asher," she warned as she squeezed her closed eyes even tighter. "One accidental slip of my eyelids and you're a dead man."

"I'm sorry. I can't help it." With his other hand, he trailed a finger along her heart-shaped jaw. "Do you have any idea how beautiful you are?"

"How beautiful I *was*. Another part of Athena's curse I neglected to mention."

"What part of the curse? That when you close your eyes you're hot again?"

Medusa's flawless forehead was furrowed in puzzlement. "Hot? No, the curse has no effect on my temperature."

Damian tried not to laugh. "I meant that when you close your eyes you look like your former self."

"Indeed." Medusa dropped his hand and twirled the ends of her silken, honey-colored hair. "In the past, when men looked upon me while I slumbered they were drawn to me as if to a goddess, and then, well, you know what happened next."

This was enough to send Damian scrambling for the mirror. He held it up and watched as, in an instant, she transmogrified back into a hybrid witch. He wiped the sweat from his upper lip and unzipped his hoodie. He'd never felt so ashamed.

"I'm so sorry," he said.

Medusa waved him off with her hand. "Don't be so hard on yourself, Asher. Men can hardly control their lusts *without* the curses of goddesses goading them, much less with them."

Awkward seconds ticked by as Damian debated what to say next. How could he resume a normal conversation after embarrassing himself with such an idiotic advance? But this conversation had never been normal in the first place.

When his tongue finally unglued itself from the roof of his mouth, he asked, "So what's so exciting about the oracle?"

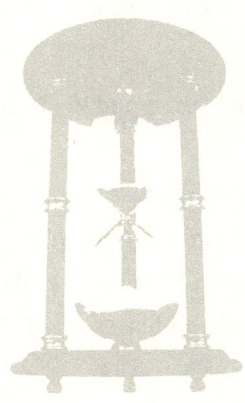

CHAPTER SIXTEEN
ENEMIES

Medusa folded her wings as the restless snakes lifted their heads and flicked their tongues at Damian. "You don't know about the oracle?"

Damian looked away from her reflection. Dawn's light was in full bloom and yet the world was as quiet as it had been at midnight. Not so much as a morning bird stirred or made a peep.

"I don't know much," he said. "That's why I'm out here."

"There's a woman, an Asher like Leto, who received a prophecy long ago. It concerned a future Asher who would finish the business she began with Apollo."

"Iris?" Damian returned his gaze to Medusa's reflection in the mirror as she disappeared into her makeshift shelter in the rocks. "I met her yesterday. She didn't say anything about an oracle, or Apollo, for that matter."

His head was beginning to hurt. First centaurs, then Medusa, and now Apollo; how could all the harmless bedtime stories read to him as a child be undeniable fact?

Medusa emerged holding a single sheet of weathered parchment. With its ragged edges and severe discoloration, Damian wondered how it was even legible.

"Iris announced the oracle in Ourania before Leto razed it." She held the parchment to the sun. The snakes eased forward, their eyes focused on the parchment as though they were helping her read. "It's quite vague, as prophecies invariably are. I thought it nonsense myself. Until you showed up."

"Iris gave the oracle to you?"

"No. I hid atop the roof of the stoa and wrote down her words as she spoke. The historians were there in droves, as was every other Ouranian, from the priests to the prostitutes, all eager to hear what the 'girl who made fire' had to say."

"And what did she have to say?"

Medusa eyed him suspiciously, as did her slithering pets. "Perhaps it's not my place to say. If you *had* been in her company, I'm sure she would have apprised you of the prophecy already, had it been prudent to do so."

Damian sighed and shifted the mirror to the opposite hand. "Is there any good reason I shouldn't hear it now?"

Medusa clicked her tongue. "Patience, Asher. If there's anything I've learned in my miserable life, it's that hastiness gives birth to affliction." She rolled up the parchment and tucked it into her robe. "Shall I answer your question?"

"Which question?" Damian had asked her to read the oracle, but clearly that wasn't happening now that the parchment was out of sight.

"How I know Leto." Medusa pointed to a copse of olive trees near the hilltop he'd spotted earlier. "Let us fetch some water and escape this sun. In the shade I shall tell you my story, beginning to end, if you wish to indulge a desert hag. At the very least, it will orientate you with the time in which you find yourself aimlessly drifting." She raised an eyebrow at him as her amber eyes flashed with jest.

"Sounds fun," said Damian.

"Excellent!" Medusa exclaimed, as though she were a schoolgirl who'd won a new playmate.

"But I'm not aimlessly drifting," he added.

Ignoring him, Medusa snatched the empty wineskin, spread her wings, and took off flying toward the trees.

Awestruck, Damian lowered the mirror as he watched the half-woman, half-bird soar as effortlessly as an eagle across the plain. He wished his cellphone wasn't dead; he would've snapped a million pictures, if only to convince himself later that what he had seen hadn't been a dream.

His mouth helplessly agape, he followed her a quarter mile to an old stone well overgrown with moss.

"Only the cultists know of this well," Medusa said. She was sitting on the edge of the well. The snakes hissed and curled themselves into coils, evidently chilled beneath the shade. "Well, cultists and outcasts, I should say. Prior to Ourania's destruction, it was used to invoke Apollo through the dark art of hydromancy."

"Do you invoke him?"

By the look on Medusa's face, it was as though she'd just been slapped. "Duna forbid it. Channeling is what created it in the first place. Her father communed with Apollo, who then corrupted her when she reached womanhood." She paused and wrung the wineskin in her hands. "I would rather be torn to pieces by three-headed Cerberus than confer with any so-called god."

"You're just saying that because it was a god you fell in love with, a god who broke your heart, and a goddess who stole your beauty." Damian watched in the mirror as Medusa's ashen face became snow-white with fear. "What's the matt—"

"Leto..." she whispered.

Behind Medusa, a tall, statuesque woman with striking blond hair stood blindfolded. She wore a scarlet robe that fell to just above her knees and leather sandals that laced up her shins. On the outer sides of each sandal was embroidered a serpent wrapping itself around a crescent moon.

"Medusa," said Leto. "It would break my heart to learn you've been speaking ill of me to my own relative."

Damian set down the mirror and looked at Leto. "How do you know I'm related to you?"

"I don't live under a rock, as some do." Leto smiled and waved a hand toward the branches, causing a breeze to blow through them. "What is your doma? Wait, let me guess. Invisibility?"

Damian's heart beat faster. "How do you know that?"

"You had no trouble passing through the wall that prevented me from requesting the conference I wish to have with you now."

"Everyone can go out of it," said Damian. "But not everyone can go in. As you probably know by now."

"But my guess was correct." Leto smiled.

"Don't you listen to her, Asher," Medusa begged. "She speaks honeyed words. They will surely poison you if you let them."

"Honeyed words, deadly eyes...all of us have our gifts." Leto took a step closer and looked, though she couldn't see, directly at Medusa. "It's how we use them that determines whether they'll become poison or salve."

Damian saw goosebumps rise on Medusa's neck. Her wings fell forward, now a coat around her shoulders.

"You've got your friend Hermes with you, haven't you?" said Medusa. "Do you feel it, Asher? The air's got a chill."

"I can't feel anything." Damian was starting to wonder how many hours had passed. "Not while I'm invisible."

"Are you really invisible?" Medusa got up from the well. "Then how am I able to see you now? Quite plainly, I see a young man, no older than twenty, wearing a queer shrunken cloak and the strangest trousers I've ever seen."

Damian pointed to the snakes still coiled tightly on her head. "Animals seem to see me just fine." He bit his lip. "I'm sorry. I don't mean to imply that you're an animal. I just meant—"

"Oh, but isn't she one?" Leto asked cruelly. "Forget the nest of snakes she has for hair and that mangy pair of gryphon's wings. What else would you call a woman with the blood of hundreds on her hands?"

"If that's your definition of an animal, then I think you'd have to put yourself in that category, too," said Damian.

Leto's nostrils flared as her mouth tightened into a straight, humorless line. "Perhaps you have a point, Damian." She leaned her head ever so slightly to the right. "Did Hermes just tell you what my name is? You know, in my time he betrayed Apollo. Maybe you shouldn't let him be your puppet master."

It was then that the messenger revealed himself, materializing at first as a silhouette, and then as the selfsame person Damian had met in the woods just the morning before.

"It seems this Asher may also be a scion of Odysseus," said Hermes, as the wings of his sandals began to flutter. "He's devised a clever scheme to try and drive a divisive wedge between my betrothed and me." He turned Leto's face to his and kissed her softly between her covered eyes.

"Oh, Leto." Medusa covered her mouth with her hand. "You would sell your soul for all eternity to become queen for a few fleeting decades?"

"Nay," answered Leto. "I swore my allegiance to become queen forever. To commence my endless reign beside Persephone, and to freely roam this realm with my husband whenever I please."

"You mentioned a conference," Damian said to Leto. "What exactly did you want to talk to us about? I assume you know my sister is here, too."

"Yes," answered Leto. "It's a pity she didn't accompany you. I am not a foe, Damian, but an ally."

"No, no, no. Cover your ears, Damian!" Medusa cried. "You mustn't let her beguile you."

"Oh, shut up, shrew," shouted Hermes, as he shot up into the air and settled upon a branch. "One more peep out of you and your next breath will be drawn inside that well."

The snakes unfurled and stood erect, tongues darting in vain toward Hermes' heels. Medusa's yellow eyes glared at him, but he was immune to her curse.

"Do leave us, Medusa," said Leto calmly. "I'm grateful for the hospitality you've shown my guest heretofore, but your presence is no longer necessary."

Medusa turned to Damian, her bleary, bloodshot eyes pleading with him not to engage with Leto a moment longer.

Damian was torn. But wasn't this why he had come here? Hadn't he left the camp with the express purpose of finding out who Leto was, and why Iris and the others were so afraid of her? He couldn't go back now. The real tale of Medusa would have to remain untold.

He set the mirror on the well and turned his back to Medusa. "I'll be all right," he whispered. "Go now before they hurt you."

He listened as Medusa's wings clapped open and her footsteps padded toward him. He tensed at the feel of her warm breath on the back of his neck.

"Remember," she said, "hastiness breeds affliction."

CHAPTER SEVENTEEN
PROPHECY

"Did he say where he was going?" Ethan asked.

It was lunchtime and Damian still hadn't shown up. Charis had spent the morning searching the six square miles of hills and farmland that were protected by the wall, an absurd task considering Damian had very likely gone invisible while abandoning his sister yet again. Charis would still have been searching for him now had her doma not reached its limit; it had taken her an hour to trek back to camp.

Chloe shook her head. "We didn't part on the best of terms last night. After I told him about the flashback—or flashforward, I guess I should say—he said that if he had my gift, he'd use it to bring our parents back."

"I'm not a betting man," said Tycho, as he reshafted a spear that had killed the boar now roasting on a spit before them, "but if I were, I would bet he left the perimeter. Young men have an uncanny way of following their noses toward danger."

"I guess going to Hades wasn't enough danger for him, then," Ethan said, regretting the bite in his words even as he spoke them.

"He just needs to blow off some steam," said Chloe, as she fiddled with the girdle of yet another robe, one Iris referred to as a chiton, which was apparently much better suited to campestral life than the heavier himation Carya had gifted her.

"He won't get far before Mania finds him," Iris said. She sat cross-legged while her daughter braided her hair behind her. "She has Apollo's brother helping her."

Chloe stopped fiddling and started pressing down her cuticles instead.

"Hermes?" Ethan asked.

Iris nodded.

Chloe's eyes darted to Ethan. "I thought Hermes was on our side."

"In the future he's on our side," said Ethan, "but until yesterday he was still as evil as they come."

The Centaur grunted as he picked at his teeth with a twig. "Everyone becomes sensible in the future, eh?"

Artemis trotted down the lane and stood slobbering beside Chloe. "Everyone but the people in charge," Chloe said, scratching the dog's chin.

"Who's in charge?" Charis asked. "The Alphas?"

Ethan knew only a little about the Alphas. His mom had told him that according to the scrolls she'd found, the Alphas comprised one of two religious groups. They worshipped the mythical gods and goddesses, while the other group, the Eusebians, bowed only to Duna. His mother never could find out what had happened to them.

In modern Petros, religion didn't exist at all. The Fantásmata only paid homage to what they referred to as "the unknown god," and that was just once a year during the Lycaea Festival. Ethan couldn't help but wonder what was really behind that festival anyway. Now that he knew the truth about coronations, he had no reason to believe Lycaea was the lighthearted holiday everyone thought it was.

"The Fantásmata," Chloe answered. "Phantoms." She looked up at Ethan as the Petrodian translation unfolded in their ears, thanks to Carya's spell. "Makes perfect sense. We never see them and know nothing about them, other than that they're sadistic liars who love control and despise Ashers."

Iris ran her fingers along her new auburn braid and closed her eyes, as if trying to retrieve something from her memory. "Do the Fantásmata ever speak of Apollo?" Tycho laid a sympathetic hand on her shoulder. "Diokles, the wicked leader I once followed..." Her voice trailed off as her thoughts traveled back in time. "He secretly served Apollo. With his dying breath, he told me it wasn't over."

"That's all he said?" Ethan asked, as a cloud settled over the sun.

Iris nodded. "He was gone after that. I waited for years, expecting another Apollonian leader to rise and take his place, but to this day no one has. On the contrary, we've enjoyed decades of peace for the first time in ages. Until Mania."

"I suppose when you have eternity to work with, it's easy to bide your time," said Chloe.

"And then I was given this." Iris turned to a small, linen-wrapped bundle beside her and picked it up. She only had to unfold a corner of it for Ethan to recognize what it was.

"An amber scroll?" He felt the strangest sense of déjà vu as he remembered standing in the lower gallery at the museum, staring at another of Iris's ancient scrolls. Now he was here, in her presence, about to be shown not just any scroll but an amber tablet, a sacred oracle.

"You know of the oracles?" Tycho asked, setting his spear aside.

"My mother was an archaeologist." When Ethan saw Charis tilt her head sideways in confusion, he repeated, "Archaeologist. It's someone who digs up old artifacts from the past to learn about history."

Charis gave a bashful nod. "I see. Has she found very many?"

"She's found two. The Fantásmata confiscated one, and shortly after that they stopped all excavations."

"And the second one?" Chloe asked.

"She kept it. She showed it to Damian, Katsaros and me. It was burnt to a crisp on the outside. It's a miracle it was still intact."

The Centaur pointed to himself with the twig. "Katsaros... you mean me? The civilized, congenial, future me?"

"Yes," replied Ethan. "You translated it for us. It was a poem about the Moonbow."

Iris gazed up at the last patch of blue in the overcast sky. "It truly was a miracle. Those scrolls are housed in the temple in Eirene. If Chloe really did glimpse the future, and I believe she did, Mania plans to destroy every last relic and oracle." She unwrapped the amber scroll and hugged it to her chest. "Thank Duna she will not succeed."

"But she *did* succeed," said Chloe, so abruptly that Artemis jumped and scampered over to Ethan, her hind end bumping into a stationary wagon filled with bushels of barley. "No one, except for me, my brother and Ethan even knows about the Alphas and Eusebians, let alone Duna and the reality of heaven and Hades. If that's not success, I don't know what is."

"You said it yourself," said Charis. "When you have eternity to work with, it's easy to bide your time. Maybe Duna has been biding his. He knew the oracle of the Vessels would come to pass."

"She's right," Tycho said, placing a hand on his daughter's arm. "But I know what you're thinking. Why did Duna allow Mania to conquer Petros in the first place?"

"It's a reasonable question," Chloe said, as if defending herself before an Enochos jury.

Ethan couldn't help but smile. Chloe had more of Damian's fire in her than he'd thought.

"I agree," said Tycho. "And it's a question all of us ask at one time or another. But we must realize that while Duna could stop evil before its roots take hold, he doesn't."

Ethan felt a fire of his own igniting deep within him. "Why doesn't he, if he has total power? The coronations would never have happened." He looked at Chloe, his heart breaking for her again as he considered, just for an instant, all she'd been through. "Chloe would never have been deceived by some dead poet and led to hell."

"Our parents would never have died." Letting her hair fall in front of her face, Chloe leaned forward onto her elbows and traced lines in the ground with her finger.

"If Duna intervened in the ways you wish him to, he'd be no better than the phantoms that control Petros in your time," said Iris. "He would have followers who fear him but do not love him. Millions of Petrodians aligned beneath his aegis because of force and not volition. That sort of loyalty is artificial. You two should know that better than anyone."

Ethan and Chloe sat silently.

Ethan couldn't argue with Iris's logic, but neither could he shake the anger still hooking its claws into his mind, infecting his thoughts with an animosity he knew perfectly well was anything but constructive. But in his opinion, his feelings were defensible, and every part of him was busy justifying his embitterment while the future of his world still languished in uncertainty. He needed rationality to return. He needed to numb his emotions, but he didn't know how. In his time, doctors had drugs for emotional imbalance. Here, he was on his own, helpless and paralyzed, like he was pinned to the bottom of a rushing river but unable to fully drown.

This is grief, he thought. *This is what it feels like to lose everything.*

Chloe stood up and started back toward the tent.

"Where are you going?" Ethan asked.

She took an elastic from her wrist and pulled her hair into a ponytail. "To change out of this stupid robe."

"I hope you're not thinking of going after your brother," called the Centaur.

Iris held up a shushing hand. "It's as it should be." She looked down at the amber tablet and cleared her throat. "Listen."

Ethan caught himself leaning forward, desperate to hear something—anything—that would divert his mind from its self-pity. He saw Chloe's feet beside him and chuckled at the hot-pink toenails poking out of her sandals. She had been to hell and back, *and* back to the ancient past, all with neon polish on her toes.

"'This oracle was delivered to me by Carya, apostle of Duna, on the twelfth day of Thargelion in the four thousandth year since the War of Heaven,'" Iris read. "'I received the oracle on the day Alexa was killed...'"—she paused, her voice cracking with emotion—"'during the festival of Therismos by a woman who introduced herself as Alexa's niece. The woman demanded that Alexa escort her to our home, but when Alexa refused, the murderess called forth lightning. A perfume merchant in a nearby booth watched Alexa fall.'"

"Mania," said Chloe.

Iris nodded and looked up from the tablet. "Carya had warned us of Diokles' daughter Leto months before. She informed us that she was a powerful Asher whose mind had been polluted with lies from the Underworld. All of us," she said, indicating her family and the Centaur, "swore to one another we would be wary of any maiden we suspected might be her."

"Alexa was the bravest among us," said the Centaur, his own gravelly voice broken by grief.

Ethan remembered his mother giving him what scant information she knew of Alexa from the scroll fragments she'd been allowed to keep. Iris had met the young girl outside a tanner's house while the latter was running from the Centaur after stealing his sword. Alexa's brother, Diokles, had led the rebel Eusebian army, employing terror and fear to try and overthrow their Alpha oppressors. Iris had nearly been corrupted by him, as had her aunt Corinna, an Asher whose doma could change her into a gryphon. Yet another myth that was all too terribly true.

"How could Alexa be Leto's aunt?" Ethan asked. "Diokles didn't have a wife, did he?"

Iris's eyes returned to the tablet and continued reading. "'After obsequies were conducted and Alexa's body interred, Carya appeared to me in the cemetery. Everyone had retired for the evening, except for me. She handed me this parchment, along with a reed, and told me to record these words:

> Knowing well that his reign would not
> last, Diokles made Corinna his wife,
> In secret they wed and in secret conceived
> the object of your future strife.
> The infant lay hidden in the dark desert caves
> and was nursed by her mother at night,

Swords were her toys in her formative years,
*   and swiftly she learned how to fight.*
Power she thirsts for, dominion she craves,
*   and every Asher to her is a threat.*
She will succeed in subduing every inch of the
*   world, and truth all the world will forget.*
Her fury will erupt from her fists like thunder—
*   behind a wall built by prayer you'll dwell,*
Meanwhile, unbelievers shall be deceived
*   by this malevolent coup of hell.*
Your devout generation will fade, die away,
*   leaving only the oracles behind,*
But these too shall perish, in time or in fire,
*   and every soul will walk through life blind.*
Iris, don't cry; though all hope seems lost,
*   Duna's faithfulness will always remain.*
A Vessel will rise when the Moonbow
*   returns, then you shall revisit*
*   these divine words again.'"*

"Well, that's heavy," said Chloe with a flippant laugh. "So what makes you so sure I'm the Vessel? And what does 'Vessel' even mean?"

"You and your brother are the Vessel," Iris said.

"Pardon me, Miss Chloe," said the Centaur. "You and Damian dropped out of the sky with your friend here while the rest of us were running for our lives. Turns out you're both Ashers who have suffered a great deal and want to see your world set right." He stopped chewing on the twig and flicked it onto the ground. "On top of that, you've arrived at a time when we could use your help the most. If that's not an act of God, please, call me a nitwit and tell me what is."

Chloe's mouth puckered and twisted as she ruminated on this.

"He's right, Chloe," Ethan said. "You're a Vessel because you carry the possibility of hope for Petros. *This* Petros, and ours."

Ethan felt his mind becoming his own again as the claws inside it loosened. Even though he had neither a superpower to offer nor a shred of esoteric knowledge to share, he refused to turn to mush and let his emotions fester. There was a reason he'd narrowly escaped death at the Religious Council building. There was a reason he'd been allowed to follow Chloe through the portal. And there was a reason he'd been the one to learn of Chloe's gifted family in the first place. He could only trust he'd find out eventually what that reason was.

"I can't do anything without Damian," said Chloe. "He's our only way of getting close to Mania undetected."

Ethan looked down at his watch, but it was dead; the trip through time had apparently done it in. "How long has he been gone, by the way? Doesn't his doma wear off after three hours?"

Chloe spun on her heel and stomped toward her tent. "I'm changing clothes and going after my brother," she yelled at the Centaur over her shoulder. "Do I have your permission?"

The Centaur nodded. "Aye. And my sincerest prayers."

CHAPTER EIGHTEEN
CAVE ONE

"Chloe, we have to be strategic about this," said Ethan from the doorway of her tent.

She sighed as she laced up her tennis shoes and rolled her mud-caked jeans up to her ankles. "I knew it was a just matter of time before you said something like that."

"Why did you think that?"

Chloe stood up and reached for the food-filled hidesack Iris had placed on the settle, then slung it across her body. "I might not know you that well, but I had a lot of time to think while I was in hell."

"And?" Ethan ran his hand along the strap of his baldric and fingered the haft of the short sword Tycho had given him.

There was something about a man with a sword that made him fifty times more handsome—at least in Chloe's opinion. She wondered if the robe she'd been wearing made her any prettier. Too late for her to change back into it now: Artemis had found it in a heap on the floor and was currently using it as a dog bed.

"And," she said, regathering her thoughts, "I couldn't help but think that the reason you invited me to the museum on my birthday was because you knew something was about to happen to me. Or was it just a coincidence that Carya appeared in the backseat of my car as I was leaving?"

Ethan laughed. "She did?"

"Oh, yeah. She gave me an enchanted walnut. Did you know her name means 'walnut'? I ate it later and it took me back to the past for the first time. Well, technically the first time was earlier that day, but I thought I was just dreaming."

Chloe stopped herself. She was talking too fast again and slurring her words. Suddenly she felt the urge to reach into the hidesack and devour the first thing she grabbed. She wanted to binge. Why was Ethan making her so nervous? There wasn't time to stress-eat over a boy!

Ethan gripped the sword and exhaled a long breath through his nose as he gazed out through the tent flaps. Arrayed in a tunic, cloak, girdle and funny boots, Chloe thought he looked like a proper warrior. He may not have known how to use his sword, but at least he looked the part.

"I wanted to say something," he said at last. "At the museum...in the cafeteria...I was just too scared, plain and simple." He turned back to her, his jade eyes sorry and sincere. "When you invited me to Astrolux for coffee, I made up my mind then that I would tell you everything I knew."

"Orpheus said you left when you saw the crowd outside the café."

Ethan shook his head slowly. "No...I left when I saw you with him."

"What? Why?"

Ethan shrugged and toed the dirt floor with his boot. "I don't know. I guess I didn't want to interrupt your date."

"You know it was far from a date."

"I know that now."

"Well, like I told you earlier about Damian, the past is in the past. Whatever you could've, should've or would've done is irrelevant now, right?" Ethan had just lost his parents. She knew the last thing he needed was to be guilt-tripped about his failure to come clean when he'd had the chance.

"I'm not so sure." Ethan scratched his neck and then lightly rubbed his forearm. "You see this?" He pointed to a faint ring of scars just below his elbow.

A line of chills, like icy ants, raced down Chloe's back. "They almost look like teeth marks," she said. It didn't make sense, though. All the dogs the Petrodians were allowed to keep as pets were tiny. If an animal had done this to Ethan, it couldn't have been a small one.

"It was a wolf. Happened when I was ten."

Ethan didn't have to continue. Chloe shuddered. Ten was how old she'd been when her parents died, when they were murdered by the councilman because her father was an Asher. But how were the incidents connected?

"What in Zeus' name was a wolf doing loose in Eirene?" It was a preposterous notion; all carnivorous animals were contained in preserves and zoos.

"I've been trying to figure that out for the last eight years." He paused and turned toward the doorway, as if pondering whether to leave. "I think..." He sat down on the settle and stared at the opposite wall where Artemis, curled into an unidentifiable ball of fur, lay napping.

"Spit it out, Ethan. What do you think?"

Ethan leaned forward, pressing the heels of his hands into his forehead. "I think the wolf was sent by the councilman to kill your father," he said, looking up at Chloe as though waiting for her to reprove him.

But Chloe was silent, eager to hear more. Could Ethan really think she'd find anything unbelievable after all she'd seen over the last few days? "Go on," she whispered, steeling herself for whatever he might say next.

"It was vocation day at school and I was at the coast with my mom. I got bored and took a nap, and when I woke up I saw your dad walking the beach. I shouted at him, but it was too windy for him to hear me. Then this enormous wolf charged me and latched onto my arm. I know it would've killed me if your dad hadn't wrestled it off."

"Why was it coming for you and not him?" Feeling her legs grow weak, Chloe sat down beside him.

"It attacked him next. I thought he was dead, but then—"

"But then he healed himself," said Chloe, a bittersweet smile on her lips and in her heart as she remembered her father's cold hands on her temples after she'd been forced to drink from the River Lethe. His doma had healed her brain and brought back all of her memories. She could see the wheels spinning in Ethan's head.

"How could you know that?" he asked.

"Because he healed me, too. In Hades."

Chloe wanted to tell him everything, from Orpheus and the tragic creatures on Circe's island, to Charon and Cerberus and the River Styx. Maybe one day they could have that coffee date at Astrolux…when they weren't on the Fantásmata's wanted list. Right now, that prospect seemed next to impossible. As long as Mania was on the warpath, Chloe knew she would never lead a normal life back home. If she couldn't change the past, her future would bring nothing but death.

"It was the most incredible thing I'd ever seen." Ethan's eyes stared into space, focusing on nothing except the memory of moments that had turned his life upside down. "After the wolf left him for dead, your dad sat up like he'd just been sleeping. All his wounds closed up on their own." He touched his elbow again. "And then he healed me."

"I wonder what my dad was doing out there. He was supposed to be at work."

"He was exploring. My mom showed your brother and me seven jars that he found in Cave One. Each one was connected to a color of the Moonbow."

"Orpheus told me the Moonbow's appearing was an omen or something."

Ethan nodded. "'The warning and the way,' is what your dad told me." He turned to her, his hand nearly meeting hers in the middle of the space between them. "He wanted me to tell you that. I'm sorry it's taken me this long."

Chloe hardly heard his apology. Her mind was still stumbling over "the warning and the way." She understood what "warning" meant. The Moonbow was how the Fantásmata knew that the "Vessel" had arrived. They knew the prophecies, too. After all, they were the ones who'd been hoarding them all these thousands of years. But what about "the way"? The way to what? She could think of only one option for getting answers.

"We have to go back there, Ethan."

"Back to where?"

"Back to Cave One, where my dad found the jars. We have to talk to him and find out what they mean and what the Moonbow has to do with any of this."

Ethan's knee began to bounce. "And what if that wolf's there and for some reason your dad's doma doesn't work?"

Chloe looked down at his baldric. "Then I hope you know how to use that thing."

As if able to detect Ethan's agitated nerves, Artemis stirred and wagged her tail at him. He stared down at the sword, then looked through the tent flaps at the pebbly path and the dusty feet passing by.

Chloe couldn't tell if he was giving himself a mental pep talk or trying to figure out how best to tell her he wasn't going. "If you don't want to go with me, I understand," she said, "but you can't talk me out of it."

"No, I'm going with you. That's not the issue."

"Then what is?"

"Your brother. Damian's life is in danger every second he's with Mania."

He had a point. The only thing she or anyone else seemed to know about this rogue Asher, Mania, was that she was, well, maniacal. The prophecy said she considered every other Asher a threat, so what would stop her from harming Damian...or worse?

"You said yourself we need a strategy," said Chloe. "Mania has to have her own, don't you think?"

Ethan's face brightened as an epiphany hit him. "She's probably using Damian to lure you and Iris to her."

"Exactly. And we're no match for her."

"Not yet." Ethan smiled. "I have a feeling those jars will be more useful than the sword."

Chloe laughed. "But it does make you look significantly more intimidating."

"That's all that matters then," he said, in his signature deadpan way.

"You ready to go?"

Ethan stood and held out his hand for her. She took it and pulled herself up, then gave him a funny look when he didn't let go.

"I have to touch you in order for this to work, right?"

Chloe could feel her hands get clammy. "Good call."

Then she closed her eyes, took a breath, and focused on her father's face as she said the words: "Cave One."

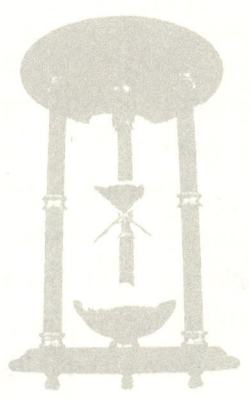

CHAPTER NINETEEN
AISON

The salty breeze was the first thing Chloe felt as sunlight flooded the spinning darkness. Whatever wormhole was responsible for transporting her through time, it was anything but cozy; it was pitch black, damp, and emitted a soft buzzing noise like a lightbulb about to burn out. Her inability to see only worsened the queasiness brought on by what she guessed was her body trying to cope with the inexplicable mechanics of time travel. She would get used to it eventually—at least that's what she told herself.

She felt Ethan lift his hand from her shoulder. Had she only imagined that he'd held her hand?

"We made it," she said breathlessly, and then bent over to wait for the nausea to subside. "I knew I shouldn't have eaten any of that boar." She groaned and tried not to focus on the surplus of saliva pooling in her cheeks. "What'd you think of the ride?"

When Ethan didn't answer, she looked up and gasped. Damian was sprinting away from her, turning invisible as he did. Ethan was nowhere to be seen.

"Damian!" She took off after him, but she knew it was foolish to try and catch up; he was a cross-country all-star after all and already she had a stitch in her side.

Chloe's mind was racing so fast she could barely keep up. Should she use her doma now to go back to the past and stop Damian from sabotaging her trip? What was he doing here anyway? She wished she could go to the future to find out what he was planning, but Carya had made it clear that traveling forward wasn't part of the arrangement.

She stopped running, partly because she wanted to and partly because she thought a lung was about to collapse, then turned to gaze at the Great Sea. The only time she'd ever seen the ocean was in ancient Petros, as Petrodians were rarely permitted to venture outside their own cities. Why had her father been out here exploring anyway, and how had he managed to do so unnoticed? But then again, he *had* been noticed, hadn't he, by some kind of mercenary wolf, a wolf that might be nearby, even now...

"Just breathe," Chloe whispered as her heart beat faster. "You have a doma. You have a brain. Use both of them."

It only took a single long exhale for Chloe to realize what Damian was up to. He wanted to save their parents, an act that, if successful, would undo everything. From Chloe learning the reality of heaven and Hades, to her and Damian hearing a two-thousand-year-old prophecy about their critical role in history, rewriting the past would assure victory for both the Fantásmata and the rulers of hell that controlled them.

Chloe knew what she had to do. When her heart rate finally normalized, she closed her eyes and visualized the tent along with Ethan and Artemis's faces. She waited for her heart to leap into her throat as the feeling of weightlessness replaced gravity. But her focus was interrupted by a low growling sound not ten feet away.

Don't open your eyes, don't open your eyes... She pressed her tongue against the roof of her mouth and tried to concentrate on the sound of the surf.

"Where did you come from?" came a young man's voice.

Chloe tried her doma again, but as she did, the man let out a blood-chilling bark, and she knew he wasn't just any man.

"I know what you are," he snarled.

Every muscle in Chloe's body tensed as she heard him coming closer. Where was that sword when she needed it?

Desperate, she plunged her hand into the hidesack and pulled out the first piece of fruit her hand touched.

"Here," she said, tossing it toward the wolf. "I promise it tastes much better than I do."

The creature laughed, and a few seconds later, Chloe heard the scratchy Velcro-like sound of an orange being peeled.

"A kind gesture," he said, taking a bite. And then a firm human hand grabbed hold of her wrist. "If you're planning on going anywhere, you're taking me with you."

Chloe opened her eyes and was astonished to see a familiar face standing beside her, his wide eyes fading from orange to yellow to hazel.

"Aison?" she said. The last time she'd seen Aison he had been serving her ice cream with Orpheus.

"Answer me, Asher." Aison bit off a chunk of the fruit, tossed the skin onto the sand and tugged on her hidesack.

As she stumbled into him, Chloe thought he smelled like fresh laundry, with just a hint of citrus and sweat. Had she only imagined that he'd growled and barked at her?

"You can move at the speed of light, is that it?" he said.

"How about you tell me why it matters so much to you?" she rejoined as she jerked away from him.

Little by little, patches of tawny hair began to sprout along his arms and cheeks, and his angry eyes glowed orange again.

Chloe commanded her feet not to move. Running would only rile him further. "You really are the wolf."

Aison growled as the orange fell to the ground. His fingers stretched five inches past their normal size and sharp claws ripped through the tips. "How do you know what I am?"

Chloe stared past him, hoping she would see her dad approaching in the distance.

"Answer me!" Aison roared, his neck lengthening as four of his teeth transformed into long incisors. "Or are you that eager to die?"

A seagull squalled as it circled overhead, as if searching for a carcass to feast on.

"You said it yourself," said Chloe. "I can move fast. And you can turn into a wolf. Your secret is my secret." She pretended not to notice his dissatisfied snort. "Now, if you don't mind giving me some space, I need to go—"

"You're not going anywhere."

Aison hunched over and fell to all fours as a repulsive series of cracking noises accompanied the appearance of canine vertebrae through his white T-shirt. His nose elongated into a grizzled snout, and with a shrill howl, his jeans ripped from his body as he kicked off his sandals, making room for furry legs. From his paws to his shoulders, he stood at least four and a half feet tall.

Chloe had to admit she was relieved to see that, unlike her prison guards in Hades who were horrific mishmashes of creatures, Aison was just an old-fashioned, regular wolf.

Granted, he was three times the size of any dog she'd ever seen, but at least he wasn't part lion.

"Can you speak properly when you're all wolfed out like that?" Chloe was sure her fear was making her delirious. This wasn't a joke, after all. Aison could take her down with a single pounce.

"Of course I can," he answered, his voice just the same as it was before.

"Great news. The conversation was starting to get good."

Aison's fur bristled. "You're lying."

"Of course I am. You really think I enjoy talking to shapeshifters?"

"Not about that." He walked in circles around her, sniffing her jeans and tennis shoes. "You lied about your doma."

Chloe didn't make a peep: there was no way Aison could know that unless his nose was a lie detector.

"You reek of Molossus." He tucked in his tail and snarled. "The Molossus has been extinct for fifteen hundred years."

"I don't even know what a mo-whatchamacallit is." Chloe wasn't lying about that one.

Aison's eyes, level with her chest, squinted up at her. "It's a hunting dog. An ancestor of the mastiff."

"I'm afraid you're mistaken." She paused and put a hand on her hip. "How would you know what a Molossus smells like, anyway?"

Aison lowered his eyes and fixed them on the surf lapping against the coast. She'd backed him into a corner, but she knew it was only a momentary advantage. She reached into the hidesack, rummaging for a knife or something else that was sharp. And then came a boy's voice shouting at the top of his lungs.

"Get away from her, you big ugly dog!"

Chloe stopped breathing as her hand clamped onto a worthless lemon. She pulled it out and turned her head slowly toward the boy, the boy she knew was Ethan at ten years old. He was just as lanky and pale as she'd remembered.

"Ethan, go back to your mom," Chloe said as calmly as she could. "The big ugly dog just wants a snack." She threw the lemon at Aison, hitting him lightly in the ribs. Aison crouched low, cocked his tail and bared his fangs, preparing to attack Ethan.

"How do you know my name?" The boy seemed more troubled by that question than having a wolf stare him down as though he were a T-bone steak.

Chloe extended her arms, one toward Aison, the other toward Ethan, and stood between them. "Aison, look at me," she whispered, hoping Ethan couldn't hear.

Aison glanced up, but didn't speak. It was clear he didn't want the boy to know who and what he really was.

"I'll tell you who I am," Chloe whispered. "I'll even show you. Just let the boy be."

Aison gave a slow nod, but his body didn't relax, nor did he tear his eyes from Ethan.

"Aison..."

The animal barked and curled his lips higher, exposing mottled gums and hungry teeth. Then he shifted his weight onto his hind legs and sprang forward, covering five yards easily with a single bound.

He was going after Ethan, and there was nothing Chloe could do to stop him.

CHAPTER TWENTY
DISCORD

This was Chloe's chance to go back to the past, to totally erase this entire encounter and start from scratch. If she could only concentrate, this trip would soon be nothing more than a bad dream.

But she couldn't go back. Something inside her wouldn't allow it, was telling her to wait. Was this the moment in time when her father and Ethan were both attacked? She closed her eyes and said a silent prayer: *Duna, don't let them die today.*

"Trying to leave without me, are you?"

Chloe's eyes flashed open to see Aison back in his human form, complete with a fresh T-shirt and jeans.

"Where's Ethan?" Her voice was breathy with panic. She spun in circles, expecting to see Ethan's crumpled body lying somewhere along the beach.

"I chased him off. He needs to learn to mind his own business."

"One could say the same about you." Chloe took a deep breath, ripples of relief replacing the tidal wave of anxiety.

"I have a feeling our businesses are intertwined."

Chloe's chest filled with heat as she fought back the impulse to punch him in the face. She'd never been one for violence, but she could make an exception for assassins.

"My business has nothing to do with murdering innocent people," she said, glaring at him with more hatred than she'd ever felt before, even in hell. This man had attempted to kill both her father and her friend. She wanted nothing to do with him, and yet that voice inside her was telling her otherwise.

"I have murdered no one." Aison came closer and whispered, "Hold up your end of the bargain and I'll tell you everything you want to know."

Chloe snapped her elastic against her wrist. She didn't have time to argue with him. Who knew what damage Damian would do if she didn't get out of there soon. She would have to take her chances bringing a shapeshifting wolf back to Ourania.

"I hope you're not afraid of the dark," she said. Then she clapped Aison's shoulder and closed her eyes once more.

(

"Damian!" Chloe yelled even before her eyes had fully adjusted to the light inside the tent.

"What in Hades is *he* doing here?" Ethan drew his sword. He was sitting on the settle, just as he had been before she'd left, only now, there was visceral aggression burning in his eyes. "You brought back *Aison*? The ice-cream guy? Is this a joke?"

Artemis sat wagging her tail on the bed she'd made of Iris's chiton.

"Molossus," Aison muttered.

"Long story. Keep your sword out," Chloe told Damian. "I don't trust him."

"Nor do I trust *you*," Aison retorted as he strode out of the tent, leaving Chloe no choice but to follow.

"Wait, we're not done in here!" she yelled, nearly bumping into him as he stopped abruptly outside the door. She stepped around him and stood in his way, as if she'd be able to detain him for even a millisecond were he to try and proceed.

But Aison didn't appear to be in a rush to go anywhere. A look of incomprehensible peace settled over his features. His strong, square jaw relaxed slightly and his gray-green eyes became misty. "It's been two thousand years," he said softly.

Ethan brushed past Aison, eyeing him closely. "Why is he here, Chloe? And where did you go?"

"Where's Damian? I'll let him explain." Chloe pressed the sides of her hands around her mouth and resumed yelling Damian's name. "Damian! I know you're here. I know what you're planning."

Aison pointed at a wooden shed not a hundred meters away. Men and boys were having lunch outside it, their hoes and mattocks strewn on the ground between them. "There's a guy dressed like you over there," he said to Chloe. "The one who ran away the second you appeared on the beach. If I'm not mistaken, it's your brother."

Chloe looked, but everyone she saw was wearing chitons and straw sunhats. "Where? I don't see him."

Aison stabbed his finger at the shed. "Right *there*. Wearing jeans and a dark blue jacket."

"How can you see him?" Ethan asked, dumbfounded.

"How can you not?" Aison's exasperated face turned red. "He's right there, plain as the nose on your face."

"He's invisible to us," said Chloe, "but obviously not to you. Where exactly is he standing?"

"Now he's walking down the road. And now he's running."

Chloe followed Aison's gaze down the hill and groaned. She hated running, a fact Damian knew better than anyone. "Ethan, you run faster than me. Mind catching up to him for me?"

"Sure," said Ethan, a question in his voice, "but I can't guarantee I could take him in a fight if he started one."

Chloe stared at Aison a moment, trying to weigh whether or not she could trust him not to take things too far were he to confront her brother. But she didn't have a choice. She couldn't let Damian escape that wall again, not without resolving a few things first.

"Aison, we had a deal, right?"

"Yeah, and I kept it." He looked at Ethan. "The boy's reached manhood, hasn't he?"

"How do you know he's the same person?" Chloe asked.

Aison tapped the tip of his nose. "Same scent."

Ethan's hands flew up. "Whoa, whoa, whoa. Would one of you please tell me what you're talking about? How did you know me when I was a kid?" he asked Aison. "And how in Hades' name do you know my *scent*?"

"Later, Ethan," said Chloe, "please." She looked back at Aison. "I'd appreciate it if you could extend our terms and not hurt anyone here."

Aison nodded. "I didn't come here to harm anyone. I'll go with your friend to retrieve your brother, and I swear not to touch a hair on the pretty boy's head."

"Thank you."

Then Aison took off, running far faster than the best sprinters at her school, including Damian and Ethan.

Ethan shot Chloe a look out of the corner of his eye. "I hope you're not leaving me in the dark."

"Only when I time travel," Chloe said.

Ethan laughed and followed after Aison, who was already halfway to the shed.

"Back so soon?"

At the sound of the familiar voice, Chloe turned to see the Centaur looming over her shoulder with a leather bowcase strapped to his back.

"I didn't go after Damian," she said. "Turns out he was here all along."

"Good news then, eh? Simplifies things a bit." He took a swig from his wineskin.

"Not really. Damian just followed me into the past—*my* past—and I'm pretty sure I know why."

"And why's that?"

"He wants to rewrite history so our parents were never killed. He doesn't understand the damage that would do."

The Centaur sighed and looked around the camp, at the dozens of men and women building new lives for themselves, literally from the ground up. Their old lives had been burned to ashes, yet not a one of them seemed aware of it, or, if they were aware, they simply didn't mind. They worked and laughed and ate and sang as if they were the most fortunate people on the planet. They had each other and they had security. They didn't seem to need anything else to be happy.

"Who wouldn't want to rewrite history if they had the chance?" he asked.

It was a rhetorical question, but Chloe felt compelled to answer anyway. "If there wasn't so much at stake, you can bet your life I'd go back and try to prevent a lot of things, starting with my parents' deaths. But that would be the cowardly thing to do, and my family is through being cowardly."

"A noble sentiment, as long as your family's not through being a family. Take it from someone who knows, Miss Chloe." The Centaur turned to her. She tried not to stare at the triangular serpent head tattooed on the bridge of his nose. "If you haven't got your family, you haven't got anything."

Chloe wondered what secrets lay hidden behind his gruff exterior and tattooed face. He obviously wasn't a part of Iris and Tycho's family, nor did she see any other centaurs walking around. But before she could ask him what his story was, she saw Damian, Ethan and Aison trudging toward her. Much to her relief, no one appeared to be bruised or bleeding.

"Can we talk about this in private?" Damian asked Chloe, staring at the ground the way he used to when their parents scolded him for something.

Chloe looked past his shoulder at the carpenters by the shed. They were shaking their heads and mumbling to each other, pointing at them with their tools. She didn't want to know what they thought of the three strangers Iris had brought to their new colony. Did they suspect she was another Mania? She couldn't blame them if they did. So far she'd done nothing to ingratiate herself with them, much less give them reason to trust her.

"We can talk farther away from them," she said to Damian, indicating the men and boys behind him, "but I think the rest of us deserve to know where you've been and why you're betraying us."

"Strong words to speak to one of your own kith and kin," said the Centaur.

Chloe held her gaze on Damian until he finally lifted his eyes to hers. "It's the truth, and he knows it," she said. "Warning Mom and Dad or whatever it is you're intending to do by following me to our past would undo everything we've accomplished up to now."

"What have we accomplished?"

Damian didn't sound angry, the way he had in the tent. Instead, sadness, verging on apathy, shaded his words. She could feel the weight of them pulling on her heart like an anchor.

"We're freaks, Chloe. Exiled from our own world and this one, too." He gestured toward the rows of tents beyond him. "We don't belong here."

Iris, Tycho and Charis emerged from the woods and rounded the corner near the shed, each with a wicker basket on their arm. Chloe's thoughts shot back to the Fields of Asphodel and the flower-filled baskets every soul there was obsessed with. Like Sisyphus, who rolled and rolled his boulder upwards without ever reaching the summit, the spirits of Asphodel labored in vain. But, Chloe thought, at least Sisyphus was aware that his monotonous lot was the gods' retribution. To those in the Fields, picking flowers was their life's purpose. It would be *everyone's* purpose if they died without knowing the All-Powerful.

It was that thought alone that restored Chloe's reason whenever she found herself fantasizing about meddling with her parents' murder. Even their deaths, which were senseless and devastating, were being used for the greater good—the good of all Petrodians, both present and future.

She couldn't trade their eternal damnation for her temporal happiness.

She wouldn't.

CHAPTER TWENTY-ONE

MERCENARY

Iris waved at Chloe, but Chloe could only manage a superficial smile in return. As her own smile faded, Iris hastened toward her.

"And you think we belong back in the past with our parents," Chloe said. "You want to just erase your mind of all we know about the Fantásmata and the fact that they want our family dead." Chloe fixed her eyes on an early evening star crowning a distant peak. If only Damian could see the Fields himself. If it weren't such a risk, she'd take him there right now.

"What's going on here?" Iris turned to Damian and rested a hand on his arm. "It's good to see you, Damian."

"Just a little sibling spat," said Ethan.

Chloe wished this *were* just a spat and not a quarrel concerning the fate of humanity.

"Did you go outside the wall?" Charis asked. Her strawberry-blond hair danced in the breeze as her eyes widened with curiosity.

"Maybe," said Damian, thinking this was a convenient change of subject. He would have loved to talk about anything other than his and Chloe's "spat."

"Don't beat around the bush, kid," said the Centaur. "If you saw something worth telling, you'd better open your yap and have out with it. I didn't save your skin for nothing."

Damian glared up at the Centaur, whose massive hand rested on the strap of his bowcase. Damian had always been the braver twin. "You know," he said, "I liked you a whole lot better when you were Katsaros."

Charis and Ethan laughed, despite the Centaur's disgruntled sneer.

"Come now, Damian," Charis said sweetly. "What have we done to so upset you that you won't tell us what you've seen?"

"No one's done anything to upset me," Damian assured her. "I just wish my sister would see that there's nothing we can do here. Mania isn't our problem." He sighed and stared down into Charis's basket as a gust of wind rushed by them. "I met Mania today. She wanted me to go with her. She wasn't scary at all, actually."

"Then why didn't you go?" Ethan asked. "You could've gotten some intel and then used your doma to leave without being noticed."

"Because," began Damian, his apathy giving in to heated conviction, "this is what I'm trying to tell you—*she isn't our problem*." He pointed to Iris and Charis. "These Ashers are the ones who should have stopped Mania, not us. I wanted to go with Chloe to the future because that's where we can make a difference. We could save our parents, and Ethan's, too."

"No," said Aison, "you couldn't."

All eyes swung to the shapeshifter, whose true identity only Chloe knew.

"Who are you?" Charis asked, as if only now noticing Aison's presence in their circle.

"The proper question is *what* are you," Chloe said, glad that two of the three men around her were armed and that one of the two women had fire in her hands.

But Aison didn't seem to mind her remark. He pointed to the back of his right hand, just below the space between his thumb and forefinger. "You see that?"

Everyone but the Centaur bent down to get a closer look. Chloe had to squint to make out a small, flesh-colored rectangle the size of a stamp imprinted on Aison's skin.

"A tattoo," said Tycho. "Pythonian. Look, there's a serpent running through the middle."

Chloe looked up at the Centaur, whose own snake tattoo was glaring at her. She turned back to Aison and said, "Why do you have the same mark as someone from this time?" But she already knew the answer: Aison wasn't from her time. He probably had more in common with Iris and the Centaur than Chloe or anyone else back home.

"The Pythonians are what you know as the Fantásmata," said Aison, flecks of orange flickering in his eyes. "They're cut from the same blood-soaked cloth as Apollo. This"—he tapped the tattoo—"is not just the Pythonian mark. Beneath it is a tag called the Lycaean Seal, and that contains everything there is to know about me, as well as the others." He looked at Damian. "And there are others, thousands of them."

Charis's pale cheeks flushed pink with impatience. "Others of what? What are you?"

"One of the young men chosen at the Lycaea Festival. I was the first."

"The first what, Aison?" Ethan said.

"Asher hunter." Aison grimaced, and his four incisors protruded from his mouth. Within seconds, his face and arms were covered with yellowish-brown fur.

Charis and Iris gasped and stepped close to Tycho, whose hand flew to his scabbard.

"Peace,' Aison said. "I'm only showing you."

Less than a minute later, Aison's metamorphosis was complete. Artemis growled at him from her post outside Chloe's tent, but at half the wolf's size, she wasn't dumb enough to provoke him.

"So *that's* how you could see me," Damian said to Aison. "You're part animal."

The Centaur cleared his throat. "Keep that in mind the next time you try to sneak by *me*, kid."

"You're the wolf that attacked Chloe's dad and me," Ethan said, more stupefied than upset.

"I..." Aison's fiery gaze fell to the earth as he dug his claws into the earth. "I cannot say. It could've been me, or it could've been a dozen other Lycaeans assigned to that area."

"You can't stay here, Aison." Chloe said, and Aison's ears and tail went limp. "We can't risk changing history if it was you who went after them. I don't think it was a coincidence that Ethan showed up there on the beach with us."

"Then what stopped him from coming after *me*?" Ethan asked. "Or going after you? If he's our attacker, he would've attacked." He stared at Aison a moment, examining him from head to tail. "He isn't the same wolf."

"It was *hope* that stopped me." Aison released the word as if it had been pushing against his lips for hours. "The second I saw Chloe and Damian appear out of nothing, I knew they were Ashers with great power, Ashers who might be able to help us."

"You mean help all the other wolf people?" Damian asked.

Aison nodded. "We're not all assassins. We do what we must to survive, mercenaries compensated with another sunrise."

"Tell us what happened to you," said Charis. Then she ducked into the tent and returned with a bowl full of water. She set it before Aison and smiled as he lapped it up.

"Thank you." Aison lifted his wet nose from the bowl. "My past is not a pleasant one, nor one I'm proud to share, but perhaps it will help redirect your perspective." He was looking straight at Damian.

"Come," said Iris. "Let's get you into the woods and back to your human form before someone sees you."

Iris led them behind the tents and up a steep narrow path lined by armies of beech, oak and eucalyptus trees whose foliage blocked the sun. The air was infused with the intoxicating scents of pine needles, mint, and honey, a virtual paradise for the moths and butterflies floating through the branches in search of the best place to feast.

It was easy for Chloe to believe that the mythical wood nymphs known as dryads dwelled here. Eurydice, Orpheus's wife, was one such nymph. Her tragic death by a viper's bite was one of the many reasons Chloe was here. Without it, Orpheus would not have been desperate enough to do the bidding of his beguiling uncle Hermes by luring Chloe to the gateway to hell; she knew him better than that. Had Eurydice lived and their marriage endured, who knew how the future would have unfolded, and what tack Apollo would have taken to stop the Vessel when the Moonbow appeared.

It was useless to speculate, but following the thread back to the moment Eurydice died only further persuaded Chloe that good really could be made of evil. Her time on Circe's island and later in hell hadn't exactly been a bed of roses, and nor had losing her old life and coming here been easy. But the fact was, Eurydice and Orpheus were together in heaven now. As were Chloe's parents. All of it, from discovering Carya in her backseat that first day at the museum to being forced by Deimos to drink from the Lethe, had prepared her for this, her one and only chance to change history.

"Have none of you ever heard of or seen a Lycaean before?"

The sound of Aison's voice interrupted Chloe's thoughts and she looked up to see him, in his human form, standing beneath an oak tree. The others circled around him slowly, cautiously, eyeing him as though he were a feral animal. He seemed genuine enough to Chloe, but she acknowledged that her judgment wasn't always spot on. She'd been naive enough to believe Orpheus, after all. She had learned the hard way that people aren't always what they seem.

She noticed that the Centaur was also staying back, eating a handful of mulberries he'd no doubt picked from one of the others' wicker baskets. Though he appeared nonchalant, Chloe had a hunch he was more interested in serving as bodyguard for the group than hearing Aison's story. She watched him remove his bow from the bowcase and set it beside him, a clear warning to the shapeshifter.

Before Aison could continue speaking, he stumbled sideways, catching himself on the oak's wide bole. Unable to support his weight, he slid down the tree, his neck and brow suddenly slick with sweat. His arms and legs began to shake. Charis tried to go to him, but Tycho held her back. He didn't trust Aison either.

Chloe gasped. "Aison!" She ran to his side and crashed to her knees. "What's happening to you?"

Aison's lips parted and thin rivulets of blood spilled between them, trickling down his chin, staining his white shirt. He raised a hand to his mouth to cough, filling it with inky blood.

"The seal," he rasped, holding up a bloody, trembling hand until, wracked with exhaustion, he let it drop onto his thigh. "Take the seal." Then he wheezed a final breath as his head fell back against the oak.

CHAPTER TWENTY-TWO

BLOOD

Chloe stared at Aison's lifeless eyes, hoping that if she looked long enough she would see a glimmer of orange. She refused to feel for a heartbeat. He couldn't be dead; he hadn't been sick or wounded. On the contrary, he'd seemed in better spirits than he had been on the beach. One second he'd been healthy, and the next, fighting for breath.

Iris stepped between Chloe and the oak where Aison reposed and held out her hand. "Come, Chloe. Leave him in peace."

"I'm going back." Chloe whispered, unable to find the strength to shout. She wanted to scream, to let her voice ring out and echo through the woods—echo until every Petrodian and dryad heard her. She would make this right. Aison hadn't deserved to die.

She reached around Iris and placed her hand on Aison's, tears welling at the shock of his cold, stiff skin. "Please go," she said to Iris. "I need space to do this."

"You've used your doma twice already today," said Ethan, standing just a few feet behind her. "Remember what Carya said?"

"Then I'll wait and go back tomorrow," Chloe said, finding her voice again. "I'll go back to the beach, to the moment I saw him, and then..."

"Then you'll try to convince him that he can't come here with you." Iris placed a maternal hand on Chloe's head, stroking her hair. "There's a reason he wanted to come with you, Chloe. You heard him yourself."

Chloe looked down at Aison's tattoo and the minuscule snake bisecting its middle. She thought of the stained-glass windows in the foyer of the Religious Council building that depicted a crescent moon and a serpent just like this one. And then she knew.

"The councilman killed him," she said, releasing Aison's hand and leaning back against Iris's legs. "Just like he almost killed Ethan." She turned to look at Ethan, recalling, with tears running down her cheeks, the moment the councilman had held the fob over Ethan's head, one touch of which could have taken his life in an instant.

"The microchip was rigged, just like the suit was," said Ethan. "It was probably programmed to kill its host if something ever seemed off."

The Centaur cursed under his breath. "By the Twins, if I ever get my hands on a Petrodian..."

Tycho knelt beside Aison and gently closed his eyes with his palm.

"He said to take the chip, didn't he?" Damian said to Chloe. "If you try to go back in time, we won't know what he's talking about."

Shakily, Chloe got to her feet and wiped her eyes, anger roiling beneath her eyes where tears of grief still stood. How could Damian be such a hypocrite? "And if I go back and save Mom and Dad, none of this is relevant." The woods went silent with her shout. Even the Centaur froze.

"So take your pick, Damian," she said in a softer but no less severe tone. "Should I go back and save our parents, promising them nothing but maybe a day, a week, a year of life? Or would you rather we stay here and fight for something that could make a difference?"

Damian pressed his lips together firmly and stuck his hands into his hoodie's front pockets. "There's a reason we're the first ones in our family to stand up to the Fantásmata, Chloe."

"Yeah, I know," she said, feeling the ground firm up beneath her feet. "It's because we're the Vessel, Damian. And we can ignore it and resent it, or we can run with it."

Damian stood so still that Chloe could have sworn he was going to make himself invisible again and take off through the trees. She wouldn't try to bring him back if he did. If he wanted to leave, she'd let him.

"I've got it," said Tycho.

Chloe turned to see Tycho pinching something between his fingers: the microchip. He had cut it from Aison's hand.

"The decision whether to time travel and spare Aison's life rests with you, Chloe," Tycho said. He walked over to her and placed the rice-sized wafer in her hand. "But I think you know what he would've wanted."

Fresh tears spilled over as the Centaur pulled a cloak from his kit and draped it over Aison's body, making his death all the more real to Chloe, all the more final. She clutched the chip. *I can't go back.*

She forced the words from her heart to her tongue and willed herself to speak them. "We'll honor Aison and our parents," she said, glancing at her brother and Ethan beside him, "by doing everything we can to ensure that their deaths weren't for nothing."

Iris put her hand on Chloe's shoulder. "I told you when I met you that you had to be quite strong if Duna saw fit to send you here. I still believe it." Iris's blood-red jasper stone was twinkling in what little sunlight had made its way to the forest floor. She placed her free hand on the stone and lifted the necklace over her head. "My brother Jasper gave this to me. He was murdered by an Alpha guardian who was threatened by Jasper's beliefs in Duna." She put the necklace on Chloe and pulled her blond hair over it. "There was a time when it kept my mind fixed on vengeance."

"And now?" Chloe asked, rubbing the cool stone with her finger.

"Now it symbolizes redemption, of recovering that which was lost. For me, it was recovering the faith of my fathers." She smiled warmly at Damian. "For you two, it remains to be seen what its purpose is."

"It represents blood," Damian said. He walked toward Chloe, unspoken apologies filling his eyes. "Flesh and blood."

Chloe nodded once, then turned back to Iris and Tycho, who now stood at her side. These strangers, these ancients from a forgotten time, were her family. They, along with her brother, were all she had in this world. The Centaur had been right: if she didn't have them, she didn't have anything. The stone around her neck would serve to remind her of that. She knew it.

She lifted the stone so Damian could see it. "Didn't the Centaur give this to you, when he was Katsaros?"

Damian sighed. He studied the rock a moment as a look of deep-seated shame washed over him. "I gave it back to him.

Another one of my prouder moments." He gave a weak laugh, and then lowered his gaze to her closed fist. "The microchip is useless here. Wouldn't Aison have known that?"

"What does it do?" Tycho asked.

"We always thought the chips were just for tracking pets," said Chloe. "Obviously, they're for a whole lot more than that."

"Killing people," Damian muttered.

Ethan pulled his dead cellphone from his pocket and popped out the SIM card. "Makes you wonder what else these do." He dropped it to the ground and crushed it with his heel. Damian did the same.

"All the chip's information is stored in a database somewhere," said Chloe. "It'd be like searching for a needle in a haystack if we tried to hunt it down."

"Not to mention there'd be no way we could hack into the computer, even if we could find it," Damian added.

"Well, aren't you a sunny bunch?" the Centaur said. "This lad risked his life following you Ashers here. If you want to honor his memory, you can start by having a little faith in him. He entrusted that blasted object to you. I'd like to think he knew you'd find out why."

Chloe had a dozen reasons to explain why she thought the task impossible, and how she meant no disrespect in thinking so. But the Centaur's imposing disposition alone had a way of discouraging arguments.

Chloe, Ethan and Damian stood in silence.

After what felt like hours, Tycho intervened. "The best thing for you right now," he said, putting an arm around Damian's shoulder, "and for all of us, is to give Aison a proper burial."

"What about this?" Chloe said, indicating the silicon chip in her fist.

"Has anything thus far been left unknown to you?" Tycho asked.

Chloe shook her head. The fact that she and those standing around her were still alive was proof enough that the god they served was faithful. He wouldn't leave them in the dark on this.

"Who has perished?"

Chloe looked up to see Archelaos, the high priest, on horseback behind the Centaur, his young attendant mounted beside him. When no one answered, Archelaos kicked his heels into the horse's flanks and trotted to the oak tree. He pointed at Aison's covered head and said, "Cael, pull back the cloak."

The attendant dismounted and did as he was told.

"No..." Archelaos stumbled off his mare and ran to Aison in panic. "No, it can't be." He took Aison's face in his hands, turning it tenderly from side to side as if to confirm his identity. When there was no longer a question, he fell prostrate onto the hard dirt ground and wept.

Ethan took the attendant by the elbow and drew him aside. "He knows Aison?"

"Aye," nodded Cael. "Aison is his nephew. Aison ran away this time last year and no one's seen him since."

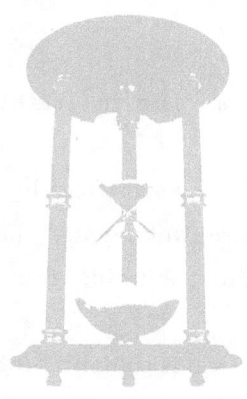

CHAPTER TWENTY-THREE
ULTIMATUM

The fetid stench of pig blood turned Hermes' stomach as he floated down the aisle of Hades' throne room. Of all the creatures the Pythonians sacrificed, swine were by far the most offensive to the nostrils, even nostrils accustomed to the sulfurous fumes of the Underworld. Hades himself, the dark lord, choked with disgust as waves of blood mixed with the fire of the far, magma-canvassed wall.

Hermes watched his master remove his horned helmet and begin to pace back and forth on the precipice, below which roared the insatiable mouth of the Phlegethon.

"I would rather they sacrifice the aphids from their gardens than one more stinking pig." Hades swung back his arm and sent his helmet spinning through the air, straight into Hermes' chest.

"The Lycaea Festival is tonight, brother," said Hermes, placing the helmet over his cap. "The purest Petrodian blood will soon rid the air of this unholy odor." He plugged his nose and offered his most charming smile.

"We don't tolerate you for your humor, Hermes," said Apollo, who was seated on his basalt throne, arrayed in his blinding panoply of gold. "Give your report, and please, spare us any embellishment."

Hermes nodded. He forced himself to remember that if he were condemned to remain sequestered here in Petros's bowels as they were, he would no doubt be equally inhospitable.

"Sires," he said, "I have told you that two Ashers have joined the refugees in the hills outside Ourania. I have reason to believe that one, perhaps both, of these is the Vessel the oracle spoke of."

Hades raised a hand toward his helmet, and with a flick of his finger jerked it toward him, the force of his pull dragging Hermes to the floor. "Have you seen the Moonbow?" With his opposite hand, Hades made a sweeping motion across the igneous wall, commanding the flow of fire and blood to cease.

"No, my lord," said Hermes, pushing himself up onto hands and knees, "but—"

Apollo held his palm beneath his lips and blew across it, his breath lighting the rows of cauldrons atop their tripods, one by one. "The prophecy was clear, brother. The Moonbow precipitates the Vessel's appearing." He stood from his throne and stepped off the dais, drawing his sword. "We all know you love a good battle, Hermes, perhaps more than Ares once did, but the time has not yet come to make war."

Apollo pointed his sword at Hermes and made three mock thrusts, laughing when he saw Hermes' hand reach for his wand, a reflex Hermes had never learned to control in the presence of his brothers.

"You see," Apollo said, turning to fence with the air, "you feel paranoia because you're itching to fight. Why don't you return to your mistress and enjoy peacetime while you can. Mania will finish off the Ashers soon enough, and your bloodlust will be sated."

Hermes sheathed his wand. "It's not as simple as that, sire. As I speak, the Ashers are with Iris, protected behind a wall the All-Powerful is using to protect them. Mania is powerless as long as they're in hiding."

"Then get them *out* of hiding." Hades' cavernous voice echoed throughout the chamber; the wind of his breath sliced the tripods' flames in half, sending skeins of smoke into the noxious air. "Every second those Ashers live bolsters the All-Powerful's plans against us."

"Our brother speaks truth, Hermes," said Apollo, bringing the sword to his side. "If we don't eradicate them, the Pythonians—from the centaurs to the aristocracy—will be subverted."

"Our hands are tied as long as the wall stands, my lords," Hermes said. "One of the Ashers, the boy, was intercepted by Leto just this morning, but the encounter was unproductive."

"Don't be cryptic. Unproductive in what way?" Apollo asked.

"I-I counseled Leto that it would be best to befriend the new Ashers rather than play the foe. B-but the young man regarded her as nothing more than a common beggar and disappeared before an inroad could be made." Hermes cursed his tongue for stuttering. He was no mightier than a mouse when interrogated by these two.

"A doma that permits him to disappear..." Apollo tapped his chin. "Perhaps you've met your match."

"Indeed, sir." Hermes paused, feeling his pride creep down his throat like a spoonful of bitter herbs. "That means one of the other two is the time traveler. In any case, I'm afraid to say that I'm far outmatched. It's my suspicion that they've come from the future to thwart our present plans. Perhaps the Moonbow rose in the time they've come from, and whatever stratagem our future selves concocted failed."

"Our future selves?" Hades bellowed. "Don't include me in your baseless hypotheses, Hermes. I will take Zeus' place in Tartarus if I've played a part in this ignominious fantasy of yours."

"His theory is feasible, Hades," Apollo rejoined. "But as you say, if it's true, our brother insults us by implying that we're at fault."

Apollo spun on his heel and pointed his sword once more at Hermes' head, only this time there was no trace of mirth in his ice-blue eyes; he'd spilled plenty of Hermes' immortal blood before, and in circumstances far less dire than these.

"I care not what the reason is for why these Ashers are here," Apollo said, "be they Vessel or minor delinquents. I only care that you dispose of them and anyone who comes to their aid, including their comrades behind the wall. If any one of them so much as sets their big toe outside that barrier, chop it off and slit their throat."

Hermes gave a humble bow, the final step before he begged to be spared Apollo's blade. "Brother, you know I can touch no one bodily. I ca—"

"I am well aware of the laws!" Apollo shouted, the luminous glow of his face fading as his ire increased. "Every day we're bound here in this rathole is a reminder of that millstone."

"Then you know that I cannot harm the Ashers, much less take their lives." Hermes folded his arms across his tunic, thankful for the bronze cuirass beneath it. If he lingered here much longer he'd undoubtedly need its protection.

"Are you so daft that you've forgotten why you charmed Diokles' daughter in the first place?" Hades moaned and pouted, his round bloated head turning a sickly shade of green. "Why do we tolerate him, Apollo? If he is our eyes, I would rather we gouge them out."

Apollo settled back into his throne and threw his feet onto the ivory footstool, a gift from Hephaestus before he, too, was chained in darkness. "Aye, and he's our ears as well, ears that had better be rid of wax right now or these words will be the last they hear."

"My ears are opened, my lord." Hermes bowed so low that he could see the whites of his eyes reflecting back at him from the slick obsidian floor.

Apollo leaned forward and drummed his fingers against his lips. "It's time to involve the child."

"Which child, sire?" Hermes said.

"Your son, you imbecile. You say you've met your match with these Ashers, that they're unreachable, unknowable behind their wall. It stands to reason, does it not, that Mania's spawn will serve as a worthy rival?"

"That boy is being spared for my sacrifice, the pure, undefiled blood of an Asher's child," shouted Hades, now rushing toward Apollo, his horned helmet lowered like the head of a charging bull.

Apollo snatched his shield from behind his throne and forced his brother back with a warning blow to his chin. "Don't be so myopic, Hades. You'll have your Asher blood the hour this inconvenience is contained. We'll maintain his innocence as much as possible, but at this juncture, it's required that we dirty his hands a bit."

Hades grunted; he held his jaw in his hand, opening and closing it while Apollo set down the shield, bowl side up. "You strike me again and I'll have Deimos and Phobos feed your rotten heart to Cerberus."

Hermes shuddered. He knew these two made no empty threats. Despite their ability to regenerate, an ability with which all souls of the Underworld were cursed, they still played by mortal rules, wounding and killing one another as a virile show of power. Hermes had lost count of the number of times his own organs had been roasted for the hound of hell.

"You give me a need to strike again and I'll weave a rug from that glaucous skin of yours," Apollo said.

Hades turned away, and with an indignant air stalked off into the shadows.

"Stand like a man, you spineless imp," said Apollo, spitting as he turned back to Hermes. "It's no wonder that the Ashers torment you so, even from afar; your affair with Mania has robbed you of all your mettle."

Hermes stood and brought his right arm across his chest, a sign of gratitude that his own skin was not yet stripped off his bones. In no small way did it hearten him to hear his brother pinning blame on Mania. "You speak truth, brother, as always. The woman has been a distraction. I've spent all my time tutoring her, training her—"

"Bedding her," said Apollo.

Hermes' cheeks grew hot. It was true he'd been Leto's lover, but only because he'd been commanded to ensure she produced an unblemished Asher's son for sacrifice once all of Petros had been purged of Duna's devoted. Since he couldn't convince her to woo any man save himself, he'd been left with no choice but to take her as his mistress, his own Persephone.

"Indeed, sire," Hermes said, "forgive me for my indulgence in such carnal pleasures."

Apollo smiled as he waved off Hermes' apology. "Your carnal pleasures have maintained Mania's trust all these years. I don't ask for your repentance, only that you will carry out my wishes."

"Anything you ask, brother." Hermes' heart beat wildly, so anxious was he to leave this place and fly through the night back to Leto.

"You will make a weapon of your offspring and your lover," Apollo said.

"Yes, my lord," said Hermes, bullets of sweat now pouring from his brow, "but you forget that the lad is just ten years old. His doma will not manifest for another eight years."

"And you forget that your immortal blood runs through his veins." A shadow fell darkly across Apollo's porcelain face. "Death will elude him for centuries. Even his sacrifice, which our selfish brother so craves, will not result in his annihilation. You must use this to your advantage."

Hermes' jaw fell slack. He took the cap from his head and wiped his perspiring face. "I am daft, like you say. Pray, speak plainly of your plan."

"I make no pretense about having a greater intellect than yours." Apollo came to Hermes, clapping his shoulder as his piercing eye winked. "I leave you to your own devices now. But should you fail..."

Apollo unsheathed his sword, cast it onto the floor and shoved his cold, steel-like fingers between Hermes' ribs. "I will rip out your liver and feed it to Prometheus' eagle piece by piece. This I will repeat for as many days as it takes me to forget your failure." He clenched Hermes hard and pulled him close. "And my memory is not short."

CHAPTER TWENTY-FOUR
CURSED

Aison's corpse was the first ever to be interred behind the refugees' wall. Every man, woman, and child gathered that evening with small cakes and libations and laid them on his grave, lamenting a man they knew nothing about, save that he was a runaway, just like them.

Archelaos had replaced his white robe with a sackcloth tunic, which he'd torn from neck to navel. He sat beside the grave mound, watching through tear-stung eyes as the last of the lamenters wandered back to camp.

"It was kind of them to mourn for him," he said, placing his hand on the ancient yew tree towering above him, its low-hanging branches like a shroud around the bereft.

"They're goodhearted people," said Iris. "They know better than most what it's like to lose a loved one."

"And you three," Archelaos said, gesturing at Damian, Ethan, and Chloe seated to his left and right, "am I wrong to presume that you, too, have lost family?"

Damian watched Chloe and Ethan give hesitant nods, neither of them willing to explain the details of their parents' deaths.

For Damian's part, he didn't want to answer questions but ask them. The afternoon had passed and not a single question had been put to the priest. Damian was doing his best to pay his respects and give the man some space, but the sun was setting now, and he refused to let the priest leave without first answering his questions. Someone had to break the silence. It might as well be him.

"How did you know he'd died?" he asked Archelaos.

Chloe slapped Damian on the back of his hand. *Leave him alone*, she mouthed.

Archelaos sank his wrinkled hands into the mound and began digging a hole. "It's all right. I feel it necessary that my grieving period be cut short." He took a dagger from his belt and sliced a diagonal line across his palm, letting the blood trickle into the hole. "On this grave, at this death,

I hereby pledge to bring to justice to he whose hand has taken my nephew's life."

The priest ripped off a piece of his garment and wrapped it around the wound. "In answer to your question," he said to Damian, "I knew only that a relative had perished in Ourania." His gaze fell to the modest headstone, Aison's name carved crudely into it. "I had no idea it was my nephew."

"But who told you?" Ethan asked. "We were the only ones who knew, and we've all been here this whole time."

"And you got here pretty quickly," Damian said to Archelaos.

Archelaos sighed as he sprinkled dirt over the hole of blood. Damian didn't have the heart to tell him that his solemn oath was useless; the man responsible for Aison's death wouldn't be born for another two thousand years.

"I knew because an envoy of the Pythonian oracles intercepted me on my journey home to Eirene," Archelaos said.

Iris and Charis shifted beside one another, uneasiness sneaking its way into their sadness.

"You break your vows as high priest by consulting with Pythonians," said Tycho, his face livid with outrage. "It's little wonder you've always been so distrusting of Iris and my daughter when your loyalty is clearly divided."

Cael, standing at attention over his master's shoulder, put a warning hand on the hilt of his sword.

Iris touched her husband's arm. "Tycho, calm down. You're jumping to conclusions."

"I don't claim to be the man my predecessor was," said Archelaos. "He led by faith and I lead by pragmatism. The Pythonians and I have an understanding."

"Do you realize that these Pythonians are the ones responsible for your nephew's murder?" Damian was unable to temper the exasperation in his tone. "They're called the Fantásmata where we come from, but they're still the same bunch of bastards."

Tycho let out a long exhale, willing his emotions to cool. "Forgive us for reacting with such passion, Archelaos. My wife and I, and our new friends, have seen firsthand what the Pythonians are capable of. The fact that you have any sort of agreement with them is—"

"Sheer idiocy," muttered the Centaur, before tramping off into the trees, yanking down limbs as he went.

"It's misguided, is what he meant," Tycho said, glaring at the Centaur's tail as it swished back and forth tempestuously.

"What sort of understanding do you and the Pythonians have, exactly?" Ethan asked, so far maintaining his civility.

"It's a simple one, really." Archelaos' eyes welled again. "I give them money when they request it, and they protect my family in return. They've sworn to spare my family from Mania's wrath, and their own, when the time comes." He turned to Chloe, his mouth quavering, reluctant to speak. "You were right. They're going to destroy the temple."

"Aison gave this to us," she said, taking the microchip from her jeans pocket. "We don't know why he wanted us to have it, though. It's technology that doesn't even exist here."

Archelaos bent low, his long nose nearly touching Chloe's palm as he studied the chip. "My god, the Lycaean Seal. This isn't technology, my dear girl, but sorcery." He straightened and held out his hand. "May I?"

Chloe set the chip in his palm. "What do you mean? What does it do?"

"In truth, I'm ignorant of its function," Archelaos said, as his old eyes squinted at the seal. "I only know that it's used to seal the missives I receive from the Pythonians. I don't even know their names, only what they write to me when they demand more gold for their coffers."

Ethan ran his hand along the scars the wolf had left him with over eight years ago. "Sounds familiar. They like their anonymity."

"Why did you call it sorcery if it's just used to seal letters?" Damian asked.

"Because the seal kills whomever does not comply with the Pythonians' wishes. It's cursed." In that moment, the high priest's olive face turned ashen as sudden terror seized him. "I fear I have already revealed too much." He closed his hand around the chip before drawing it to his heart. "I pray you let me keep this, Chloe. I cannot, in good conscience, leave it here with you. It's only a matter of time before its dark magic descends upon you."

"Let him have it, Chloe," said Damian.

"But Aison gave it to us," she said firmly.

"And how do you know his motives were pure? You knew virtually nothing about him." Damian stopped himself from continuing. He wanted to add that they did know one thing about Aison: he was a Pythonian, and a murdering, shapeshifting one at that. Surely his sister didn't need reminding.

Chloe stared down at Archelaos's closed fist. "He didn't want to hurt us."

"Don't be naive, Chloe." Damian stood up, no longer caring whether he hurt her feelings. They had bigger problems to worry about besides making sure they weren't being insensitive. "He was playing you. He followed you here so he could kill as many of us as he could. He was probably expecting the chip to take out more people than just himself. If you keep it, there's a chance it still will."

The priest opened his hand as every eye fixed on the dormant chip. Damian couldn't help but wonder if it was leaking its poison into the air right now. How did it kill people, anyway? He didn't want to find out.

"What do you guys think?" Chloe said, looking up at Iris and Tycho.

After a few long seconds, Iris finally answered. "I've been trying to consider what I would do if I were in your place."

"And?" said Chloe.

"And I wouldn't risk the lives of those I love for the sake of knowledge."

"Give it to him," said Charis. Though no one had asked her opinion, she wasn't one to withhold her thoughts until someone asked for them. "It's too big of a risk to keep it."

"Why not make your decision the democratic way?" said Archelaos. "I will not take the chip from you by force."

"The Centaur isn't here to vote," said Chloe. "But he'd want me to keep it."

The high priest sighed as he stroked his wispy beard. "Centaurs are just as devious as Lycaeans, my girl. Whatever the Centaur has told you in the past, my advice to you is do the opposite."

"All in favor of giving Archelaos the chip," said Damian, "say aye."

Charis, Iris, and Damian were all in favor, making it a tie vote.

With the help of his attendant, the priest got to his feet. "I think I deserve a vote as well. I'm in favor of the notion, and therefore take this burden upon myself."

Damian looked away from his sister, feeling her grief as if it was his own.

Cael returned in a matter of minutes with the horses, and the priest was helped onto his mount.

"I'm afraid you won't be welcome here after what you've divulged to us today," Tycho told him.

"Understandable, my friend. If and when you require my assistance, you know where to find me." Archelaos reined his horse toward the trail before looking once more upon Aison's grave. "If you receive news of my death, do me the honor of burying my bones beside his."

"You have my word," said Tycho.

When Archelaos was out of earshot, Chloe stood up and placed upon the burial mound a small bouquet of hyacinths and lilies tied together with twine. "I will honor your memory," Damian heard her say. "I still have faith in you."

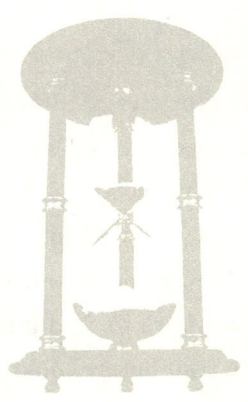

CHAPTER TWENTY-FIVE
HERMOGENES

Hermes stayed away until sunrise, hoping that the brightness of day would make his proposal—his *orders*—for Leto more palatable, even sweet, if possible. He had never met his son before. Hermes had made it clear to Leto on more than one occasion that he didn't want to learn anything about the boy, not even his name. He'd already let himself grow dangerously close to her; he couldn't afford to form a bond of any kind with their child.

Today, however, he would not only meet the boy but also inform him and his mother of Apollo's nebulous plan, a plan Hermes had been assigned to carry out. He knew of only one way to ensure Leto's compliance, and that was to appeal to her love for him, a love he only wished he didn't share.

He flew over the courtyard wall and settled onto the lone branch of the poplar tree that Leto had smitten with lightning just days before. The house was quiet, save for the barking dog below his feet.

"Get away, you!" he snapped.

He didn't want to wake Leto. He needed more time to prepare a speech whose fervor would command obedience, a Herculean labor considering his mind felt like a cart half sunk in mud. The longer he sat, the more he realized that it wasn't for want of ideas that his thoughts were stagnant; he could not will himself to corrupt a child, much less his own.

Up to this time, all the mortals Hermes had ever lied to and led astray had been grown men and women, no longer innocents with hearts as impressionable as clay. He'd found it took very little guile to tempt adults toward wickedness, so long as he pandered to their selfish desires. Children were different. Their consciences had not yet been silenced by the raucous demands of the flesh, or soul-consuming avarice. They still saw the world as a bright rose blossoming before them. To wrong anything, or anyone, within it would be to trample it.

Leto emerged from the colonnade, her eyes searching for the yapping mutt presently leaping to reach the wings of Hermes' heels. His breath nearly left him when he saw her, for he'd never before beheld her in the sun. The silvery streaks of her flowing hair shone like rivers under starlight. Her ivory complexion was a moon in the long gray shadows of dawn.

Leto had been just eighteen when he'd met her in the desert, a woman by the world's standards yet still a child in desperate need of love. Love had been all she'd ever wanted, and love he had lavished on her in return for her loyalty. It had not seemed shameful to him to ratify an agreement of which she was completely oblivious.

To her, their affair was as natural an arrangement as Orion or Pisces in the heavens. Bringing the boy into it would prove to her that his affection was disingenuous, and, to be fair, in the beginning it had been. Now, he rued the hour he'd bewitched her with promises of love and conquest. He'd corrupted her heart, and she'd stolen his. Soon, he would drive her to break it.

"What are you doing up there, you silly bird?" Leto called, laughing as the dog ran circles around the tree.

"I didn't want to wake you," Hermes replied.

"You never come in the morning. Is something wrong?" She came closer, seeking to discern from Hermes' countenance whether he spoke the truth. He prided himself on his talent to deceive, but she'd seen through him before, in tender moments of intimacy when his affiliation with hell was temporarily forgotten. In those times, he didn't exist in reality, but in a dream.

"Not at all," said Hermes.

The dog had stopped barking. He had lifted his forepaw and pricked his ears toward the courtyard wall, focused on the green lizard scurrying across it.

"I wanted to see you in the daylight, my flower." Hermes leapt down from the tree and pulled out his wand, which now appeared as a yellow daffodil, the narcissus she loved so well. "For you."

Leto took the flower and kissed his cheek. "I feared your brothers had hung you over the Phlegethon by your wings." She nudged his sandals with her bare toes.

"Mama?"

Hermes' eyes jumped to the colonnade and the statue of himself, called a herm, which the Alphas believed warded off evil, an imbecilic notion that benefited no one except the merchants who sold them. Beside the herm stood a young boy wearing a loincloth and rubbing his sleepy eyes. He was a redhead, just like Hermes.

"Go inside, Hermogenes," said Leto. "I'll be right there."

The boy took a step forward, shielding his face from the rising sun as he regarded Hermes. "Who are you? And why are there wings on your sandals?"

"I..." Hermes felt as if Apollo's sword had pierced straight through his lungs. He could barely breathe as agonizing pressure permeated his torso and numbness gripped his limbs. He stumbled rearward and caught himself on the tree trunk.

"He's a neighbor," Leto said to Hermogenes. She waved the daffodil for him to see. "He brought us this narcissus. Isn't it beautiful? He picked it while shepherding his flocks."

Hermes frowned. Did the boy have no idea who his mother was? Did he not know that everyone in Ourania was either dead or hiding from her?

"Why does he have wings?" The lad grinned. "Can he fly?"

"Don't be ridiculous." Leto rushed to him, shooing him back with the flower. "Now go inside and get yourself dressed." She spanked his bottom and the boy scooted into the house, glancing back over his shoulder as he went.

"You named him Hermogenes?" Hermes asked as air refilled his lungs.

"As you know, it means 'born of Hermes.' Don't worry yourself, my love. He thinks I named him after the herm." Leto laughed. "He knows nothing of the true gods, and I intend to keep it that way, in deference to your wishes."

A sharp pain, like the pinch of a pair of calipers, bit down on Hermes' heart. He knew he'd been wise to keep his distance these ten years, but never did he expect that a single glimpse of his son would affect him so profoundly. Hermogenes' resemblance to him was uncanny. Even the boy's mellifluent voice was his, as was the cleft chin, broad shoulders, and oval face full of freckles.

Hermes had never experienced boyhood, and if he followed through with Apollo's plot, Hermogenes' own would be cut short. He would become a fiend like his parents. Innocence—the belief in herms and the fascination with flying—would melt like snow at Hades' gates.

"Did you really come only to bring me this?" Leto asked, caressing her cheek with the daffodil. "I cannot even keep it."

With a flick of his finger, Hermes changed the flower back into his wand. Taking it by its end, he pulled Leto into his arms. "I came to—"

The hound resumed its barking at the wall. This time there was no creature to excite it; the dog was looking directly at something, or someone.

Hermes leaned in and whispered into Leto's ear. "We have a visitor. You must conjure a strong wind to buffet him. Hurt him, but don't kill him. We need them alive."

Leto tried to conceal her grin as she nodded. "The time for befriending the Ashers has come and gone." She balled her hands into fists as the dog chased the unseen trespasser around the wall's perimeter.

Hermes twirled the ends of her sun-streaked hair. "The boy had his chance to accept your hospitality."

All thoughts of pacifism, which had disarmed him the moment he saw the boy, fled Hermes' psyche as he was seized by an alternative plan: trap the Asher. Hold him captive to lure the others. Apollo would be satisfied, and Hermogenes' innocence would remain intact, a fact that would please both Hades and Hermes, but for two very different reasons. The former desired a pure sacrifice; the latter a guiltless life for his child, one untainted by the gods for as long as possible.

The dog was now jumping at the wall, yapping at the creature only he could see.

"Panther, come!" Leto whistled, but when the dog wouldn't obey, she extended her hand toward him, shaking the earth beneath his paws. The dog jumped, tucked in his tail, and took off toward the house. "Good dog."

Hermes also retreated into the shelter of the colonnade as Leto's arms stretched forward. "Be swift," he called.

"What's happening?"

It was Hermogenes, his little voice like a morning lark.

"A storm is coming," grunted Hermes, refusing to incline his head toward the boy. "Go hide underneath your bed."

"But my mama's out there."

Hermogenes went to the fountain just as whirlwinds of dust began to spin, advancing like infantrymen toward the wall.

"Boy, it's not safe there!" Hermes shouted, pulling his cloak around his nose and mouth.

The poplars and myrtles started to sway as the wind howled around them, yet Leto stood like a pillar in their midst, untouched by the storm she conducted. Within seconds, the sky was cast with an eerie pall as storm clouds were marshaled overhead.

Hermes thought that even Poseidon, who had ruled the seas, would have been impressed by Leto's power to rally the winds, and control their direction and speed. If the Great Sea would obey her, no doubt she'd rule the world and forget about her masters below.

"Get back inside before you get hurt!" Hermes yelled at the boy.

But Hermogenes latched onto a stone dolphin's nose and dug in his heels, stubborn just like his parents. "Mama!" he cried out, but Leto didn't hear; his shout was a quiet whisper in the wind.

The pergola groaned; the wisteria vines whipped against each other as the beams beneath them shook. Sharp pellets of rain shot down from the sky like murderous darts, followed by hailstones the size of a fist.

A peal of thunder sent Hermogenes to one knee, but still he held his ground, craning his neck forward as the fierce wind pushed him back. Every muscle in his skinny body straining, he proceeded toward his mother, his footsteps faltering as he fought to stay upright. He didn't seem to notice when a lump of ice crashed onto his head and fell with a thud to the sodden ground, nor did he cover his ears as the wind shrieked like a harpy. He merely rubbed his eyes and continued forward.

Leto was shouting something at the Asher, but her words were garbled in the stormy melee. She had no idea that her son, who heretofore was ignorant of his mother's power, was reaching for her robe. When she felt him tug, she spun around with a fury so raw that with one look, blue bolts of lightning tore from the clouds and struck in a circle around them.

The boy screamed and darted back, faster than a hare through a thicket, and joined Hermes beneath the colonnade.

"I told you to get back inside," Hermes growled.

"Is Mama *making* the storm?" Hermogenes was trembling as primal fear besieged his nerves and stripped his face of color.

Hermes reached for his wand, and then stopped himself from forcing the boy into the house. It wasn't his job to protect Hermogenes' innocence. The child was guilty the day he was conceived, marked and sentenced to suffering.

The black hound, Panther, rubbed against Hermogenes' leg, whimpering as his tail slowly wagged. They stood there, the three of them, watching Leto orchestrate this most unorthodox hunt. Somewhere out there, perhaps just behind the wall, or maybe a furlong removed from it, the Asher was fighting. Even if the Asher couldn't feel the impact of the raging elements swirling around him, Hermes knew that his concentration was being tested. And concentration, for every Asher, had to be keen for a doma to operate.

Hermes wanted to help, to fly out above the storm and see if he could use his own powers to further fracture the Asher's concentration. But the second he exposed himself, Hermogenes would know that the gods were real. He would set his heart on becoming one, thereby making himself an enemy of Apollo. And Apollo had no patience for ambitious mortals, even half mortals like Hermogenes.

"Why is she doing this?" Hermogenes' honey-sweet voice was now soured. He clutched the dog's scruff as he leaned against the animal for strength against the gale.

Before Hermes could concoct a lie, Leto lowered her hands, signaling the deluge to end and the winds to cease. "He's getting away!" She whipped her head back to Hermes, who stared at her dumbly. "What are you waiting for?"

Still Hermes said nothing; he glanced at Hermogenes, hoping Leto would intuit his concerns.

"Hermes!" she roared. "Seize him, or I'll send a bolt through his skull."

"Hermes?" Hermogenes said, his copper eyes wide and glistening.

Hermes dipped his brow to the boy in both affirmation and shame, and then took flight over the wall in pursuit of the Asher. He looked back over his shoulder, catching his son's awestruck expression as he studied those golden wings.

CHAPTER TWENTY-SIX
ANSWERS

"Wake up, Mr. Centaur," whispered Chloe for the seventh time. She'd never seen anyone sleep so hard, especially in so uncomfortable a position. The Centaur was standing in an olive grove, leaning against the largest tree, his chin resting in a narrow crook between two boles. His bowcase hung from the branch nearest his snoring bald head, and his sword was propped next to his fingertips, its bronze tip sunk into the dirt.

Ethan picked up a fallen limb and pointed it at the Centaur's side. "I'd stand back," he said to Chloe.

She did so, backing all the way to the path. She knew better than to disturb a sword-carrying Centaur. "Please don't kill him, please don't kill him," she whispered.

Ethan reached out another inch and poked the Centaur gently in his flank. As she expected, the Centaur bucked, snatched his sword, and swung it around with a whoosh.

"What in Zeus' name do you think you're doing, boy?" the Centaur said, lowering his sword, but just halfway.

"Trying to wake you up," shouted Chloe, holding up her palms in surrender as she walked toward them. "You know, it doesn't do any good to lie down next to all your weapons if you sleep harder than a rock."

"Neither does it do any good to criticize a Centaur when he's armed and you're not." The Centaur grinned as he directed his sword at Chloe.

"With all due respect, Mr. Centaur," said Chloe, "you're full of crap. I don't know why you try to play the tough guy all the time. We all know you're more bunny rabbit than bully."

Ethan held his hand over his mouth to keep from laughing.

"You think that's funny, do you?" the Centaur said to him. "It's amusing to you, is it, to cast aspersions at your elders?"

"She's just joking, sir," said Ethan, dropping the limb. "Please, put the sword down. We only wanted to ask you something."

"Whatever it is, the answer is no thank you." The Centaur stuck his sword in the ground and turned back to his tree. "I need my beauty rest."

"I think maybe you're so grumpy because you're bored," said Chloe. "I'm the same way."

The Centaur cleared his throat then covered a yawn with his hand. "I'm in a poor mood, Miss Chloe, because the dawn has only just broken and you've awakened me rudely, in the fashion of thieving hoodlums."

"Just because we wear weird clothes doesn't mean we're hoodlums," said Ethan. "We came here because we wanted to tell you that we agree with you about Aison. We don't think he wanted to harm us."

"That's all very well," said the Centaur, spinning around to face them once more, "but what does it have to do with anything?"

"Except for Tycho, everyone voted that we give the chip to the high priest," Chloe said. "You weren't there to vote, so we lost."

"That two-faced, yellow-bellied greybeard had a say, did he?"

"He took the chip," said Ethan. "He said it would curse us, maybe even kill us, if he didn't."

The Centaur shook his head. "Nothing but poppycock, if you ask me. That man doesn't have an honorable bone in his body."

"That's what we think, too," said Chloe. "Something about him—"

"*Everything* about him," the Centaur said. "His predecessor Anatolius would kick open his grave if he heard his successor was conferring with Pythonians."

"And giving money to them, too," added Ethan.

"Righteousness embodied." The Centaur sighed. "Mark my words: he deceived the others."

Chloe smiled. "I knew you'd say yes."

The Centaur shifted his weight as he yawned again. "You must be hearing things, Miss Chloe. I've agreed to nothing."

"I was getting ahead of the conversation," said Chloe. "You know the high priest has ulterior motives, so it stands to reason that you'd want to find out what those motives are, does it not?"

The Centaur scratched the tattooed serpent atop his head. "If you're proposing that I take part in upsetting the universe with your time-traveling shenanigans, I'll have you know I'd rather scrub the priest's crusty feet every day for a year."

"We're not upsetting the universe," Ethan said. "We're trying to fix it. Duna gave Chloe her gift for a reason. You wouldn't be here with Iris and Tycho if you didn't believe that domas are meant to be used for good."

The Centaur glared at Chloe. "Aye, they are meant for good. But in the wrong hands, they work only evil."

"So because the Ashers have one bad apple, you're not going to trust the rest of us?" Chloe asked. "That doesn't seem fair."

The Centaur scratched the rust-colored stubble of his chin. "And what would you have me do concerning your ill-fated friend?"

"Come with us back to the first Lycaea Festival," said Chloe. "Help us find out what the chip does and why Aison wanted us to have it."

"Why do you need my assistance? I have no doubt you two would fare perfectly well on your own."

"You were a Pythonian, weren't you?" Ethan said, regarding the Centaur's tattoo.

"And what of it?" he snapped. "I know nothing of that blasted pagan festival. It was founded long after I broke free from Python."

"Python?" Chloe said.

"Another name for Phoebus Apollo," the Centaur said. "One part ray of the sun, the other part snake of the pit. It was his fall from heaven that cursed all of Petros with his depravity and pride." He spat and took his bowcase from the tree. "He's the far-striker, the great archer whose arrows destroy far more than men's bodies."

"You don't need to know about the festival," Ethan said. "We just need you to help us infiltrate. I have a feeling they don't let just anyone behind the scenes."

"You're right about that. The mark of Python and the *synthēma* are required to participate in any ritual."

The word *synthēma* translated in Chloe's ears as "passwords." "Do you know the *synthēma*?"

"As much as I've tried to forget their blasphemy, I'm afraid they're as ingrained as ever."

"Good," said Chloe, ignoring the Centaur's scowl as she patted his back. "So they'll let you in. Ethan and I will wait for you until the ceremony ends. We'll be back in time for lunch."

"You'd better not go anywhere dressed like impious hooligans," the Centaur said.

Chloe looked down at her faded blue jeans and oversized plaid shirt. "Fair enough."

"But"—the Centaur pointed his hairy finger in Chloe's face—"if you leave me behind, I will do everything in my power to visit you in the future after I die. And I swear the Katsaros you meet then will be anything but pleasant."

Chloe extended her hand for the Centaur to take. "Again, fair enough."

☾

Damian's skin tingled as he flexed every muscle, straining to make himself invisible. His hands were bound with iron shackles, and heavy fetters were fastened around his ankles. Hermes and Leto sat around the hearth enjoying unappetizing bowls of porridge and conversing in tones too low for Damian to hear. The boy, who was a miniature of Hermes, sat on the floor a few feet from him, rolling a leather ball back and forth against the wall.

"What's your name?" the boy asked.

"Darling, I told you not to speak to him," Leto said, pointing her spoon at Damian.

"Why is he dressed so strangely, Mama? He's wearing trousers like the outlaws do."

"Because he *is* an outlaw, Hermo," she answered.

Damian turned to Hermes. "Hermo. So he is your son."

The god's face burned red as he snatched a rag from the empty stool beside him. "I should have done this earlier." In a flash, he flew to Damian and gagged him with the rag. "Be grateful I don't cut out your tongue, you little maggot."

The boy called Hermo let the ball roll down the uneven floor. His face held the ecstatic expression of an orphan who'd just learned his family wanted him after all. "Is that true, Mama? The flying neighbor is my father?"

Leto's eyes fell to her porridge and stayed there for long, soundless seconds. She folded her lips and crossed her arms as she scooted back her chair and glanced up at Hermes, who was still brooding over Damian.

Damian could almost the see the battle being waged in Hermes' brain. He parted his lips to speak, sealed them and paced a few steps. Then he floated to the top of the open ceiling, where the hearth smoke masked his face. Damian was sure the messenger would leave this place this second if it weren't for his obligation to serve as prison guard.

"I'm not an imbecile," Hermo lifted his little voice to his elder. "You gave my mother a flower this morning, and I look like you, too. You're my father, aren't you?"

"Don't be a pest, Hermo." Leto rose and laid a firm hand on her son's slight shoulder.

Damian studied the boy's eyes, watching as his joy dissolved to confusion, then sadness, and finally anger.

"Why have you been away all this time? Why do you want to keep it a secret?" Hermo needled his father as the latter descended slowly to the kitchen floor.

"To protect you," Hermes answered, in a tone that was almost gentle.

"Protect me from what?"

Hermes unsheathed his wand and waved it at the ball, propelling it back to its owner. Hermo picked it up and gazed in awe at the magical staff, his freckled cheeks reflecting its golden gleam. "The gods really do exist." He looked to his mother. "Are you a goddess, Mama?"

"Not yet, my sweet," she cooed. "Not yet. And neither are you a god."

"Not yet," the boy echoed.

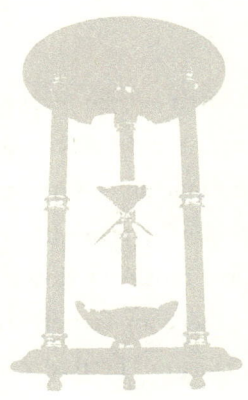

CHAPTER TWENTY-SEVEN
LYCAEA

It was just after sunset on a mountaintop Chloe had never seen before, not even in her history books. The Lycaea Festival, she knew from her time, was held in all four colonies in Petros on the same day each year; she had no idea where the festival had originated.

Around her danced at least a dozen priestesses dressed in animal skins and carrying long sticks wrapped in vines. On some heads lay wreaths of ivy, while other dancers wore bull-shaped helmets. They were chanting and singing gibberish, their discordant notes interrupted by sporadic shrieks and squalls as a frenzied rhythm directed them from rows of frame drums and tambourines.

Around the perimeter, hundreds of observers looked on, their silence a stark contrast to the clamorous spectacle before them. Men, women, children, even infants in their mothers' arms, were gathered, all of them transfixed, waiting patiently to see what this new festival was about. What were they to make of hysterical women clothed in skins, dancing and shaking sticks?

Chloe knew that the Lycaea Festival was an occasion for dressing up in funny wolf costumes and eating candy until it hurt to breathe. There was even a band of drummers, and castanet and rattle players, but the music was harmonious, not wild and abrasive like this. Here, the percussionists' faces were dripping with sweat, their bloodshot eyes glazed over as they punched the drums with their knuckles, pounding them again and again, smearing the leather membranes with dark crimson streaks.

In the midst of the commotion was a bronze wolf the size of the brazen bulls she'd watched chase down Ethan's parents. Its eyes, the only part of it that was painted, were bright orange and seemed to follow Chloe as she stepped closer to the Centaur.

She watched as two men, arrayed in white, approached the statue, their arms full of logs. A teenager followed closely behind, holding a torch with two hands, the flame of which enlivened the wolf's hard eyes. As the men began to stack the logs, one of the priestesses stopped dancing and leapt onto a rock, then forcefully raised her stick, a gesture that seized the audience's attention. Unlike her peers below, her robes were royal purple, and atop her raven hair rested a laurel wreath.

"My fellow Pythonians," she said, her orotund voice traveling easily to every ear. "On behalf of the holiest among us, the oracles of Python, whose presence here would be too glorious to behold, I welcome you to the inaugural festival of Lycaea. Henceforth, this shall be an annual celebration to honor almighty Python."

She paused and scanned the sea of faces, ensuring that every eye was upon her. With a proud smile, she continued. "Today marks the first occasion in which Python's true identity shall be revealed." A collective gasp swept through the throng. "The Eusebians have preached to you that the gods—Zeus, Poseidon, Apollo—are nothing but made-up entities, mythical deities created by clever poets to enchant the populace with tales of woe and valor. Let it be recorded here, on this day, that no greater lie has ever been told."

"Here we go," the Centaur muttered.

It was only then that Chloe noticed that many of the people around her were not people at all, but centaurs, and they all had the same serpent tattoo on their faces.

The priestess dropped her stick on the grass below her. It writhed for a few seconds, then hissed and slithered toward the wolf. "Python, the serpent of the Great Sea, is just one of the many forms with which the preeminent god identifies."

The crowd murmured as the snake made its way up into the center of the logs just as the third man touched them with his torch. The serpent neither squirmed nor tried to flee the sudden blaze. It simply let itself be devoured by the hungry onslaught of flames. A few seconds later, it unhinged its jaws and bit into its own flesh, expediting its death.

"Do you wish to know the name of the god, the most powerful god, who has ordained this festival," the priestess said, "who has looked upon us all with favor and afforded us the honor of calling upon him by name?"

The crowd cheered. Toddlers jumped up and down, feeding off the excitement of their parents and siblings.

"Let us see who among us is well versed enough in our Pythonian lore to guess his name."

The priestess raised her palm; silencing her sisters and bidding them stand still. Another stick was handed to her, only this one was shorter, and made of gold: Hermes' wand. The priestess lifted the wand overhead and waved it at the sky. The pink puff of cloud directly above split down the middle, taking the form of twin dolphins gliding through the dusk.

"Apollo!"

It was the Centaur who had shouted the answer, though the priestess didn't see him. She merely acknowledged the whole of the crowd with an approving nod of her head. There were more gasps and utterances. Chloe held her gaze on Hermes' wand, trying not to cower behind the Centaur. She'd experienced its power. If these people knew what it was capable of they'd be running, not marveling.

"Who said that? Come forward at once," said the priestess. Her expression was pleasant, welcoming, but Chloe knew better.

"Don't go," she said, elbowing the Centaur in the leg.

He stepped forward. "Trust me," he said behind clenched teeth.

Ethan took the Centaur's place beside Chloe and touched her hand. "It'll be all right," he whispered.

She wanted to believe Ethan. Have faith, she told herself, remembering Orpheus's final words to her. She tried to block out the words that had preceded those, the ones about Apollo's mission to destroy her. But, inevitably, those were the ones that replayed in her mind like a mantra. If she were found to be an Asher, she'd be dead in minutes within this pit of Pythonians. Just because the immortals couldn't harm her didn't mean their disciples couldn't.

She watched the other centaurs sprinkled throughout the assemblage, all of them dwarfing their neighbors. They regarded the Centaur suspiciously as he approached the priestess, whispering to one another as they craned their necks to get a better look.

One of the other centaurs stepped forward, his muscles just as bulging and his face just as ugly as the Centaur's. The only difference between them was that this one had a full head of curly black hair and a tattoo darker—fresher—than the Centaur's. "He's a Eusebian!" he cried.

The priestess beckoned to the centaur. "Step forward. Explain yourself."

The crowd parted to let him through as the centaurs' murmuring grew louder, their discomfiture more apparent.

"He's right!"

"He follows the Asher!"

Chloe squeezed Ethan's hand. There was nothing they could do. They couldn't even speak to each other without someone hearing.

The accusing centaur genuflected before the priestess, and Chloe gave a relieved sigh when she saw he wasn't armed. "My name is Solon, my lady. I beseech you, don't let this centaur's mark of allegiance fool you," he said. "He is no Pythonian."

The priestess's countenance darkened as she looked down on the Centaur. "Does this man speak truthfully?"

The Centaur didn't hesitate to respond. "It is true—"

There was a roar from the crowd before he could continue, but the priestess quieted them with a swift stroke of the wand across the air. Mouths continued to move, but no sounds were emitted. She'd struck them mute.

"Silence!" the priestess bellowed, her voice chillingly masculine in her anger. "This is not some jester's court or chorus stage, but an assembly of order. You will conduct yourselves with the civility of the gods if you wish to enjoy their favor." She turned back to the Centaur and her woman's voice returned. "Now defend yourself, if you can."

"I was saying, my lady, that it's true what my brother Solon has said. But his charge contended that my loyalty still lies with the Eusebian blasphemers."

The priestess's knuckles went white around the wand. "Does it not?"

Chloe prayed in silence.

"My association with Iris and her husband Tycho is no more, my lady," the Centaur said. "I joined them because my life was in danger and I had no other recourse. She broke me free from Diokles' prison and I followed her, knowing her doma could protect me from the rebel army."

The centaur called Solon rose from his position of reverence and raised a finger to speak. "If I may, my lady. He broke his centaurian oath once before and was promptly ostracized by the herd. Even if he is telling the truth, his cowardice still violates the oath."

"What is the punishment for dishonoring the oath a second time?" the priestess asked.

"His eyes must be gouged out," Solon answered coldly, "to symbolize his blindness and the spiritual darkness to which his treachery has banished him."

Chloe's stomach shrank into a nauseated knot as she fought to keep her hands from flying to her mouth. She wanted to shout, to call the Centaur back to her so they could get out of there. But there was no way she'd get enough space, let alone enough stillness, to use her doma now: they were surrounded by enemies.

The priestess looked in amusement at the captivated faces of the crowd. The priestesses giggled amongst themselves, enjoying the prospect of the Centaur's pain.

"What is your name?" she asked the Centaur.

"My name, when I had one, was Katsaros."

"You must be joking. That name means 'curly-haired.'" The priestess gave a chuckle, eliciting waves of devilish laughter from the people. "Where has your curly hair gone, Katsaros?" she asked mockingly when the laughter settled.

"It was shaved off the day he was exiled," answered Solon. "He keeps his head shaven as a sign of his shame."

"I see." The priestess tapped her chin as she stared at the Centaur. "And have you not chosen another name for yourself? Falakrós, perhaps?" The audience snickered again; the name meant "bald."

Chloe clenched her fists. Ethan's jaw tightened. The Centaur was being humiliated, and their hands were tied.

"Only creatures of worth are given names," said the Centaur. "My worth was stripped from me the day I betrayed my vow."

"Tell us, that your account might serve as a word of caution for my brothers and sisters, how you first betrayed your vow." The priestess stepped aside, making room for the Centaur on the rock beside her. "Stand here so all may hear."

The Centaur jumped onto the rock and looked quickly at Chloe. His eyes gave away nothing. If he was in control of the situation, she couldn't tell.

"It's shameful, my lady," he said to the priestess. "My greatest weakness was exposed, the selfsame weakness that prevented me from bringing harm to the Asher when I had a thousand chances to slice her throat." He looked at the priestess, pausing to see if she might relieve him of this task, but she didn't speak. The subtlest movement from the wand in her hand was enough to encourage his resumption.

"I find it difficult to take the life of an innocent, someone who has done no harm to our cause or our people." The Centaur lowered his head. "I wished to present myself to you here today to publicly confess and repent of my repeated failures as a Pythonian and a centaur." He ran his hand across his tattoo then looked up at the dolphins still sailing overhead. "The dolphin, I have always believed, symbolizes both Apollo's majesty and his mystery. I can only hope that it also suggests his mercy, for dolphins are known to rescue men from drowning. I ask for his mercy now."

"You demonstrate great bravery by coming here today and speaking up as you have." The priestess motioned for the Centaur to step down from the rudimentary platform. "It's not every day I see a criminal come forth, willing to have his eyes plucked out in return for his soul's absolution."

The crowd grew restless in anticipation of the Centaur's punishment. Chloe dared not say a word. She inched closer to Ethan, preparing herself to use the doma if the Centaur sold them out. He couldn't really be betraying them, could he? She turned to Ethan, hoping his expression might indicate whether it was better to stay put, or leave while they were still anonymous. But his eyes were closed and his face strangely serene. She realized he was praying. What else could they do?

"If that is the fate I must embrace," the Centaur said, "then I shall embrace it and give praise to Apollo for upholding justice."

The priestess turned to Solon and waved him away. "You shall be awarded five drachmae for your loyalty." Solon nodded gratefully before disappearing into the throng.

"You are wise to see mercy in the dolphin," the priestess said to the Centaur, directing the wand to the sky. "Apollo, as I'm certain you know, is the god of prophecy. He glories in symbols, portents, and omens. I could have chosen any of his sacred creatures to place in the clouds, such as the hawk, the griffin, the snake, all of which speak of his judgment and wrath." As she thrust the wand upward, the dolphins merged and formed a balance scale, one side of which was elevated high above the other. "But the dolphin is a creature of peace, of balance."

Chloe looked around. Everyone seemed as stymied as she was by the turn of events. But she knew the Centaur wasn't off the hook, not yet anyway. The dolphin scales weren't even, after all.

The priestess tucked the wand into her belt and clapped her hands three times. Two of the drummers left their places and scurried off into a colonnade surrounding a circular limestone structure, a temple, Chloe guessed. A loud series of shouts echoed against the columns, turning the attention of the crowd away from the priestess, but only for a moment.

"Today marks the beginning of a new and hallowed season," proclaimed the priestess. "And in his unsurpassed wisdom, Apollo has chosen to christen it with both the tears of atonement and the blood of sacrifice." She reached down and placed a hand on the Centaur's shoulder. "Mercy shall be yours, as will your reinstatement as our Pythonian kinsman, if you prove your loyalty before your elders and peers."

Half the crowd cheered while the other half folded their arms and rolled their eyes with displeasure. They would rather see pain inflicted than mercy extended.

The two musicians who had been dismissed now tarried outside the colonnade, holding a man between them; a sack covered his head and his wrists were bound by rope.

"Bring him!" the priestess called.

The men started forward, but their prisoner leaned back and dug in his heels, resisting them with all his strength until the guards landed punches in his sides.

"Katsaros." The priestess sang the Centaur's name with ironic sweetness. "How fortune has smiled on you today. Not only do you share with us all the honor of ushering in the age of the wolf and Lykaios Apollo, but the stains of your past shall be cleansed and forgotten."

"And by which form of absolution am I to receive the god's far-reaching mercy?" the Centaur asked. He hadn't yet turned around to see the prisoner standing just ten yards behind him, beside the bronze wolf and the fire burning beneath it.

"The form of killing an innocent," said the priestess. She pointed over the Centaur's shoulder, directing his gaze and everyone else's to the wolf and the trembling captive. "You must prove to us that your weakness no longer controls you. Slit the boy's throat and feed him to the burning belly of the wolf so that our father Apollo might be glorified by the aroma of a pure and spotless sacrifice."

With a nod to the musicians around her, the haunting rhythm began again, as did the inelegant dance of the priestesses. They encircled the prisoner, chanting louder and louder as they huddled to form a compact ring around him. Lowering their voices, they raised their suntanned arms, blocking him from view.

The music died abruptly. The priestess took the Centaur by the hand and let him to the circle. "Reveal the offering!"

The priestesses bowed in unison, and then backpedaled away from the prisoner. The sack that had covered his head now lay crumpled at his feet.

"Aison!" Chloe gasped.

CHAPTER TWENTY-EIGHT
PRODIGY

Aison was just the same as when she'd met him on the beach, only he was dressed not in jeans and a T-shirt, but a bright white robe that glowed gold in the torchlight. His eyes darted around the ring of priestesses, searching for a gap he could escape through, but there was none. Even if he did slip past them he'd never evade Hermes' wand, or the sadistic crowd hungry to see him sacrificed.

Chloe leaned over and whispered in Ethan's ear, "We can't let the Centaur kill him."

Ethan didn't seem to hear her. "They just chipped him." He nodded toward Aison.

Chloe's heart skipped a beat when she saw that Aison was holding his right hand, around which was wrapped a blood-soaked linen bandage. She looked away as the high priestess stepped down from the rock.

"Katsaros, do you accept this offer of mercy?"

"I do, my lady."

The priestess smiled. "Excellent. Now go into the temple and recite the sacred words of the Pythonian oath so that Apollo may hear."

One of the priestesses left her post behind Aison and led the Centaur past the colonnade, into the shadows of Apollo's temple.

Babies began to cry as the evening chill swept in on the breeze. Sinister whorls of black and gray replaced the pastel shades of sunset. Thunder bellowed from above and below, evoking images of the Underworld swirling in Chloe's head. It was just beneath their feet, after all: the Styx, Cerberus, the River Lethe, all of it.

Chloe shivered as she watched the scale-shaped cloud rip apart and regather into the snarling face of a wolf. She couldn't just stand around waiting to see how this would all pan out. She'd already been still too long. She nudged Ethan's arm. "The seed Hermes gave you."

Ethan looked at her quizzically.

"Do you still have it?"

Ethan nodded slowly and then patted his pants pocket.

"Give it to me."

He stared at her with stern, disapproving eyes, but when her eyes stared back with equal stubbornness, he relented, pulling the pomegranate seed from his pocket. "You don't know what you'll turn into," he said.

"I have to try." She took the red seed and studied it. *Duna, help me.* She didn't have a plan, only that prayer. It would have to be enough.

The Centaur reemerged from the wall of columns. With shoulders stooped and head bowed, he looked smaller, weaker, as if years of life had been drained from him. He staggered as he walked, leaning on his escort for support. His mouth hung open, his unblinking gaze was vacuous. Chloe wondered if he was drunk or drugged, or pretending to be. *Duna, let him be pretending.*

The priestess led him into the circle, straight to Aison's side. Kissing the Centaur on the cheek, she placed a dagger in his hand.

The crowd began to chant: "Lykaios Apollo! Lykaios Apollo!"

Chloe placed the seed on her tongue and swallowed it quickly. Whatever she did, she'd have to be fast; the high priestess would waste no time dispatching her with Hermes' wand—if Chloe wasn't overtaken by the brainwashed mob first. She could only hope she'd either transform into something huge and terrifying, or something small and discreet.

She squeezed Ethan's finger. "Just play dumb."

Her skin began to itch, as if her entire body had been bitten by a swarm of mosquitoes. Next, her gums started to throb as the metallic taste of blood filled her mouth.

Ethan slowly backed away, pointing briefly to his upper teeth.

Chloe touched hers. Two of them had become long and alarmingly sharp. She held in a scream as another pair forced their way through her gum line. *Go,* she mouthed.

Ethan turned and faded into the crowd. Chloe hoped no one would know he was associated with her; this was no place to be aiding and abetting an interloper.

A burning feeling replaced the itchiness on her skin and rushed down to the tips of her fingers and toes. Short, dark-blond hair sprouted on her hands and her nose began to stretch. She heard the crack of cartilage as her ears lifted and enlarged. The coarse fur proliferated until it covered her body from head to toe, rubbing uncomfortably against her clothes, the seams of which she could feel tearing apart.

"Wolf!" someone beside her cried out in terror.

Better milk it, Chloe. She fell forward onto what used to be hands and knees. She looked down. Instead of hands, she now had two gigantic paws, each one outfitted with four bone-colored claws.

She sniffed the air with her new nose, taking in a profusion of scents simultaneously: the sweat in the ruined clothes beside her; the rain sitting heavily in the pregnant clouds; the smoke rising beneath the bronze wolf's belly; the fear of all who watched her; and lastly, the most overpowering of all, a vile odor she couldn't identify. All she knew was that it originated in the high priestess, whose attention was now being directed to the interference of a wolf.

Chloe wanted to growl, or bark, or howl, whichever came first. It didn't matter. She'd have to be intimidating if she had any chance of saving Aison, not to mention Ethan and the Centaur, though the latter she didn't exactly feel like saving. She'd deal with him later—if there was a later.

Remembering what Aison had looked like at his fiercest, Chloe ducked her head, pinned back her ears, and bared her teeth. She locked eyes with the priestess and yelled as loudly as she could, the effort translating into a deafening bark. Her audience packed in closely to one another. The babies' crying went quiet as their mothers covered their mouths.

Chloe had command. Now she just had to keep it.

"What magnificent prodigy is this?" the priestess shouted. Her face displayed not fear, but elation. "Apollo has smiled upon our bronze idol and sent us one of flesh and blood as a sign of his favor. Do not fear the beast, but worship it." She collapsed to her knees and stretched her arms in front of her, prostrate between both wolves.

Chloe decided to try a different tack. She raised her ears and relaxed her tail into a neutral, comfortable position. Opting not to pant like a common canine at the park, she set her jaw and made eye contact with as many people as she could. One by one, like a row of dominoes, the people in the crowd knelt and folded forward in worship.

"Do you wish to die slowly?" The high priestess's voice was as clear as a bell as it lashed out at Aison. "Bow at once, both of you."

Aison and the Centaur did as they were told. Every eye in the crowd was either closed or focused on the earth, waiting for permission to look elsewhere. The only creature still standing was the bronze wolf, whose fiery eyes had been fixed on Chloe since she arrived.

Hands and knees scooted aside as Chloe made her way to the wolf. She spotted Ethan easily because his hair was shorter than anyone else's, and gently pawed at his arm. When he lifted his head, she growled and gave an aggressive bark, then clamped down on his wrist, yanking him forward. He got to his feet and stumbled behind her as she dragged him the rest of the way.

Looking up from her reverent posture, the high priestess's eyes glittered with dark delight. "Do you wish us to sacrifice another virgin in the fire?"

Chloe nodded. Then she jerked Ethan sideways, letting him loose as she nudged him toward the Centaur with her snout. She forced herself between the three of them, taking care to ensure that some part of her legs and feet were touching them.

Ethan bowed.

The high priestess chanted with the deep, unctuous voice of a god: "Lykaios Apollo! Lykaios Apollo!"

The rest of the cult followed suit, repeating the mantra over and over as the clouds began to rumble and churn.

This was it, the small window Chloe needed.

Aison was looking up at her, his hazel eyes moist with tears, his body quaking. "Please don't kill me," he pleaded.

Chloe closed her eyes and took a breath, inhaling his debilitating fear, the Centaur's stupor, and the mushrooms that had induced it.

Ourania. Iris. Tycho. Charis. Chloe repeated their names in her head, envisioning their faces and the camp as clearly as she could. Darkness spun around them like a cyclone, enveloping them in the weightless cocoon that would soon shuttle them to safety.

"They're disappearing!" cried a woman nearby.

But the high priestess didn't stop chanting. Who was she to question the mysterious ways of Lykaios Apollo?

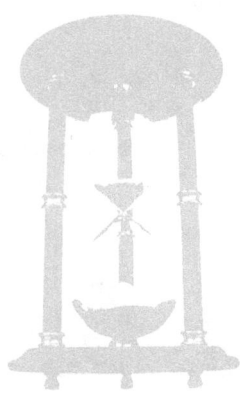

CHAPTER TWENTY-NINE
PARADOX

For what felt like eternity, no one said a word. The world around Chloe looked like a dream she was seeing only in her mind's eye. The trees appeared as an imposing wall of incubi, the wind blowing through them the rush of their steel-tipped wings. The starlings' song was strident, like Stymphalian birds. Even the tranquil stream trickling behind her was reminiscent of the pitch-dark Styx over which Charon had ferried her.

Her body, which she perceived was human again and fully clothed, felt dazed and disconnected, as though it were trapped back on that mountain, or bound beside the bronze wolf. She dipped her hand in the stream, hoping to be refreshed by its coolness, but the water might as well have been mud. Her tongue was dry, but she couldn't bring herself to drink.

"Thank Duna!"

Chloe squinted at two forms as they passed through the shadowy wall of demons. *Trees*, Chloe told herself. *You're back in Ourania. You're in a forest.*

"Chloe?" It was Iris's voice. "Chloe, can you hear me?"

As Iris came closer, Chloe's vision sharpened around her auburn hair. Her face faded into focus. Chloe smiled. "It's good to see you."

"And you." Iris took her hands in hers and kissed them, then pulled a wineskin from her sack. "Drink up. You'll feel better soon."

On Chloe's right, the Centaur lay sprawled on his back, staring at the sky like an idiot high on nirvána, a psychoactive powder prescribed for overanxious adults. Next to him was Aison, who was sitting in a ball, his knees pulled into his chest, his spindly arms trembling atop them. He glanced at Chloe a few times, but still looked too traumatized to speak. They *all* looked too traumatized to speak.

"Is that..." began Tycho, looking at Aison.

Chloe nodded. "We went back to the Lycaea Festival. The first Lycaea Festival."

"You did what?"

"Please don't be angry, Tycho." Chloe turned to Aison. An abandoned puppy couldn't have looked more pitiful. "We got back here just before they were going to kill him as a sacrifice to Apollo."

"You could've been killed," Tycho shouted. "You *all* could've been killed."

Iris watched her husband as he paced back and forth, settling down a little more with every step. "Now's not the time, Tycho. They're alive. Aison is alive. Let's praise Duna for that."

Tycho stopped, sighing loudly. "Anyone care to tell me why the Centaur looks as drunk as blazes?"

"It's a long story," said Ethan. "They made him go into the temple and swear some kind of oath. They must've drugged him while he was in there."

"Mushrooms," Chloe added. "I smelled them on him while I was the wolf. Aren't they hallucinogenic?"

"Some kinds are," replied Ethan.

They both looked down at the Centaur. His glassy gaze bounced from one part of the sky to another, following some unknowable hallucination.

"Please tell me you have a second doma and you weren't turned into a Lycaean," Iris said to Chloe.

"I ate a pomegranate seed," she answered flatly. It had been one of the more normal parts of her day.

Tycho crouched next to the stream and splashed water onto his face, shaking his head in disbelief as it ran down his neck, darkening his light-blue tunic. "And where exactly did you get a seed that turns one into a wolf?"

"Like I said," said Ethan, "it's a long story."

"Over dinner," he said, "I want to hear it."

Ethan nodded.

Tycho cupped his hands in the water and took a long drink.

Ethan walked over to Aison and sat beside him, making sure there was plenty of space between them so Aison wouldn't be startled. "How's your hand?" he said.

Aison looked down at the bandage.

"They put something in it, didn't they?" Ethan said.

"How do you know that?" Aison's eyes flashed to Chloe, then all around him as a fresh wave of fear washed over his face.

"Take it easy," said Ethan. "You're safe now. We're not Pythonians."

"Then who in Hades are you?" Aison winced as he gripped his hand.

"We're Ashers," said Iris. "At least, Chloe and I are." She put her arm around Chloe's shoulder. "As well as my daughter and Chloe's brother."

"Where are they?" Chloe asked, looking through the trees as the last nightmarish shadow fell away from them, revealing their benign green leaves. "Are they back at camp?"

Neither Tycho nor Iris spoke for several seconds. The Centaur hummed to the infernal rhythm of the Lycaean drums.

"Damian's gone missing again," said Iris. "Charis is out looking for him, but her doma won't last much longer." She squeezed Chloe's shoulder.

Chloe chewed on her lip to keep from yelling. Why was Damian acting out like this, leaving the safety of the wall a second time without telling anyone? Did he have a death wish? Was he hiding somewhere close by, waiting for her to go back to Cave One again so he could stop their parents' death? Or was he just trying to infuriate her? If so, he was definitely succeeding.

"Ashers," Aison said, looking warily at Iris and Chloe. "My uncle says you're Pythonian-bred menaces. He says you were created to destroy the memory of Duna by hoarding glory for yourselves."

"I wouldn't believe everything your uncle says," said Tycho. "The high priest belongs in the temple the way a horse belongs in a chariot's carriage."

"How do you know my uncle is the high priest?"

"Because we've met you before," said Chloe. "My Python-bred doma allows me to travel back in time. Long story short, if it weren't for us you'd be an immortal shapeshifter living two thousand years from now, hunting down Ashers so they won't rise up and restore the memory of Duna to our world. Despite what your uncle told you."

"And for the record," Ethan said, "in a different timeline the chip in your hand is the cause of your death."

Aison shifted uncomfortably as he picked at the bandage. "That's impossible. Becoming a Lycaean grants immortality."

"Maybe if you stay loyal," Chloe answered wryly.

Aison carefully unwrapped the linen, revealing a green goopy poultice covering the chip. "I suppose I should thank you for saving me, then." He pushed the mass of herbs until the round wound was visible.

"If you wanted saving, sure," said Chloe, finally feeling like herself as she took a swig from the wineskin.

"I never wanted to be a Pythonian. I hope my uncle doesn't think so. They fooled me in Limén. A gang of centaurs said they had work for me in a quarry." Grimacing, Aison scraped around inside the hole and pulled out the chip. "I guess you know what happened after that."

"*I* don't know," Iris said, tears welling in her eyes.

"They kidnapped me and hauled me off to Mount Lykaion." Aison jammed the heel of his left hand into his right, matting down the poultice. "To be sacrificed."

Iris's tears broke like water through a dam. "I'm so terribly sorry."

Aison shook his head and gave a nervous smile. "I was a fool to leave Eirene in the first place. I only wanted to see the world."

Chloe knew just how he felt. Before her eighteenth birthday, before her doma had changed everything, she, too, had dreamed of an unbridled, unrestricted exploration of Petros. She wanted to escape her aunt and uncle who, while not strict or abusive, were so aloof that she and Damian could only interpret their indifference toward them as hatred. She had wanted to escape Damian, who outshone her in every way and always seemed resentful that they were related. She wanted to escape the colony of Eirene and see what the other three were like, and if any other lands lay beyond them.

But, like every other Petrodian confined to their colony of birth, exploring anything outside of school and study was out of the question. She had turned to her cartoons, to Rhoda and to Farley the dragon, and lived vicariously through their adventures, which were boundless and as free as the birds. Never in a million years could Chloe have imagined that one day she would indeed become an explorer, and that the people and things she saw would never be believed back home.

But now, if she were to be honest with herself, there was much she wished she couldn't see.

"Just before you were killed," Ethan said to Aison, "you told us that the microchip holds information about you."

"Aye." Aison turned the chip over and handed it to Ethan. "Believe it or not, the bloody thing's cursed. My name, where I came from, the day I was sacrificed—or supposed to be—is all encoded by some godforsaken magic."

"Or technology," said Chloe. "It's a tracking device, too. It has to be. That explains how the Pythonians knew you died here."

"We'd be wise to get rid of it," Iris said. "You heard what Archelaos said about it."

Aison crossed his legs and leaned over them, his worried face gaunt with exhaustion. Chloe found it hard to believe this was the same person she had met on the beach. He was childlike now, fragile and innocent; still a naïve young man who'd only wished to see the world. It was as if the sacrifice, or perhaps the chip itself, had changed his demeanor entirely into the volatile shapeshifter she'd encountered.

"What did my uncle say?" Aison asked.

"That it might harm us if we stayed too close to it," said Tycho, staring at the chip in Ethan's hand.

"He feared you might have been disingenuous about your reason for coming here with Chloe," said Ethan. "He said that you leaving the chip with us after you died was a trap. So, after all of us had voted on whether or not to keep it with us, he took it back with him to the temple."

Aison shook his head in frustration. "That isn't true. I was there when they implanted the seal in my hand. The incantation said nothing that could be even remotely construed as a death curse, not on myself or anybody else. Besides that, curses don't exist."

"So curses don't exist, but men who can turn into immortal wolves do?" said Chloe.

Aison stood up and scanned his surroundings. "Where is my body buried?"

Ethan put the chip in his satchel. "Nowhere," he said. "You didn't really die, remember? It's a paradox thing."

"I still know it wasn't the chip that killed me." Aison looked to each one of them, as if seeking their affirmation.

"There's no better explanation," Iris said. "Your symptoms came on so suddenly—"

"A weapon is a perfectly reasonable explanation," Aison interjected. "Did you check my body to see if perhaps an arrow had pierced me?"

"There was no weapon," said Tycho, stirring the water with a stick. "Not one we could see, anyway."

"What do you mean?" Aison asked. "What sort of weapon is invisible?"

"Poison," Tycho replied. He stood and flung the stick into the stream. "But that doesn't make any sense either."

Just then, the sound of a woman crying mingled with the wind and the starlings.

"Charis?" said Iris, eyes frantically searching the trees.

In an instant, Charis appeared among them, sniffling and dabbing her cheeks with the hem of her cloak.

"Charis, what's wrong?" Tycho said, embracing her.

"Artemis," she said softly. "She's dead." Her arms fell to her side as she sobbed into her father's shoulder.

"How?" Ethan asked. "She was fine yesterday."

Charis lifted her head and stood there silently, breathless for half a minute as she waited for her sobs to abate. "I found her in Chloe's tent beside the sack of fruit you gave her, Mama. It must have poisoned her."

CHAPTER THIRTY
POISON

C hloe's heart beat like the Pythonian drums, pounding rapidly, furiously, louder and faster as the revelation hit her: she'd given Aison an orange back on the beach. *She* was the one responsible for killing him.

"I poisoned Aison." She felt like she was reciting the words of an oral essay for school, perhaps a line from a letter or an ancient play. They couldn't possibly belong to her.

"Chloe, that's impossible," said Ethan. "We were with you the whole time. You didn't give him anything."

"I gave him an orange." She looked at Aison. His was the only face not stricken by surprise. "When I met him on the beach back in time. I threw it at him as a distraction."

Aison lowered his head and looked away in shame.

"I thought he was going to attack me. I'm so sorry, Aison," she said.

Aison swallowed hard, then picked up a stone and sent it skipping across the stream. "It isn't your fault," he said. "You were defending yourself, for one thing. And you didn't know an orange would kill me, for another."

"He's right," said Tycho, "in more than one regard." He walked over to Aison and held out his hand. "The seal isn't cursed. And, praise Duna, neither are you."

Aison smiled, the first real smile Chloe had seen him give, and shook Tycho's hand. "Praise him, indeed."

Iris stood and went to Charis, wrapping a consoling arm around her waist. "Don't you worry about Aison," she whispered. "He isn't a wolf anymore."

Charis looked over her shoulder at Aison. "If the seal doesn't kill people, then why did you want Chloe to have it?"

Aison drew a deep breath, fingering the wolf-shaped brooch at his shoulder. "The only thing I know about my seal is what I've told you. It identifies who I am, or rather, what I was supposed to be."

"You told us it identifies all the thousands of Lycaeans who came after you, too," said Chloe.

"Thousands?" Aison shuddered.

"Aye," Tycho said. "One every year at the Lycaea Festival. They celebrated the sixth last evening."

Aison wrapped the bandage around his hand. "Because I was the first, perhaps the seal given to me is unique. Perhaps it has a dual purpose."

"And I have a hunch Archelaos knows what that purpose is," said Chloe.

With an agonizing groan, the Centaur rolled over and got to his hands and knees. His normally tanned skin took on a greenish tint as he started to perspire. "I feel like I'm going to..."

"Vomit?" said Tycho.

The Centaur shook his head. "No. The other end." He jumped up and bolted into the trees as everyone struggled to hold in their laughter.

When he was out of sight, Chloe belly laughed for the first time in what felt like years. Her laughter spread to Charis and Ethan; theirs transferred to Iris and Tycho, and finally Aison was infected by it, chortling so hard he cried and was sent to his knees.

The Centaur reappeared a few minutes later, pressing a finger into his sweat-bedewed forehead. "I had the strangest, most terrifying dream," he said. Then, startled by something unseen, he jerked and glanced around the woods, eyeing the foliage, stream, and cloud-streaked sky above him with suspicion. "Where are they?"

"Where are what?" Iris asked. "Here, drink some water. It'll help your headache." She took the wineskin from Chloe and handed it to him.

"Where are Zeus and Cronus? I saw them a few minutes ago." The Centaur searched their faces, each one still flushed from laughter. "Why do you all look at me as though I'm some grog-besotted sap? I saw them. Ferocious men as big as mountains." He gestured toward the brook. "They'd drain this brook with a single gulp."

"You were drugged," said Tycho, "with ceremonial mushrooms at the Lycaea Festival. You went there with Chloe and Ethan. Do you remember?"

The Centaur twisted his mouth and took a swig from the wineskin. "So it wasn't a dream."

"Everything up until the point you got drugged was real," said Chloe. She paused, envisioning the moment he'd spoken up at the ceremony, endangering not only him, but Ethan and herself as well. "Why did you do it?"

The Centaur hung his head. He knew exactly what she was talking about.

Tycho paced toward the Centaur. "Would you mind telling us what, precisely, you did?"

"Save your breath," Chloe said to the Centaur. "Your throat's probably sore from all the talking you did earlier."

"Back your oars, Miss Chloe," the Centaur said, his olive complexion returning.

"Why? I'm only going to tell them that you presented yourself to the high priestess—a lovely lady, might I add, full of hospitality—and would have slit Aison's throat yourself had I not eaten the seed and saved all our hides."

The Centaur stomped his hoof. "You've not been in our world one week and yet you still have such arrogance. You may be an Asher, my lady, but that doesn't make you omniscient. You cannot rightly judge everything, least of all my motives."

"Make your defense," Tycho said to the Centaur. "You must see how rash your actions seem to the rest of us. We're not accusing you of treachery, or even imprudence. Please enlighten us so we may understand your true intentions."

The Centaur clenched his jaw, pawing the gravel as he poured water along his neck. "Despite the turbulence of our journey there, my wits did not escape me once we arrived on Mount Lykaion. I knew what I was doing. I knew I would be recognized, and I knew the risk it would present.

"But I also knew that it was possible, and in fact probable, that the high priestess would propose an alternative to punishment, one meant to display mercy only as a minor character in the night's drama. The major player, as in every tragedy, was catharsis. The high priestess wanted her audience to put themselves in my place, to feel their own hands taking the blade, and to equate their own freedom, their own repentance, with the killing of an innocent."

Chloe's breath chilled in her lungs as a dead calm fell over the forest. The water stood still as glass. Every breeze and bird ceased to move as all mourned in silence for the sacrificed.

As the sun slipped out of the clouds, Ethan asked, "What if you'd been wrong? You would've had your eyes gouged out, and then what?"

"Then you and Miss Chloe would've traveled back five minutes to tell me to keep my cake hole shut." The Centaur chuckled, but no one else seemed to find his words funny.

"That's what you think." Chloe couldn't keep a straight face; she laughed, too.

"But you didn't know that Chloe would be able to save you with the seed," Ethan said.

The Centaur pointed to his right hip. "Do you not see the dagger ever at my side?"

Ethan examined him closely, cocking his head sideways. The Centaur grinned. There was no dagger to see.

"Centaur, I'm sorry to say the drugs haven't cleared your system yet," said Ethan. "You left all your weapons behind last night."

"He's toying with you," said Charis. "He carries Carya's knife. The one she used to free my mother and him from prison at Ēlektōr."

"Why must you spoil the fun?" the Centaur said. "I was going to show them." His hand hovered over the invisible object sheathed at his hip. "Like this." His hand clutched the air and left a hole in his fist that a hilt could fill. A thin column of light appeared in his hand. It began to pulsate, buzzing as it brightened to a bold electric blue.

Chloe moved closer, eyeing the diaphanous blade from all angles. "Does it work?"

"It cut through iron bars," said the Centaur. "Of course it works. And had you stayed put a little longer, you would've seen for yourselves. I'd have cut Aison free and dared anyone, even the high priestess with Hermes' silly staff, to challenge me."

"I mean no disrespect," Aison said, "but I confess I favor Chloe's plan over yours. I'm not sure you could have prevailed against so many." He eyed the dagger with caution, second-guessing his choice to offend its owner. "Though your bravery is laudable. Unsurpassed, I should add."

"No need to kiss up to me, kid," said the Centaur. "I'm only free to use this when innocent lives are on the line."

The Centaur lifted the glowing knife to his shoulder, holding it sideways with the flat of the blade face up. With a guttural roar, he reared back and flung it across the stream, where it veered left, spun in the air at a sharp right angle, and sliced through the trunk of a young juniper, sending the top half toppling onto the bank.

The knife's errand wasn't done yet. Adjusting its course, it curved upward and cut away scores of leaves from a dozen trees lining the brook. Then, lowering its tip as if to nosedive, it sped across the water, tip touching the surface, skimming in a brilliant blur as water shot up like miniature geysers along its sides. Only when the Centaur lifted his hand did the dagger decelerate and circle back to him, floating on the air like a fairy.

"I changed my mind," Aison said, as the dagger slipped into its invisible scabbard.

"And how was I supposed to know you had a magical knife?" Chloe said. "I wasted a perfectly good magical seed for nothing."

The Centaur shrugged. "So I forgot to tell you."

Chloe's fingernails dug into her palms. "We'll never get anything done as long as there are secrets between us." She looked around the circle. "Between any of us."

"You're right, Miss Chloe. Sometimes the horse part of me overrides the man part. Will you forgive me?" The Centaur's brown eyes showed that he meant it.

Chloe's hands relaxed. "If you'll forgive me for not trusting you."

The Centaur looked down as he picked at his callused hands. "I never gave you reason to."

"But today you have." Chloe went to him, drawing his eyes back to hers. "Magical dagger or not, it took guts to do what you did." The Centaur's cheeks took on the subtlest shade of pink as he smiled. "Because of you, we've proved that Aison is innocent."

Tycho pulled his family close. "There's one we cannot trust yet."

"Archelaos," said Chloe.

"Yes, but also one of our own."

Chloe knew whom he was referring to before she'd answered with Archelaos's name. She just didn't want to admit it.

"Your brother," Ethan said.

"Did you have any luck locating him, Charis?" Iris asked. Charis shook her head. "It's all right. It's an impossible chore."

"He'll come back," said the Centaur. "Just as he did before."

"That's if Mania lets him leave of his own volition this time," said Chloe. She turned to Tycho, conviction steeling her bones. "I know you have reason to distrust my brother, but I have greater reason than anyone to doubt him, and I still believe that deep in his heart he's good."

"I want to believe that, Chloe," Tycho said, laying a hand on her shoulder. "But there comes a time when we must face the truth about those we love. When we have to let them go."

Chloe closed her eyes. Quick snapshots of her brother's face, irrepressible memories of all the times he'd hurt her, and the sting of the fateful day he'd abandoned her, flashed and burned in her brain.

"No," she whispered, willing herself to forget the past, just like she'd promised she would. "You're wrong about him.

And even if you aren't, there's no way in Hades I'm ever letting my own brother go."

Before doubt or self-pity could poison her thoughts, Chloe took off into the woods, an unfamiliar fire of fervor propelling every footstep, filling every breath. She would keep walking until she found him.

CHAPTER THIRTY-ONE
PAWNS

Damian's stomach tightened and growled at the robust smell of stew lingering in the air. His captors had enjoyed three meals in his presence and hadn't spared a single nibble for him. Hermogenes had tried sneaking him an apple, but the second Damian reached to remove the gag, his parents noticed and snapped their disapproval. They'd retired to bed hours ago, leaving Damian under the watch of Panther, who snarled when Damian breathed too loudly or even rubbed an itch on his nose with his shoulder.

Never in his life had Damian felt his body revolt against him as it did now. Previously he'd been sick enough to vomit only a handful of times, and that was only in reaction to routine vaccines and had been readily remedied with a pill. He'd had sore muscles from track and wrestling practices, and even broke an arm when he fell on it wrong. But none of that came close to rivaling the discomfort he felt now.

His throat was so parched that he could no longer tell his tongue to swallow, nor could he move his stiff ankles without drawing blood from the iron chains wrenching his skin. Too dehydrated to sweat, he felt himself baking in the sticky heat of the wilderness; it seemed evening's cool would never come.

Hadn't Leto called him an ally? This was some way to treat one. A day or two more without water and he'd be dead. He wondered how many other people had died two thousand years before their birthday. Maybe what they said was true; maybe there really was a first for everything.

He jumped as a cold pair of hands grazed the back of his neck and untied the rag. "I didn't want it to be this way."

It was Leto's voice. She gently pulled away the rag, then flung it onto the floor as she strode to the hearth. "I'd hoped we could be friends." She grabbed a spoon and hastily filled a nearby bowl with stew. "Wine or kykeon?"

"Pardon me?" Damian rasped, desperately eyeing the amphora of wine beside her.

"To drink. Wine or kykeon?"

Damian blinked. "Anything. Please." He'd never been one to beg, but he would if he had to.

Leto sighed, took the jar by the neck and poured the wine into a wide black bowl. Just hearing the sound of liquid spilling into the vessel heightened Damian's thirst a hundred fold. She held the bowl to his lips. He hardly breathed as he drank it down. It didn't taste at all like cough syrup this time, but honey-sweet nectar of the gods. It was only on the third refill that his taste buds sensed the abhorrent, herb-like flavor he remembered.

Leto laughed at his disgusted expression and served him the stew.

"Thank you," he said.

Leto didn't answer; she just lifted a spoonful of vegetables to his lips. After he'd had enough to appease his stomach, he paused, and she set down the bowl.

"I didn't want it to be this way, either," he said.

"I offered you my friendship yesterday," Leto said, the subtlest breeze blowing back her silvery white hair as she spoke. "And you rejected it. You came here today uninvited and unseen, like a rat looking to steal my cheese or make a home beside my hearth. Two offenses in so brief a time hardly persuade me that you've come here with pure intentions."

"I came here looking for truth." Damian rolled his neck from side to side. He'd never sat in one position for so long.

Now that his thirst was slaked, he wanted nothing more than to lie down and stretch his limbs as far as he could.

Leto lifted another spoonful to his mouth. "You can thank your doma for your shackles. They're the only way to ensure you stay put once your power returns."

"When does *your* power stop working?"

Leto pounded her fist into the floor, causing Panther to whimper as thunder shook the columns, and rattled the pots and bowls. The pot hanging over the hearth squeaked as it swung back and forth in a violent gust of wind.

Damian closed his eyes and mouth to keep dust and rocks from blowing in. *I get the point*, he wanted to say.

"My doma operates when I tell it to," Leto shouted above the thunderous refrain still echoing around them. "And it stops when I command it."

Damian opened his eyes just wide enough to see her hovering six feet above him, arms extended toward the east and west as twin thunderbolts crisscrossed the courtyard, carving a flame-red X through the dusky fabric of sky.

"You'll wake...your son..." Damian strained to speak through the din of howling wind.

"It matters not. He's already seen who I am." Leto dropped to her feet, signaling the thunder to cease and the winds to blow softly once again. She drew her blood-red cloak across her shoulders. "The All-Powerful might have created me, but I don't belong to him, nor does the doma with which he endowed me."

"May I ask you a question, or will you throw another tantrum?"

A smile tugged at Leto's lips, but she twisted it into an indignant smirk. "No one save for immortal Hermes has spoken to me with such insolence."

"I guess we Ashers all have a bold streak."

The smile escaped. "You may ask it. And I will control my temper."

Despite her promise, Damian braced himself. He took a breath. "Why do you want to own the world when you yourself resist belonging to anyone? Why can't you leave Petros alone and let the people worship how and whomever they want to?"

Leto threw her hands onto her head and looked up at the gibbous moon rising over them. "You fancy philosophy, do you?"

"I fancy people being able to do whatever they please. I don't fancy tyrants who manipulate the world to align with their own private agendas."

Leto lowered her arms to her sides and looked on him with something much deeper than pity. Lines of anguish etched her face. Sorrow glimmered in her eyes as they fought to withhold their tears. Her hands, normally rigid, poised to command the weather, interlocked as she clasped them to her chest. Just like Chloe's did whenever she was sad or afraid, Damian noted. Leto's long hair fell like a platinum shield across her face, forbidding him from witnessing any more of her emotions.

"The world is cruel, Damian," she said, turning her sharp chin toward him. "The people within it, the gods below, are all heartless, selfish creatures who do just as you say. But whether aristocratic tyrant or common merchant, they are all gods in their own eyes, displaced deities seeking a throne. And they'll deceive, abandon and kill anyone who stands in their way."

She showed him her face, lovely in its sadness as her radiant complexion shone even brighter in the moonlight, her tears like crystals on her cheeks. He made himself look away.

"My cousin Iris killed my father." The crystals melted and slipped down her ivory neck. "For her beliefs in Duna, the All-Powerful," she said mockingly. She wiped her cheeks and knelt in front of Damian. "And do you know what is cruelest of all?"

Damian watched Panther slip into the shadows behind Leto, his tail between his legs.

"She oversaw the death of the gryphon Corinna, who was my mother. She fell dead, a dozen arrows in her back, before my father's eyes. And Iris did it all because she wanted a throne for herself."

Damian knew there had to be another side to this story, but it would do no good to probe for it now. "I'm sorry about your father. I lost my parents, too."

Leto's face softened at this, but only for a moment before fresh anger filled it. "I can see in your eyes that they were murdered as well." Damian nodded. "By whom?"

"By someone we call the chief councilman. He hates Ashers. That's why we're here."

"You're not here to hinder me?"

"I can't speak for anyone else," Damian said, measuring his words carefully; one wrong syllable and she'd stir another storm. "But I'm here because I wanted to see who you are for myself."

Leto drew back, eyeing him askance. "And have you made your judgment? Have you decided who you think I am?"

"I know you're not a monster. You're not Mania. You're hurt, you're angry. Just like I am. The only difference between us is that you've made an enemy of the entire world."

He held his breath, certain that any second she'd unleash her fury to prove him wrong, to show him she indeed was Mania, through and through. But she remained still, pensively studying his face as if hoping he had more to say.

"And how do you view the world, the world that allowed your parents to die and will kill you as well if it gets the chance?"

"I view it as another victim." Footsteps padded behind him. He heard Hermogenes yawn.

"Father said we shouldn't talk to him, Mama," the boy said.

"Your father isn't here now, is he?" Leto answered sharply. "I am master of this house, not he. Now go back to bed."

Damian looked over his shoulder as the boy, shoulders stooped and feet shuffling, turned the corner. "The world is a victim, just like your son is," he said, turning back to her.

Leto's gray eyes narrowed. "What do you mean? My son is a victim of no one."

"I'd be willing to bet his birth wasn't an accident. I don't know much about the so-called gods, but I know every step they take has been carefully strategized. Your son, even you, you're both just pawns on their board game."

Leto picked up the bowl of half-eaten stew and threw it against the pot. Whipping back around to Damian, she stretched her arms toward him as a forceful wind gathered the dust from the floor and spun it into a small cyclone. It grew wider and taller and faster by the second, and then shrank as quickly as it had appeared.

"I told you I'd hold my temper, and I'll keep my word," she said, clearly using every bit of self-control she had to keep her fingers curled. "But if you ever slander the name of my beloved again, that whirlwind will just be the beginning of your woes."

She smiled and bent down closer to whisper, "I may not be able to kill you, but I can still make you suffer until you pine for the Styx." She stood and pushed a wind into the lamps, extinguishing their light and sending ribbons of smoke into the sultry air.

It struck Damian with perverse amusement that this was what he deserved: to be held prisoner by a capricious witch who could kill him with a snap of her fingers. After all, he'd been the one to leave his own sister in Hades, chained and tormented by the embodiments of evil. It didn't matter that Chloe had forgiven him; justice required more than an apology.

No sooner had Damian closed his eyes to sleep than the temperature dropped fifty degrees, causing his teeth to chatter. He brought his knees to his chest and buried his face between them. He felt a blanket fall across his shoulders, then looked up to see Hermes standing over him, wand in hand.

"I want to see it," Hermes said.

"See what? And have you been here this entire time?"

"Aye, but I kept my distance." He patted Damian's shoulder. "We wouldn't want our pet Asher to get chilly now, would we?"

"Go back to hell, Hermes."

"I shall." Hermes' jovial demeanor turned dark. "And I shall take you there with me if you don't do as I ask. I wish to see my future self betray Apollo. And you will take Leto with us so she can see with her own eyes that you're a liar."

"You're afraid she'll find out that what I said is true."

Hermes bore down on Damian's shoulder and squeezed into a pressure point with his thumb. With his opposite hand he pointed his wand at the chains binding Damian's feet and cut them off. "You're the one who should be afraid."

He stuck his wand into Damian's back, pushing him onto his feet.

"Uh, slight problem, buddy," Damian said.

Hermes pressed the wand harder, twisting it into his spine.

"Easy. I just wanted to inform you that I can't travel in time, and my sister can only go backwards. Neither one of us can show you anything that hasn't happened yet."

"I don't need your rotten domas. I need your brain." Hermes drew back the wand and stashed it at his side. "It will only hurt a little."

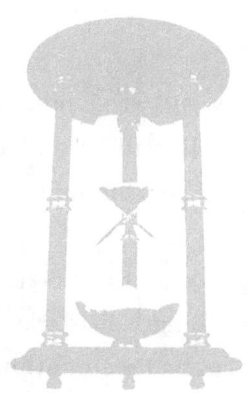

CHAPTER THIRTY-TWO
MNEMOSYNE

W e'll have to make this quick," said Leto, combing her hair with her fingers as Hermes lowered her gently onto the sand; Damian he'd dropped carelessly from three feet above. "Hermogenes won't sleep much longer."

"He'll sleep just fine," Hermes replied. "I made him drink water before we left."

"Water will only send him to his chamber pot."

Hermes grinned. "Not when it's filled with valerian."

He directed his wand at Damian and the blindfold covering his eyes. "Hold still." Damian froze as Hermes pulled off the blindfold and summoned it into his satchel. "The shackles stay."

Despite his close eye on the Asher, Hermes wasn't too worried about him escaping. They'd traveled halfway around the world, and Damian had seen nothing of their journey. He'd wander for weeks before finding civilization again, if he didn't die first.

"Where are we?" Damian asked, shivering as snow flurries danced around him. They were standing at the base of a peak that had long been forgotten, accursed by Zeus after the Titanomachy of eons past.

"Mount Othrys," answered Hermes, "the oldest mountain in Petros."

Leto drew her cloak across her nose and mouth. "It smells of death here."

"This place *is* death." Hermes crouched down and collected a handful of snow. Though the earth was covered with snow, it failed to conceal the stench of ichor, smoke and charred skin saturating the soil beneath. Somewhere, bones of Hermes' own limbs lay buried.

"Want to tell me what we're doing here?" Damian's voice quivered in the cold.

"You mortals are so fragile." Hermes removed his cloak and with a flick of his wand covered it with fur. He draped it over Damian's shoulders. "We're here because this is where the mechanism is."

Damian threw his bound hands toward the sky. "Thanks. That tells me a lot."

Hermes turned to face the mountain. He'd sworn to Hades and Apollo that he would never speak of this place, much less return to it. They had assured him that doing so would be futile since they had eradicated all the Titans, save one, and every remnant of their existence.

But Hermes had to try. He had to put his doubts to rest by proving that what the Asher said was false. Never had he so much as fantasized about forsaking Apollo. However, the fact that Hermes was suddenly so hellbent on making sure he never did only made him suspect it was true. Just yesterday, Hermes had violated Apollo's command by sparing Hermogenes and using the Asher as bait instead. Two thousand years was a long time for resentment to germinate and bud into betrayal. This mountain was proof that even the strongest alliances could be shattered.

"Mnemosyne, guardian of all mankind's memories!" Hermes exclaimed, the bitter air searing his eternal lungs. "It is I, Hermes, protector of travelers, and with two such Petrodians have I come to request one hour with the *pýli*, the machine wrought by the Cyclopes before snow erased the glory from Othrys."

Beneath his feet, Hermes could feel the mountain rumbling. He seized Damian and Leto by the hands lest he need to snatch them away from a crashing avalanche. He didn't expect the goddess to act hospitably. After all, it had been he, along with his Olympian brethren, who had banished her family to Tartarus.

But an avalanche didn't come. The quaking shook away snow from the craggy face, revealing a cave's mouth that was the shape of a screaming skull. There were even two concave recesses above it resembling the sockets of eyes that could see far better than any god or mortal. The goddess was inside, waiting.

Hermes dropped their hands. "Come." But the others didn't budge. "Don't stand there like a daft pair of mules. If she wanted to harm us, she would have done so by now."

"I'm thinking I should have taken my chances in hell," said Damian.

Leto blew into her hands and scowled at the snowflakes gathering on her boots. "You still haven't said plainly why you've dragged us all the way to a desolate wasteland just to see some useless old relic. It probably hasn't worked in centuries. I can't imagine it worked to begin with if it was crafted by one-eyed barbarians."

Hermes took a breath and turned to her. With as much equanimity as he could muster, he said, "You expose your ignorance when you speak so disdainfully about a race you've never seen. I have seen the Cyclopes and they were far more intelligent than the cream of Petros's elite."

"I suppose with heads the size of a gourd, they would have sizable brains." Leto laughed.

It was all Hermes could do not to slap her. Who was Leto to mock the sons of Titans, men who had aided Hephaestus in his forge, built entire palisades in a single night, and crunched the bones of impudent maidens just like her for supper? He had felt unparalleled relief when Cronus banished them to Tartarus, but never would he stop respecting them.

It was arrogance like Leto's that made Apollo's job so simple. All he had to do was let men believe they were supreme in strength and intellect, and that nothing, neither on Petros nor beneath it, could best them. Even the Pythonians believed, deep in their hearts, that they could defeat Apollo should he emerge from hell as a foe. This much Hermes had heard them say with his own ears.

If Duna ever did permit Apollo to roam freely as the gods once had, Apollo would take up his bow and wage the briefest, bloodiest war in history, and doubtless break the oath between himself and both his brothers. Indeed, he would see to it personally that Hermes and Hades were chained nearest the sweltering heart of Petros's core. After all, the proclivity for uprising coursed through their ichor veins.

Hermes turned and gazed upon the snow-covered plain before him. Steel clashing against steel, Apollo's arrows whistling through the air alongside Zeus' bolts…the sounds of the Titan War were still etched in his memory. And why wouldn't they be? After all, the memory holder herself stood behind him.

Mnemosyne could force him to relive every excruciating blow and witness the bloodshed a second time if she so desired. In the blink of an eye, the *pýli* could show him the moment Cronus and his ten siblings were herded like cattle to the volcano north of the mountain. Hermes could hear again their pleas and ululation as they were thrown into the fire, leaving Hades, Zeus and Poseidon to divide the world among them. He could again witness Apollo's smug, satisfied expression, content to bide his time until his armies were ready.

Hermes felt a heavy somberness descend on him like a rain-soaked mantle. Duna's eyes were on him now. He could feel them boring a hole through the restless machinery of his mind and surveying the emptiness of his soul.

He heard the All-Powerful asking him: *Was it worth it? Do you not regret rising against me?*

"Leave me!" Hermes shouted. He pressed his hands to his ears, but Duna's voice could not be silenced. It continued: *Are you prepared to learn the truth? Are you prepared to act upon it?*

Hermes reached out and grabbed Leto and Damian once more, this time by the tender bend in their elbows, and dragged them into the cave.

"Despite your reputation, you are unwise, Hermes." The goddess's voice echoed throughout the main chamber as a spectral glow materialized before them.

"Do not fear her, the Titaness has been subdued," he whispered, assuring himself more than he was assuring the mortals standing beside him.

The light intensified as a woman's body slowly took shape within it. "You cannot serve two masters," she said. "You've brought yourself to the place where your road diverges. You must choose which path to take."

Hermes widened his stance and searched for the eyes still hidden in the lambent haze around her. "I have not come to alter my path, only to use the mechanism, if it's possible."

"Your path, cousin, shall alter you."

Leto stepped forward; Hermes could sense the aggression boiling in her hands. "As long as his path does not lead him to sequestration inside some damnable mountain," she said, "I think he will be just fine."

Hermes took her wrist and pulled her back. "Your insolence will get you in trouble one day if you don't learn to hold your tongue."

Hermes doffed his cap and bowed his head. "Mnemosyne, forgive our intrusion, as well as our impertinence. You were— you are—the last of the illustrious Titans, heaven's unequaled protectors. I must say I'm astonished that even now you try to protect me, messenger of the one who vanquished you."

As if throwing aside a cloak, Mnemosyne cast the light off her shoulders, revealing her full, unobscured splendor. Her beauty had not diminished one iota since Hermes had last laid eyes on her all those centuries ago. She was a temple statue come to life: tall, regal, and immaculate. Her entire being—hair, skin, eyes and robes—was the color of white clay, brighter than snow in the sunshine. Despite her station here in this cold corner of the world, her bearing was dignified, fearless, and ineffably peaceful. Why did she not wish to hurt him as Apollo had hurt her, Hermes wondered.

"The burden Apollo gave me was not light." Mnemosyne's voice was resonant and full, as if flowing through water. "He left me here not as a display of mercy, which he does not possess, but as a monument to his pride. For through my memories, the blessed gift by which I'm now cursed, he can forever remember the victory he won at the price of his own soul."

"Each of our souls was sold far before the Titanomachy, goddess," said Hermes, as his frigid blood caught fire.

Mnemosyne lowered her head, the circlet upon it lightly reflecting the scarlet of Leto's robe. "Duna's forgiveness reaches farther than I once thought. Have you never heard him call to you, Hermes?"

Her soothing voice coaxed his gaze upward into the porcelain pools of her eyes, but he dared not speak. He could not acknowledge that he had indeed heard Duna's voice, and it wounded him more deeply than any strike of Apollo. He wished his own memories of heaven, of his life before the War, could be erased. He'd drunk from the Lethe on countless occasions, but the river had the reverse effect on him: it sharpened his recollections, magnified his regret, and made the suffocating shell of hell all the more insufferable.

"I wouldn't know his voice if it shouted to me from Olympus," Hermes said.

Mnemosyne turned her face toward the shadows. "I pity you, then. Perhaps in time your ears will regain their sensitivity."

Leto's fingers twitched at her side. She pressed her lips together to keep from insulting the goddess a second time.

"This will be over soon," Hermes whispered to her.

He unsheathed his wand and turned it into a torch. "If you will direct me to the mechanism, fair cousin, we will depart before dusk."

Without turning her head, Mnemosyne pointed at Damian. "Answer this first. What business do you have with this boy? And tell me truthfully, how is that I have no memory of his existence?"

"I'm an Asher," Damian said. "And so is my sister."

Hermes jabbed him in the side. "Who gave you permission to speak?"

With a sweep of her arm, Mnemosyne ripped the torch from Hermes' grasp and held it to her face. Its luster, compounded by the radiance of her skin, shone like the evening star. "He needs no one's permission!" Her voice shook the stalactites over their heads, each one an arrow poised to drive straight through their skulls. "Do you understand?"

Hermes flew to the torch and clasped it with both hands, trying with all his strength to wrench it from her fingers.

With a single breath, Mnemosyne created a wind that rivaled Leto's and sent Hermes cartwheeling into the wall. "Don't make me remind you of the Titans' strength."

The threat did not fall on deaf ears. Hermes knew full well the power the Titans possessed. It was not for want of force that they had lost the war to Zeus, rather, the want of loyalty. What Hermes and the other Olympians lacked in brawn they more than made up for with cunning. They'd won the giants and Cyclopes to their side, procuring enough brawn to defeat a hundred Titans, let alone a dozen.

"Forgive me," Hermes said, every joint and tendon throbbing.

If Mnemosyne had heard him, she didn't show it. Her attention was turned to Damian; he stood before her as stolid and stiff as a soldier awaiting a reprimand.

"I've always wanted to meet an Asher," she said, holding the torch's light on him now, examining him from head to foot.

"It's nice to meet you." Damian held out his hand.

Rather than taking it, the goddess cut off his shackles with one flick of her finger. "You come from the future?"

"Yes, ma'am," Damian answered. He glanced at Hermes, who was still slumped against the wall, licking his wounds. "Hermes brought me here because he wants to see whether what I said was true."

Mnemosyne leaned in and caressed the side of his face, peering at him tenderly as though he were an exotic pet or her own newborn babe. "You're the one the oracle spoke of. The Vessel. I've been waiting for you."

"Actually, my sister and I together are the Vessel."

Before the goddess could speak another word, three flaming arrows pierced her chest, sending a spray of icy golden fluid onto Damian's face and clothes.

"Apollo!" Hermes gasped. He watched in terror as the Titaness's body was dragged into darkness.

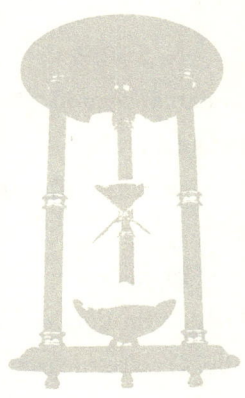

CHAPTER THIRTY-THREE
CHIONE

Damian rushed after the fallen goddess, stopping only when he saw the colossal crater in the limestone floor. One more step and he would have followed her into it.

"You told me Apollo and Hades couldn't cross into our world," Leto shouted at Hermes.

Damian pointed at the hole. It looked bottomless. "I haven't seen too many portals to hell in my life, but I'd say this is one of them."

Hermes flew past Leto and landed at Damian's side. "Aye, and a secret one, it would seem. Perhaps that's why Apollo housed Mnemosyne here." He jumped up and hovered over the abyss. "I know you can hear me, Apollo. Is my theory correct?" He began flying in circles above the crater. "You claim I'm the clever one, but I see you've been concealing your craftiness all along."

Damian stepped back. He didn't want to be around when three more arrows came whizzing out of there. The walls of the crater began to thunder, the vibrations rattling his ribs. He took off for the exit, taking Leto's hand as he ran by.

"No need to scamper off like a scared rabbit, Asher," Hermes yelled. "Neither Apollo nor I can harm you, nor any other deathless god for that matter."

"But you can push me into hell," Damian called back as he picked up his pace, lungs already burning from the altitude.

"And what makes you think I can't do the same?" Mania halted and reached her arms out in front of her, summoning the snow from the ground. "I could push you into Hades before you take your next breath."

Damian had no idea which way home was—home for the time being, anyway. But given his options, he'd rather wander aimlessly on his own than take his chances with these two. He closed his eyes, and felt his hands and arms begin to tingle.

"Hermes!" Leto shouted. "Damian's disappearing."

Hurryhurryhurry, Damian thought.

But his doma wasn't fast enough. In a flash, Hermes was in front of him, binding his wrists in a new set of shackles.

"Take him back to Ourania," Hermes told Leto. "I'll follow once I find the mechanism."

"Be careful," she said. "Try to stay in one piece."

Hermes laughed halfheartedly. "I make no promises but this," he said, pulling her close and kissing her forehead, "I will come home to you." He paused, tasting his next words before he spoke them. "And to Hermogenes."

The miniature blizzard Mania had conjured died away, the snowflakes settling onto their heads and shoulders. Sheets of snow cascaded down the mountain as it erupted again with another rumbling warning. From the mountain north of them, thick plumes of smoke were rising.

"I think that might be a volcano getting ready to blow," said Damian.

Leto and Hermes turned to look, then held one another tighter. Were they not evil megalomaniacs trying to take over the world, Damian might have felt sorry for them.

"Come with us now, Hermes," whispered Leto. "No matter what that stupid machine shows you, you've already betrayed Apollo by coming here."

Hermes sighed as he took in the dreary scene of smoke and infinite snow.

Damian could only imagine what history these plains and peaks contained, much less what Hermes, this notorious menace of the ages, had endured under Apollo's reign. One thing was for sure—he didn't envy him.

"I was telling the truth," he said. "You helped us—my sister, and Ethan and his parents. I have no reason to lie to you. I can tell you exactly what the *pýli* would've shown you."

Hermes cast a defeated look back at the crater as a wall of fire sealed its mouth. "I should have predicted this moment. All of us who fell from heaven are nothing if not fickle. Our loyalty is never fixed."

"And where is your loyalty now?" Leto asked him.

"With you," Hermes said, taking her hand. "And with whatever twist of fate awaits us."

He turned to Damian and stared down at the shackles. "It would seem these are no longer necessary." He touched his wand to each ring and snapped them open, then sent them spinning into the fire.

"Thanks," Damian said, rubbing his wrists. The snow actually felt pleasant against his chafed skin. "Now take my hands." Leto and Hermes looked at him as if he'd just sprouted another head. "It's safer to be invisible right now, don't you think?"

"You want to help us?" Leto asked.

The surprise on her face made Damian wonder if anyone besides Hermes had ever shown her kindness.

"This is a thank-you to you, Hermes," he said, "for what you did for us in the future." As Damian reached out to take their hands, a numbing wind swept through them, so strong it nearly knocked them to the ground.

"What was that?" Damian looked around. Sitting three feet in front of him was a round block of ice the size of his floor mirror back home. Around it pulsated a silvery orb from which tinkling music emanated.

"The *pýli*," rasped Hermes, his voice hoarse from the cold, dry air. "What in Zeus' name is it doing out here?"

"In Duna's name, it's here because he deemed it be."

Damian's wind-stung eyes darted in all directions in search of the female speaker until, finally, he noticed not a person, but an iridescent sphere floating near the ice. "Look." He pointed to it. "How many goddesses live out here?"

The sphere expanded to twice its size then turned to sapphire blue. "I am not a goddess," it declared. "Chione is my name. I am a messenger, as Hermes is, except that I serve the true god. The only god." The sphere glimmered as it grew once again, stretching to the length of a human.

"Your father Poseidon has surely missed you all these years," said Hermes, a wry smile on his face. "No doubt he dreams each night of his daughter and the endless snow that follows her."

"Yes, as Maia above misses you," Chione said. "The chasm between heaven and Hades is no greater than the one in her heart, Hermes."

Hermes' smile vanished. "What have you to do with the Cyclopes' machine?"

Chione floated to the ice and, resting upon it, thawed it to reveal a bronze, clock-like device surrounded by dark wood. It was sleek and streamlined, as modern-looking as anything Damian had ever seen.

"Mnemosyne entrusted it to me ages ago." The dial in the center of the *pýli* shimmered as Chione spoke. "She was wise enough to know that her proximity to Hades' void was no coincidence. It was only a matter of time before some curious soul came hunting for it."

The fire roared behind them as though desperate to pulverize the snow and everything on it. Chione rose higher into the air and extended a sinewy arm of blue light toward the cave. With a flick of her finger, the fire went out, the flames replaced by opaque layers of ice. This only angered Apollo further. The mountain quaked as the volcano beyond them expelled black smoke like a factory chimney.

"Um, maybe we should take this conversation elsewhere," said Damian.

"Peace, Damian," Chione said, her voice like the metallic chime of a harp. "You mustn't bow before Apollo's tantrums. He can kick and he can scream, but he cannot bring peril to Petros's land."

Damian waited for Hermes to refute her claim, but he kept silent, eyes fixed upon the machine as though hypnotized.

"Would you like to see what you came for?" Chione said, her glowing arm now stroking the top of the *pýli*.

Leto linked her arm with Hermes' and whispered into his ear. Damian didn't dare tell her it was useless to try and keep secrets from the All-Powerful's messenger.

"I am weary of running," Hermes said, making no effort to conceal his response. "Running to and fro through Petros. Running through the portals to do my brothers' bidding. Running from the omnipotent eye of the All-Powerful, who created those who endeavor in vain to destroy him."

He removed his cap and tapped it twice with his wand, transforming it into a gold tiara. Leto's gray eyes turned the same color as the tiara elevated past her face and rested atop her head.

"Sometimes, my flower," Hermes said, "I pray to him."

Leto's head tilted left, her expression a resounding question mark.

"I ask that you would love me not for the power you think I possess but for my heart," Hermes said. "That is to say, what's left of it."

Leto's eyebrows arched as she felt the tiara shrinking. She unhooked her arm from Hermes' and slid off the crown, tears springing to her eyes as it shriveled and tarnished, turning into a tangled knot of common weeds.

"Why are you so cruel, Hermes?" She glanced at Damian. "Damian was right about you, I'm just a pawn." She flung the tiara into Hermes' chest. "From the night you appeared to me at Ēlektōr, your mission has been to win my loyalty through grandiloquent speeches and intoxicating promises of power."

Damian noticed that the phantasmal bobbing ball called Chione was fading. If she had eyes beneath that blue facade, they were probably rolling. How many thousands of lovers' arguments had she been privy to since the dawn of man, or the dawn of immortals, for that matter? Damian was willing to bet she could predict their words verbatim before they spoke them.

"We made pawns of each other," Hermes said, lifting a hand to Leto's cheek.

Leto recoiled. "You are the most pathetic creature." Her words dripped out slowly behind gritted teeth, each one more vindictive than the last. "You are lower than a creature. You are scum." She stepped toward him, pressing a finger into his chest. "You are excrement. If I were Apollo, I'd have buried you in the vilest dump of hell the second I had the chance."

Hermes blinked rapidly and staggered back, absorbing her verbal blows as if they were delivered on the ends of spears.

Damian looked away, considering whether he should create some distance between himself and the bickering couple. He knew that if he'd been behaving rationally, he would take advantage of their squabble by escaping while he had the chance. But for reasons he couldn't explain to himself, he wanted to stay. And something, perhaps his conscience or a benevolent inner voice, was telling him that he should.

"I cannot deny that I deserve such vitriol," said Hermes when he recovered his breath. "The anguish it causes me, like a javelin through the heart, testifies to my love for you.

There was a time, I admit, when your words touched me like a feather. They were immaterial, forgettable..." He paused, and with caution, took her hands. "But I do love you, Leto. As sure as the snow falls in this blighted hinterland, I love you."

Leto shook her hands free and jerked her chin at Damian. "Where am I in the future, Damian? In your interactions with this silver-tongued cretin, did he ever make mention of his desert flower?"

Damian glanced at Hermes. He didn't want to tell her the truth: that he'd never heard of Leto before he traveled back here, not from Hermes and not from his teachers.

"Your silence answers plainly." Leto rested her cold eyes back on Hermes. "Once you used me for your own clandestine purposes, you discarded me like scraps for the hellhound."

Chione rushed between them, blocking their view of one another should Leto's doma rise up against Hermes' wand. "Stop this nonsense," she said.

Leto and Hermes turned away, the former pouting and the latter sulking like a chided child.

"The future is yours to see. That's why I have been sent." Chione pointed at the machine still nestled in the snow. Damian, for one, wanted to see what it could do.

"We came here," Leto said, in a low, composed tone that belied her temper, "to put Hermes' nerves at ease." She dug the toe of her boot into the ground and kicked snow into the air. "But you always knew what the future held, Hermes, because you knew, beyond the shadow of a doubt, that your heart will be as black and villainous in two thousand years as it was the day you were cast from heaven."

Leto swept her arms up and over her head, summoning the winter winds to her side. Chione leapt in front of the *pýli*, another arm appearing as she stretched herself in front of it.

"I won't touch your precious *pýli*," Leto shouted to Hermes as the winds propelled her above the plain. "Nor shall I touch a hair on your head, my darling, as long as you stay out of my way."

Then, increasing the winds with a spin of her finger, she flew down and wrapped her arms around Damian's chest. "Tell the gods you serve to mind their own affairs," she barked at Hermes over her shoulder.

Damian wriggled and squirmed, he even bit the side of Leto's arm, but she continued to fly. Behind them, blue veins of lightning cut through the sky, rendering any pursuit impossible.

"I've had enough of gods and Ashers," she whispered.

"So this is the part where you make me suffer until I 'pine for the Styx,' right?" Damian squeezed his eyes shut as the thunder boomed beside him.

"This is the part where you help me."

"Help you do what?"

"Become mightier than the gods."

CHAPTER THIRTY-FOUR

REFLECTION

May I come in?"

Chloe finished securing her chiton to her shoulders. She'd started to pick off all the dog hair Artemis had left behind while napping on it, but stopped when her tears blurred her vision. She wiped her face and turned toward the door of the tent. "Sure."

"You're ancient-looking again," Ethan said with a smile.

"I'm going to assume you're talking about my outfit."

"Oh, yeah." He laughed, realizing his mistake. "You don't look ancient. You look fine."

Chloe bit her lip to keep from looking disappointed. What if violet wasn't her color? What if her hair looked awful in a bun? There were no mirrors around to show what she looked like, and for once in her life she actually wanted to know.

"It's late. Why aren't you in bed?" she asked, before the silence became even more awkward.

"Same reason no one else is." Ethan looked outside, to where one campfire was still burning bright. "We want to know what you're planning."

"I would've thought that was obvious." Chloe crossed the tent, picked up the hidesack, which was now only half full, and slung it over her shoulder. "I'm going to find my brother. Did they send you in here to talk me out of it?"

"Iris and Tycho did, yes." Ethan drew the tent flaps together. "But I'm not going to try."

Chloe took a breath. She'd been preparing to give him an impassioned spiel about blood being thicker than water. After that, she was going to tell him she was willing to take the risk because she'd never be able to live with herself if she didn't. But instead, Ethan was looking at her somberly, as if he already knew all of that.

"I know it won't do any good," he continued. "I'm sure Mania will be a breeze after dealing with Hades."

Chloe couldn't help but burst out laughing at his unintended joke.

"What? What'd I say?" he asked.

Chloe leaned against the back of the settle. "Mania will be a breeze. And thunder, and lightning, and maybe some hail and a snow flurry or two."

"And you're not intimidated by any of that?" he asked, too preoccupied to be amused.

"I would rather Mania's doma be sheep shearing, but like you said, I've lived through worse."

Ethan sighed and stepped into the center of the tent. Maybe it was just shadows from the oil lamps falling across his face, but Chloe thought he looked tired, like he hadn't slept in days. She remembered the first few nights after her parents had died, and how she'd counted the stars to try and lull herself to sleep. The one time it had worked, she'd been so overcome with renewed grief when she woke that she avoided sleep for nearly a week until the doctor made her take a pill. Sleeping had made their deaths feel like a bad dream; it was a terrible trick of her unconscious, one that took months to escape.

"Try to rest, Ethan. I'll be fine." She gave her most convincing close-lipped smile, but she could see it did nothing to reassure him. "Really. Don't worry about me."

"We both know that's not going to happen."

"What, the-me-being-fine part, or the you-not-worrying-about-me part?"

"The me-not-worrying part."

Chloe felt her face grow warm as he came closer.

"I just lost my parents," he said. "I'm not going to sit on my hands while you go out there and face the weather monster."

Chloe laughed. "She doesn't sound so scary when you call her that."

Ethan cracked a smile, then reached out and placed his hand on hers, brushing the top of it with his thumb. "I'm serious. I walked away when I saw you with Orpheus that day at the café because I had no clue who he was. But I know everything now. Well, almost everything. And I'm not walking away."

Chloe relived the moments she had stood on the sandbar at Lake Thyra, watching the portal to Hades appear as a silver mist on its surface. She'd been too enthralled by Orpheus's lyre-playing to realize what she was stepping into.

An idea hit her. "Orpheus..." she whispered.

Ethan pulled his hand away. "Orpheus? What about him?"

"His power. I watched him hypnotize a witch who was seconds away from turning me into an animal. For life. I know it could work against Mania."

Ethan sighed and ran a hand through his hair. "It's a good theory, but there's a slight problem: you can't travel forward in time. And even if you could, there's no guarantee Orpheus would believe you or want to help you."

"I don't have to travel to our time. I can go to his time and bring him here."

"But there's still the other part of the problem. He'll have no reason to believe you."

A breeze blew through the door and the air suddenly got colder, sending chills up Chloe's arms. Either a cold front had just rolled in, or an immortal was in their midst. She had a hunch she knew which it was. She looked at Ethan. "Hermes?"

Ethan drew his sword and held it before him with both hands.

"Sheathe your sword," came Hermes' voice, as mellow and deceptively suave as ever. "I come here peacefully with but one request: that you accept my aid in the matter of the poet Orpheus."

He appeared in the center of the tent, holding his golden staff at his side. With a snap of his fingers it morphed into an olive branch. He held it out to Chloe. "Take my wand if you suspect my intentions are foul."

Chloe snatched the branch from him and held it behind her back. "I don't suspect. I know. The last time you and I met, you picked me up at the gates of Hades and dropped me off in the Fields of Asphodel."

Hermes didn't laugh or grin or wink, as she'd known him to do in the past. On the contrary, he regarded her with eyes as tired as Ethan's, and equally sincere. "And according to your brother, I betrayed Hades."

Chloe took a step toward him, half tempted to wield the wand and see what it would do. "Where is he? Where's my brother?" she demanded, her anger brimming from deep inside her chest.

"With Leto." Hermes' eye was on the branch as it slowly changed back to solid gold. "Or Mania, as she's affectionately known. She took Damian during our excursion to acquire this." He slipped a large leather sack from his shoulder and pulled out a bronze clock encased in a wooden box.

"I don't care about a dumb clock. Where did she take him?"

Hermes shrugged. "To her home west of here, perhaps. But then, all of Petros is hers to hide in. And no one, not even I, can approach her without first confronting her fury."

Chloe and Ethan exchanged glances. Despite her efforts to see past what was surely a ruse, Chloe couldn't help feeling that Hermes was going against his nature and being honest for once. There was just one more thing she wanted from him before she let him explain why he was there.

"Take off your sandals," she said, pointing the wand at him, "and toss them over there."

"You've leveled the playing field," said Hermes, throwing them onto the mat. "A wise strategy. But I told you, I haven't come here to play games."

"Does that thing have snow on it?" Ethan asked, pointing at the clock. It was covered in white powder.

"Aye. It's been kept safe at Mount Othrys since the dawn of time as you know it."

"What does it do?" Chloe asked. "What does it have to do with Orpheus?"

Hermes beckoned her with his finger. "I'll show you." He turned the clock around, revealing a small black circle the size of a drachma. "Look and see."

"You must think I'm a special kind of stupid," said Chloe.

Hermes went to the table and set the clock on the edge. "Would it put you at ease if I showed you how the mechanism works?"

"Maybe," Chloe replied.

"Very well." Hermes knelt down, took off his cap and pressed his right eye against the circle. Nothing happened.

"Maybe snow got inside the gears," said Ethan, with his usual dry wit.

A muted light spread against the wall behind the table. Small gray figures curled up from the bottom like shadow puppets stretching to life. There was the sound of faint voices as the figures, now grown and consuming two-thirds of the gossamer-like screen, began to move. And then, as if the light were a TV monitor that had just been switched on, the shadows became suffused with color and a full background bloomed into view behind them.

A tall mountain loomed in the middle, overlooking scores of soldiers and horses. Three giant creatures five times the size of the Centaur, with dozens of heads sprouting out of their necks and twice as many hands, tore chunks of rock from the earth as if they were flowers and flung them at the opposing ranks; their targeted shields splintered and fell underfoot. The bodies, now exposed, became pincushions for falling arrows.

Chloe lifted her eyes to the top of the screen, where a silver chariot led by two black steeds raced through the low-hanging clouds. The driver, his hair and panoply gleaming gold, was the ruthless archer. Though she'd never seen him before, she knew instinctively that this was Apollo.

"What's this?" she asked Hermes.

He lifted his arm and pointed at the right side of the screen. Three Cyclopes were marching onto the field. Hermes, clad in armor, floated over their heads, a red guidon flapping at the end of his wand. Above him, dark clouds spun in circles, clashing against one another, creating thunder so loud it shook the mountain and made even the giants jump.

When lightning flashed, Chloe could make out a bearded face among the clouds. "Zeus," she murmured under her breath.

The army beneath Zeus' clouds halted as Apollo's chariot landed near the enemy lines, a spear's reach from the front-rankers. But instead of advancing toward him, they laid down their weapons and fell to their knees, then lifted their palms in supplication. As if in response to their surrender, an eagle swooped down from the ether and circled overhead, crying out triumphantly in sharp, staccato shrieks.

Sounds of lament drowned out the eagle's taunts and the bird perched on Apollo's shoulder. A thunderbolt crashed behind the chariot's carriage and dragged itself along the ground, directed by Zeus' unseen hand. A wide fissure was left in its smoky wake.

Chloe gasped. She could almost smell the sulfur of the Underworld rising out of it. The defeated foe had no choice but to march toward it.

Hermes leaned back from the clock. The light, and the war it depicted, faded instantly. "The War of the Titans," he said, his voice quavering. He looked haggard, as if the clock had aged him fifty years. "Five hundred years after that, it was Zeus who was deposed, and all the Olympians with him."

"So that machine is like a live-action history book?" Ethan asked.

Hermes looked at the space on the tent wall where the grisly scene had been depicted. "One's own history can be seen through the *pýli*. Every smile, every moment of ecstasy, every tragedy and tear. It was created by the Cyclopes to preserve the memories of the immortals."

Chloe willed herself not to pity him. She had to remember that Hermes had been deceiving people for eons. If his present distress was genuine, it was the least of what he deserved. "What does that have to do with us?" Her cold tone was harsher than she'd intended.

Hermes stood. "I have a theory that the *pýli*'s capabilities transcend reflection into the past. Its guardian, Mnemosyne, seemed to indicate as much when I encountered her at Othrys." He locked eyes with Chloe and planted a hand over his heart. "As surely as I stand before you, she told me she'd been waiting for something, or someone, called the Vessel. She said this after your brother informed her that he was from a future time."

"And where is this Mnemosyne person now?" Ethan said, drumming his fingers along the hilt of his sword.

Chloe was almost positive that Ethan still didn't know the first thing about sword fighting, but even so, she was still grateful he had it.

"In Tartarus, I would assume," Hermes said. "Her abode was close enough to a portal for Apollo, or one of his minions, to hear our conversation."

"Sounds like ol' Lykaios Apollo doesn't want us to have the film projector," said Chloe.

Hermes scrunched his brow. "The what?"

"That," Chloe said, gesturing to the clock.

"Indeed." Hermes sighed. "He knows the cycle of conquest better than anyone. Each day he's driven by his maddening fear of subjugation. He also knows the oracle, and has stationed spirits and Pythonians throughout Petros to inform him of any rumors of the Vessel. Should it emerge, and emerge it has, he'll be ready to act."

DIANA TYLER

"Why are you telling us this?" Chloe asked. "Don't you fear subjugation, too? You're on his side, remember?"

Hermes' cheek twitched as he glanced up at the door.

If he wants to leave, he'll have to use it, Chloe thought. Right now Ethan was blocking his way. "Aren't you on his side?" she said.

CHAPTER THIRTY-FIVE
IMMORTAL

L eto stood in the doorway looking at Hermogenes, who lay on his bed, his chest rising and falling peacefully. It was just the two of them now. For ten years she'd dreamed of becoming Hermes' bride and eclipsing Persephone's legend. Now a new prospect burned inside her heart, that of wedding power alone and erasing the immortals from memory. Mania—*fury*—would supplant Apollo, Hades and Hermes, and Duna in heaven would quake as his renown also drew to an end.

But one thing stood in her way, something her sleeping son possessed.

"You forgot to gag me," said Damian from his shackled spot in the kitchen.

Leto ignored him. Hermogenes stirred and turned onto his side. What had her own father thought when he watched her sleep? Had he wondered what doma lay dormant in her veins, the way she wondered now as she stood over her own offspring? If her father had survived to see the first storm she ever conjured, what would he have done?

She already knew the answer. He would have used it to carry out his mission. Within an hour, he would have decimated the temple in Eirene and murdered its priests in cold blood, just as he'd intended before Iris thwarted him. Not a single soldier would have been mobilized, for Leto's doma was more powerful than a hundred armies combined. Together, as mortal counterparts to Zeus and Athena, Hermes and Leto would have ruled the world.

This fantasy is what most consumed Leto's thoughts when sleep eluded her, which it did almost nightly, ever since the oracle had been given. She dreamed of a palace all her own, and lavish banquets with the finest meats and delicacies. She pined for festivals devoted solely to her and her father, of standing within a chariot in the midst of a grand parade. She longed to hear the people chant her name and adore her as the women of old adored Demeter.

But more than the wealth, the tributes and adulation, Leto wanted reunion with her father, whose spirit, thanks to Iris's fire, was now adrift in some hazy vale of the Underworld. The instant she became queen of all, she would free him and put Hermes in his place. Hermogenes would understand. His father had never loved them. Even the crude plan arising in her mind was for her son's own good, and if he was wise he would realize it one day.

"Just so you know," said Damian, "my sister is one of the smartest girls in school. I'm pretty sure she knows you're using me as bait."

Leto turned and strode to the kitchen. "Is that supposed to concern me?"

"I'm just saying, you could be waiting a long time if you think she's coming here to find me."

"And what's her alternative?" She sat down at the table and crossed her legs comfortably. "She's your sister. Do you mean to tell me she'll leave you here to suffer my cruelty?"

Damian popped both thumbs and gazed off toward the stone dolphins.

"Your reticence tells me you think she *would* leave you here." Leto poured a cup of wine and sipped it slowly.

Damian's eyes jerked back to hers. "No. She's not like me."

Leto set down her cup and leaned forward, chin resting in her hands. "Ah, how terribly fascinating." She smiled and waved at him. "Go on, I love a good story. Especially a tragedy."

He knitted his brow and leaned against the hearth beside him. He felt like a mouse trapped beneath her cat's paw; he had no choice but to let her toy with him. "She was kidnapped and taken to Hades, which at the time I thought was just a made-up place meant to scare little kids into following the rules."

Leto laughed. "I once thought the same, until Hermes emerged from its depths. I've never had the privilege of visiting the realm of the dead, but I would wager that he represents it rather well."

Damian's eyes shifted to the mountains, their peaks washed white by the moon and stars. "It was a miracle she made it out of there. No one helped her." His eyes fell to his tattered shoes. "Including me. And with my doma, I could have."

"So," said Leto, taking a long, satisfied drink of wine, "even in the future, mankind is as heartless and selfish as it is today." Damian turned away from her the same way that Hermes did whenever her conversations with him went sour. "I don't say this to condemn you. I state only an objective truth, namely that the nature of man will remain unevolved till the end of time."

"People are not always selfish," Damian said.

"Of course not. Feeding my child is unselfish, as was my choice not to stop Hermes' heart with a lightning bolt this afternoon. But when our lives are at stake, or our most sacred desires, our strongest impulse tends to supersede all virtue. And that impulse is pride, of honoring, favoring and preserving ourselves above all."

Panther wagged his tail and curled up next to Damian's hip. The dog always lay next to Leto on chilly nights. Whenever there was noise, even the faintest rustling of leaves outside the courtyard walls, he barked and burst from the door to seek out signs of trespassing. She'd lost count of the number of times he'd tempted Hermes' wand by snarling at him at midnight, daring him to come one inch closer toward his mistress.

Panther was perhaps the only selfless creature Leto had ever known. His sole purpose and favorite pleasure was keeping her safe. She'd done nothing to earn his loyalty or protection, and yet he behaved as though he owed her his life.

"I don't understand," said Damian. "You talk about selfishness like it's a plague or something, and yet everything you do is selfish."

Leto rose, accidentally stepping on Panther's tail. The dog yelped and ducked under the table. As she knelt in front of her prisoner, an owl, Athena's most beloved bird, hooted from atop the dolphin fountain.

"Tell me," she said, "what did you feel that day you chose to leave your sister in Hades?"

Damian shrugged. "I don't know. Anger, fear..."

"And a modicum of guilt, I'm sure," Leto added. "But your innate sense of self-preservation prevailed, as it always does. It does no good to fight it."

She stood and tilted her head toward the twinkling stars, which seemed to be peering down at her like a thousand inquisitive eyes. "The way I see it, Damian, those with the strongest wills are those to whom life is kindest. I was created to be an outcast, as were you, but I, and I alone, create my destiny. If that's selfish, then so be it."

"And is it your most sacred desire, to use your phrasing, to become better than the gods?"

Hearing the edge of amusement in Damian's tone, Leto pointed at the gray owl, which was still watching from a distance. "The owl is Athena's bird. It symbolizes her wisdom because of its talent to see clearly in the black of night." With a yell, she reached toward the heavens and pulled together myriad clusters of clouds. "But even this goddess, for all her valor and sagacity, is not invincible."

The newly formed thunderhead crackled and groaned as light began to flicker within it. In the next breath, a red streak of lightning ripped from its belly and struck the owl at the first flap of its wings. The bird dropped to the ground, a tousled heap of feathers on the paving stones.

"That owl didn't do anything to you," said Damian. "You didn't have to kill it to make a point."

Leto divided the storm cloud into harmless wisps and sent them floating over the mountains. "Did you not hear what I said? The owl belongs to Athena. And I will tolerate no creature, no matter how virtuous or lovely, whom the gods have claimed."

"You can play god all your life, Leto, but what happens when you die?"

She smiled, the sting of her doma still pulsing in her fingertips. She'd been waiting for him to ask her that.

"You'll die and go to the Underworld," continued Damian, "just like everyone else who doesn't believe that Duna is the All-Powerful."

Leto went to the table and snapped her fingers in front of Panther's face. The hound sprang up, eager to hear her command. "Take the owl, Panther," she said, pointing at the dead bird. "Go!"

The dog dashed into the courtyard and happily carried away his supper.

"The answer to your question is simple," she said, stirring her wine with a ladle. "Ambrosia."

"Ambrosia? The stuff the gods eat?"

"Precisely. It's their lifeblood. And my way to immortality."

A look of bafflement crossed Damian's face as he stared down at his shackles.

Leto reached forward and grasped his arm, feeling his muscles tense beneath her hand as he leaned away. "Your sister is going to help me get it."

"She won't help you. No matter what you say to try and convince her."

"Oh, but I think she will." Leto reached for the knife hidden in her girdle and pressed its blade to Damian's throat. "As you said before, she isn't like you. She won't leave you to die." She trailed the blade lightly around his neck, laughing when he flinched and shut his eyes. "At least you'd better pray she doesn't."

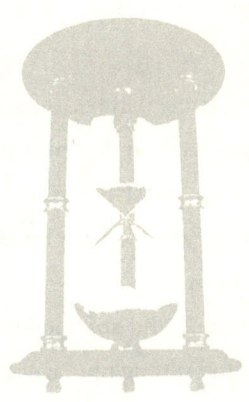

CHAPTER THIRTY-SIX
FREEDOM

There were few things Chloe missed from her time, but one of them was definitely a cup of hot coffee. The sunrise, although beautiful with its peaceful shades of peach and lavender, was hardly enjoyable when seen through stinging, sleep-starved eyes. The music of the morning birds might as well have been clanging cymbals or violins played by toddlers; each note exacerbated the splitting headache that had been going strong since midnight, the hour Hermes, Ethan and the others had finally gone to bed.

I wonder if Hermes' wand can make coffee? Such were Chloe's thoughts as she gazed into the cirrus clouds, imagining them as froth on the top of a mouthwatering cappuccino.

"Tea?"

Chloe jumped. Iris sat down next to her on the hillside, a stone's throw from the breakfast bonfires now starting to flicker.

Chloe looked down at the nondescript cup of tea. It smelled like dirt. "I was just daydreaming about having a cup of coffee."

"What's coffee?" Iris set the tea between them.

Chloe's mouth twisted. How did one describe coffee? "It's like tea. But better. A thousand times better." She rubbed her head. "It's especially good when you're sleep deprived and feel like crap."

Iris tapped the rim of the cup. "So is this. Try it."

Chloe held the cup in both hands and tried not to inhale. She would rather suffer her headache than drink liquid dirt, but she didn't want to be rude. "What is it?"

"Ironwort." Iris said the word as if it were the most poetic in the universe. "It's one of Petros's most healing herbs."

"No wonder it smells so bad." Quickly, before she could talk herself out of it, Chloe took a sip, immediately fighting the reflex to spit it out. The bitter concoction slid like slime down her throat. "Ironwort's a good name for it."

"It isn't pleasant to drink, but it's good for you."

Chloe fought down another swallow. "I have a feeling you mean that metaphorically."

Iris smiled and leaned back onto her hands. "Perhaps I'm speaking of Hermes, too. I can imagine that forgiving him, let alone trusting him, is not an easy drink to swallow."

Chloe thought back to just hours before, when Ethan had given the *pýli* contraption a whirl. She hadn't been there in the Folóï Forest when Hermes had appeared to the Rosses and Damian. Five seconds into viewing the encounter, the mystified messenger had melted to the floor and alternated between covering his eyes and groaning as he watched, like a nosy pedestrian gawking at a car crash, his future betrayal play out. Within minutes, he had been virtually apoplectic.

The second the scene showed Hermes handing Ethan the seeds that guaranteed the mortals' safety, he let out a terrified cry and pulled Ethan back from the machine. Once he regained his composure, Hermes sheepishly admitted that Damian had been right; Hermes' fate was to help the Ashers.

"You should have seen Hermes when he foresaw the future," Chloe told Iris. "I've never seen a man look so afraid."

"Becoming an enemy of Apollo is no small thing," Iris said.

Her blue eyes dimmed, and Chloe couldn't help but wonder what memories were flashing behind them.

"Not to mention," Iris added, "until he trusts Duna to light his path, he's wandering aimlessly through a self-made darkness, with neither a purpose to fulfill nor a home to return to."

Chloe shuddered as Hermes' impish face flickered and grinned in her mind's eye. "He's the one responsible for the literal hell I've been through. How can I trust someone whose purpose up to now has been to destroy me and my family?"

"*Don't* trust him."

Chloe drew up at Iris's words. "What? Really?"

"Forgive him. Only then will you be able to see him clearly for who he is."

"But he didn't even ask me to forgive him." Chloe spilled a splash of tea as she set it on the grass. "He probably doesn't even know what 'apology' means."

Iris sighed, then reached out and touched the jasper stone that hung from Chloe's neck. "My mission in life, after I received my doma, was to avenge my brother. Day and night, the only thing I could think about was killing the man who ordered Jasper's execution. It was my purpose, or so I was convinced, to assassinate every last Alpha and Pythonian who had brought such pain and sorrow to my people. I felt I was doing what Duna had neglected to do. I thought I was being just."

Chloe's breath caught in her throat. She reached again for the tea. "And what were you really being?"

"I've had many years to ponder that same question, and there are many answers that suffice." Iris reached into a small satchel attached to her belt. "Ethan told me about the cave your father was exploring before he died."

"Ethan said my dad found seven jars in there that had something to do with the Moonbow."

Iris nodded and closed her fist around the object she'd pulled from the pouch. "The jars are now with Gennadius in Limén."

"And Aspasia?"

Iris froze. "Aspasia died six months ago. Did I tell you about them?"

"I met them when I traveled back in time," Chloe said, "before we came here and stayed at their house. Charis was just a little girl." She smiled and placed a hand on Iris's shoulder. "You and Tycho gave me some great advice then. You're good at that."

Iris smiled and lightly touched Chloe's hand. "They took me in when I was like Hermes, wandering, searching...running from Duna." She plucked a blade of grass and twirled it between her fingers. "The dried calendula flower Aspasia gave me has a sacred jar all its own. Its orange petals represent healing, and the hot desert sun that would expose my need for it."

Iris opened her hand, revealing an emerald oval, no larger than a pomegranate seed. "This, as the future has shown you, will be hidden away with the other artifacts, but I cannot part with it yet."

"It's beautiful," Chloe said, watching the gemstone sparkle as a shy ray of sun winked through the clouds. "What does it symbolize?"

"New life," said Iris. "The kind that springs forth from forgiveness."

"You forgave the man who ordered your brother's death?"

"Yes." Iris looked down with fondness at the emerald. "And the executioner himself. It was he who gave this to me. He expected me to kill him and bring my brother justice. I wanted to. It was the moment I'd been waiting for, the chance I'd been chasing since the fire first escaped my palms."

"Why didn't you do it?"

Iris tapped the jasper stone in Chloe's necklace. "Because of Jasper. Of all the people I knew, my brother had the most compelling reason to retaliate with violence against those who mocked him for his beliefs in the All-Powerful. He was ostracized, beaten, imprisoned on numerous occasions, yet he never once uttered a single syllable of complaint." A solitary tear trailed down Iris's cheek. "He would only repeat the words I've been saying to myself more and more: 'I give thanks that I've been found worthy of suffering disgrace for the name of Phos.'"

"Phos..." Chloe envisioned Orpheus's face, surrounded by the otherworldly cloud she'd last seen him in. "I've heard that name before. Who is he?"

"Hope," Iris smiled, wiping the tear away. "Redemption. As Duna's son, he's the embodiment of all things pure and righteous. It was Jasper's belief in Phos that got him killed."

"And where is this Phos person now?"

D I A N A   T Y L E R

Iris cast her gaze to the purple mountains, still shrouded in shadows as they slept soundly beyond the sunlight's reach. "In heaven, letting Apollo's rebellion unfold; waiting for us to call upon Duna to end it."

Chloe felt the all-too-familiar heat of frustration in her chest. "Why wait? Why doesn't he just stop it now and let everyone see him do it?"

"Because, unlike Apollo and Hades and every other man or god who's ever set himself up as tyrant, Duna and Phos do not force themselves upon us." Iris took a breath and looked up. Two falcons soared low over the valley, gliding downward with folded wings. "But they do pursue us—Ashers, Pythonians, orphans, widows, the whole world. But the day is coming when the world, and everything in it, will be theirs again, with no evil left to trouble it."

"I was born two thousand years from now, and that day still hadn't come," Chloe said, watching the falcons arc upward and fly into the clouds.

"Duna's patience is long. Long enough to wait for even the likes of Hermes to emerge from darkness." Iris placed the emerald in Chloe's hand. "Forgiving my brother's killers freed me just as much as it freed them. If not more."

Chloe felt the gem vibrating in her palm, punctuating Iris's words.

"It doesn't matter if Hermes never asks for your forgiveness," Iris said. "You'll be bound by bitterness unless you release him from the dungeon of your thoughts."

Chloe clasped the jewel tightly before putting it back in Iris's satchel. "I don't think I could forgive myself if I lost it. But I'll remember what you said."

She stood up and helped Iris to her feet, then gulped down the remainder of her ironwort tea. Amazingly, the stuff had worked. Her headache was gone. Her eyes no longer felt like they were being pricked by forks. She felt awake, energetic, and strangely optimistic. "I do feel better. Thank you."

"The heart, the soul and the body are connected, Chloe. When one is sick, the others suffer. When one is depleted, the others falter and grow weary. Tend always to all three, and you'll find a contentment that no being, whether on Petros or below it, can destroy."

The sound of footsteps treading on gravel made Chloe turn around. It was Ethan.

"Hermes is awake..." He paused when he saw their faces. "Sorry. I interrupted something, didn't I?"

"Just girl talk," said Chloe, pretty sure she'd never used that phrase before. In the past, any time she wanted to talk she went to her diary. It was refreshing to confide in a real person. "Hermes still wants to do this?"

"Right now I think he just wants to eat more honeycakes," replied Ethan. "The Centaur said Hermes needs to put some meat on his bones. I guess honeycake making isn't part of his wand's repertoire."

"I don't recall seeing any food during my stint in Hades," Chloe said. "I imagine he could use a good breakfast." She felt her own stomach start to growl.

"Sounds like you could, too." Ethan smiled when her stomach grumbled even louder. "Want me to bring you back something? Quail eggs? Salted fish? Barley stew?"

Chloe frowned in disgust. "It's okay. I'll see if I can get in on the honeycake action." Maybe if she asked nicely, Hermes would make her a pot of coffee to go with it.

CHAPTER THIRTY-SEVEN
ORPHEUS

So far, Chloe was still alive. She'd taken Hermes' advice and transported them back five hundred years to Orpheus's time. The only name Hermes had given her to focus on was Mount Parnassos, home of the muses, and apparently Orpheus's favorite place.

Hermes fell flat on his back when the time travel was over. Holding his stomach, and with his lips sucked in tightly, he rolled slowly onto his side.

Chloe took the wineskin from her sack and set it on Hermes' chest. "I should have warned you that eating eleven honeycakes probably wasn't the best idea before taking a ride in a wormhole."

"That was incredible!" Charis exclaimed, her pale cheeks flushed and her red hair wild. "Can we do it again?"

"After we get Orpheus," Chloe said. Hermes groaned in opposition. "We'll have to if we want to get back."

She turned back to Hermes. "Is this the right place? It's kind of hard to breathe."

Hermes suppressed a belch, pushed himself up to a sitting position and pointed to a mountaintop half covered with snow. "Aye. Liakouras is up there. The highest peak of the mountains."

"Well, you know what they say," said Chloe. "Go big or go home." They blinked at her, clearly not knowing that's what they said, whoever "they" were.

"How do you know Orpheus will be here?" Iris asked Hermes.

He poured water into his hand and splashed it onto his face. "I don't. But it's my best guess."

"Great." Charis plopped down to the grass and lay back, closing her eyes. "Wake me up if you need me."

After a few more seconds of rest, Hermes got himself up and flew five feet into the air, holding a hand to his ear.

Iris was quick on the draw. She held out her hands, emitting a small flame of warning. "No flying, remember?"

Chloe took his wand from her sack and pointed it at him. "I have no idea how to work this thing. Don't make me turn you into a newt or something."

Hermes, still hovering, pressed a finger to his lips. "Shhh! I can't hear over all your yammering."

"Hear what?" Charis said, lifting herself onto her elbows.

Hermes fluttered a few yards forward, toward the mountain, stopping abruptly behind an olive tree. Two seconds later, he vanished.

Charis stood up and marched in a circle around the tree, looking it up and down. "How did he do that?"

Chloe shrugged. "No idea. I didn't know he could do that either."

"It's my cap."

Charis jumped at Hermes' voice behind her. "You scared me to death!" she shouted, yanking the cap from his head. "Where did you go?"

"The Corycian Cave. Orpheus is there, wailing like an alleycat."

"Eurydice must have died recently," said Chloe.

"Such was my deduction as well." Hermes jerked his cap from Charis's hand. "Come. I'll lead the way."

What was it with Orpheus and caves, Chloe wondered. On the day she met him he'd taken her to the Psychro Cave, which contained a portal to the creepy zoo on Circe's isle, where she almost became the latest attraction. If there were any mysterious-looking pools in this cave, she was keeping her distance.

((

The sound of Orpheus's crying was as painful to Chloe's ears as his music was beautiful. It echoed through the cave's main chamber, filling it with a sorrow so strong it was almost palpable. The darkness, already difficult to navigate, was made all the more disorienting by the musician's heartrending cries and sporadic gasps for air. It sounded as though he was being tortured. In a way, she realized, he was.

An orange flame floated out of Iris's hand, only slightly illuminating the claustrophobic space of stalagmites, stalactites and water droplets falling from the roof. From her opposite hand emerged another fireball; five times the size of the first.

Orpheus's sobbing stopped. "Leave me!" he shouted.

Chloe could barely make out his dark figure slumped against the farthest wall. "Orpheus, it's me, Chloe." No sooner had she said the words than she remembered that her name meant nothing to him, and nor would it for another twenty-five hundred years.

"Calm down, Orpheus," said Hermes, his tone like that of a master pacifying his riled-up dog. "I come as a friend."

"Uncle..." Orpheus growled the word, then rose and charged Hermes, grabbing him by the throat.

Chloe's hand twitched over the wand in her sack. She'd throw it to Hermes if things got bloody.

"It is I, dear nephew," Hermes managed to say as he lifted up his empty palms. "Please. I'm not here to set a snare."

Orpheus grunted and shoved Hermes hard into the wall. "Apollo took your wand, did he? Have you come to request the use of my lyre so you can lull him to sleep and retrieve it?"

Chloe winced as Hermes cracked his neck back into place. "*I* took his wand, actually," she said.

Orpheus glared at the three women standing before him. His gaze fell to the wand. He clearly knew what it was capable of. "I don't know you."

Chloe's heart ached when he lifted his eyes to hers. They were empty, hopeless, reddened by a grief that wouldn't subside. The first time she'd seen him, she'd been struck by the beautiful blue color of his eyes. Now they were totally gray, the color of the cavern to which he had exiled himself.

"I know you don't." Chloe lifted her sack over her shoulder and carefully took out the *pýli*. "Not yet. I'm from the future. You and I become friends in, oh, about two and a half thousand years."

Orpheus returned her smile with a withering stare. He turned to Hermes. "This must be the most pathetic ruse you've ever devised."

"It's no ruse," Hermes said. He pointed at the machine. "We need your help, but there will be no gimmicks or traps to obtain it. You have my word."

"Your word is worthless," the poet snapped. He wheeled around to face Charis and Iris. "Don't believe a word that proceeds from this miscreant's mouth. Whatever he's promised you in return for your presence here, it's a lie from the pit of hell."

"He's promised us nothing," Iris said. She stepped forward and sent a tiny light, no bigger than a candle's flame, in front of the *pýli*. "This device of the Cyclopes proved to us that Hermes is different. Let it prove to you that you know Chloe. Then you can decide whether to help us or turn us away. We will leave you if you wish it."

Orpheus's pupils constricted as he marveled at the flame that had come forth effortlessly from Iris's hand. "You are goddesses, then. I gather you are Hestia," he said to Iris.

"We're Ashers," said Charis. Then she vanished, appearing that same second in the entrance of the cave fifty yards away.

Orpheus stumbled back toward the corner they'd found him in. "I know of furies. Harpies. I know the muses that reared me, and the dryads to whom my beloved belonged. But never in my life have I heard of the Ashers."

"The Ashers were created long after your time, nephew." Hermes went to the *pýli* and took it from Chloe's arms. Before any objections could be made, he turned the device around and set his right eye on the circle. "I remember it as if it were yesterday."

As Hermes spoke, half of the limestone wall before them turned as black as tar. A low rumbling sound crawled across the darkness, accompanied by the quiet howl of the wind.

"What is this? Stop this madness," Orpheus protested. But he didn't make a move to stop it. His curiosity, or perhaps his fear, was getting the better of him.

Jagged lightning flashed on the wall, illuminating a diminutive grove of olive trees in the lower left corner.

"I'm hiding there." Hermes pointed at the trees. "And so is Asher. The very first."

Innumerable stars studded the sky as a full moon slid slowly into the frame. The midnight storm subsided.

"Asher..."

The voice was quiet and deafening all at once. It wasn't a human voice, and it seemed to come from the moon itself.

"Duna," Iris whispered. She and Charis fell to their knees in worship.

Chloe stood frozen, both petrified and awestruck.

A man, small as an ant in comparison to the vastness of space above him, tiptoed out of the trees. He, too, fell to his knees as a fingertip, as big as the moon, drew a vibrant red arch across the smoky black palette of sky. The first band was followed by ribbons of orange, yellow, green, blue, indigo and violet.

It was the Moonbow.

"Record what you see, Asher," said the voice, as the finger faded into the moon's white aura.

The man opened his hands to the sky. "But, my king, I have neither stylus nor tablet to do what you say." With a despondent cry, he tore his tunic and plunged both hands into the earth.

Chloe went closer, squinting at the tiny man to see what happened next.

"You have trusted me all your life," said Duna. "Trust me now. Take the stylus I've placed in the earth and receive your doma, the first of many your line shall bear."

Asher leaned toward his right side, sinking his hand deeper into the soil. When he brought it out, a stylus was wedged between his fingers. Chloe's heart beat faster as her eyes jumped to a small mound of mud moving beside him.

"By the gods," said Orpheus, "what is happening?"

"A miracle," Iris said, from her prone position on the floor.

The amorphous sludge beside Asher tightened, its round edges evening out as it stretched into a rectangular tablet. A column of hazy light appeared beside him, like the mist that had surrounded Carya on several occasions. The column spun to face not Asher, but its onlookers. A bare foot stepped out of it, followed by another as the mist vanished like a vapor.

It was Carya, but Asher didn't seem to realize she was there.

"She wasn't there that night," Hermes whispered.

Carya walked forward, her body growing taller with every step as the fresh scents of lavender and lemon permeated the air.

"She's here," Chloe said.

Hermes lowered the *pýli* away from his face, but still Carya's form grew bigger. "I'm sorry!" he shouted. "Take the mechanism. I'll never use it again." He dropped the device and cowered like a cornered animal, covering his face with his hands.

Chloe wondered why he was so afraid of a teenager, and a female one at that.

Carya was now standing before them in three dimensions. Chloe could smell the sweetness of her wine-colored hair mingling with the aroma of herbs that followed her everywhere she went. Then she began to speak.

"I do not come to harm you, Hermes,
  so be not anxious or afraid,
I come with news of Leto and the
  plan that she had made.
She yearns to strike Duna's name from
  history, to rise above Zeus and Apollo,
To silence her rivals, destroy every Asher,
  leaving no faith for Petros to follow.

All she lacks is one bite of ambrosia, and
*   for this she keeps Damian in chains.*
An age of darkness will surely descend
*   if that substance fills her veins.*
There is but one way to stop her, so
*   listen to these words well:*
Orpheus must save Hermogenes, and
*   Chloe must undo the spell."*

The bejeweled coronet on Carya's head glittered in the flames as she gave a slight bow and stepped back toward the plain cave wall. All eyes but hers moved to Orpheus, now holding his lyre at his side.

"I have half a mind to think this strangeness nothing more than a perverse hallucination," Orpheus said. "I've been living alone in this squalor so long that perhaps I've lost my sanity."

"You haven't," said Chloe. "I thought the same thing the day I met Carya in my car."

She smiled at her friend, remembering when Carya's reflection had appeared in the rearview mirror and she had given Chloe those ludicrous walnuts. Chloe had been positive she was going crazy, but curiosity had compelled her to eat one of the walnuts regardless. She'd convinced herself she had nothing to lose. That simple bite had changed her life, just as the bite of ambrosia could change Leto's.

"Why not see where the hallucination takes you, Orpheus?" Charis said, a mischievous twinkle in her eye.

Then Chloe saw it, the piece of Orpheus she knew from before. The goodness she'd seen in him when he'd saved her from Circe. The compassion she'd observed when he met her outside of time and asked for her forgiveness. His was a poet's heart, and she knew it couldn't bear to see the world in turmoil, even a world that had crushed him.

CHAPTER THIRTY-EIGHT
AMBROSIA

I have one request," said Orpheus, as the last speck of Carya's mist evaporated.

Chloe glanced at the *pýli* on the floor. "You want to see Eurydice."

"How do you know her name?"

"I told you. I know you, Orpheus." She picked up the *pýli* and carried it to him. "Put your eye there," she said, pointing to the black circle.

"It will only sting a little," Hermes warned.

"I'll endure any torture to see her face again," answered Orpheus.

Charis and Iris sighed in unison; Orpheus was a romantic, that was for sure.

"Wait," said Chloe, her heart falling to her stomach. "I forgot. You can't see Eurydice in the future because you haven't lived it yet. I'm so sorry, Orpheus."

Iris approached, twin flames hovering above her. "But *you* can see the future, Chloe."

"Yes, but I never saw Orpheus and Eurydice together," Chloe answered. "He only told me they had reunited in heaven."

Tears welled in Orpheus's eyes, filling them with a heartbreaking shade of blue. "That will more than suffice," he said.

As Chloe raised the *pýli* to her eye, a long, green-speckled tail burst from the shadows and wrapped itself around the device. Orpheus and Hermes pulled against it, but the creature was too strong. Without a struggle, it broke free from their hands and disappeared into the darkness. The *pýli* clattered to the floor.

"What in Zeus' name was that?" Chloe said, clutching Iris.

A loud splash sounded from somewhere deep inside the cave, followed by an ominous hissing noise that weaved, like a ghost's whisper, throughout the labyrinth of rooms.

"Orpheusss...isss...mine..."

Chills ran up Chloe's neck. She had heard such a hissing voice before, the first time her doma had manifested and taken her to an ancient ship that Iris and Tycho were aboard.

"Scylla?" she said.

"Scylla's lair is in the Great Sea," Iris whispered.

"It's Echidna," Hermes said.

The creature's tail, strong and scabbed, crept around the rock closest to Charis.

"Charis, watch out!" Chloe shouted.

Charis vanished, reappearing in a split second beside her mother as the serpent's tail extended into the center of the room; it was at least fifteen feet in length.

Where's this thing's head, Chloe thought, gripping Hermes' wand at her side.

And then it—*she*—peered around a pillar that reached from floor to roof. The snake was a woman—at least, part of it was.

From the neck down, Chloe thought her hideous, as Scylla was. Her brown, bloated belly was distended from whatever her last meal had been. But her head and face were striking, more beautiful than Circe's, which made Chloe wonder why the world's most evil women were also gorgeous. Her black hair, shiny as silk, cascaded to the floor in luxuriant waves. Her eyes were amethyst and hypnotic, and drew Chloe further into them the longer she looked.

"It isss Orpheussss' desssstiny to dwell here forever with me..."

"Go back to Hades, you stinking witch!" Orpheus yelled. He ran across the cave and fetched his lyre. "Cover your ears," he said, as he set his fingers to the strings.

As Chloe and the others obeyed, Echidna emitted an ear-piercing shriek, drowning out Orpheus's music, neutralizing its effects.

"It isn't working," Chloe shouted.

Echidna smiled, her brilliant white teeth beaming in Iris's flames as they floated like lanterns above her head. She stuck out her long, forked tongue and pierced one of them, making it sizzle into smoke. Then she uttered a high-pitched scream with such superhuman force that the lyre fell from Orpheus's shaking hands.

The instant he bent down to get it, the serpent's tail raced toward him and snatched the lyre, then raised it high overhead where it dangled mere inches from the largest of Iris's flares.

"He isss uselessss to you without thissss, isss he not?" Echidna intoned. "I've alwaysss wanted to learn how to play like Orpheussss. But sssince I have no handsss, I shall have to be content to use hissss..."

Orpheus drew a dagger from his belt and pressed its tip to his wrist. "I would sooner hack off my hands and watch you eat them than play a single note for you."

Echidna's body stiffened as she lifted her head higher until it grazed the ceiling. Her tail lowered the lyre nearer to the fire. "Sssooo you will not be needing thissss..."

Before she could burn the lyre, Chloe took the wand in both hands and pointed it at Echidna's face.

Tape.

As soon as the word popped into Chloe's mind, a silver piece of duct tape appeared across Echidna's mouth. The monster tried to scream, but only a muffled shout was heard. Her tail swung the lyre toward the flame, but in a flash, Charis was in the air to intercept it and vanished to who knew where.

Chloe breathed again. The lyre was safe. And now for the rest of them...

Hermes clapped his hand on Chloe's shoulder. "Well done. The wand is fond of you."

Echidna was struggling to reach her sealed mouth with her tail.

"Or maybe it's just *not* fond of her," Chloe said, watching as the serpent part of Echidna began to thrash and flail. "I think we've worn out our welcome."

Iris held out her palms to Echidna. "I doubt you'll be able to withstand a tunnel of fire as well as you do a single flame." Two walls of fire streamed out of Iris's hands as her face contorted with pain. The flames formed a fence around Echidna's body, rising around her so only her raven-black head was visible. "Hold still and you won't be harmed," Iris shouted.

The four of them backed away toward the cave mouth, eyeing the beast as her fierce tail tore through the flames.

Chloe raised the wand once more and aimed it at Echidna's lips.

"What are you doing?" Hermes said.

"How will she eat if she can't open her mouth?"

Hermes sighed. "You want to spare the life of the creature that would kill us all if she had the chance?"

Chloe lowered the wand and looked at him, silently weighing whether the decision to save Echidna was the right one. "Duna gave *all* of us life, even monsters like her. As far as I'm concerned, it's his job to take life away, not mine."

Chloe pointed the wand at Echidna again, this time envisioning the tape being peeled from her mouth. The wand obeyed.

Echidna wasted no time using her freed vocal cords to hiss curses and scream at the flames. "Ashersss, you will never defeat ussss... Apollo...shall alwaysss...win!"

Chloe stepped into the sunlight, then called back over her shoulder, "It's not over till the fat monster sings."

☾

"Did she say anything else?" Ethan asked. "I mean, did she give you any more details about the ambrosia?"

Chloe rubbed the sleep from her eyes as he handed her a cup of ironwort and sat beside her.

This time the scent of the tea turned her stomach only slightly. "Thanks." She took a sip, trying her best to imagine it was a cinnamon-sprinkled latte. "And no, not really. She just said that it's the reason she's holding my brother hostage."

Ethan stared into the campfire, stroking the light brown stubble of his chin.

"What are you thinking?"

"The ambrosia she wants has to be back in time somewhere," Ethan said. "That has to be the reason she has your brother."

"To get to me," Chloe said. "To use my doma." Ethan nodded. "I can't help her, Ethan. If I do, she gains immortality. If she gains immortality, the world is worse off than it was when we got here."

Ethan turned to her, his expression grave. "If you don't, she'll keep Damian prisoner forever. Or worse."

"Yes, worse," came Hermes' voice.

Chloe turned to see him hovering in the air, honeycake crumbs tumbling from his mouth.

"I know Leto better than anyone," Hermes said. "She is many things, but merciful is not one of them. She has only two uses for Damian: to hold him hostage until you help her, or to kill him if you refuse."

Chloe gazed over at Orpheus. He was standing beside the paddock in which a group of colts loped and kicked up their heels. His lyre protruded from a leather sack one of the refugees had given him after he'd serenaded the children, and many adults, to sleep the night before.

The poet had been here only a few hours and already he was a celebrity. The women couldn't walk by him without blushing and fanning their faces. The teenage boys desperately wanted to learn how to play and charm as he did; this second they were off searching for instruments or making them. The older men, no doubt feeling inferior in this hero's presence, had brandished their swords and were fencing with one another instead of working. A few were engaged in foot races, churning up dust as they sped past. Chloe could almost smell the testosterone in their sweat.

She couldn't help but think of Damian. He would outrun every one of them if he were here. "That's why we have Orpheus," she said.

Ethan shifted and threw another log on the fire. "It's not enough."

"What do you mean? All Hermes has to do is take us to Mania's house. We'll take cover somewhere and guard Orpheus while he plays his lullaby, then Damian can disappear and come find us."

Hermes lowered himself to the ground and dusted the crumbs from his hands. "One problem. Unless Damian knows we're coming, and by some miracle has use of his hands to cover his ears, he'll be just as susceptible to Orpheus's lyre as Leto. There'll be no getting him out if he's unconscious."

"Then we carry him out," said Chloe. "Not a big deal."

"That's if everything goes perfectly, Chloe," said Ethan. "And there's no guarantee of that. The lyre's effects aren't instant. Mania could hear Orpheus start playing and then go completely berserk."

"She could make ten times the noise that Echidna did to mute his music," added Hermes.

Chloe had thought of that, but she couldn't afford— *Damian* couldn't afford—for her to succumb to fear and what-if, worst-case scenarios. She had to be positive. But she also couldn't be dumb.

"Then what do we do? Just let my brother die? Just let Mania destroy the world and rule it the way she wants to?" Chloe's heart tightened in her chest. Hot tears rushed to her eyes and blurred the orange flames before her. How could she live with herself if she failed to save the future—and lost Damian in the process?

"You have to help her," said Hermes.

Chloe pulled the wand from her belt and pointed it at him. "So that's what this is about, this whole I'm-a-changed-man act of yours. You've just been waiting for the right time to convince me to help your beloved maniac become invincible." She took a step toward him, waving the wand in circles. "I should've known better than to forgive you. People like you don't change."

She lunged forward, and the image of an overweight platypus flashed through her brain.

Ethan grabbed her wrist and snatched the wand from her hand. "Don't," he said, pulling her back. "He's right."

"What do you mean 'he's right'? Don't you see how he's been playing us?"

Hermes stood up and doffed his cap. "Quite the other way around. My intention is not to play games with you, but with Leto. What you must do, you must do alone. But this should help you." He placed the cap in Chloe's hand.

"Fine," said Chloe. "I'm listening."

CHAPTER THIRTY-NINE
ADMISSION

ermes looked around, ensuring that there was no one near enough to eavesdrop. "Go to Leto," he said. "Tell her, with indubitable conviction, that you'll happily assist her if she unshackles your brother and lets him go. This she has to do first, you must tell her, because you rightly cannot trust her. Then," he said, floating in circles around the fire, "you travel in time, fetch the ambrosia and bring it back."

Chloe put on the cap. It was more comfortable than it looked. "And what do I do with this thing?"

"You put it on, of course. Simply by wishing it, you will make yourself invisible and free your brother. Then you steal the ambrosia from Leto before she eats it."

Chloe sighed, fiddling with the frizzy ends of her hair. "I can't just shut her mouth like I did with the serpent lady?"

Hermes shook his head. "Her winds are too strong. You'd have to do something more permanent, something that would prevent her from opening her mouth ever again."

"And I won't let her die," said Chloe. "At least not on my watch."

Ethan stood up and stuffed his hands in his pockets the way he did when he was trying to tame his frustration. "But what if you have to? It could come down to that, Chloe. You have to be prepared to kill her with Hermes' wand if you have to."

"No," said Chloe, a sharp edge of vehemence in her voice. "Then I'd be no better than she is. Duna will make a way. He hasn't let me down so far."

Ethan exhaled loudly through his nose and interlaced his fingers on the back of his head.

Chloe smiled. Ethan was an expert temper restrainer.

"Desperate times call for desperate measures," he said. "I'm not telling you to do it. I'm just asking you to be ready."

Chloe's body got warm. She set the tea aside and stood up. "I couldn't live with Leto's death on my conscience, Ethan. It's easy for you to tell me to kill someone when

345

you're here sitting on the sidelines." She regretted the words as soon as she'd said them, but it was too late now.

A long silence passed before anyone moved.

Finally Ethan returned his hands to his sides. "I know what it's like," he said softly, a hollowness filling his eyes. "I killed someone."

Chloe thought she hadn't heard him correctly. Even if Ethan were capable of such a thing, when would he have had the chance to do it? And then the answer came to her.

"At the Religious Council building." The question sounded more like a statement.

Ethan nodded and clenched his jaw, his lips straightening into a thin hard line. "One of the councilman's guards, just after your brother and my parents escaped." He closed his eyes, both eyelids quivering under the strain of those dark memories. "I had no choice."

Chloe went to him and placed a hand on his shoulder. "Ethan, I'm so sorry."

"You have nothing to be sorry for," he said flatly. "It was my decision to kill him. I chose my life over his."

"But if you hadn't done it..."

Ethan stepped away, out from under her touch. "If I hadn't done it, nothing would've changed."

"That isn't true."

"It *is* true." He pivoted to her, taking a moment to compose himself. "Even if I'd been killed, everything would have played out just the same. My family and Damian would've escaped, you would've found them without me, and I'd be dead, in heaven, sitting on the sidelines just like I am here."

Before Chloe could say anything, he closed the gap between them, standing mere inches away from her. "I'm not proud of what I did," he whispered, "but I don't think I was supposed to roll over and do nothing. And I don't think you are, either. Just be ready."

"Forgive me," Hermes said. Tears filled the messenger's eyes. His hands shook as he lifted them and pressed them to his heart. "The blood you shed, Ethan, covers not your hands, but the hands of all the gods. It was we who created war. It was we who ushered death into this planet. The world suffers the repercussions of our perfidy."

Despite herself, Chloe's heart sank at the sight of Hermes. Standing there weeping, absent his cap or wand, he looked like a common beggar or homeless transient. She didn't want to pity him. Up until now, she'd still been suspicious of him, half expecting him to whisk her away to the Fields of Asphodel like he'd done before.

Iris was right. Bitterness had taken hold of Chloe's heart, but this was her chance to break free of it. Sure, there was still no guarantee that Hermes wasn't up to something, but the tortured look in his eyes was genuine, she knew that much. Right now, in this moment, he was

347

a different god; he was a god pleading with mortals to forgive him.

"Forgive me," he repeated, dropping to his knees as he clasped his hands and held them against his brow. "For all the pain I've brought to you, and all the lies I've told. I swear, and may Duna strike me if my tongue speaks falsely, I will never again work evil against mankind, nor hoodwink any Asher." He prostrated himself across the rocky ground and stayed there for a long while.

Her mind made up, Chloe transformed the wand into an olive branch. She tapped him gently on the shoulder. "You gave this to me once, and I refused it. I hope you'll accept it from me now."

Hermes lifted his head, tears spilling from smiling eyes as he beheld the branch and the green leaves sprouting from it.

Chloe offered her hand and helped him to his feet. "This belongs to you," she said, holding out the wand.

Hermes took her other hand to his lips and kissed it softly. "You reminded me of something just now." He lowered her hand and stepped backward. "Keep the wand. You are far more worthy of it than I am." The golden wings of his sandals buzzed like hummingbird wings as he levitated off the ground.

"Where are you going?" Chloe asked.

"Somewhere I should have gone ages ago," he answered. "I'll return before nightfall." And then he was off, arms outstretched like eagle's wings as he weaved across the sky, disappearing over the dewy, sunbathed hills.

Chloe secured the wand in her girdle and looked back at Ethan. He sat on a log, spinning a stick between his fingers. She sat down next to him, praying silently for the right words to say.

"That was big of you," he said. "While you were talking to Hermes I tried to imagine me forgiving the councilman for what he did to our parents." He shook his head and tossed the stick aside. "I think I'd rather take a tour of the Underworld." He gave a half smile, but it didn't last.

"The Underworld is worse. Lots worse," said Chloe. "It's strange, but I feel better than I have in a long time. Free... relieved...I can't explain it."

"I think I get it. Our emotions can take their toll on us if we hold onto them too long."

"Exactly. It's as though my anger toward him was bleeding into the rest of me. Like poison."

Ethan leaned forward, laughing quietly to himself.

Chloe felt her cheeks flushing. Had she said something wrong? Was there food in her teeth? Had the ironwort stained them brown? "What are you laughing at?"

"Nothing. It's dumb." He pressed two fingers to his lips, as if to stop himself from saying whatever it was he was obviously thinking.

"Please tell me," Chloe said, trying her best not to sound whiny. "Don't make me use the card."

"What card?"

"The card that says this could be the last time we talk, and therefore you'd better tell me." She laughed, but he didn't seem to find it so funny. "Sorry. Everything's going to be fine."

"No, you're right." Ethan took a deep breath and cleared his throat. "I do need to say something."

"Can I say something first?"

He hesitated. "Sure."

"It's my turn to ask for forgiveness. What I said about you just sitting here on the sidelines, that wasn't true. And it was a terrible thing to say."

"But that's what I'm doing, isn't it?" Ethan indicated the log beneath them. "I'm not like the rest of you. I'm not an Asher, and I don't belong here." His gaze drifted to the sheets of rain falling on the horizon. "I don't belong anywhere."

"You *do* belong here," Chloe insisted. "You just don't know it yet. Duna has you here for a reason." She squeezed his hand. "I know it."

Ethan's whole body relaxed as he nodded his head slowly and turned his knees toward hers. "You know, you're good at giving pep talks."

Chloe smiled and let go of his hand to point out a faint double rainbow peeking through the rain. "I never get sick of seeing those." She could feel Ethan staring at her. *Now* what was it? Was there a smudge on her face?

"Can I say my something now?"

There was an unfamiliar tone in his voice that made Chloe's palms get clammy. She could feel her upper lip starting to sweat. Her throat was suddenly swollen, and all she could do was nod.

"Do you remember what I said when I saw you in the stairwell back at the Religious Council building?"

Chloe tried to think back, but all she remembered was Ethan holding a gun to her face. "You asked me who I was."

Ethan laughed. "After that. After you told me it was good to see me."

"Oh. I don't really remember. You probably said the same thing back to me."

"I said it was good to see you, too," Ethan said, "but it was a gigantic lie."

Chloe's eyes skimmed the hillside for a dark hole she could crawl into. Finding none, she sat there, dumbstruck, waiting for the strength to walk away with some semblance of self-respect.

"Chloe, there's not a word strong enough to describe how I felt when I saw you again. It was the best feeling in the world."

Chloe closed her eyes, letting his words echo and sing in her ears. When she opened her eyes again, the rainbow seemed a thousand times brighter. She knew exactly the feeling he was talking about.

"You're not saying anything," Ethan said.

Chloe held up her forefinger, silently shushing him as a smile filled her face. She wanted to savor this. "What does my smile say?"

Ethan took her hand in his, and with his other hand he touched her face, pulling her closer as a wormhole of a different sort enveloped her. His kiss was a doma all its own, and she was powerless against it.

CHAPTER FORTY
KRATÍRAS

K ratíras was perhaps a more cursed place than Mount Othrys, for it was here that the Titans and Olympians first made contact with Petros after their banishment from heaven. Three hundred and sixty rebels had been sent spiraling through the cosmos, each of them secured to a meteorite by shackles they could not shake. Not until they collided with the coarse sands of this foreign world did the chains fall away and their trek to Othrys begin.

The crater that had resulted from the impact was over a mile wide and over three hundred feet deep, forming a perfect circle in the middle of the desert.

It had been Hermes' job, along with the others gifted with flight, to escort the rebels out of the pit. How different things would have been, he mused, if he'd refused to assist them, if he'd left them there to bake in the sun for all eternity. How much less suffering would the incipient race of humans have had to endure?

He had so much to atone for. He'd wronged Iris countless times, and the record of his own offenses against the All-Powerful could fill this crater a thousand fold. Duna would be a fool to forgive him as Iris had.

The sun overhead burned Hermes' uncovered head and scorched his skin. It was as hot as Tartarus here. If he were Duna he would chain him here, in this very spot, never to move again for the rest of time. That was what he deserved, after all: a judgment no milder than the one Apollo had sentenced for the Olympians and Titans before them.

"Why are you here, Hermes?"

Hermes' heart beat wildly as fear, greater than he'd ever felt, even before Apollo's sword, swept through him. He knew that voice. It was the one that had called all life into existence, and the one that had decreed his exile.

"Duna?" he said, laboring to control his anxious breaths as he stretched himself along the basalt ground. He heard footsteps approaching, but dared not look for fear his eyeballs would melt in their sockets at the sight of Duna's glory. Not even Cronus's magnificence came close to rivaling the aura of holiness that clothed the All-Powerful.

"Do not be afraid." Duna's voice was as peaceful as rain and yet as fearsome as thunder. "Since you were created, I have heard everything you've ever said or thought, desiring one day to discern contrition in your words."

The shadow cast by Duna's form felt like the shade of an oak against Hermes' back. Duna's presence never failed to bring relief.

"You have never been far from my thoughts, Hermes. You may have broken my heart, but you never left it."

"I am unworthy of such love, my creator," said Hermes, his whole being trembling with awe. How foolish he'd been to have once deemed himself divine, and to have viewed Hades and Apollo as such. Comparing themselves to Duna was like parasites posing as lions. That Duna was not mocking him now was astonishing.

"Are you truly repentant?" From the nearness of his voice, Hermes knew Duna was kneeling beside him.

"My heart aches with shame, my lord." Hermes lifted his chin so that he might project more clearly. "I have spent centuries trying to outrun my guilt, but it pulls me down like an anchor."

Duna placed a hand on the crown of Hermes' head. "Be thankful for that anchor, my son. So many of your brothers and sisters were lost in the sea of their hubris long ago; now nothing draws them back to me."

"Please, tell me what I must do to earn my way back through heaven's gates."

Restlessness festered in the marrow of Hermes' bones. He could almost smell the stench of his sins. The weight of them crushed his soul from all sides. He had to do something to purge himself, even if it meant repeating all twelve labors of Hercules, or staying here to bake in the sun until the skin peeled off his flesh.

"You only need to trust me. Turn from the unrighteousness of your past and never think on it again. I will make all things new, my son. Your future is in my hands."

Duna's voice fell like dew upon Hermes' ears, a mere whisper of life-giving wind. He couldn't help himself; he began to weep, the mercy radiating from the All-Powerful almost more than his inferior frame could take. When he could cry no more, he started to laugh, for the stench was fading and the weight was falling away.

"I trust you, Duna. I want to be made new."

Duna held his palm against Hermes' forehead. His warm touch sent a surge of heat through Hermes' body, starting in his right foot, traveling all the way up to his head, and rushing like lightning down his side. Then it stopped as his toes continued tingling.

"You are clean. Think no more of making restitution. Grace is a gift I freely and joyfully give."

Hermes wanted to turn and kiss his creator's feet, but he knew the light that covered Duna was sacrosanct. One touch of that light would still his heartbeat, an effect that would be irreversible, despite his immortality.

"Your mercy is more vast than the heavens, deeper than the Great Sea. Your righteousness more mighty than Olympus." Hermes felt his adulation bubbling up from within him, unrestrained and overflowing. He would have continued had Duna not laughed and touched his shoulder.

"Your words bless me, Hermes. Such poetry rivals that of Orpheus. But time is short, and there is something I must show you." He removed his hand from Hermes' brow and stepped away. "Stand, and keep your back to me as you send your gaze out over Kratíras."

Slowly, his body as weak as if he'd been sleeping for days, Hermes rose and turned to face the crater. What he saw took his breath away. The basin, once nothing but an enormous layer of thick sediment, was now a smooth mirror through which he could view perfectly the vault of cloudless sky.

"Tell me who you see," said Duna.

The edges of the crater darkened as a pale oval face materialized in its center, followed by a smattering of freckles, and lastly a percipient pair of copper eyes with red hair spilling over them. It looked like Hermes, and yet the man was far too young.

"Hermogenes," Hermes said, his eyes flickering in the sunlight. "But...but he's just a boy." He indicated the mirror. "This shows him nearly fully grown."

"It's difficult, even for immortals' minds, to fathom the nature of my infinitude," Duna said. "I created time. I am not limited by it."

"You know the end from the beginning, and the beginning from the end," Hermes sang softly, recalling a heavenly chorus he thought he'd long forgotten.

"Keep watching."

The image of Hermogenes' face faded as his mother's profile took its place. Leto was older, with tiny lines framing her eyes and mouth, and more silver in her hair; even so, she took Hermes' breath away. As she parted her lips to speak, Hermogenes appeared before her, clothed in white robes, his head shaven.

"You always wanted to be an Asher," she said tenderly to her son, "and now that your eighteenth year has come and gone, I know you are grieved. It breaks my heart to see my boy so crestfallen."

"I only desired a doma in order that I might serve you more completely and become a son you could be proud of." The lad hung his head. "Now, for the rest of my life I will be known only as Leto's bastard."

Leto rushed to him and threw her arms around his neck. "Mark my words, Hermo. This day shall bring an end to your sorrows. I will give you a gift far better than any doma stored away in Duna's coffer."

Hermogenes lifted his head. "What gift?"

"A long life with which to rule and reign beside me," she said, her gray eyes flashing as they did whenever she lied.

"The boy is half immortal," Hermes protested to Duna. "Surely he must know that his days are destined to be long."

No response from Duna. He didn't need to give one; Hermes knew what Leto was plotting.

"Mama, you are not making any sense. It's impossible for me to become—"

Leto gripped her son's shoulders and gave him a shake. "You know better than to tell me what is impossible."

Hermogenes closed his eyes, waiting patiently for the chastisement to end.

"I'm so sorry, my love." Leto kissed his forehead and dropped her hands onto his. "There is a way. A way that will please the lords of Hades as well as serve to advance us one step closer in our quest to subvert their sovereignty."

Hermogenes brought her hands to his lips and kissed them. "Tell me what I must do, Mama. I know that all things must bend to the will of Mania."

Leto smiled as she drew a dagger from the hidden sheath on her thigh. "You must be sacrificed upon Olympus. And then shall Hades mingle your blood with the ichor of the gods."

The surface of the mirror began to move like waves on the sea, obscuring the two faces until they had receded into the walls of the opposite rim. In less than the blink of an eye, the crater floor had returned to bedrock.

Terrible despair gripped Hermes' heart. It had pained him enough to prepare, however briefly, a libation offering of his son's pure blood. But to see Apollo's plan brought to fruition was almost more than he could bear.

"Why have you shown me this?" he asked, inclining his head toward Duna.

"This is what the future could become should the Ashers succeed only in preventing Leto from obtaining immortality. Her legacy would continue within a man whom not even death can conquer, not for centuries."

"So it's not already decided."

Hermes' head spun as he tried to separate the future from the present while at the same time making peace with his past. He'd always thought time was as steady as the Styx, moving immutably in one direction only. That had all changed the day Chloe tore through Iris's fire tunnel. Were it not for that, he would be with Leto this second, plotting the immolation of Eirene.

"The refugees behind the wall have been praying ceaselessly since the night Chloe and Damian joined their number."

A silver bowl of water appeared in the air before Hermes' chest. He nodded his thanks and drank as Duna continued.

"The Vessel has bolstered their faith, as it has restored yours. I honor my people's prayers by giving you this warning." He waited until Hermes' thirst was slaked before saying his final words. "Your son must be spared."

As Duna walked away, Hermes piped up with a single request. "Please, if you wouldn't mind indulging me before you go. Why did the oracle prophesy one Vessel, and yet the Ashers are two?"

Duna neared him again and placed a fatherly hand on his shoulder. "You're not the only skilled strategist in the cosmos, Hermes. Apollo has been expecting one individual, has he not?"

Hermes smiled. "Of course. And by that strategy the Vessel was able to escape the future snare set by my brothers."

"The theory you posed to Apollo was correct," said Duna, the warmth of his glory like a hot spring gushing around Hermes. "The Moonbow was the signpost, as it has always been."

"So you could even hear the conferences held in Hades."

"As I told you before, my son," Duna whispered, "I have heard your every word. I have waited for you to call upon me as a father watches by moonlight for his son who has wandered astray."

Hermes felt Duna's glory slowly departing as the relentless sun began to beat down on him once more. All at once he knew the kind of father Hermogenes needed, and with not one ounce of guilt, nor stiver or shame left to stop him, he made up his mind: that's what he would become.

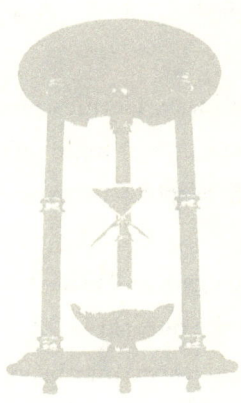

CHAPTER FORTY-ONE
MISSION

T hank Duna!" Chloe exclaimed.

Beside her on the ground, Charis jumped from her sleep. Only Chloe and Ethan had stayed awake, waiting for Hermes to come back from whatever errand he'd suddenly felt compelled to run.

"You haven't done anything yet, have you?" Hermes kept his voice low over the crackling fire.

"If we had," replied Chloe, "either Damian would be here or I'd be...well, dead, probably."

"Chloe..." Ethan murmured as he squeezed her hand. He'd been holding it so long she could hardly feel it.

"It was just a joke."

"It's no laughing matter, Chloe," said Hermes.

Chloe thought Hermes looked different, changed somehow. "Where have you been?"

"To the place where war and tyranny began." Hermes' visage brightened as he looked up at the twinkling stars, as if he and they shared a secret. "Ironically, it's there that I was cleansed of all the blood I've shed and all the lies I've told."

Charis sat up and rubbed the sleep from her eyes. "You've been with Duna, haven't you?"

Hermes nodded and held a hand to his chest. "Aye, and I have each of you, as well as those absent, to thank for helping rescue my wayward soul."

He looked at Chloe, his moist eyes smiling at her. "Your obedience has sent ripples out through the waves of eternity. And by Duna's grace, one of them touched me."

"They've touched all of us," Chloe said. "It pains me to say it, but without your help, we wouldn't have Orpheus."

"And we wouldn't have the *pýli*," added Ethan. "It's not every day you get to see a visual record of the first time Duna ever spoke to mankind."

"Ah, but you forget that without me you wouldn't be in this predicament to begin with," Hermes countered.

"Don't give yourself too much credit, Hermes," said Chloe. "If you hadn't agreed to join Apollo and Hades' little mission to rule the world, I'm sure they would've found some other flying, wand-wielding madman to fill the role."

Hermes chuckled, then gestured to the wand sheathed at her side. "Now who's the madman? Or madwoman, I should say."

Chloe removed the wand then pointed it at him playfully. "Touché."

"Congratulations, Hermes," said Ethan. "It's good to see you happy."

Hermes' smile faded as the notes of a lyre came floating through the trees, followed by the sound of footsteps.

"Orpheus!" Chloe shouted. "Stop playing or you'll put us to sleep."

The music stopped and Orpheus stepped into the firelight. "My apologies. I'm a bit rusty. I must be at my best if I'm to sedate this villainess. When, exactly, do we march out?"

Chloe looked at Hermes. "I just remembered. The plan you laid out for us earlier didn't include Orpheus."

"It does indeed," answered Hermes. "We need him for another purpose, one of no slight importance."

Orpheus's skeptical eyes narrowed to slits as he lowered his lyre to his side. "What purpose?"

"That of saving my son."

Orpheus shook his head slightly, as if doing so would make Hermes' words make sense. "You have a son?"

Hermes nodded.

"With Mania?"

Hermes nodded again, but more hesitantly this time.

"This is news to us as well, Orpheus," Ethan said.

Chloe took a deep breath. "It's in the past. It's forgiven. Don't be angry, Damian."

She turned to Hermes and asked softly, albeit through gritted teeth. "Would you mind telling us why you didn't mention your son before?"

"I was ashamed, which is itself a shameful thing to say." Hermes' eyes fell to the fire, where they lingered for long, still moments. "After my time with the All-Powerful, shame no longer dwells in me, least of all concerning my flesh and blood."

"I'm glad, Hermes, I really am, but can't we just focus on getting my brother back right now?" Chloe could feel her nerves starting to unravel as she thought of Damian in chains in some dank cell, expecting to die at any moment, probably wondering if she knew he was there and, if she did, whether she cared.

"Duna showed me the future," said Hermes. "A potential future, I should say. And in it, my son, Hermogenes, is sacrificed to Hades by Leto's hand. This abomination assures him immortality, or so she has convinced him, even if the ambrosia is withheld from his mother."

"What do you mean, 'or so she has convinced him'?" Charis asked. "He cannot be granted immortality?"

"Quite the contrary. With half ichor in his veins, he's already nearly immortal. Leto only means to use his sacrifice as a vehicle to gain her closer access to Hades' throne."

Orpheus plucked a sad, single note with his finger, and its sound seemed to echo to the moon. "What would you have me do?"

Hermes paced a few steps, head down and hands joined behind his back. "The lad, as all boys do, adores his mother. As such, he will not stand to see her precious ambrosia taken from her. He will intervene, and afterward bear even more affection for her."

"So Orpheus needs to put him to sleep," said Ethan.

Hermes stopped walking. "Exactly. While Chloe distracts Leto, Orpheus will sit outside his window and start to play. Charis, it will be your responsibility to bring the boy back here, behind the wall, as soon as you can."

Charis grinned. "I can do that."

"What can I do?" Ethan asked.

"Wait for us," said Chloe. "And if you don't mind, pray while you're at it. Hard."

Hermes beckoned them to their feet with an urgent wave of his arm. "Come now. Let us finish this before dawn. Orpheus's music is more potent beneath a theater of stars."

Charis and Orpheus followed the messenger down the hill, but Ethan held Chloe's hand tightly.

"Ethan, I have to go," she whispered. "I'll be back, I promise." She lifted herself up and lightly kissed his forehead.

"I want to go with you," he said. "I don't care if it's dangerous. I just want to be with you."

Chloe lifted their interlaced fingers and brought them to her chest. "You are with me. Right here."

It was well after midnight when Leto spotted the party making its way toward her walls. They stood out starkly on the open road, the stars like lanterns beaming down on them. *They are wise to approach as friends*, she thought.

"It appears you were correct." She turned to Damian, who was still chained inside the kitchen. "Your sister comes for you. Unless you want to watch her die, you'll let her make her deal with me."

If Damian's glare were a sword, it would have pierced clean through her skull. She smiled at him, amused by the hatred burning like cinders in his eyes. She'd never been looked at with such contempt; she had killed any who had come close to regarding her in such a way.

She went to the courtyard gates and flung them open. It had been ages since she had had real company. She looked around, taking in the disarray of what had once been as pristine as the Eirenian temple, every tree and flower planted by the touch of Hermes' wand. She wasn't expecting visitors, and the house was such a shambles.

With wide, slow strokes, her arms sent swift wind to sweep the dirt from the floors and carry away any remaining rubble from where the lightning had struck the owl. The owl's carcass, half eaten by Panther, she left as a subtle warning.

She plucked a larkspur and stuck it behind her ear as she strode into the kitchen. "This will be the last night I enjoy wine," she mused, pouring a cupful. "After this I shall sustain myself with nothing but nectar and sweet ambrosia."

"Have you ever stopped to think that maybe *nothing* will satisfy you?"

Leto clenched her fists, restraining the fury within them. "Immortality always satisfies," she said.

"Uh-huh. And that's why things are going so well for Hermes and Mnemosyne, wherever they are."

"Silence!" Leto took a damp rag from the table, stormed over to Damian and secured it over his mouth. "You're awfully bold for a man no better off than an unlucky lamb picked for slaughter."

She waved at the party halted at the gates. "Come in, my friends. My doors are open to you."

There were three in total: two girls—one the Asher, she presumed—and a young man, a handsome chap with hair as long as a woman's and downcast eyes fixed shyly on his sandals.

"I hope you don't mind that I didn't come alone," the blond girl said. "Charis brought us here, and my new friend from the village gave directions."

368

"I don't mind at all," replied Leto, smiling cordially at each of them. "They may leave now. When your brother is free, your friends can guide you back."

Chloe turned to her companions. "I'll see you later."

The pair gave her long, unwilling stares.

"I swear on the graves of my beloved mother and father," Leto told them, "your friend will reunite with you shortly." This, paired with a solemn bow of her head, seemed to satisfy them. They threw their cloaks over their heads and set off into the shadows.

"Tell me," Leto said when they were out of earshot, "how did you know I wished to see you? Did that miscreant Hermes pay you a visit?"

The girl's head cocked sideways. "Hermes? Why in Zeus' name would he want to help me? Do you have any idea what he did to me where I come from?"

"I can imagine," said Leto. "He cares for no one's interests but his own."

Chloe folded her arms and sighed bitterly into the cool night air. "You can say that again."

Leto smiled. She couldn't help but feel a sort of solidarity with this rival. After all, an enemy of Hermes' was a friend of hers—at least for another few hours.

"What is your name?"

"Chloe. And it was Carya who told me my brother was here. Do you know her?"

A sour taste crept up Leto's throat. Indeed, she knew the messenger. Carya had appeared to her just after her father died, speaking in rhymes like a blathering fool, making not one iota of sense except for what she'd said about Hermes, whom she called "the beguiling imp of Hades." Carya had warned Leto not to listen to his lies. She'd said his promises were empty and that he would only bring more heartache to her already woeful life.

But Leto had seen no other alternative. If Duna, whom Carya claimed to represent, cared anything about her, he would have done more than send down some spindly waif who offered only worthless words of caution. He would have stopped Hermes from exiting that fissure to begin with. He would have swooped Leto up from her homelessness and given her a new family, a new purpose, a new life.

Leto knew she had become Mania long before Hermes' charms won her over. Her heart had turned black the moment she knew the All-Powerful had left her to rot in the ghostlands of Ēlektōr.

"I don't know how you tolerate that singing loon," Leto hissed at Chloe.

"Her rhyming does get a little annoying."

"As does her nosiness."

Leto glanced around at the nearby poplars and atop the pergola. She wondered how many times Carya had perched among the trees to spy on her late-night lessons with

Hermes. She was probably here now, weeping in silence over the deceased owl or Damian's present plight.

Carya's compassion turned Leto's stomach. Even on the morning Carya had appeared, her crystal eyes seemed to pierce straight to her soul. They'd wept at what they saw, and she'd pleaded with Leto to take her words to heart. Maybe if she'd done more than speak eloquent words. Maybe if she'd done something to free Leto from her undeserved circle of Hades. Maybe then she'd have received Carya's message in a more favorable manner.

"Did she tell you what it is I request of you?" Leto asked, shoving the messenger's cherubic face from her mind.

"She mentioned something about ambrosia. I'll be more than happy to get it for you, on one condition."

Leto tapped her foot impatiently. "I have almost as little tolerance for conditions as I do for Carya."

"I want you to let my brother go first. I think I know better than to take you at your word."

"Even when I've given it to you under oath, sworn on my parents' graves?"

Chloe nodded. "I'm afraid so."

Leto couldn't help but grin. "Very well. Come." She led Chloe to the kitchen and pointed to Damian. "I had no choice but to muzzle him. He's mouthier than the harpies."

"I get it." Chloe removed the rag from Damian's head. "I probably would have done the same." She went to the table and brought him back the bowl of wine.

371

Damian began to whisper to Chloe, but she held up a warning hand for him to see. "Remember what I told you, Damian." One more word from him and she'd slap him unconscious. She didn't always need her doma to make people obey. She helped him to his feet and gave him a hug. "I'm sorry I didn't get here sooner."

"I'm sorry I got here at all," he said, as he glared once again at Leto. "Everything we heard about her is the truth."

Leto smiled, pleased. "I'm glad to hear I've lived up to my reputation. I'll unlock his shackles, but first you must separate from him and maintain your distance. I know how his doma works, and I won't let you fool me with it."

"Perfectly understandable." Chloe backed up to the hearth.

Once the shackles and fetters were loosed from Damian, he stood, but didn't move.

"No thank-you?" Leto asked. "You're a free man now. At least thank your sister."

He looked at Leto coldly and bent down to tie his shoe.

"Fine. Be gone with you. Wait by the shed outside the wall. Panther will keep you company." The dog wagged his tail and lifted his snout to lick Damian's wrist, red and raw from the iron's abrasion. "If I see him stray, I'll know you've left. But you know better than that, hmm?"

When Damian gave a half nod, she said, "Excellent."

It was then that she saw it: a faint gold flicker winking at her from the folds of Chloe's cloak.

CHAPTER FORTY-TWO
CORINNA

Leto waited in silence as Damian rounded the corner and disappeared from the courtyard. Then she crossed to Chloe and placed her hands lightly on her shoulders.

"May I take your cloak?" she asked. "You must be burning up here so close to the hearth."

Chloe pulled the garment closer. "No," she said abruptly. "Thank you. I'm cold-natured."

Leto gripped the cowl with both hands and tugged Chloe backwards. "I insist," she said, swinging her against the table.

Chloe struggled to right herself and her cloak fell open, exposing the end of the golden wand that gleamed innocently in the firelight.

"I knew it," Leto growled, knocking the full amphora from the table. The red wine pooled like blood on the floor. "Hermes did betray me and send you here. And with his wand, no less." She lunged for it, but Chloe's hand was too fast.

"You wanted me to come, didn't you?" Chloe pointed the wand at the wine-stained floor. "Hermes told me not to mention him to you."

"I should say not. He doesn't want to take the blame for my murder."

"I didn't come to murder you. This is for self-defense. I didn't show it to you because I'd hoped we could be civil with one another. Showing your host one's weapon, even a defensive one, doesn't exactly scream, 'I come in peace.'"

"So we make a bargain, then," said Leto, her heart rate slowing as reason returned to her. "I don't harm you with my powers, and you don't harm me with Hermes'."

"Sounds fair to me. Now where, or should I say when, do I find this ambrosia you're looking for?"

Leto raised an eyebrow at the wand. It reminded her, for a moment, of Eros's arrow. "To the dawn of Petros, when immortals and men still dwelled together, long before there was enmity between the gods."

"Sounds safe."

"It'll be safe enough, especially for an Asher. All you have to do is go to the cape of Tainaron, find Eros and Psyche on the eve of their wedding day, take the ambrosia prepared for the bride, and bring it back."

Chloe picked at her fingernails. "And what if I can't?"

Leto considered this as a strong wind rustled the trees. She would have no problem killing the girl's friends if she failed to obtain the ambrosia, but she couldn't let it come to that. She needed the ambrosia, and quickly, before Hermes could hatch another plot against her.

"You can," she said, "and you will."

"How can you be so sure?"

"Because I'm going with you."

⟨

Chloe knew Hermes and the others might never forgive her, but she was going to change the plan and risk her life in the process. It was only a matter of time before Leto took the wand, and Chloe was willing to bet she'd use it for far more than self-defense; sooner or later she would use it, along with her own doma, to take down her rivals and wipe the Ashers from the face of Petros, just as she'd planned all along. Once the ambrosia was in Leto's system, all bargaining and talks of peace would be over.

Chloe couldn't let that happen.

"Hold onto me," she told Leto, wrapping her hand tightly around the wand. She had the feeling that if Ethan were here, he'd tell her to knock Leto out cold while she had the chance. But she knew in her heart that he knew better than that. Like her, he had to believe deep down that killing Leto wasn't the answer. And that maybe, just maybe, Leto could change.

Leto wrapped her fingers around the back of Chloe's girdle, and Chloe jumped at the fiery heat of her hand.

"I beg your pardon," said Leto blithely. "My hands get a little warm whenever I feel threatened."

"Well, I hope you don't feel threatened by darkness and a little motion sickness."

"Are you stalling?"

Chloe sighed. "No. I'm just warning you."

She closed her eyes and quieted her mind long enough to focus on the single word Damian had whispered to her before he left: *Corinna.* The black tunnel rattled and shook as the buzzing sound popped in her ears. Bright flashes, like tiny lightning bolts, electrified the swirling shadows around them. They were going somewhere, that was for sure.

"How marvelous," Leto shouted, her hand much cooler than it had been seconds ago. She wasn't threatened in the least. She was enjoying this. "It's like a storm."

A few minutes later, the rattling stopped and the flashes faded into a deafening downpour of rain. When the tunnel disappeared, Chloe could see the faint silhouette of a mountain range, backlit by the cloud-covered moon. There seemed to be nothing and no one around. Where had she brought them?

"This is the *desert*," Leto yelled, pushing Chloe away from her. "We're supposed to be by an ocean."

"How do you know?"

"Do you smell the sea?"

"All I smell is rain," Chloe said, trying to suppress any signs of fear. *Let this be the right place*, she prayed, *and the right choice.*

"I'll prove it to you." Leto stretched out her arms to the storm overhead, and with a slow, controlled exhale, turned the sky as bright as noon with rapid bursts of thunderbolts.

Chloe saw a giant cage fifty yards ahead, and a bird, ten times the size of an eagle, peering at them from within.

"Mother..." Leto dropped her arms and took off for the cage, then fell on her knees before it. "Stop!" she shouted at the sky as she lifted a defiant fist into the air. The rain ceased. The lightning fled. The clouds broke apart. The full moon was free to shine again.

Chloe threw off her hood and approached the cage, standing a safe distance away. The gryphon's yellow eyes were staring at Leto, the black-tipped talons of her front feet clawing at the wooden platform on which she was perched.

"Mother, do you know who I am?" Leto said, her voice higher, sweeter than before, like a child's.

The gryphon's tufted tail swung back and forth. Using her lion-like paws, she jumped off the platform, landing in front of the cage's log latch. Motionless, the two looked at one another as rain slid down the bars and splashed their faces.

The gryphon opened her mouth as if to speak, but only a soft squawk came out.

Then, as if she was standing right beside her, Chloe heard Carya's words whisper in her mind: *Orpheus must save Hermogenes, and Chloe must undo the spell.*

The first part she'd understood, as had everyone else. If all had gone according to plan, Orpheus, Hermogenes and Charis would be back at the village now, enjoying a celebratory cup of ironwort tea. But the last part had been brushed over, forgotten about as seemingly more important things, such as winning over Orpheus and getting away from the crazy snake lady in one piece, stole their attention.

Now, however, Chloe realized it was just as important. The spell Carya referred to had to be about this, about Leto's mother.

"Corinna's cursed," Chloe whispered. She went closer to the cage, slowly unsheathing the wand. "I'm going to try something."

Leto turned around and eyed the raised wand in Chloe's hand. "If you hurt her, I will kill you."

"You think I don't know that?" Chloe closed her eyes and prayed aloud. "Duna, I know this isn't the body you gave Leto's mother. I ask you to use this wand to heal her, to undo whatever curse made her this way." She kept her eyes shut, continuing to pray in her head.

"Something's happening," Leto shouted.

Chloe opened her eyes to see the gryphon's charcoal feathers being shed from her body, revealing smooth white skin. Two wings of pale violet unfurled and fell around her like a cape. Her hooked yellow beak shaped itself into a human nose as her head shrank, and auburn waves of hair tumbled down onto her bare shoulders.

"Leto." Corinna smiled as she coughed and brought a trembling hand to her throat.

Leto laughed and cried simultaneously as she reached through the bars and joined hands with her mother. "You know me?"

Corinna cupped Leto's chin in her hand. "I knew somehow I would see you again," she said, looking at Chloe and the wand still hanging from her hand, "just as I knew I would one day be released from that prison, either by death or the benevolent hand of a god." She looked at the feathers blanketing the cage floor. "It was transforming me, replacing my soul with that of a beast. Your name," she said, stroking Leto's hair, "was one of the last ones I could still remember."

Tears spilled shamelessly from Leto's eyes as she looked back at Chloe, whose own eyes were welling as she thought of her reunion with her father in the Fields of Asphodel, an occasion just as miraculous as this.

"Let's get you out of there." Chloe reached up for the log just as Leto ripped the wand from her belt.

"You think you're so clever, don't you?" Leto roared. She pointed the wand at the log and split it cleanly down the middle.

"Leto, what are you doing?" Corinna asked, stepping back into the cage.

"Come with me, Mother." Leto reached for her mother's hand. "The poor sap thought she'd changed my mind, but she's only given me an even stronger advantage."

"Please, Corinna," Chloe said, as the rain began to sprinkle on her face, "talk some sense into your daughter. She wants me to take her back in time to get the ambrosia that will make her immortal." What Chloe saw in Corinna's eyes made her blood run cold. She gasped. "No! I thought *your* curse was the one I was supposed to break."

Leto threw back her head and gave a devilish laugh. "I'd planned all along to come back for my mother and father. You rearranging things did little to inconvenience me." She pointed the wand at her mother, and a scarlet robe appeared on her body, followed by leather sandals on her feet.

Chloe looked at Corinna, clearly seeing now the deviousness radiating from within her. Every word she'd said had been a lie, and Chloe's brilliant plan had blown up in her face.

"I'm curious," Leto said to Chloe, "about what exactly you expected to accomplish by bringing me here."

Chloe didn't answer. What good would it do to try and explain her reasoning to someone who was incapable of comprehending it? She'd hoped that helping Leto get her mother back would change her heart, that their reunion would grant Leto a contentment that far outweighed the attainment of endless world domination, and that she would realize it.

But Leto hadn't gained contentment, just an accomplice. Chloe wouldn't be surprised if Leto killed her mother in cold blood if she ever stood in her way. Luckily for Corinna, though, she was cut from the same cloth as her maniacal daughter.

"So you want to save your father even though he turned your mother into a monster and kept her inside a cage," Chloe said.

"It wasn't always going to be this way," Corinna said. "Diokles has chosen to keep my true identity a secret until the time comes to show Petros who I really am."

"Well, the secret's out now, isn't it? How will Diokles react when he sees his killing machine is back to being a woman again?"

"Come now, Chloe," said Leto, beckoning her with the wand. "Don't worry your silly little head with such useless questions. It's time to hold up your end of the bargain. I let your brother go, and now you fetch me the ambrosia."

Corinna kissed her daughter's cheek. "I always knew you would grow up to be brilliant. Your father will be so proud."

"I'm not taking you to get the ambrosia, Leto," Chloe said. "And without me, you can't get back to the future to carry out your threats."

Corinna flapped open her wings, their span nearly as wide as the cage behind her. Even without her sharp beak and pointy talons, she was no less intimidating. It took little imagination for Chloe to consider what she could do with those wings, like carry her over the Great Sea and drop her into the middle of it.

"Don't be careless with your words," Corinna warned. "They could get you into trouble."

"I've never meant anything more sincerely in my life, Corinna. If you want to kill me, so be it. I happen to know that death isn't all that bad."

Leto sneered as dirt collected around her feet and wind whistled through the cage. "Death, perhaps not. But dying... I can make it so terrible you'll wish you were never born."

"Then do it," Chloe challenged.

Corinna bent down, ready to charge her, but Leto gripped her arm. "Don't. I need her alive a while longer."

"I told you, I'm not helping you," Chloe repeated. Ethan's face flashed through her brain, followed by the feeling of his lips upon hers. What she wouldn't give to kiss him one last time.

"You don't need her, Leto," Corinna said. "Your body may die, but your name shall live on forever. Make an example of her. Tomorrow we can take her to the temple and show Petros what happens to anyone who fails to cooperate with Diokles' daughter."

She looked at Chloe with sadistic joy, her eyes like the snuffs of dead candles. "Her screams will ring out through the streets and fill every plain and valley. And no Asher will ever dare defy you again."

CHAPTER FORTY-THREE
PRISONERS

V ery well." Leto waved the wand, effortlessly creating a pair of shackles.

Chloe closed her eyes, half tempted to leave this place now and be done with it, but she knew she couldn't. She'd never forgive herself for saving her own skin while leaving the world worse off than it had been before she'd traveled back in time to begin with. With Diokles, Leto and Corinna in league with each other, who knew what havoc they could wreak throughout Petros.

It was her fault, and she was resolved to die at Leto's hands. Ethan would understand one day, at least she hoped he would.

"You don't have to do this," she said, her voice shaking as Leto slowly made her way toward her through the pouring rain. "You don't have to kill me, or anyone else. You can have your family back and take them to the future to meet your son. You can start over together."

"Why would I want to do that when I can stay here and kill Iris?" Leto grabbed Chloe's wrists and secured them in the shackles. "She'll be so surprised to see me here, don't you think?"

She yanked Chloe forward and led her past the cage where a lone tamarisk tree waved flimsily in the wind along the sheer cliff's edge, as if asking to be struck by lightning. She pushed Chloe to the ground, locked a pair of fetters around her ankles, and created heavy chains with which to bind her to the tree's slender trunk. The smell of hot metal filled the air as the wand glowed orange in Leto's hand.

"As a thank-you for what you did for my mother, I've decided not to kill you." She smiled as lightning illuminated the long dark drop below them.

Chloe wondered how many dead men's bones were down there, and how long it would be before hers joined them.

"That's not even me creating the storm," Leto said. "It's your beloved Duna. You're not worth wasting my power on, anyway. I'll give him the pleasure of taking your life."

Chloe's heart skipped a beat as she saw it appear, band by band, color by color in the yellow haze of moonlit sky still untouched by the storm. The Moonbow was there, watching her. *I can die now, right here. If this is what Duna wants for me.*

"Leto!" Corinna shouted.

Leto silenced the wind with her fingertips and craned her neck toward the cage. "No," she whispered, then gathered her robes and ran to her mother.

"Chloe."

A voice had whispered in Chloe's ear, and she tried to turn around. It was Ethan's voice, but she couldn't see him. She watched as the Centaur's blue blade sliced through the shackles and fetters.

"I tied up Corinna in the cage," Ethan said. "Stay here, I'll come back for you."

"What...how..."

"I'll tell you later. Just stay here," he repeated, letting his hand linger on hers a second longer, allowing her to see his face, if only for an instant.

Chloe felt a rush of air as he ran past her, and she breathed in the slight scent of his sweat mixed with rain. *Protect him*, she prayed.

"It's the other Asher!" Leto cried out above the thunder's din. She ran toward Chloe, open hands raised to the sky, the wand nowhere in sight.

"Hurt her and I'll kill you," came Ethan's voice.

Chloe watched the wand zoom toward Leto in a golden blur, striking her square in the chest. Leto reeled back with a yelp, then found her balance and gnashed her teeth at the air.

"Who are you?" she barked. "You don't sound like Damian. I command you to reveal yourself."

Another blow, this time strong enough to knock Leto down and send her over the cage's threshold. Before she could stand, a new latch, this one nearly two feet thick and made of steel, appeared across the bars. They were trapped. Inside, Leto ran to the bars and screamed until her lungs finally gave out and she collapsed to her knees.

"Chloe." Chloe jumped at Ethan's whisper in her ear. "We can't leave them here," he whispered, "and we can't take them back to Ourania, either. It's too dangerous."

"Take me to the cage," said Chloe.

She knew just where to send them, as well as another spell she could undo; she only hoped this idea would turn out to be better than the last.

Ethan took her hand, his body appearing on her left side. She couldn't wait to get home and find out how he could be here right now. Slowly, they made their way to the far side of the cage. Chloe grasped a bar lightly, careful not to make a sound. She mouthed: *Ready?*

Ethan nodded.

Corinna bawled and savagely beat her wings while Leto dragged her nails along the cage's wooden floor, sparks flying from her fingers. Chloe knew that if she didn't move quickly, Leto would burn her way to freedom. She closed her eyes and envisioned the island. She had never wanted to see or think about it again, but it was the only place she knew where Leto and Corinna could live without harming anyone.

Except for maybe one person.

Aeaea.

Chloe concentrated on the name and the beautiful sorceress it belonged to, a woman who would waste no time turning Leto into a rodent at the first sign of assault.

The lightning gave way to the darkness of the wormhole. Inside the cage, fury raged, increasing in volume and intensity until Chloe was sure the prisoners had escaped. She could feel the heat of their breath on her skin and the wind from Corinna's flapping wings. Sparks from Leto's hands flew through the air, intersecting with the tunnel's erratic flashing as Leto continued to claw at the floor.

And then, the salty smell Leto had wanted all along, followed by the feeling of warm soft sand underfoot and the familiar chirping of a bird, a parakeet whose name Chloe remembered was Erato, the first of Circe's pets she'd met that day with Orpheus.

The sun's hot beams tore through the tunnel, revealing the calm, aquamarine-colored ocean and the low-flying seagulls hunting for fish. Still clutching Ethan's hand, Chloe gazed eastward at Circe's palace. Already, Erato, or perhaps some other of Circe's winged spies, was flying toward it, no doubt to inform its mistress of her guests.

I'm here to free you! Chloe wanted to yell at the bird, but she decided to let her actions speak for her.

She took the wand from Ethan's free hand and directed it at the compound, then waved it in small, smooth circles, completely aware of how ridiculous she must look to Ethan, who had no idea who or what lay behind Circe's walls.

He nudged her side. Nothing was happening. Even Leto and Corinna had paused their tantrums.

Shouts and laughter spilled from the courtyard and trickled through the surrounding shade trees, followed by the sound of clapping hands and swinging gates.

The prisoners were free.

Chloe could see them, an army of young men, running into the ocean, embracing it as if it were their dearest love. They splashed themselves again and again, dove down like ducks and reemerged only to go under again. She'd never seen such happiness, such rejoicing over something as simple and common as ocean waves.

"Stop, all of you!" cried Circe.

Chloe's eyes swung back toward the courtyard to see the witch's magenta robes sweeping out of the shadows and onto the sparkling sand. She marched toward the men, at least a hundred of them, then stopped when they turned to face her, drawing the swords from their scabbards.

"Let us be, if you wish to keep your head!" cried one.

"My princes," Circe said, her tone now sweetened at the sight of their weapons raised, "I fear you're making a grave mistake. In your human state, you're mortal and will be met with death one day, and perhaps very soon, on your voyage home. Stay with me. I have treated you only with kindness."

"You've treated us as dogs and slaves," shouted the same man.

His comrades affirmed his words with rounds of whoops that might never have ended if the man hadn't raised his hand to silence them.

"From this day forward," he continued, "no man, save he without sense or regard for his soul, will set foot upon this island. Far and wide, all Petros will know that Aeaea is accursed and its chieftain as black-hearted as Hades."

Circe bowed her head and backed away. What else could she do? *She* was the helpless creature now, alone, abandoned, and nearly forgotten. All she would have left once they departed was a frieze of the men's frightened faces, each one etched with torment, forever depicting the terror they'd felt when Circe's spell overtook them.

"Help us!" Leto shouted from the cage.

Circe approached. A man of equal beauty trailed behind her, his eyes downcast on the hem of her robe. Chloe had a hunch this was the parakeet, Erato. Circe claimed he was named after the muse of lyric poetry. For reasons unknown, he remained loyal to her, so perhaps he was the one she truly loved.

"Have you done this?" Circe asked Leto, circling the cage as she gestured at the sailors, who were chopping down branches with their swords. "And what abhorrent hybrid is in there with you?"

Leto spread her hands at her sides and cast her gaze toward the cloudless sky.

"What are you doing?" Circe asked, an amused smile on her face. "Do you expect Zeus to swoop down from heaven and release you?"

"Strike her, Leto!" Corinna called out.

"I'm trying," Leto shouted back. Her domas were drained.

Chloe knew she and Ethan had better leave before theirs stopped working, too.

As if he'd read her mind, Ethan squeezed Chloe's hand. "Time to go."

Chloe looked once more at the cage, where Corinna was crying and Circe was laughing as Leto pounded her fists on the floor.

"Laugh while you can," Leto said, looking up at Circe from beneath her disheveled mess of hair. "When my powers return, I'll send a lightning bolt straight through that pretty throat of yours and you'll never laugh again. You won't even be able to weep as you choke on gurgling blood and feel flames consume you from the inside out."

"We'll see about that," said Circe. "This island, if you haven't heard, is filled with wondrous vegetation. My warning to you: choose carefully what you eat. There is a fate worse than death, as the sailors behind me can attest. And if I'm dead, you will not avoid it."

Peas in a pod, thought Chloe. Then she sheathed Hermes' wand and set her thoughts on Damian, Orpheus, and the glow of a warm campfire.

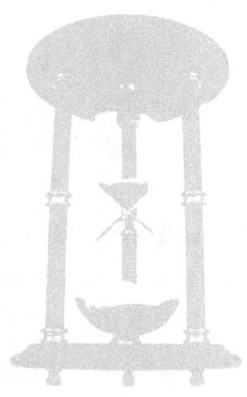

CHAPTER FORTY-FOUR

MEMORIES

S trange music, unlike anything Chloe had ever heard, flooded the walls of the wormhole as her eyes adjusted from the blackness to amber shafts of light. The rhythm of the instruments was joyful, and the drumbeat full of life as a chorus of voices began to sing.

"Sing! Sing! Sing!
Make music and lift up your hands!

DIANA TYLER

Darkness has been defeated!
Love and light forever stands!"

Ethan wrapped his arm around her waist. "Chloe, look."

Chloe recognized downtown Eirene only by the dome-shaped Religious Council building at the end of Eiríni Boulevard. Before it stood an aluminum stage, on which a band was playing instruments she'd never seen before.

The area was foreign to her in every way. The sidewalks, typically reserved solely for use by council employees, were crowded with people. Men, women and children lifted and clapped their hands, singing and swaying to the song. Some held long-stemmed roses, olive branches and balloons, waving them high over their heads. Many more balloons were tied to streetlights and open doors, from which delicious smells were wafting. The younger children sang with their mouths half full of pastries as they gleefully flicked icing off their fingertips.

In the middle of the street danced teenage girls, each one waving multicolored streamers, and executing graceful pirouettes and long leaps through the air. They were dressed in white leotards covered with golden sequins, which made their movements all the more mesmerizing. As far as Chloe could tell, the only thing that distinguished one from another was the color of the tiaras atop their heads. The foremost rows of dancers wore tiaras of various shades of red, while those immediately behind them were crowned with resplendent hues of orange, followed by yellow, green, blue, indigo and violet.

The Moonbow's colors, Chloe thought.

"Ethan," she said, linking her arm with his, "where—I mean *when*—are we?"

As the young girls moved down the boulevard, the band's song died down and an old, gray-haired man stepped onto the stage. Chloe recognized him instantly, for he was only one of nine men permitted to live so long: the chief councilman.

"No..." The colors around her faded away as her vision focused only on his feeble frame. "He's still here." She stood on her tiptoes and spun around in circles. "We have to find Damian."

"Eirenians, I welcome you to the five thousandth festival of Therismos," came the councilman's voice through a nearby speaker. The crowd erupted with applause and beat their branches together as his face appeared on giant screens beside the stage. "It is with this festival that all of Petros celebrates the bounty of the harvest and the elders of our land. It is they, the old and wise among us, who keep our traditions alive, and pass down to our youth the oracles and myths of the ages. By these we learn, and in learning we defend against the wiles and schemes of the evil one."

Another roar of applause, so loud that it caused the shop windows to shake.

Chloe's breaths became short. She could feel Ethan's elbow grow hot beneath her own. There had never been a Therismos Festival in her time, much less speeches that made mention of the "oracles" and the "evil one." Did he mean Apollo? She knew Apollo controlled the councilman, and yet he clearly seemed to view Apollo as an enemy.

"The harvest time symbolizes abundance," the councilman continued, "and mankind's dependence upon the All-Powerful for the sustenance that gives us life. It represents the cycle of sowing and reaping, and the truth that everything we plant, either by word or by deed, produces fruit. It also has a personal significance for me, an Asher whose doma manifested during the olive harvest some two thousand years ago."

Chloe stopped breathing altogether as the councilman drew two fingers to his temples and held them there in silence. "Some would call my gift a curse, and perhaps sometimes it is. When I'm very still, I can hear the suffering below our feet, the travail of Apollo's enemies and the souls who chose to follow Python, Lykaios, and every other infernal iteration under which he placed his standard."

The people froze, and even the children stopped eating as everyone hung on his every word and watched him wipe tears from his eyes.

"It is my great suspicion," he said, before clearing his throat, "that I would be on the pathway to the pit if four brave Ashers and their comrades had not risked their lives so long ago to save mine. And, more than that, they saved my soul."

Ethan bent down and whispered in Chloe's ear, "Chloe, it's—"

"I know," she said as the hair on her neck stood on end. "Hermogenes."

The councilman gripped the edges of the podium, his knuckles protruding from his spotted, arthritic hands. "I often think my doma has been given to me as a reminder of that hell from which I've been spared. For what else can a boy become if all he's been taught proceeded from the mouth of a tyrant?"

"Duna's grace prevails!" came a shout. It was Damian's voice, and it was echoed by a hundred others chanting the same three words.

The councilman's visage glowed and a warm smile settled upon the pallor of his features, transforming him into someone almost completely new—at least in Chloe and Ethan's eyes.

The last time Chloe had seen him, he'd been channeling Apollo inside the council building's sanctuary. He'd called her a heretic, a traitor, and a threat to Petros, while lamenting the fact that he wasn't permitted to kill her. Before that, he'd stood with her in the past, perhaps right here where they stood now, staring up at one of Mania's storms with searing hatred blazing in his eyes. "The final Asher," he'd called her.

And why wouldn't he have hated her after she'd spilled his blood to win favor with Hades? He must have spent his entire life observing her sly manipulations, clever lies and heartless conquests. He'd learned from them—that much was obvious—but he must also have resented them. Why else was her memory no longer honored? Why else would he have devoted his entire, nearly immortal, life to annihilating the Ashers?

She knew he hated them because she'd hurt him, and perhaps also because no other Asher had intervened to stop her. Until recently.

"Damian Zacharias," said the councilman, straightening up as best he could into a posture of formality, of respect, as he focused on a face in the front row.

Chloe's stomach lurched as her eyes found the back of Damian's blond head and his broad shoulders pulled back.

"It is your family we honor this Therismos, for it was you and your sister Chloe..." The councilman paused and brought a hand to his brow, shielding his eyes from the late afternoon sun as he scanned the crowd looking for her. "It was the two of you, and your friend Ethan, who saved me from what I might have become, who carried me out of a home of war and unrest to one of peace."

He made a mild gesture toward the Religious Council building behind him. "It's taken five years to complete, but the renovations are finally finished and the temple is ready to be unveiled. We have Lydia Ross and her team to thank for that."

The crowd clapped and cheered as the screens zoomed in on Lydia and dozens of others waving and smiling outside the dome.

"Mom," Ethan gasped. His eyes were fixed unblinkingly on his mother's face, his breath unmoving in his chest, as if the slightest twitch would make her vanish.

When the applause had faded, the soft melody of the last song began to play beneath the councilman's voice.

"On behalf of the Eirenian Council, and the Ross and Zacharias families, I invite you all to congregate here tomorrow morning for the sunrise dedication of the temple. Until then, enjoy the music and food of the festival." He waved a farewell and carefully made his way down a ramp before disappearing into the sea of faces.

"Come on." Chloe took Ethan's hand and cut through the dispersing throngs, making a beeline for her brother.

"I'll meet you back here," said Ethan. He kissed her cheek and took off running toward the dome, to his mother.

A cool breeze wrapped itself around Chloe's body, carrying her forward despite the heaviness taking hold of her limbs. The beat of the drums and thrum of the strings fell away as her senses tunneled around the image of her brother and the two others standing beside him. Now she knew why Ethan had stared so intensely at his mother on the screen. She felt distrustful of her eyes. She stood motionless, breathlessly quiet; waiting for the rest of her body to confirm that what she saw was real.

And then: her mother's laugh, high and light, fluttering gently into her ears; the woodsy scent of her father's favorite cologne, filling her mind with childhood memories, of climbing onto his lap and nestling against his neck.

"Daddy," she whispered. "Mommy..."

Her mother's laughter faded as she turned to Chloe with a smile. "The woman of the hour is finally here." She opened her arms wide for a hug and Chloe ran into them, nearly knocking her mother back.

Mrs. Zacharias stroked Chloe's hair as she kissed the top of her head. "Did you and Ethan have a nice drive in? We heard there was a storm down your way in Ourania."

"Ourania?" Chloe asked, still clinging to her mother as her throat tightened with imminent tears. "What were we doing in Ourania?"

"You go to university there, silly," her mother said, pulling back. "Honey, are you feeling all right?" She pressed a palm to Chloe's forehead. "You feel a little warm to me."

Chloe turned to Damian and, with one look, she could see that he knew.

"Maybe you're a little dehydrated," said Damian. "Come on. I'll show you where the drinks are."

"Not before I get a hug from my little girl." Mr. Zacharias stepped over to Chloe and drew her into his arms. "It's good to have you home, sweetheart."

No Fields of Asphodel. No monsters watching nearby. No memories washed away then returned at the shores of the River Lethe. No daunting journey ahead. Just this. Just her father's heartbeat against her ear and the unyielding warmth of happy tears trailing down her cheeks.

Chloe followed Damian under a purple-and-gold pavilion selling snacks and festival souvenirs. She grabbed a package of peanuts and pretended to read the label. "Damian, please tell me—"

"I know," he said gently, his eyes bluer than usual, softer. "I fell asleep last night, I don't know when, and woke up in a dorm room three blocks from here." He turned and looked down the street, scratching the back of his neck. "I'm studying theology." He smiled. "And you and Ethan are history majors."

Chloe stared at him, shock and joy and bafflement and bliss all swirling around inside her, making it almost impossible for her to speak.

"You don't remember anything else?" she managed.

"A little. I remember that our whole changing-the-timeline thing is common knowledge here. It's in the history books and everything."

Damian glanced at the group of kids in the corner of the pavilion who were hiding behind rainbow-shaped hand fans. Chloe could tell by their stiff bodies and hushed voices that they were trying to eavesdrop on them.

"They don't remember," one boy whispered. "How can they not remember?"

"Hey," said Damian, whipping his head toward them. That one stern word sent them scuttling off, their abandoned fans strewn on the ground.

He turned back to Chloe and sighed. "We'll remember more eventually." He pulled a piece of paper from his pocket and handed it to her. "Mnemosyne, a woman I met when I was with Leto, must've left this for us, or sent it somehow. I found it on my desk."

Chloe took the paper and unfolded it carefully. It was a letter written in Próta, the letters and markings of which translated themselves in a shimmering blur before her eyes. She skimmed the note in silence.

Greetings to Chloe, Damian and Ethan,

Before I deliver my message from the All-Powerful, I wish to inform you, Damian most of all, that I am no longer stationed at Mount Othrys, nor am I bound by Apollo in the heart of Tartarus, as you might have suspected after our meeting that day, two thousand years ago.

The instant I was dragged to Hades' depths, Duna sent one of his messengers to release me, and restore me once more to the courts of heaven. After meeting you, Damian, one half of the promised Vessel, my presence at Othrys was no longer necessary since the world's memories are now secured, preserved in pious hands.

The fact that you are reading this missive testifies to your victory, by Duna's strength and provision, over Mania and the darkness of her legacy, the memories of which the three of you alone now carry with you.

As for your own memories—the ones formed in this era presently foreign to you—they shall return, little by little, over the course of the coming months. Some will come back sooner and sharper than others, while others may be delayed and remain dim for quite some time. I tell you this so you will not be afraid, or think yourselves crazed or deceived. Such things, I understand, are difficult for mortals to comprehend, and so I urge you only to trust and give thanks for this most blessed gift of reunion with your families.

You have my word, as guardian of all Petrodians' memories, that the friends you left behind lived well, happily, and long. They wait for you, as I will wait for you, within the gates of heaven. Until then, cherish the days both behind and ahead, and forget not the things you have fought for.

Mnemosyne

CHAPTER FORTY-FIVE
DÝNAMI

The next evening, Chloe and Ethan sat on the beach at Ourania, a place they had seldom been to, at least not in the world they knew; the government had had strict rules about when and where one could travel. But here, now, there were no such rules. Petrodians were free to go where they wished and do what they wanted, according to the divinely given laws Chloe's ancestors followed in ages past.

There was no Fantásmata, no coronations, no dictating who would bear children and where one

404

would work, and no Lycaea Festival held in secret honor of Apollo.

Chloe straightened her arms and leaned back, enjoying the rush of the tide as it lapped on her ankles and shins, and caked her feet with sand. The orange sun bobbed lazily on the horizon as a sheet of rain slanted into it from a solitary patch of gray. There would be a Moonbow tonight. She could feel it.

"I think it's safe to tell me now," Chloe said, casting a furtive glance around the beach, ensuring there was no one around to hear.

Ethan didn't need her to expound. He reached into his jeans pocket and slowly pulled out the small black chip that had been implanted in Aison's hand. "I wasn't sure it had survived the time hop back here. I took it from Aison after we got back from the Lycaea Festival and hid it in my satchel."

Chloe sat up, dusting her hands on her thighs. "I don't get it. The chip is what made you go back in time?"

"With Iris and Tycho's help. They're the ones who helped me figure it out."

"Figure what out?"

"That the chip was created to help its owner manifest domas, at least the domas of Ashers who'd been around it."

Chloe took the chip from him and studied it, looking for some sort of telltale sign of its power. But there was nothing to indicate that it was anything more than an ordinary microchip. "How could you possibly figure that out?"

"Let's just say the campfire needed some stoking and..." Ethan lifted his right palm to the sea and winced slightly as a thin yellow flame broke through the flesh and sailed out over the waves.

"And *that* happened," Chloe said, as she reached for his other hand. "That's incredible."

Ethan watched the flame until it disappeared, then closed his fist and rested it on the sand. "Tycho made the connection that perhaps I could use it to find you. And with Duna's help I did."

Chloe brought his hand to her lips and kissed his knuckles. "Thank you for saving my life. I should have said that a long time ago."

Ethan smiled, his green eyes appearing bluer beside the sea. He took her hand in both of his and set them on his thigh; she could still feel the heat where the fire had flowed. "I should have said the same to you, back at the Regional Council building after I found you in the stairwell." He kissed her eyebrow. "You disappeared before I had the chance." He kissed her lips. "Before I had the chance to say a lot of things."

Chloe rested her head on his shoulder and dropped the chip into his lap. "I guess we know now why the high priest wanted it so badly. I wonder how it was made."

Ethan shrugged, picked up the chip and squeezed it tightly. "I don't know, but I know how it's going to be destroyed," he said, and stood up.

"Destroy it? Why?"

Ethan turned to her, his expression grave, his body rigid. He didn't have to explain. Chloe knew. The chip had helped save their lives—and the world, as they knew it—because it had been in Ethan's possession. In the wrong person's hands, however, it had the potential to cause unprecedented damage that Petros might never recover from, especially now that there were more Ashers in existence, and therefore more powers to imitate.

Chloe nodded. "Do it." No sooner had she uttered the words than the chip went flying into the Great Sea, to rust and disintegrate into oblivion.

Ethan sat down beside Chloe and pulled her toward him, his lips just inches from her own. "I'm just back to regular old me now."

She leaned into him, kissing him softly as she held the back of his neck. "I love you." The words slipped effortlessly from her lips as her heart hammered inside her chest. She hadn't meant to say them out loud, but by the look on Ethan's face, it wasn't a mistake.

He held her, whispering those same three words in her ear as the sun's crown dipped beneath the horizon, making room for the Moonbow to shine.

☾

Below the dark surface of the water, the sea nymph Eione was swimming, searching for the dýnami forged long ago in the molten bowels of Mount Aetna.

"Foolish mortals," she said, grinning as she spied the dýnami—the power—sinking further into the murk. But how could they have known that the dýnami could only be destroyed by the volcanic fires that formed it? Its origin was kept secret for a reason.

Only Apollo and his former cohorts knew the Asher whose blood had imbued the object with powers even the Olympians would envy. Straton, he was named, for the army his sacrifice would raise, when the time was ripe. An army created for reasons unknown, for Apollo never acted first. Instead, he waited for the All-Powerful to incite him.

But as fate would have it, it was Eione, a lowly goddess compared to the vaunting rulers of Hades, who now snatched the dýnami for herself and tucked it into the sea-foam folds of her dress. She could feel its strength pulsing like a heartbeat next to her skin, as if asking her to unleash it here, while the sea was asleep in shadow.

Eione remembered the first time she had seen its power, when Straton swam past the nereids' caves and stole her favorite hippocampus from the stable. He then sped off toward the sky, too fast for her to catch up. He returned the animal hours later before inviting himself to dine with her and the other sea nymphs, fifty in total. He charmed them all with his tricks and jauntiness, boasting and telling jokes well into the night over honeywine and figs.

Straton could have taken any one of Nereus's daughters for a lover, but his escapades were just beginning. There were many more goddesses to enchant, many more mythic realms for his mortal feet to find.

It was from Straton alone that Eione had heard of the dýnami. It became the ocean-dwellers' chief source of gossip as rumors swirled about its owner and what he could do: fly like an eagle, swim like a dolphin, create tablets of clay from dry earth. He was a shapeshifter like Nereus and a sorcerer like Circe, able to turn into whatever beast he wished and craft objects out of air.

But Apollo, as was his nature, had failed to honor his end of the bargain with Straton. Straton had offered his blood—his life—in return for equality with Apollo and his brothers. But only a few weeks after the Dýnami was issued from Hephaestus' forge, Straton was overpowered by the hounds of hell and dragged to Tartarus to molder along with his memory.

A surge of adrenaline coursed through the sea nymph's veins as she darted and weaved through the waves, her keen eyes fixed on a faraway reef, behind which lay the entrance to the River Styx. A train of bubbles streamed from Eione's nose as she laughed, envisioning the look on the gods' faces when they saw her, dýnami in hand, sneaking into Tartarus to rescue them.

They would defeat Apollo. They would rule again. And the Ashers would fear their names once more.

FATE OF THE ASHERS

Book 3 in The Petros Chronicles series
www.dianaandersontyler.com/signup

THE PETROS CHRONICLES
FATE OF THE ASHERS

CHAPTER ONE
EIONE

The sea nymph could smell the sulfur now. She was fast approaching the hidden gateway in the reef, a place no immortal free to wander the upper realm ever dared to go. But Eione had good reason, for in her hand she held the dýnami, the coveted seed-sized object forged by Hephaestus thousands of years before. She knew Tartarus's prisoners would treat her hospitably. They would have to if they desired escape.

Eione jerked as a translucent eel slid out of its hole, brushing against her arm as it snaked its way past her. She took a slow, deep breath. She couldn't startle so easily if she expected to make it down the River Styx where the flesh-eating serpent swam. *You have the Dýnami*, she said to herself, *so stop acting like a sniveling waif.*

Her hand trembled as she reached through the anemones, feeling for the stone door behind them. A chill shot up her spine as her fingertips trailed across algae as slick as slime. Curious clown fish peered at her as if to ask what she was doing so close to Hades.

Mustering her courage, the sea nymph pushed against the wall. The response was a violent rush of fire-hot bubbles that sent her hurtling backward, and the clown fish with her. She looked up at the anemones swaying like saplings in a storm, their bright colors stark against the gaping blackness where her hands had been. The portal was open.

"It's time," she whispered, swimming forward, holding her breath as the mortals did, afraid of drowning, afraid of death.

The bubbles burned Eione's skin, spurring her to swim faster toward the Styx. She could see and feel nothing; darkness clung to her like a shroud as the noxious scent of sulfur grew stronger, the unmistakable stench of death.

For what seemed like ages, she wandered blindly, unsure whether she was swimming, floating, or being pulled by the current. At last she saw light: the red glow of lava at the end of the tunnel that had led her from the sea. It spilled, churning and roaring, into the pitch-black Styx below.

Though Eione could feel her limbs again, she could not see them as they ripped through the water around her. She was invisible, just like the Asher called Damian, about whom she'd heard rumors on the beach.

The dýnami was working, pulsing like a heartbeat in her hand. She sped ahead, diving headfirst into the lair of the serpent, whose job it was to incapacitate any visitors, save for the souls of the dead. But she escaped his notice easily, swimming freely through the world's most hated river as though it were a summer stream on Olympus.

Cerberus's nap was not interrupted as the sea nymph waded to shore, her dark dress dripping wet. His gray serpentine tail twitched only a little as she walked through Hades' gates, leaving not a single footprint in the sand.

"You do not know what you are doing."

Eione knew the voice, as did all the immortals. Her gaze rose to the top of the marble wall, on which Hermes, former messenger and captain of Apollo, sat watching her.

"And you do not belong here," she hissed back, careful not to wake the sleeping hound.

Hermes removed his dog-skin cap and kicked his dangling legs. "I may no longer be allegiant to Apollo, but that doesn't mean I cannot summer here if I wish." The golden wings of his sandals fluttered. He floated down the side of the wall and stood before her, his copper eyes surveying hers before fixing on her fist, which was clenched tightly around the Dýnami.

"How can you see me?" Eione asked.

"Duna's power exceeds all other forces, for he created them. This thing you wish to do..." He twisted his cap in his hands as sharp distress fell like a shadow across his face. "Well, to call it unwise would be an understatement."

"It's unfair that Cronus, not to mention both our fathers, is locked inside the abyss." Heat flooded Eione's chest. She ground her teeth to keep from shouting. "Apollo was never fit to rule. He's a tyrant. He—"

"None of us are fit to rule, Eione," Hermes said, fitting the cap back on his head as he scanned the artificial sky that spread like a dull, dirty sheet above their heads. "His reign, like this world, is a sham. Nothing good has ever come of immortals pretending to be greater than the All-Powerful, nor will it ever."

Eione's mind flashed with images of her father, Nereus, on the day he'd taken his daughters and hid them inside the caves they now called home. In return for the promise of their safety, he gave himself over to Apollo, letting Apollo drag him away in chains through the halls of hell.

Of all the gods, Nereus's appetite for power had been the least, yet his existence alone was threat enough for Apollo. And so, along with dozens of other ill-fated gods, Tartarus became his abode. The prisoners' freedom had been an impossible dream for the spouses and children they'd left behind...until today. Now, with the dýnami found, there was a way, a flawless way, to save them, and nothing Hermes said could change Eione's mind.

"I did not come here to be proselytized. Step aside, or I shall make you step aside." Eione's eyes narrowed as a ball of fire rose from the porcelain cup of her palm.

"And I did not come here to prevent you from carrying out your plan." Hermes didn't seem to notice the flame hovering dangerously close to his face. He wasn't afraid of her, an observation that made Eione want to scream.

"Good." She pushed past him, gliding effortlessly through the wall. "The smell of your burning flesh would no doubt disturb the dog."

"You're naïve if you think Cronus and our fathers will tolerate more peace in this world than Apollo has." Hermes hovered above her head, following her closely as she trudged up the rocky hillside. "The ichor in their veins runs hot with selfish ambition. You've seen this with your own eyes."

Eione stopped and shot her eyes up to him, her cold, ichor veins roiling with impatience. "And yet here you are, Hermes, a flawless example of one whose proud heart has been humbled. Surely you cannot tell me that it's impossible for our fathers to be softened as well and to forsake the old ways."

To her surprise, Hermes offered no reply, and neither did he continue to fly beside her as she swept up the excess fabric of her garment and ran ahead. She knew her reasoning was sound, and even he, master of tricks and schemes, could not deny it.

"Then I will pray for such a miracle," Hermes muttered under his breath as he watched Eione disappear over the hill.

It was true, what she had said. Never in a million years could he have predicted that he would one day humble himself enough to lift his eyes heavenward. His stubbornness had been just as unyielding as Apollo's, his delight in deceiving just as great. And yet, despite his deeds and intentions, Hermes had been changed, transformed, and, more miraculous than that, forgiven.

No longer was Hermes a peon of Apollo, nor a reprobate ever on the run from the righteous wrath of Duna. He was a child of the All-Powerful, and a helper of mankind. Who was he to say that his metamorphosis could not be replicated in one, or perhaps all, of his immortal brethren, whose souls were no blacker than his once was? He knew better than to assume Duna's power knew any limit; he could rip Tartarus from the heart of Petros and set it beside his throne if he so wished. Hermes only knew that his ways were immutably unknowable, a notion he was still getting used to.

Cerberus began to bark. Hermes could hear the guttural heaving erupting from the canine's flanks.

"Oh, shush!" Hermes called to him. The dog grew quiet, as he always did when he heard Hermes' voice. It had been two thousand years, Hermes reflected, and the dumb creature still didn't know that Hermes was a traitor here.

Hermes soared back to the wall and sat upon it as he fashioned a honeycake with his wand and threw it down to Cerberus. The hound swallowed it whole and wagged his tail like a pup.

"If only the gods were as docile around me as you are," Hermes said, throwing cake after cake into all three of the dog's wide jaws. "Perhaps then I could speak to them civilly and diplomatically, as the Petrodians do."

Cerberus whimpered and rolled onto his back, readying himself for a belly rub. Hermes chuckled and jumped down next to him. In a rapid blur of movement, the dog leapt to its feet and lunged toward Hermes, snarling as a large paw planted itself on his arm, ripping through Hermes' skin as if it were wheat to be threshed.

Hermes sprang up onto the wall again, glistening ichor spurting uncontrollably from his forearm, falling like rain into Cerberus's wide, foaming mouths.

"I taught you well," Hermes said, wincing in pain as he waited for the wound to heal. "Feigning peace until ready to attack is one of the greatest strategies there is."

Cerberus growled. His hackles were raised proudly as he stalked the length of the wall, daring Hermes to come down again.

"Thank you for the reminder, old friend." And with that, Hermes flew across the sky toward Petros's crust, leaving the Styx and its sentry behind.

AFTERWORD

I hope you enjoyed *The War of the Ashers*, the second installment in The Petros Chronicles series. If you don't mind, I would appreciate it if you could head over to Amazon, Goodreads, or your preferred website of choice and leave a brief review of this book. Your help in spreading the word is gratefully received and encourages me to keep reaching others through my writing.

Also, I invite you to join my Greek-mythology-related mailing list at www.dianatylerbooks.com. Each month I do fun things like send exclusive short stories and run giveaways, all related to books and/or Greek mythology, of course.

ACKNOWLEDGMENTS

Every morning, I wake up and realize how extremely blessed I am, not just because I get to do what I love every day, but also because I have the support and assistance of amazing people who have enriched both my writing and my life. The Petros Chronicles series has been a tremendous journey, one I surely wouldn't have completed without the motivation, encouragement, and tips and advice offered by the following people:

My husband Ben, my #1 fan who puts up with my writerly quirks, moods, compulsions and extemporaneous brainstorming sessions.

My mom Barbara, who has always nurtured my dream of becoming a published author and patiently listens to me vent and cry on the bad days.

My beta readers and proofreaders, Jaime and Kara:. You have no idea how invaluable your encouragement and feedback has been to me. Thank you for shooting straight with me, catching my mistakes, and enjoying the story. I owe you the moon and so much more!

My editor, Penny, at Book Cover Cafe. Words fail to adequately convey just how grateful I am for an editor who not only polishes and corrects, but also affirms and educates. Thank you for shaping me into a better writer, page by page.

The team at Book Cover Cafe, who always do a fabulous job of typesetting, design, and e-book conversion.

ABOUT THE AUTHOR

Diana has been writing all her life, starting with her own versions of Teenage Mutant Ninja Turtle comics when she was four. She's always been fascinated by Greek mythology and comic-book superheroes, all of which inspire her fantasy novels. She's also a gym rat who loves to pretend she's Wonder Woman while lifting heavy weights, and swinging from rings and pull-up bars. She co-owns CrossFit 925 in San Antonio, Texas with her husband, Ben.

Diana currently writes entertainment and media-related articles for movieguide.org, and runs a popular blog for writers at www.dianaandersontyler.com. When she isn't writing or working out, she can be found playing Scrabble with her husband, watching Marvel and Pixar movies, pinning recipes on Pinterest that she never gets around to cooking, and reading, of course.

MORE FROM DIANA

www.dianatylerbooks.com
www.dianaandersontyler.com

You can also contact her through

Facebook:
facebook.com/dianafit4faith

Twitter:
@dandersontyler

Instagram:
@authordianatyler